I0685904

THE **KISSING** SCHOOL

YOU CAN'T STAY YOUNG AND NAIVE FOREVER

CREATED BY

JORDAN URTSO

COVER DESIGN BY SCARLETT RUGERS.
EDITED BY SARAH NORTON.
CONSULTANT EDITOR MORGAN SHEA.

For The One Who Took My Place.

Girls and Boys

"Ummm, Helloooo? Don't you think you guys are being a little . . . *melodramatic*?" Sosie Hinkhouse sat boredly on top of a cart of library books and yanked a silver tube from her midnight-blue cardigan pocket. The smell of watermelon lip gloss filled the fusty air.

Three of Sosie's girlfriends circled around on the floor Indian-style, picking at their dried cuticle beds and peeling the split ends from their hair. They were hanging out in their usual spot: a hidden nook of The Bluffdale Preparatory School for Girls' Library buried behind a cluster of shelves. The mood was rather depressing, compared to their usual upbeat gossip sessions. After all, the shabby crawl space that the four had grown to love would soon be vacant.

All good things must come to an end, though . . . right?

Sosie's gaze zoomed across the cobwebbed shelves. What was so depressing about escaping some gloomy old library for good, anyway?

"Tomorrow, we'll be surrounded by muscles and after-shave for the first time in our pathetic, little lives, and the three of you are acting like you're being shipped off to prison! What's the deal?"

"We're nervous," Juliet Bigsby piped up from behind the Blairstown University brochure she held tight in her hands. She blinked down at a mirage of blindingly white smiles, khaki skirts, and a line of perfect, gold calligraphy reading: "The closest to perfect life can get." Her frizzy perm scuttled down her neck in golden kinks as she sat straight to search her out-of-season slouch hobo for a protein bar. "At least I am," she muttered.

Juliet stared longingly at Sosie's long, sleek locks of perfectly blonde hair from below. Right around the era of maxi-pads and braces, Juliet had been introduced to Sosie Hinkhouse and Nala Middleton, the two most beautiful girls at Bluffdale Preparatory — and probably in the world — during cheerleading auditions, and ever since had longed to belong to their very exclusive coterie. After years of body butter and hairspray, it seemed she had finally secured her spot. For now.

Juliet's body-glitter glinted like fish scales on her cleavage, as she twiddled the brochure beneath her chipped manicure. Her cardigan stretched with every inhale, and her gigantic breasts bobbled inside. The truth was, the thought of seeing boys tomorrow for the first time ever made her queasy.

"So, when do boys study French?" Nala Middleton asked innocently, tossing her brown, shimmering hair behind her toasted shoulders. Nala was Sosie's best friend. She flipped through the

August issue of *Food & Fit to Fit*, landing on a spread of German supermodel Konstanze Eichelberger, who was posing in a claw-foot, vintage bathtub and blowing bubbles at the camera. "Girl's best friend is the one who never lets her go unwashed," the caption read. Nala admired the perfectly suntanned legs peeking out from the throng of foam. All she had ever wanted since she first got her polished little fingers on a fashion magazine was to travel the world as a model. She would see Buenos Aires, Bali, Florence, Johannesburg, Tokyo . . . she would wear Michel St Pierre's fall collection around London, sign autographs in Sao Paulo, and attend all of the hottest fashion shows in Sydney, Milan and Madrid. She was certainly pretty enough to be a model, after all. Everyone said so.

Nala's golden eyes were riveted on Konstanze's strangely symmetrical face, wondering how many hours it took to airbrush out her pores.

"Boys will study French with us, because — you know — it's like, the language of romance." Sosie jumped onto the floor to join her girlfriends and snagged the bathtub issue of Konstanze, whose swollen lips pouted at the lens. "Ew! She has total fish face after all of those lip injections." Sosie plunged onto her stomach, kicking her legs over her back so that her one-size-too-big flats dangled floppily over her. "So, I need to tell you girls something. I sort of . . . met a guy." Sosie casually chewed on a hangnail as the stares overawed her. "Earlier this morning," she added. Nala, Juliet, and another girl, Tessa Van der Pool, dropped their jaws and stared. No longer were they playing hair-salon with their malnourished blunt cuts. Sosie had seen a *boy*, or so she said.

"And I have a freaking unicorn." Tess rolled her ice-blue eyes, prodding around on her cell phone and twisting her deco ear studs boredly. "Say what you want, but even us jaded laymen know that that's impossible. In Bluffdale, you don't just *meet* a guy."

"Don't you have a broom to fly, somewhere?" Sosie snapped.

Tess arched one tweezed, black eyebrow at Sosie, shoveling her arms beneath her boobs so that her brand-new, mint-green plunge push-up peeked through the buttons of her blouse. "Bite me."

Sosie weaved her fingers through her hair, trying to avoid Tess's fake, apple boobs staring right at her. "For those of you who aren't pretentious bitches, his name was Gino Blackthorn, I think. And he was like, the most beautiful thing I've ever seen."

Juliet stacked her curls into one huge, unmanageable bird's nest bun on top of her head, her nerves burbling beneath her milk-white pores. "Sosie Blackthorn. Hmm. It has a nice ring to it."

Tess giggled snootily. What was Juliet getting so excited for? She probably wouldn't even be able to snag a boyfriend until senior year, when pickings were super slim and boys were starting to get desperate. Nala would probably fall in love the first week on campus with some jock on the lacrosse team, since she was so perfect and all. They'd exchange promise rings, hold hands around the local artisan shops, spoon-feed each other tiramisu, vacation in the mountains. They'd put the wet rag in drag.

Sosie was admittedly pretty in an I-don't-care-about-anything sort of way, and Tess had read somewhere that some boys liked the whole "natural" look, so Sosie would likely be settled down by junior year. She and her beau would order pizza, get stoned, and play weird, post-apocalyptic video games for their entire lives. As for Tess, she was beautiful, smart, and had legs for days. What wasn't to like?

Juliet blinked her squinty blue eyes, marveled by the idea of quiff-cuts and sweat-sprinkled skin sprawled across the Blairstown lawn, toking on cigarettes, jamming to classic rock through tiny earphone beads, plucking at guitar strings. Never having met a boy before, or even seen a decent picture—with the exception of a vague diagram of the naked male body in

Pre-Male Anatomy and a couple of illustrations in young adult fiction books — she tried to imagine a really muscular girl with short hair and a beard. *Gross.* "What did he look like?"

"Ummm . . . he was tall, had dark hair, brown eyes, scruffed chin," she shrugged.

Tess calculatedly strung her black hair, ripping a lotion sample out of Nala's magazine and taking a whiff. Mmm . . . toasted vanilla and shea butter. Anything to keep her mind off the fact that Sosie Hinkhouse had supposedly met some gorgeous, stubbly, dark-haired dreamboat on the white sands of Bluffdale beach.

Sosie propped up on her elbows. "I swear, he was like, Nala with a penis."

"Awesome!" Juliet batted her clumpy eyelashes jealously while the other girls groaned at Sosie's use of the word, penis. "So, how'd you guys meet?"

"Yeah, Sosie. How'd you guys meet?" Tess smirked.

Sosie rolled her eyes. She didn't really want to say anything else, especially since Tess was behaving like a jealous, little girl on Christmas morning. *Sorry I unwrapped Ken, and you unwrapped Baby-Wets-Herself.* She glanced down the hall where one of her classmates, Kiki Weames, was browsing the music section for trans-psychedelic hits of the sixties, still reeking of hookah and fish from her meditation on the beach that afternoon. Her face was glowing, and her hair — waved by the salt-water and ocean breeze — now tumbled loose from a floppy, camel-brown hat. She was wearing sand-splattered thunderbird moccasins and an ivory maxi skirt.

Kiki glimpsed Sosie from beneath her humongous hat, smiled crookedly at her, then grabbed three or four CDs and shoved them into her all-organic, handloom blue boho bag. Then she pressed one finger against her lips and pursed her mouth, like it was their little secret. Kiki had always been a free spirit, but recently she was more than just a "nonconformist." She had become an outright rebel. Stealing from the library the day before the big move was her final testament of revolt.

Kiki clomped up to Sosie and her friends, the stolen goods thwacking against her hip as she breezed by. "Hey you paper shakers! Better get back and start packing, soon!" she said.

Tessa smudged her thumb into her lipstick, fluttering her eyes up and down Kiki's questionable attire. Wasn't Halloween in October? "Can't imagine you have much to pack since you're like, one with the wind, or whatever."

"Wind or not, I still gotta brush my teeth." Kiki flashed a yellow smile down at the girls who in unison thought, *those things have been brushed before?* She then slammed her hand against her hip and narrowed her bushy eyebrows. "Welp, I better haul ass. The cafeteria's selling all-vegetarian grub for the road tomorrow, and I want to get there before the tofu runs out."

Like that would ever happen.

"Later," she called out, just before thumping down the stairwell on her moccasins, her natty, brown hair floating behind her gracelessly.

"She's so weird," Tess whispered when Kiki was gone, jumping onto her feet. "Anyways, I'm outtie, too! I have a million things to pack, and I need to get in a Pilates sesh before I box up the heels." Tess hitched up her socks and tossed her backpack over one shoulder, already feeling her muscles tighten at the thought of a spine twist. "*Ciao!*"

"Ta-ta!" Sosie squealed in fake falsetto as Tess vanished down the stairwell. Thank goodness she was gone! She could be such a little witch.

Sosie glanced back at Juliet, who was still hungry for details about Gino and taking it out on her protein bar. "Okay, so you want to know how we met?"

"Uh-huh!"

Sosie's eyes burned with secrecy. "It was about noon," she said, "and I had been lying out on the beach since like, ten, and I was starting to get sun poisoning on my ass. So, I got up to wash the sand out of my bikini before heading home, and that was when I saw him. A perfect blur of bare-chested tanness! He was just standing there, dripping with sweat like an ice cream cone, watching me. I almost thought I was having heat stroke, or I was so dehydrated that I was hallucinating him, but then he held out his hand."

Juliet bit into her nail polish, her body humming with nerves. "So what happened next?"

Sosie sat up, playing with the fringe on her thong-flat sandals. "Next, he said hi."

She continued to tell Juliet and Nala all about Gino. He grew up in Elkins, an all-boy county about forty-five minutes outside of Bluffdale. He attended The Academy of Windsor. He had been really bored recently, and decided to break the rules and cross into their city on a whim. He was eighteen, too, and would be transferring to Blairstown University the next day with the rest of his class . . . so long as he didn't get caught trespassing, that is. And, most importantly it seemed, Sosie was the first girl he had ever met. "I just can't stop thinking about him," she said, flipping over Konstanze Eichelberger's "2 Simple Short Cuts on Your Way to a Thinner and More Confident You."

What — binging and purging?

Both Nala and Juliet watched Sosie rustle deeper into the magazine, perusing diet regimen after diet regimen.

"Maybe you just like him?" Nala piped up finally.

Sosie blinked down at a black and white perfume spread. She had spent eighteen years of her life without boys. The closest she ever came to liking someone was the girl crush she had on Nala, who was so flawless it was almost impossible not to love her. She literally made everyone else in the room look like one of those naked oriental yeti things. So, maybe Nala was right, as she always seemed to be. Maybe this was what it felt like to have a small crush.

The bell sounded, and Sosie, Juliet, and Nala bounced up, sifting their canvas floral backpacks and leather totes from the pile of library junk. "*Ugh,* I have a million things to pack, and I just have to knock out Pilates before even looking at my pumps!" Sosie mocked, tossing the fitness magazine into a recycle bin. It was trash, anyways. She was going to be a pizza fiend until the day she died of cheese overdose, and no stupid model was going to tell her what to eat.

As the girls skipped down the cliff of library steps, they couldn't miss the atrocious banner dangling from the polyurethane crown molding above. It read: "As you go forward, seniors, always remember the leading principles of Bluffdale Preparatory. And never forget: Your great destiny begins tomorrow." It seemed sweet, but everyone knew what the faculty was really trying to say: make us look good, and find a husband.

No pressure or anything.

Once outside the library, Sosie clambered out of her cardigan and fanned herself with evening air. "It's like my body is turning into freaking goo! You're nervous too, right?" she asked Nala, who also had stripped down to a ribbed tank. Perhaps they didn't know much about the real world, but getting naked was practically second nature in an all-girl city. What was there to hide in a town filled with other boobs?

"Totally nervous," Nala said, breathing in the thick, salty air. She'd miss the beach. "Mostly for Kissing Class. I mean, it's one thing that we'll have to like, make out with a bunch of strange boys — but it's another thing that some old man is teaching it."

"Oh yeah! Professor Leatherhead, or Leatherhood . . . or Leathersomething."

"Leatherwood," Nala sniffled, peering through the courtyard masked with orange sunset. "The thought of some old man assigning my lips to someone else's makes me want to gag."

"Chill out, La. You're gonna break out!" Sosie teased. "And Kissing Class isn't just about making out. It's about relationships . . . girls and boys. You know — whose natural perspiration makes another's love bone tingle. Chemistry. Stuff like that," she shrugged. "Besides, it will be fun! You, me, *Professor Leatherwood* . . . boys."

The girls jogged up the dormitory steps as night fell. Their Laurent Le Blanc luggage sets were all packed an hour later, and flung into a mountain of other jacquard suitcases and faux leather travel trunks. Sosie stripped down to her freckly ass and plunged into her bleak twin bed. Nala threw on her French, rose satin pajama set and featherweight foam eye-mask.

Thirty minutes later, Sosie was drooling over memories of Gino, snoring to the rhythm of Nala's 'Nature Sounds' playlist, an echo of rainforest dripping through her computer speakers. Nala tossed and turned, wide-awake beneath her azure-blue floral duvet, her almond hair splayed across a matching pillow sham. Kissing 101 sounded like the most ridiculous class *ever*. Professor Leatherwood would probably hook her up with some greasy, crusty lumberjack with halitosis. Suddenly, it felt like a ball of ice had lodged in her stomach. A fog of possibilities ransacked her mind, as she curled beneath the cover, her head an explosion of headache at the stringency of her eye mask.

And then, just as daylight began to drip through her seaside blue window treatments, the alarm clock rang, and Nala realized she had tossed and turned the whole night long.

It was time to move.

Welcome to Paradise

Sosie Hinkhouse, Nala Middleton, Juliet Bigsby, and Tessa Van Der Pool were all stuffed on a transfer bus early the next morning, eating yogurt parfaits and browsing through Blairstown U pamphlets. Juliet slammed her nose against a glass window, blinking across as the bus wound near the university. The campus appeared with a plethora of hickories, lakefront bluffs, and hordes of men sprawled out on the lawn. They were tossing footballs shirtless, skateboarding, passing out beneath the willows, strumming guitars, listening to light rock. They were so *cool*.

"How many do you think there are?" Juliet asked Tess, who was smacking her lips at her reflection in the window.

"Thousands? I don't know."

Juliet took another glance. The campus was so beautiful she wanted to dive right in. The architecture was one big, Gothic explosion, with stained glass windows and flying buttresses. She felt like royalty approaching her castle. Alert the butlers!

"See that building? That, if I remember correctly," Juliet fumbled through the tattered pages of the catalogue tucked in her lap, "is the Library. Huge, isn't it? They call it Fifteen Floors of Bores."

Tess rolled her eyes and ripped her makeup mirror from her plum bucket bag. She was fifteen floors of bored right now, and Juliet's whining was only making things worse. "Are you a little scared, Jules?"

"I think everyone is," Juliet replied, watching the gold embossed BU entrance gate slip open.

"Not everyone," Tess replied. Ooing at her reflection, she noticed her hollowed-out, ghostly cheeks staring back at her. She had been living off of rice cakes and pomegranate juice for weeks, trying to look extra skinny for the abundance of boys roaming around campus, and it was starting to show on her face.

Juliet hugged her knees to her chest. "It's okay to be scared."

Tess jammed the pocket mirror back into her bag. Juliet could really be so naïve. "Well, I'm not scared," she said. "Men are horny creatures. They just want someone to show off to their horny friends. It's all a big beauty contest for women, and an even bigger contest for men. You know, who's carrying the shiniest trophy. And scared *isn't* sexy." She rifled through her bag, snagging a packet of breath mints. "Trust me, Jules. I'm only trying to help." Tess danced her fingers through the crook of Juliet's bangs, frowning her red lips at her. "By the way, you should probably invest in a bigger purse. So you can like, carry around a brush and some makeup." Her fingers tangled in a wad of blonde frizz. "And you should definitely look into a Brazilian blowout!"

Juliet sat in pitiful silence, wondering if her hair was really as tragic as it was frizzy. But there was no time to flirt with a flat iron. The bus halted suddenly, and the girls hopped onto their oxfords and moto boots, scrambling for their bags. They had arrived!

Miss Iris, their Bluffdale Prep housemother, waltzed her short, stubby legs up and down the aisle. "So, this is where I say goodbye," she said, teary-eyed.

Just outside, the chiseled words "Alistair Dwelling Place" glistened from slick, polished stone building, and the girls at the front of the bus trampled onto the lawn. They wheeled their bags across the short-trimmed sward, breathing in the scents of jasmine and chlorine.

Sosie lunged onto the green, her pale, blonde waves winding in the breeze. She tipped her gold-rimmed circle shades onto her nose. *This was it!* This was what she had been waiting for her entire life. The courtyard was even more beautiful than she had imagined: green willows, budding cymbidiums, wooden benchmarks engraved with initials. The campus was a freaking wonderland of stone-stacked buildings, crawling green ivy, and amber-flaked sidewalks. The real Blairstown far exceeded those lame pictures they showed in class.

"Ready to find our room?" Nala asked. She held her adorable nylon duffle in her left hand and her vintage-chic buttercup book-bag in her right. The weight of the luggage pulled at her shoulders. Where were those muscly boys when you needed them?

"Ready," Sosie nodded. They eagerly climbed the dormitory steps, and Sosie wedged the door open with her combat boot. "Welcome to paradise."

Little Chunk of Heaven

Sosie and Nala slipped inside and circled the buzzing lobby. Hundreds of girls they didn't recognize were pouting about their misplaced luggage and the elevator that was stalled on the fifth floor.

Sosie dodged a herd of caffeinated girls sipping lattés as they ran for the staircase. They sprinted clumsily, arms piled with crap, and vanished up three flights. As for the two working elevators that remained, four or five bright-eyed freshmen counted out loud as both approached the bottom floor.

"7! 6! 5!" the group bellowed together, bouncing along with every floor. Sosie rolled her eyes. *This is going to be a long day*, she thought, wondering where exactly she had packed those pain pills.

Once the noisy flock had piled into one of the elevators — and after the doors had shut — Sosie relaxed. "Good riddance!" She was two perfectly infuriating minutes away from a splitting migraine.

Suddenly, the foyer felt empty. There was a series of water paintings dangling from the teal, wooden planked walls, and a cute tea station that felt very nineteenth century France. A simple meet-and-greet buffet of raspberry lemonade and oatmeal raisin cookies had been set-up in the back, and a syrup-brown front desk hid behind artificial ball topiaries nearby. Behind the desk, a woman with silver hair and tortoise-shell reading glasses clicked her fingernails against a keyboard.

"Follow me, La." Sosie grabbed Nala's hand in hers, zooming between packs of baffled freshmen. One chick with a pixie-cut slammed her ugly, brown satchel against the floor and whined, "Where am I supposed to be going?" Her beady, black eyes dissected the crowd. Where was her bag boy? Where was her champagne? Where was her freaking room?

"Excuse me." Sosie cleared her throat as she approached the front desk, mining through her purse in search of her welcome envelope. The old lady impatiently tapped her ugly, Bordeaux-painted fingernails against an eggshell-white coffee mug with the words *World's Best Something* scribbled on it in poor cursive. She certainly was a *something*. Behind Sosie, the same pixie-cut girl was stuffing her cheeks with a cookie and yammering into her cellphone, "Where the hell are you? I'm by the food." A litter of girls were tapping their brand new Lucite, cutout oxfords against the tile, tittering into their cardigan sleeves, already gossiping about their unfamiliar cohabitants. Everyone was so obnoxious.

Finding the envelope finally, Sosie flung her wrists onto the desk and shoved it forward. "We received this, but no information on boarding."

The woman dropped her cat-glasses to the end of her nose, narrowing her thinly plucked eyebrows and snatching the paper from Sosie. "Give me a minute," her voice cracked as she noisily clanked the buttons of the keyboard.

Sosie stood with Nala, staring blankly across the lobby. There were hundreds of unfamiliar girls scattered around, taking shots of raspberry lemonade, delving through their knock-off designer totes, splashing bronzer on their necks, and slyly sipping coconut rum out of their salmon-pink crocodile flasks. Sosie winced. She'd be sharing Alistair Dwelling with a few neighboring primaries from cities near Bluffdale: girls they had totally smoked in dance and cheerleading competitions. Girls with ingrown toenails and mustaches. She hated all of them already.

The woman behind the desk loudly swigged her vanilla roast as she read the computer screen carefully. "So you two are the ones, huh?" she said finally, grinning wickedly down on them. "Well, come with me, then." She jumped onto her flats and jangled loose keys from her hand, stuffing them into a pocket. "Grab your things," she demanded as she slid between the two. Both girls got a fresh whiff of her nauseating potpourri perfume, and Sosie moaned as her stomach flip-flopped and she was forced to re-swallow some of that morning's breakfast.

She and Nala followed the brisk, peppery bun to an opened elevator. "Seventh floor," she commanded Sosie, once aboard. Sosie pressed the button, and the elevator door closed. A jingle of classic jazz trickled through the speakers as the elevator started up. "I'm Miss Marilyn," the woman said. "Your new housemother. Curfew is ten o'clock sharp Sunday through Thursday, and otherwise, midnight. Boys are restricted from the dormitory after hours. Any deviations from this rule are only acceptable with a permission slip signed by a BU professor or Principal Dotie. Otherwise, make arrangements for a fresh manicure, because if you break the rules you'll be scrubbing the scum off of the community restroom toilets until you puke in one."

"Good to know." Sosie nodded.

The elevator door sprung open and Miss Marilyn waddled out. "No music or television during study hall hours." She barreled down a hallway crammed with freshman girls dancing to Britpop in their underwear, scuffling through their knock-off Laurent Le Blanc monogram canvas suitcases, and flinging their cutaway bikinis through a fog of hairspray. "Try to vacuum twice a week. We get a lot of sugar flies during the fall."

As Sosie and Nala wandered the hall, their combats trotting in unison as they dodged hairdryers and bath salts, a girl with strawberry-colored Edwardian braids and a blush-pink rose crown stared wide-eyed back at them as she flossed. "Woah! You two are like, freaking models! Lana, come check this out! These girls are like, freaking models!"

Nala batted her long, black eyelashes at Edwardian braids and her Goth friend, Lana. She loved being called a model.

"Thanks, dolls," Sosie said, dragging Nala away before she started talking runway. Besides, it wasn't anything out of the ordinary, being praised by a pair of poorly lined lips, that is.

Marilyn stopped at room 779, the last on the floor. The door was painted powder blue with a charming, pigeon-sized window for a peephole. "Here we are," Marilyn coughed, tugging the keys out from her tweed blazer pocket. "Don't lose your keys or you'll have to pay a fine." She nudged the door open.

Sosie slipped through the entry and chucked her duffel and book bags beneath a bed before bellyflopping onto the mattress. Nala followed after her, dragging her suitcase and blowing her hair out of her face. The room was spacious and decorated like a French boutique: a total upgrade from their flat in Bluffdale.

"Why'd we get such a big room?" Sosie hummed as she rolled on her back. There was something suspicious about the twin, bo-ho-chic canopy beds and dappled pearl table lamps. It was almost too perfect.

"Is something wrong with it?" Nala wondered.

Sosie blinked up at the ceiling.

"Nothing's wrong with it." Miss Marilyn rolled her sleeves up her white, veiny arms and thinned her lips.

"Come on, Marilyn. It's not mold, is it? Tell me I don't have to sleep in one of those hideous asbestos facemasks." Sosie hopped off of her bed and unzipped her luggage. If asbestos were the problem, she'd probably just cut up one of those hand-knitted scarves she had received for Christmas from Juliet and wear it around the dorm like a motley tube. At least this year she lived in an area where an ugly muffler might come in handy.

"No asbestos, and no mold. And for that matter, no more questions!" Marilyn brushed her fingers over her bouclé-knit, one-button skirt suit. Her breasts surged from the top like twin pyramids.

"Take 'em," Miss Marilyn said, offering up a pair of matching keys. "Before I fine you for wasting my time."

"Thanks for the grand tour, Maryls." Sosie rolled her eyes as she snatched up both keys. Even if Miss Marilyn was some hideous, four-foot-eleven recluse, she didn't have to be such a wet-towel. After all, moving day was supposed to be the most exciting day for the girls since their February vacation to that little ranch outside of Bluffdale. Even though churning butter hadn't been all the hoopla Miss Iris had made it out to be, Tess, in a moment of weakness, had squirted herself in the eye with milk straight from a cow's udder. Which made the trip entirely worthwhile, Sosie thought.

Marilyn stuck near the bedroom door, picking flakey, powder blue paint from the hinges with her sharp fingernails. "Phone the front desk if you're planning on having visitors," she screeched, pointing out a vintage, princess telephone with a spiral chord. "We leave for dinner soon." Marilyn swooped out the front door and yanked it shut behind her.

Sosie slipped beneath her warm, cotton voile quilt. Why was it that all dormitory rooms had to be as cold as a meat freezer?

"Our little chunk of Heaven," Nala chirped, breaking into her perfectly packed bag. She couldn't wait to color-coordinate her reach-in closet. "Think our parents bought this place for us?" she asked Sosie as she unraveled a brand new peplum dress. Nala tried to imagine what her parents looked like — as she always did when she brought them up — but couldn't. She had never seen them before, only heard from her old housemother, Miss Iris, what they looked like. Both had dark hair and deep, suntanned skin. Her mother's eyes were hazel, and her father's were brown. Nala was "the perfect mix."

"Maybe they did," Sosie groaned as her eyes drifted shut. She was exhausted. One set of blackout curtains away from hibernating until December. "They'd have to be pretty rich to afford it."

"Hope so." Nala kicked her combats off and folded her legs Indian style, clinging to the price tag of her newest purchase. *Rich parents.* Would that, by association, make her rich? Because her shopping addiction wouldn't go well with a crummy trust fund. "Hope we get our bank accounts soon," she said, flattening a pair of wrinkled, rose-bloom skinnies against the floor. "I've been having these nightmares about it. They always seem normal, at first. I'm trying on this *gorgeous*, ruby shift dress in a boutique off campus. I mean . . . *gorgeous*! And there's this heavy-banged sales rep hovering over me while I change. Totally naked, stripping down right in front of her as she watches me . . . seriously creepy now that I think about it, but still besides the point," she giggled. "Then, suddenly, the floor caves in and I start to fall. I fall until I sink knee-deep into a pool of debt collection papers.

And every time, I wake up the same way. Soaked in sweat, staring at my closet." Nala took in a deep breath and gulped. At least she'd never have to see that lame spear closet again. "I just want to know if I'm sitting on a pile of cash or if I'm burying myself in loans. Rich or poor. Too much to ask?" Nala nibbled on her teal ombre nails. In two long weeks at the Monetary Analysis Assembly, she'd find out.

"Ever stop worrying?" Sosie yawned. "Even for a minute?"

"I'm not sure," Nala shrugged. She scooped up a few bottles of her favorite No. 3 perfume from Jon Matinee, hopped up and began to organize them around her vanity. An antique, crème treasures desk was something she had wanted since she'd paged through her first furniture catalogue in eighth grade, and now here it was — slightly more distressed than she would have picked herself, but still charming. The drawers were sizeable, but reeked of spoiled wine, and in the far right shadow of the first bin, the cursive initials "J & G" had been chipped into the wood. "What would you guess 'J & G' stands for?" Nala asked, running her fingers across the engraving.

"Hmm. Junk and Groin?" Sosie laughed.

Nala hated talking about anything penis-related, but those genitalia-slang overhead slides in Pre-Male Anatomy had been too cheeky for Sosie to ignore. Junk and groin were fast moving up her list of favorite inappropriate things to say. "Don't get your panties in a twist, La. Probably just some losers in love a few years ago."

Nala shoveled her twenty-some lipstick tubes into the top drawer and slammed it closed. Sosie slipped off of her bed and shoveled through her purse. A candy bar had melted and coated the bottom of the lining in thick, gooey chocolate, but she kept digging, anyway. Even though her fingertips were sticky with caramel, she needed those painkillers. She finally found them, and popped open the bottle and poured three tiny, purple pills into her hand. "Bottoms up," she cracked, throwing her head back. The pills tasted dry and chemically on her tongue as she tried to swallow them.

Suddenly, an ear-piercing alarm shook the dormitory walls. Sosie and Nala could hear screechy, bedroom doors creaking open and a chorus of girls squealing. Sosie jogged to the bedroom door and wedged it open. She watched as her neighbors reapplied lip gloss and combed out their knotted hair ends, lined against the hallway like kids in matching pajama sets waiting for Christmas gifts. "Nala, get out here!" Sosie said. Nala slipped her pedicured toes back inside her boots, and tiptoed to the doorway.

"Report immediately to the cafeteria. Dinner is served in ten minutes. Report immediately to the cafeteria. Dinner is served in ten minutes," an automated voice reverberated through the speakers.

Nearby, a smoky haired, hefty girl and a giant, six-foot red-head, locked up their bedroom door and raced for the elevators, their thighs smacking together as they ran. Sosie rolled her eyes. Was this how it was going to be for every meal? A rat race for the cheese? The cheese being . . . the boys.

"There's Juliet," Nala said, pointing down the hallway to a bush of yellow curls. Sosie locked the door and followed. Juliet Bigsby's frizzy hair had been combed through with gel and slicked back against her scalp, styled half-up, half-down doo. She still looked undeniably frumpy.

"Juliet!" Nala yelled over the noise. Juliet smiled cheesily as she maneuvered through the crowded flat. It was good to know she hadn't yet been forgotten by Nala Middleton: Bluffdale Goddess, and soon to be Blairstown Queen-bee.

"You girls on the seventh floor, too?" Juliet ran a finger over her mouth. Nala's lips were so perfect and full that Juliet couldn't stop staring at them.

"779," Nala smiled.

"I'm in 717," Juliet said. "The one freaking room that shares a wall with the community restroom. Milly Hodge told me that Miss Iris told the school that I had 'bladder issues,' and now the two of us are stuck falling asleep to the sound of flushing toilets."

Camilla Hodge was a pale-skinned, tragically unsocial bookworm who tutored Juliet, and occasionally Sosie, back at Bluffdale Prep in exchange for social status. She had honeydew-blonde hair usually prepared in French braids, thin lips, and spunky, clean-cut rectangular glasses that made her look like a boy.

"Doubt it," Sosie said. "Have you forgotten that Tess, your bitch of a best friend, is a class-A shit-stirrer?"

Juliet remained peculiarly mute. Sosie had a point.

A group of fifteen girls waiting to catch the next elevator all stuffed aboard as it opened and clicked the button for the first floor. Sosie, Nala, and Juliet slipped in, their toes just an inch away from the door as it slid closed.

"I'm nervous," Juliet squealed into the silence, stuffing her hands into her pockets and pulling out a carton of breath mints. She wouldn't be caught dead introducing herself to sexy, new boys with kettle-corn breath. "Want some?" she offered, flicking the lid off. Sosie grabbed a few and popped them onto her tongue. Peppermint wasn't her favorite, but it would hold her over until dinner. Nala shook her head.

The elevator doors opened on the first floor. Standing before the exit, Miss Marilyn clapped her ancient hands through the air until the crowd encircled her. Sosie could have sworn she saw dust escaping her goofy clap. "Time to fill those bellies," Miss Marilyn horsed in her old lady voice. "Follow me."

Marilyn elbowed the door open and shuffled down the steps to the courtyard. Once outside, a few girls expanded their individual campus maps and traced their fingers along the paper as they walked. Sosie, Nala, and Juliet were the last out of the dormitory doors.

"I think I may throw up." Juliet threw her hands over her mouth. In the distance, she could see a few peppercorn-haired boys dressed in blazers racing down the steps of the male dormitory, Marlborough Hall. One was sort of cute. They were the first boys she had ever seen in person, and not from a window on the bus. "Oh god. What do you think boys like to talk about?"

"Greasy, bar food," Sosie shrugged. "If you're gonna hurl, mind doing it near the bushes?"

"She'll be fine," Nala said, scooping up a hank of Juliet's blonde hair and playing with it. She noticed that Juliet's anxiety-triggered eczema had re-surfaced behind her ears, making her skin look like something straight out of an extra-terrestrial science fiction mag. *Now I may throw up,* Nala thought, but kept silent.

Sosie swallowed as her eyes took in the massive dining hall. A patriotic banner was hooked across the gables, reading: "Welcome Freshmen to Blairstown University." Not very original, but it would do.

Marilyn charged up the steps to the dining hall and clapped her hands again. The crowd of girls restrained their can't-wait-to-meet-the-boys giggling and blinked through the fading sun-rays up at Marilyn. How dare she stand between them and their future husbands? "This is where you'll be eating your meals," Marilyn said, making note of the Gothic Revival architecture. As if anyone cared. "The breakfast buffet opens at six a.m. and closes at nine a.m., sharp. Don't be that girl caught ordering eggs benedict at nine oh one. It's just embarrassing." She squinted at the girls. "Lunch opens at eleven a.m. and runs until three p.m. Dinner is at seven. Any questions?"

No one raised a hand.

"Well then," she piped, "follow me."

The entry doors were flung open and the parade of girls pushed inside. Screams echoed from the ceilings as the girls hair-tugged, elbow-gutted, and accused each other of trampling brand new organic boots. Sosie, Nala, and Juliet hung back.

"Gino may be behind those doors, Sos" Nala said, scooting forward. The hype of the first coed meal wasn't all that thrilling to her, except for her best friend's possible reunion with Gino Blackthorn. Nala knew herself better than to get worked up over juvenile boys with boob-obsessions. Miss Iris had mentioned a few times the male preoccupation with busty women. Nala's boobs were a perky b-cup. She liked them, even though they weren't turning any heads. Regardless, she couldn't help but feel too mature for the boys she had spotted briefly about campus — from a window on the bus. Maybe she'd start the year off dating an urbane senior well versed in European wines — one of the captains on the BU rowing team. Better him than some freshman pervert, she decided.

"How do I look?" Sosie asked, rubbing her hair flat. If she had brought a purse, maybe she wouldn't feel so naked. Suddenly, she didn't know what to do with her hands.

"Great!" Juliet said, positive she would blow chunks in the garden if she kept quiet. "You're totally gorgeous, Sos," she added brightly. But "Sos" felt weird coming out of her mouth, and she immediately wished she hadn't gone there. When Nala said it, it almost sounded like a full name. "Here comes Sos wearing that flirty, leopard-print cardigan," for example. But when Juliet said it, it just sounded like a mistake. "Hey there Sos — ugh — ieeeee." Juliet cringed. There was no room for her in Nala and Sosie's duet.

Nala brushed a blonde wisp from Sosie's face. "That Gino Blackthorn guy isn't going to know what hit him."

Sosie nodded and skipped up the stairs, cleaning up her lip gloss with her fingers. Even if Gino Blackthorn wasn't inside, hundreds of other dreamy, snowboard-bodied hunks would be, and she'd be damned if she didn't make a lasting impression on every single one of them.

Sosie glanced back at Nala and Juliet who were both hanging by the sidewalk, waiting on her. Sosie finally pushed the dining hall door in. "Take a deep breath, girls. Our lives are about to change forever."

Something About Girls

Gino Blackthorn pushed his thick, brown hair out of his eyes and yawned. Maybe it was only 7 p.m., but the bus ride from Elkins over to BU earlier that morning was exhausting, and all he wanted to do was roll a joint from his pot plant, appropriately named Doobie, and smoke it until he passed out. But Doobie now belonged to Christopher Thumb—a junior back at The Academy of Windsor—and Gino was perfectly and groggily awake. He slunk down the buffet line, filling his plate with smoked brisket, grilled flank steak, and gourmet mac and cheese. He'd left his plant behind, but he sure as hell was eating like he was stoned.

Near the seafood, a girl with scary-big eyes pinged a few shrimps onto her plate. Gino waited impatiently, grunting a little. Were all girls this slow? Before moving on to the tilapia, the girl blinked up at Gino, shrieked, and suddenly dashed toward three girls who were tampering with their honey-lime glazed ahi tuna at a faraway table.

"What are they so scared of?" Gino asked his buddy Knox Ritchie, who was debating between the stout beer short ribs and the tangy-sweet slaw and pulled-pork burger. A few more girls stumbled below the surfeit of ceiling frescos, latching onto each other's cardigan sleeves and examining the boys thoroughly. They were scientists ogling rats. Which man shall find his way through the maze and to the cheese first?

"Intimidated, Blackthorn. They're intimidated by us," Knox said. He furrowed his eyebrows at a heap of little, black fish eggs thrown into a bowl. Maybe he'd eat them if there were a girl to impress, somewhere. Knox scooped a mound onto his plate. "Want to make a bet? Which one of these 'aspiring-models' will go skinny-dipping in the rowing lake first—will it be 'mosquito bites' in the corner," he pointed out a slender redhead who was bluntly nipping through a see-through blouse "or Skeletor by the punch bowl?"

"My money's on the asshole eating the weird black shit." Gino grabbed a roll of bread and took off.

"Sounds good to me!" Knox followed, his notch lapel cotton blazer twining behind him as he strolled coolly by. All around, girls dropped their forks just to watch Gino and Knox walk. Gino's cool, brown eyes; his deep, olive skin; his big, muscular shoulders. Knox's sandy-brown hair flopping into his eyes; his lips curving perfectly; his suntanned skin glowing beneath the chandeliers of golden teak crystal.

Oh yeah. They were hot.

Gino plunged into an opened club chair and stabbed into his steak. Medium rare, just as he liked it.

"Dude, how can you eat?" Rocko Borai rubbed his short, stubbly hair and then dropped into a chair next to them.

Rocko was always hanging around Gino and Knox, even though they didn't really like him much. He'd wear deep V-necks, he'd fist pump, he'd carry around handles of whiskey at every party he attended, he'd steal his friends' lame jokes, he'd walk shirtless around the gym. Rocko was just *that guy*. He scratched his short, black buzz again, wishing he had a drink to sip on. Brandy, maybe. Scotch. Gin. He didn't really care what it was. "You think all of them are wearing bras and panties?" He asked. His eyes zoomed across the room. There was something about this brunette across the room. "Dude. You guys check her out, yet?"

"Who?" Knox asked, rolling up the sleeves of his blazer. He seriously doubted that he and Rocko would have the same taste in women, but there was no harm in looking.

"The one wearing that jacket-thing," Rocko said.

"They're all wearing those jacket-things."

"Yeah, but she's wearing hers well. Like . . . reeeeaaaaaal well."

"Make him shut up," Gino muttered, licking his fingers.

"Hold on. I want to see her," Knox said. "If she's really that great." His eyes zoomed around the dining hall. There were a few cute girls slurping harvest tomato soup out of their bread bowls near the Victorian grated chimney. There was a pretty senior out on the terrace sipping cabernet as she mulled over her friend's plate of bruschetta; her grungy, neo-bohemian bangs spilling into her eyes. There was a platinum blonde strutting around on crocheted platform booties, showing off her bed hair. And then . . . finally . . . at the center table . . . a girl with golden-flaked eyes, windswept brown hair, and a cute chin dimple panned into his view. Her fingers clasped around a red-apple juice box while she listened to a girlfriend of hers brag about her aubergine polyester-charmeuse bedspread that was so *to die for*. The girl was Nala Middleton. She dragged her fork across the bacon bits of her blue cheese wedge.

"Wow." Knox swallowed hard. He had never seen anything so beautiful in his entire life. Not even the intense sapphire-blue view from his water skis. Not even the Newport Plum-sprinkled highlands of Elkins. Not even during sunset. He took a distracted drink of water. "Who is she?"

"Dude, who knows," Rocko shrugged. "All I know is, our lives sucked until today. Didn't they? Melons and cucumbers were the closest we had come to boobs and shaved-legs. We were like . . . horny zombies. Dead, but filled with testosterone."

Knox cleared his throat as he ignored Rocko, and watched the girl bite into a crouton. He'd never believed in love at first sight. It sounded so lame just a couple of days before, like V-necks and fist pumping. Like Rocko. But suddenly, it was as clear as his underground aquified, three-times purified, sparkling water. Love at first sight had hit him straight in the eyes.

"Damn it." He gulped his drink. "I *need* to know her."

"Go introduce yourself." Their friend Emmitt Fink, a.k.a "Brains," shrugged inside of his navy, cashmere blazer from across the table, as if it were so simple. Emmitt's savvy, rimless glasses slipped down his nose as he debated between herb-mustard salmon and lemon-pepper tilapia, both slapped on his plate. Were they both prepared gluten free? Why didn't he check the nutrition facts? Damn it. Did the chefs use soy? He stared down through his glasses at his pitiful plate.

Gino yawned noisily as he looked around at his suddenly silent tablemates. Knox was staring hopelessly at that brunette girl, Rocko was ogling some girl's thong strap peeking out of the top of her mini skirt, and Brains was fondling his inhaler. Gino clanked his fork against his plate. Boring, boring, boring. They were all boring. He'd known this was going to happen. They'd move to Blairstown, and Knox, Rocko, and Brains would all become big, boring wanks.

Knox ripped his eyes away from Nala with great reluctance. He'd meet her, eventually . . . even if it killed him. But not today. "So, Blackthorn. You talk to that girl, yet?"

"What girl?" Gino asked.

"*What girl?*" Rocko taunted. "That blonde girl you met in Bluffdale, dipshit."

"Oh, her? No." He shrugged. And so what if he had? It would be none of their damn business.

"What was she like?" Brains slipped to the edge of his deep-buttoned, tufted dining stool and vacuumed plain yogurt through his teeth. White goo flecked his face. He looked at Gino with a gaze both pitiful and needy, like one of those kids in the "feed-the-hungry" ads.

"Told you everything already."

"All right. Then tell us again. What'd she look like?" Rocko licked his lips at the G-string panties.

"Skinny with blonde hair," Gino said, stabbing at his smoked brisket. "I can't remember her name." He took an annoyed drink of water. He thought of hot summers back in Elkins when he, Knox, Rocko, Brains, and a boy named Max Umminger would sneak-off to a wetland swamp with a bottle of whisky and hit Knox's monogrammed golf balls into the marsh until everything went black. They'd barbeque and shoot shit with pellet guns. They'd smoke cigars. They'd climb eight-foot crags and flip off. But things were going to be different now that they were living in Blairstown. Girls were apparently a needy distraction; some sophomores, juniors, and seniors hackling at their boyfriends for freshly brewed sweet tea and watermelon salad already.

At least he had that to look forward to.

"Was she hot?" Knox asked.

Gino closed his eyes and let his neck dangle over the back of his chair. Maybe the girl he had met back in Bluffdale was a total knockout. Maybe she did have thin legs and speckled, rosy skin. Maybe her sun-kissed eyelashes were really cute, and her raspy voice made him a little horny. But, who cared? She was just some girl he had met on a beach when he got bored and decided to blow off football practice. Why was it a big deal? He wished he had never told anyone.

Gino peeled his eyes open, although his head still dangled down the back of his chair.

There.

A crimp-haired blonde dipped her fried chicken strips into a puddle of ranch dressing. It was that girl. Sosie. Frisky as usual — at least, from what he had known about her — arguing with some snob about carbs. "There are no carbs in hamburger meat, Tess. Read a freakin' book!"

"Is that the girl?" Rocko asked suddenly.

Gino snapped his head back up.

"Dude, I know you heard me. Is that her?"

Gino looked back again. By that time, Sosie had moved on to a slender beak of sparkling apple cider, and was cheersing her group of friends.

Gino watched her take a drink. "That's not her," he lied casually, messing-up his bushy, brown strands of hair with his fingers.

Rocko straightened up and flattened out his blazer. "I'm going back for seconds," he said, eyeing the waiters replacing the salad bar with raspberry-rhubarb pie and amaretto apple streusel cupcakes. "Anyone else?"

Brains shook his head and slumped backwards into his chair. If he wanted a something, he'd have to browse the nutrition details on every dish. Nut and gluten allergies made it impossible to casually grab a dessert.

Rocko paraded off smugly, making suggestive eye contact with a second-year on the dance team on his way to scout for anything espresso flavored near the pudding, while Brains picked at the tasteless arugula on his dinner plate. "I don't get it. He's such a prick, and look," Brains said, pointing at Rocko who was already chatting up some girl. His phony smile glistened. The hot, honey-blonde, yoga-bodied dancer batted her gigantic eyelashes up at him while he complimented her personality. "You're adorable," Brains heard Rocko say while he gave her a pervy wink.

"Let me tell you something about girls," Gino said. "Something that Coach told me back at Windsor," he added, starting to regret his decision to pass on dessert. Two-a-days began bright and early the next day, and he was beginning to think he should carbo-load on something awesome before he got his ass whooped into even better shape. "Tell 'em what they want to hear, and they'll do anything you want them to."

"Anything?" Brains gulped, feeling an enormous amount of pressure. Power wasn't something he wanted: not the way Rocko, Knox, or Gino did, anyway. Brains would be perfectly content settling down with someone sweet and maternal, someone who could make a kick-ass pot roast and would sit with him to watch the sunset spill over the mountains from their humble, wrap-around patio.

"You should listen to Gino," Knox said dolefully, spooning up the soggy croutons that floated in his French onion soup. "One time, Gino told me to run through the circle drill during practice to help with ball security. Hardly fumble at all, any more. Remember that, Blackthorn?"

"Yeah," Gino nodded. "You used to be such an asshole out on the field."

Rocko returned then, carrying with him a plate of espresso crinkles and a used napkin "Gentlemen." He slammed his food onto the tabletop, shook out the napkin, and read from a marker smudge. "I present to you Shanna, apartment number 349." With a smirk, he rolled up the napkin and buried it in his blazer pocket. The boys looked across the flat to the same girl Rocko had met near the pudding station, now cupping her Dance Captain jacket sleeves in her hands and whispering to three, similarly-dressed "Hip-hop Alliance" friends about—they assumed—Rocko.

"She's a sophomore, enjoys ballet, and bakes the finest cake balls at BU." He chuckled under his breath, avoiding some cliché sexual innuendo. "By tomorrow's eve," he said, slipping cockily into his seat cushion, "I will have seen, and fondled, her boobs."

Gino rolled his eyes. Knox whispered, "Dear Lord, help that woman."

As the cafeteria began to empty, Gino took one more look at Sosie. She was sitting contentedly, picking at her cheesecake and laughing at her friend, who seemed to pour sparkling cider down her blouse. He needed to remember her, everything about her. Her skin. Her eyes. Her lips. He had to remember.

Because beginning tomorrow morning, Sosie was the first thing he needed to forget.

King Leatherwood

Nala Middleton and Sosie Hinkhouse strolled together across the Portuguese walkway, linking arms, Sosie's swollen eyes hidden behind a pair of mirrored, pink lenses. They were both wearing their stuffy, newfangled uniforms: purple and ruby knit sweaters, plaid skirts, knee-high socks, and black and white sneakers. Sosie was wearing a cream, cable knit scarf with matching legwarmers. August was *not* too early to start dressing Fall-mod.

Blairstown University was some sort of extravagant bubble world, the girls were beginning to notice. Sosie caught a glimpse of the snow-drenched mountaintops in the distance, and imagined a weekend up in some secluded cabin with Gino Blackthorn, Nala, and whatever hot jock Nala was seeing — probably some hunky boy with designer watches and flowy model hair. They would cozy up before a fire, slurping marshmallow hot chocolate and playing a racy version of truth or dare.

Nala observed the square-mile lawn. It was sprinkled with violet million bells and patchy Chinese redbuds. It was all very romantic . . . and sort of cheesy.

"Last night was like, the worst sleep I've ever gotten." Sosie tried to roll out the crick in her neck. Maybe if she hadn't stayed up all night thinking about Gino, she'd actually have an operable body. Why hadn't she been able to find him at dinner? Had he lied about attending BU? Or, did they catch him in Bluffdale and expel him before he had the chance to attend Blairstown? Not knowing was agony.

"Why didn't you say something? I would have made you tea," Nala piped.

"That's *exactly* why I didn't say anything," admitted Sosie. Tea was her least favorite beverage — ever — especially when it was hot. But Nala was such an angel, Sosie couldn't stand to destroy one of her dreams, like making use of that creepy, piggy-shaped teakettle Miss Iris had bought her for graduation. Nala would be thrilled at the opportunity to try it out, and Sosie would be her poor, sick, sleepless guinea pig.

Nala drew her shoes over the walkway. She practiced smiling once or twice. She was focusing on making a good impression on her first BU instructor. Especially since it was Professor Leatherwood: the silver haired, nicotine-stained, coffee-breathed Kissing teacher. At least, that was how she pictured him.

"Will you be totally honest with me?" Nala asked, pulling at her sleeves. Sosie nodded, and started to braid the ends of her totally flat, one-dimensional, blondest-blonde hair. "Am I easy to like?" she asked. "I mean, do people generally — do they, like — do you think. . . ." *Ugh.* Why was it so damn difficult to just ask a question, sometimes? "Let's say you need a favor. Do you ask me, or do you ask some tech-nerd with a photographic memory and an Einstein GPA?"

"Duh. You," Sosie said. "And afterward — to show my appreciation — I buy you one of those pumpkin spice lattes you hate to love, and drag you to an ice-skating rink to watch all the clumsy girls fall," she added. "Because you used to be one of them."

Nala grabbed her face in her hands and blushed. No one was supposed to know about her embarrassing figure skating career in Primary, back when she dressed in little burgundy couture leotards and went by the nickname "Bunhead." That was Bluffdale. Primary. Childhood. This was college. Blairstown. Boys.

"Look, I can tell you're nervous." Sosie flipped her hair behind a shoulder and stared the Kissing 101 building up and down. It was kind of cute, in a gothic sort of way. "Just do your brainiac thing, and Professor Leatherwave will 'A-plus' your ass right into Kissing 201!"

"Leatherwood, Sos." Nala said. "And maybe you should lay off the swear words. Boys aren't into it, 'member?"

"Did I say ass? I meant rump!" Sosie poorly faked an English accent. "Oh, don't fret, my little a-class bumblebee. That darling professor of ours will surely pass your hotsie-totsie rump straight into sophomore year. Cheerio!"

"I wouldn't be so sure."

"Don't worry about him. He's just some loser who never got married. If all else fails . . . unbutton!" Sosie stuck out her chest and watched Nala tense up. Even if Nala was her best friend in the entire world, she couldn't resist playing a little, raunchy joke on her every once in a while.

Nala grabbed her arms. Joking or not, She wasn't about to unbutton her blouse and show off her b-cup goods to some pervy, fifty-something nut job who probably collected nudie pics of collegiate girls for a hobby. In a big way, she already felt sorry for Professor Leatherwood.

Kissing Schools, as they had come to be known, were the strictest form of private university in the country, and had been for centuries. From birth, babies were separated into same-sex cities according to their gender. Places like Bluffdale or Elkins carried on like any other school district, only attendees were restricted to the grounds. Girls never saw boys and boys never saw girls. Both never met their parents. They were taught according to their gender — women were educated on the fundamentals of motherhood and home economics, while men were educated in business, medicine, engineering, or another subject leading to a professional career.

Some parents sent their kids off to single-sex boarding to preserve their innocence. Others claimed it built great character, weakened distraction, produced the finest academic graduates across the globe. Many just wanted to get rid of their children while they sailed the Virgin Islands sipping cosmos and baking in the perfect, 80-degree breeze. And a handful had attended such boarding programs, found love, lived great lives, and wanted the same for their offspring.

Naturally, though it was all so unnatural.

The rules of all Kissing Schools across the country were pretty simple: find a mate and marry within the years at school, or never find a mate and volunteer ten years of your life to the system. It was all so fifteenth century. If an attending student went four years without tying the knot, his or her fate for the next decade was decided by a couple of stuck-up, toffee-nosed graduates. Females without a proposal by their fourth and final year were granted an embarrassing homecoming back to Bluffdale (to nanny and instruct Primary school girls, to run dinky boutique stores and restaurants, or to join the housemaid bureau), a job opportunity to lecture at BU as a professor or become a waitress, saleswoman, or housemaid within BU grounds, or to live as an outcast on some topless beach somewhere and pray she wasn't sued for tarnishing her academic contract. Men without fiancés were delivered a similar fate—although bachelors would raise and instruct Primary school *boys*, of course. And it seemed to hold that after ten years of working on campus or in a single-sex city, few staff members ever left. The institution warped them somehow, like those criminals who come to love prison.

Most parents who liked the idea of single-sex cities and Kissing Schools were either seriously stringent and traditional, had gone through the system themselves and came out of it with bright and beautiful futures ahead of them, or truly wanted to mold their children into what they believed to be the best of their potential as human beings and—debatably more important—as spouses. Just as Blairstown University promised, a BU education was "the closest to perfect life can get".

Still, many students didn't really understand why graduating with a fiancé was so important? Perhaps the coupling rate was a marketing tool for the school, just as the Ivy Leagues had once used alumna I.Q. scores and successful business ventures to gain attention. Or maybe married life was simply . . . close to perfect.

The girls climbed the steps of the building and read what was carved in large, gothic lettering into a plaque of gneiss stone: Kissing 101. Nala speculated whether she'd love or hate showing up at 9 a.m. Monday through Friday, her lips ready to pucker up, though she remembered Sosie vaguely promising that Kissing 101 was about a lot more than just . . . making out.

Sosie rolled her pretty, green eyes, hating the intensity of the morning sunlight plunging through her shades, and kicked the door open.

Inside, the classroom appeared a square of two rows of five flipper training tables. The room was already mostly full. A gang of boys were huddled around a desk counting colored bra-straps through see-through blouses. And in response, the girls hid behind their hands and giggled. How were they supposed to kiss such brave little idiots?

Nala and Sosie took two of the last seats available, which happened to be at one of the twin front desks. "Ugh, I look like such a teacher's pet," Sosie groaned. If Professor Leatherwood ever pulled a fast one, and called her out when her hand was obviously not raised, she'd plot hideous revenge, like throwing a red sock in a load of his white laundry, or writing a raunchy love-note signed by him to Principal Dotie. Sosie tossed her bohemian book bag onto the desktop and began shuffling through the rubbish. She wished she was one of those type-A, organized freaks—the one who always had a pencil ready—just like Nala.

"Can you believe he's late?" Nala squeaked, sinking into her chair. Looking over a shoulder at the noisy classroom, Nala's eyes narrowed on a group of boys who had noticed her back. She sort of waved, and mustered up a cute, laidback grin that showed off her perfectly round lips. "Yo, sweetheart," a juiced-up guy with a peach-fuzz goatee said. "I think I'm in love with you." He licked his crackled lips back at her.

Ew. That was the last time she'd do that!

"Ah-ha! Here it is!" Sosie blurted out, ripping a pathetic scrap of notebook paper from the receipt pool at the bottom of her bag. She flattened it with her arm against the table and cleared her throat. "Dark hair, thick eyebrows, tan skin," she began to read.

"What is that?" Nala asked, peeking over Sosie's scarf.

"This is my 'Gino Blackthorn' cheat sheet. I wrote it the day I met him."

"Mighty paranoid of you."

"Well, I didn't want to embarrass him by like, forgetting what he looked like! You know I have the worst memory." Sosie dragged out her lip gloss tube from her bag. "Dark hair, thick eyebrows, tan skin, muscles, straight teeth," she read as she soaked her lips in tangerine goo. "Don't worry. I didn't write anything dirty, Sister Nala. Your eyes won't burn if you take a peek."

Nala blinked her wispy, long-lashed eyes. She wasn't the prude killjoy everyone made her out to be. And just because she didn't want to study some bizarre Gino Blackthorn checklist with spilled froyo crusting over the word "sizeable" (Yikes. Where was that going?), that didn't mean she was on the path to a nunnery.

"When you see him, you'll remember him," Nala said.

"You think? Maybe he's in this room right now." Sosie pushed her thin side-bangs behind her ears and slyly glanced over her shoulder, scanning the room. There were a couple of boys with brown, fox cuts, but both were like, five-feet tall and hideous. Another boy was particularly dreamy, but way too clean-shaven to be Gino, and had sandy, over-gelled hair. Sosie never expected Gino to be an easy find, of course. In all of her dreams about him, their first meet at BU was always somewhere dark and sexy with crystal teardrop chandeliers and sophisticated lounge futons.

"Whatever. I'm happy he's not here," Sosie said, stuffing all the outpour of her messenger back inside and tossing it under her desk. "I probably wouldn't remember him, anyway."

Just as Sosie cleared away all of her crap, the classroom door coasted open. A worn, Italian leather briefcase the color of tobacco slipped inside the room first. After it came a tall man in a navy, bar-striped, long-sleeved button-up. He marched up to the blackboard and started to write.

"It's the professor," Sosie whispered coolly under her breath. "He looks kind of hot."

Nala watched the professor scribble his name across the board and afterward, dust off his chalky fingers on his slacks. His hair was chestnut brown with a bit of wave to it, and the skin at the back of his neck was olive-tan — probably the aftermath of some fancy water-skiing competition he had spent all summer at the lake preparing for. A poor man's Kentucky Derby. His arms flexed, and she guessed that he was hiding a firm, athlete's body beneath his stiff business wear.

The professor turned and flashed a crisp, white smile. *Woahhh.* Her heart flipped inside of her. He wasn't exactly the three hundred-pound, balding asshole she had expected when his corky name popped up on her BU first-semester schedule. This Professor Leatherwood had perfect, glowing skin, no wrinkles, and a cute, buns-of-steel soccer-butt. "So, this is all of you?" he asked curiously, barreling his hazel eyes over the quiet bunch. His lips curled into a sweet, nervous grin. "This is my first class," he admitted, unbuckling his briefcase and ripping out some papers.

"Looks like we snagged the best seats in the house." Sosie elbowed Nala in the ribs. "Professor Leatherwood is a *babe.*"

Leatherwood flipped through a small sheaf of papers as he circled around his desk. "Should I take attendance, or should I just that trust all of you are here?" Was that supposed to be a joke, or not? The nerves in his voice made him sound young, like one of them.

Was this a practical joke? One of the senior boys messing around?

One boy piped up from the back of the room, "Attendance is overrated." His obnoxious water polo buddies praised him by howling some cheesy chant. *OH-VER-RAY-TED!* Sosie rolled her eyes and hid her face in her palms. *How much more hooting could she stand this early in the A.M.?*

"All right, settle down. We won't do attendance today, but be ready next time," the professor said.

He sat against the front of his desk and grinned excitedly. "My name is Professor Leatherwood, or Mr. Leatherwood, or King Leatherwood if you want. Does everyone know what this class is?" he asked. No one answered. One girl was blatantly texting away on her razor-thin cellphone and coughing to hide the sound of her keyboard buttons. Another boy flipped through a mixed martial arts catalogue, yanking on his friend's blazer sleeve to whisper loudly, "the rear naked choke."

"Well, does anyone have any questions, then?"

From the back of the room, Knox Ritchie whipped his effortlessly waved hair out of his face and threw his hand in the air. His eyes stuck to Nala. *Beautiful. Perfect. A freaking goddess.* His knees weakened. He prayed to grab her attention.

Professor Leatherwood pointed, and Knox jumped onto his European imported boat shoes and cleared his throat loudly. Sosie turned around at the sound of his cough and found herself admiring his eyes, which looked sort of emerald in the lighting. The boy with the over-gelled hair. Pretty hot. A little short. She chipped absently at her green nail polish.

Knox relaxed, and tried to grin as he stared wishfully at his crush. What the hell was it that made Nala so damn distracting? His eyes bounced to Professor Leatherwood, who was tapping his plain, russet loafers against the tile, waiting for some sort of something to be said. A pair of russet loafers was the last thing on earth Knox would be caught dead wearing in the summer. "Yeah, I was just wondering," he said, "What's the point of this class? Can't we just watch a video or something, and then make out with whoever we want to?"

Everyone laughed as Knox watched Nala for some sort of reaction. Nothing. Not yet.

Professor Leatherwood folded his arms and tried to sound professional. "Thanks for the question. What's your name?"

"Knox Ritchie," he announced, like it was something to brag about. Sir Knox Hamilton Laroche Ritchie the third: President of the BU Yacht Club, Founder of "Men in White Collars," a rowing steersman, and—this just in—insanely in love.

"Knox. Never heard that name before. It's cool," the professor said. "And regarding the question, I think I was wondering the same thing when I was in your shoes."

Nala watched the professor groom his chin stubble with his chalky fingertips, leaving behind a little white residue. God, he was cute—and not in a usual sort of way. Everyone else was thinking the same thing, so it didn't hurt Nala to admit that he was gorgeous and twenty-something, even though he was completely off limits, right? She just couldn't help herself. Even the ink stain on his shirt pocket was mildly endearing.

"Look, I'll be honest with you," Professor Leatherwood said. "Taking a class on kissing just seems unnatural—I get it. But the actual purpose of this class is to talk about dating. Communicating. Getting to know girls better. Boys better. How to socialize with one another. What to talk about. Or more importantly, what *not* to talk about." The class giggled. "How to compliment a girl," he stared for a second at Nala. "How to tell her she's beautiful. How to sound like you mean it," he said, suddenly looking away. Her stomach sunk. "Like it. Despise it. It's a school tradition and you need this credit to graduate." He shrugged. "Can't imagine why you're complaining about it, Mr. Ritchie. Look at all of these beautiful women." He winked at Knox and exaggeratedly examined the room.

The professor's eyes circled around the class once before he came back to Nala. She was wrapping her hair in a tendril twist and letting it unravel down her spine. She looked calculatedly bored, like she could feel him watching her but was too nervous to look up. She had a long, ballerina neck, and sexy, full lips. Her eyes finally peeked up at him, and he felt his chest tighten at the sight of her. She was . . . beautiful. And then, he kind of smiled.

Wait. Did he just check out a student?

Oh, How the Mighty Have Fallen Asleep

"**A**ny more questions?" Professor Leatherwood managed to choke out before anyone noticed the stupid, mesmerized grin that thrashed his face as he stared down on Nala.

The class seemed bored to death; no one spoke up. Professor Leatherwood considered throwing a game of heads-up, seven-up into the mix to liven up the students, but he didn't want to be that pathetic teacher who was always trying to make the students like him. Wouldn't that be just the thing for his shortcomings list? Right below unmarried and without children.

Suddenly, the classroom door swung open. Some boy with messy, chocolate-colored hair wearing a vintage fleece hoodie struggled inside and nodded to the professor with a dazed and swollen, red-eyed glance. "Sorry I'm late," he mumbled under his breath. He pulled his pocket hoodie to cover his face.

"No problem! Find a seat," the professor said. "To be honest, I expected worse on the first day. Most of you ditching for the cafeteria food, or something." The boy hunted for a seat. Knox Ritchie popped up and flagged down an open one next to him.

"Here she is, ladies and gentlemen—Sleeping Beauty," Knox howled while the mystery boy ripped off his hoodie and slipped his fingers through his uncombed hair. Suddenly, Sosie felt her heart plunge into her stomach. Sweatshirt boy was Gino Blackthorn. He looked drained and sort of pissed off, and his brown hair was sprinkled with sweat and matted to his forehead. Must have been tired. Regardless, he was close to perfect in a grungy, half-asleep sort of way. His linen cargos were covered in mud, wrinkled, and stained with flecks of toothpaste, and Sosie figured he had slept in them.

Knox's devotees clapped their hands while Mr. Sleeping Beauty cruised down the aisle toward the empty seat.

"Next time, remember to wear your uniform, please," the professor said. Gino waved his hand as he dropped into his seat. *I hear you, and I couldn't possibly care less,* he seemed to think.

The professor started to speak again. Knox yanked on one of Gino's kangaroo pockets and pointed at Nala as she wisped a long, brown hair out of her lip gloss distractedly. "God must be blessing me for all of those times I donated old dumbbell weights to the rec center," he whispered, admiring the sheer, skin-colored tights hugging her spider-long legs from afar. "Maybe he'd give me her if I offer up my truck for public transportation." He was joking, but still slightly curious if that would work. He was willing to do it . . . for her.

Knox didn't just want Nala for fun. He was somewhat sensitive and totally serious when it came to love, especially for a guy. In his mind, he had already built up a perfect image of his married life after BU. He would wed some model with totally unique and displaced cheek dimples and perfect, flowing hair who'd enjoy touring the coast in a luxury yacht. They'd live off of white wine spritzers and calamari for a year, wearing only bathing suits and blasting Euro-techno through the boat's sound system. She'd be shy, but adventurous, and he'd love showing her off to greasy, rich Europeans. And she'd be his, and only his.

Professor Leatherwood soon proposed that all of his students commit to completing a "10 Facts About Me" assignment by the end of class. After forty minutes of fairly impressive quiet, the bell rang, and everyone started to pack up. The professor whistled over the noise of zippers and scraping chairs. "Drop off your essays here!" he called. The pile matured rather pathetically, and he realized that he was running a circus. Introducing the ringleader, Professor Leatherwood, and his twenty mindless elephants. Don't feed them, or they'll mock you and your frivolous assignment.

"Should I go talk to him?" Sosie asked Nala, indicating Gino with a jerk of her head. It was either then or later in the quad. There was no way she'd be having her second run-in with him in the cafeteria, with a tuna salad croissant juice dripping on her hand as they reminisced about the time they shared the ocean with *plenty* of tuna; though most of them were alive.

Nala glanced at Gino. He looked like he'd punch anyone that breathed his air. "Maybe you should catch him when he's fixed his hair, and doesn't look so . . . out of it."

Sosie shrugged. She had to agree . . . he did look a little sleepy. But maybe he was only so dazed because he had been waiting for her to show up in the courtyard sunbathing, or reading some dopey romance novel he'd make fun of, or spooning raspberry punch into a stupid, $300 designer thermos she'd purposely throw away just to cause a scene, or drooling over half-naked martial arts seniors practicing Muay Thai on the lawn. Maybe Gino was just having a moment because he really, really missed her.

Sosie snatched her book bag from the floor and narrowed her view. "What's that saying, La? There's no better time than the present?"

Squeezing past Knox and a few other boys with disturbingly similar side parts, Sosie snuck up behind Gino and clapped her hands over his face before she could stop herself. "Guess who," she squealed, hating herself immediately for sounding so . . . tenth grade. Silence pounded in her ears as students shuffled by them for the doors. Why wasn't he saying something?

Guess who? How annoying. She was acting like a total kindergartener! *Practically one binky away from hiccups and drool*, she agonized.

Gino grabbed Sosie's hands from his face finally, and threw them away. His eyes found her. Immediately, he was pulled back to the afternoon on the Bluffdale beach. She had been wearing a strapless, fire-coral bandeau top and matching bikini bottoms. Something about the ocean had made her hair crimp, and her cleavage pop up with cute, baby freckles. "Name's Sosie," she had said after diving into the ocean and coming back up with a handful of sand and a pocket-sized conch shell. "I've never met a boy before." Gino remembered how funny she had been when she bragged about the perks of being flat chested. "I can get away with wearing backless halters even though they're kind of slutty."

She hadn't changed much in the last few days, besides her outfit. Of course, what did he expect after two days? Rhinoplasty? Wrinkles? Her hair was straighter and tucked beneath her cable scarf, making her look like she had a pixie-cut, and her lips were a little wetter, but he was positive that she was that same girl he'd met on the beach.

Cute. Blonde. Freckly.

"Surprise!" Sosie concentrated on covering her mortification with a smile and wiggled her stubby fingers by her hips. Gino didn't give her a hug, or shake her hand, or kiss her cheek, or anything, but she rationalized that he wasn't exactly Mr. Social Butterfly. Apparently, he was Mr. Sleeping Beauty. Oh, how the mighty had fallen . . . asleep. "Glad to see you aren't in jail," she said. "Or expelled. Or dead!"

Gino repositioned his backpack on his shoulder and started to walk, though he could still make out thin, blonde locks hanging by his side. There was nothing wrong with Sosie, but the last thing he needed was some distraction. Two-a-days would be starting soon, and Coach was already on him with tackling drills. He needed to focus on football if he wanted to start as a freshman.

"Don't take this the wrong way, but I didn't think I'd see you again," Sosie added once the line of backpacks began to shrink. "But here you are! BU! Totally cool we're here, right?"

Professor Leatherwood sat at his desk a few feet away, paging through the over-achievers' descriptive documentation of their monotonous lives. Sosie needed to shut up . . . now. If Professor L heard her talking about Gino's little rendezvous in Bluffdale, Coach could find out, and his football career—BU, and professional—would disappear quicker than he could say "sack that quarterback." And if Gino didn't have football, who was he?

"Do you ever think—"

"Stop," Gino finally snapped. Sosie yanked her mouth shut, and gulped loudly. He stuffed his hair out of his face for the hundredth time. Pretty, green eyes stared sadly back at him, and he realized Sosie was more than just a day at the beach. She'd be there—same corridors, same classroom—until graduation, staring pretty, green eyes his way.

Why was it so hard to tell her to leave him alone? Just to let him thrive in miserable peace. It was always easy to tell guys to piss off. But not her.

The crowd was building behind them while they hogged the doorway and threw blank stares at each other. As much sense as it would make to walk through the courtyard and discuss football, the incident, the need for discretion, Gino just wasn't the kind of guy to shake hands and be friends, or do anyone any favors.

"Well?" Sosie pinched her sweater cuffs in her hands and tried not to pout.

Gino cleared his throat, attempting to forget what stood in front of him. Trying to make it . . . her . . . a vacant memory. "I don't know you, and I don't want to know you. So please, just leave me alone."

Money Green Blood

"How do you think murder charges are perceived here? Would I be seen as mysterious and twisted, or just plain psycho?" Sosie slurped her cappuccino, the foam clouding her cosmopolitan-pink lip gloss, and waved at Juliet Bigsby from across the lawn. Juliet was relaxing beneath the sun in kitty shades and an embarrassingly orange plastic visor. Today was one of the most crucial days of their entire lives, but all Sosie could think about was Gino Blackthorn and his sucky memory.

"Depends. Would your victim be missed?" Nala asked.

"By the football team, I suppose." Sosie shrugged and dug through her bag for her circle shades. "And maybe by that cradle-robber, Miss Hart. Always hanging around the gym like some kettlebell junkie," she added. "Even if I don't go through with it—you know, murdering him and all—I'm still never going to speak to him again. Let it be me who said it first: a boy who treats you like relapsing pneumonia deserves to be chopped up like tuna sashimi and thrown into the lake. Or—whatever—the silent treatment works, too."

The girls flopped down next to Juliet, Tess, and Milly, who were flipping through a book, lathering up on suntan lotion, and scraping the grime from their soft suede moccasins. Sosie flipped her wrist and read her watch. 11:57 a.m. In three minutes, the MAA—or Monetary Analysis Assembly—would commence. At every boarding school that later paved way into 'Kissing Schools'—schools like The Bluffdale Preparatory School for Girls and The Academy of Windsor at Elkins—student bank accounts and financial statements were considered restricted documenta-tion, so the freshman class at Blairstown University was always brainlessly unaware of their trust funds until the MAA was held. In other words, they had no idea if they were poor or rich, or comfortably floating by.

The administration at these feeder schools always claimed to hide such crucial information from students for a purpose; basi-cally to hold off on teaching kids about money until they were mature enough to handle it. All of the BU brochures read the MAA was held to "properly and carefully 'lay' pecuniary issues on unfamiliar and undisciplined minds so that currency trans-mutes into its apposite value at the proper age."

'Lay.' As if it were a cozy blanket. *Phhh.*

It had been rumored that old, crabby Kissing School alumni got together one autumn afternoon and decided in their haze of Bloody Marys that high school seniors were still too immature to be exposed to money problems, and that university life was a more appropriate environment in which to cognize the value of a dollar. Apparently—after chucking a disturbingly huge bag of Benjamins at the gold embossed entrance gate—their wish was Genie Dotie's and every other principals' command. And even more apparently, those same loose-leaf white tea sipping and crumpet eating octogenarians had assumed that most students would respond to their undisclosed bank accounts in a frugal manner, preparing themselves for the worst possible scenario by spending conservatively. Yet, those girls spent and spent and spent up until they were sitting at the MAA, biting their nails nervously, terrified they were all as poor as dirt.

The crowd heard the jarring sound of nails clanking against a microphone. Standing on the steps of Alistair Dwelling behind a podium, Miss Marilyn was clenching a mic and glaring through the mob of burgundy and plaid. She looked as mad and thoroughly annoyed as ever. "Welcome to the Monetary Analysis Assembly, a tradition we cherish here at Blairstown, and take very seriously. There's something special about tradition, no?" she asked in monotone, carelessly and unsurely, as if she'd rather be watching her favorite telenovela and eating peanut butter and banana ice cream straight out of the pint. "Now that you're all mature enough to make grown-up decisions . . . and don't make me regret saying that . . . we are pleased to lay before you—"

Lay. Again.

"—some information regarding your trust funds. And just know that—no matter how big or small the number floating around in your piggy banks—we are here to help and support you. To mold you all into the best versions of yourselves. To make you all the best future wives you can be." She spoke like she was both pissed that she had never been anyone's wife, and pissed that she had to memorize some cliché speech that was supposedly 'cherished tradition;' tradition that no longer applied to her. *It was like cherishing cowshit.* "That being said, there will be round-the-clock counselors available at your convenience for the remainder of the week if you at all feel the need to discuss the information we are about to reveal to you any further. Because here at Blairstown, we *care.*"

That's comforting.

Marilyn sifted through the packet of white envelopes in her hands, as carelessly assembled as her puke-green blazer and cat-shaped, rhinestone earrings. "So . . . ugh . . . let's get this thingy started. When I call your name, stand and accept your envelope." The swarm of French manicures and tweezed eyebrows was a fatigued and sweat-spritzed mass, sitting Indian-style on their ascot picnic coverlets, dabbing their makeup-caked foreheads with handkerchiefs.

Nala relaxed her head on Sosie's lap and pulled her eyes shut. The roost of Alistair Dwelling was just high enough to block the thrashing late-summer sun from her eyes. "Did you remember to bring the sunblock?" Nala asked, running her mint-green fingernails over her arms.

"Not that I encourage it, but here," Sosie said, ripping out a pocket-sized sunblock tube from her hobo bag. Even though Sosie's skin was porcelain white, she was a big fan of the "burn and peel" method of skincare: no sunscreen, no aloe, just tanning oil and virgin piña coladas.

Tess glared down over oversized butterfly sunglasses to paint her toenails. "Should it be like, one-thousand degrees in the middle of August? I mean, hello? This isn't the Sahara desert!" She repositioned the tissue underneath her armpits. Had anyone else forgotten to double-coat her deodorant?

Juliet flipped a page in her thrilling romance novel, the first of the "Love, Sea, and Mistress Chronicles", and gushed over the sexy illustration of the character, Jean Dubois, wearing nothing but noir trousers and a flamboyant, French scarf. Tess rolled her eyes as Juliet released a mascara-black tear. Not only was that book so four years ago, but it was also a complete waste of totally decent paper.

"He dies, Jules," Tess snapped, ripping the soaked tissue out of her cardigan sleeves. "In some pleasure-craft boating accident. Like a total loser."

"He sacrifices himself to save Fiona . . . ." Juliet butted-in, trying to find the illustration of Jean Dubois sinking into the frozen ocean while Fiona flagged down a helicopter with her tragically blue hands and demanded they organize a search group. "He deserves a proper burial," Fiona sobs a few sentences later to her future love, the chief of Search and Rescue. Damn, that girl moved on fast.

"If you've already read it, why are you torturing yourself?" Tess pushed her sunglasses back through her hair and squinted her eyes. "Each time you start from the beginning, you kill Jean all over again. Some might think that classifies you as cruel."

Cruel? Juliet wasn't cruel for loving some schmaltzy fiction book. "Leave me alone. I like it," she said, stuffing her nose back in her book and continuing to read. Only now, Jean was sort of ruined for her, and Fiona was just some money-hungry, fickle tramp. How had she not seen that before?

"Ahem," Miss Marilyn cleared her throat over the microphone to gather attention. She was dressed in a flocked peacock skirt, a long-sleeved turtleneck, a green blazer, a goldenrod conch shell necklace, and worst of all, dolly shoes a size too small. The bloated skin of her feet poured through each opening.

Marilyn flipped the first envelope beneath in her fingers, wisped a silvery hair from her eyes, and read, "Ginger Holdsberry, room 111. Come up and claim your prize."

From the lawn, a girl with sherbet-orange hair and snow-white skin jumped onto her ballerina flats and bounced up the stone steps toward the podium. "For your eyes only," Marilyn suggested as she handed over the envelope. Ginger jogged back and practically belly-flopped on top of her pudgy friend. She ripped the letter open and started to read. Halfway through, her pasty lips curled under and she began to cry.

"Look at her. She's ugly *and* dirt poor," Tess said, watching Ginger wipe her salty tears with the hem of her chambray button-up. The entire crowd gasped. That could have been any one of them, fossilized with debt . . . and it still might be.

Juliet gulped and imagined herself dirt poor, too, scraping by with Sosie's leftover sandwich crusts and Nala's never finished yogurt parfaits. *Gross.* Yogurt had to be the worst food since broccoli. But on the bright side, at least she'd be skinny. Skinny and poor. And then she thought about it levelheadedly: her future would consist of fishing for quarters under the tufted chesterfield sofas in the main foyer and re-selling cassette tapes and the L.S.M. Chronicles at some pawnshop just off of campus. Having a gorgeous body like Nala wasn't quite as important as purchasing the new Jon Matinee perfume or indulging in seven-dollar seasonal hot chocolate or *not* working at some rinky-dinky pawnshop with other underprivileged students like Ginger Holdsberry.

The envelopes in Miss Marilyn's stack where being passed around so unconventionally that Juliet couldn't tell if her nerves were getting the best of her, or if her gut was trying to warn her about her empty trust fund. "That will be seven fifty-three," she could hear herself saying in her I-hate-my-job voice, her nametag bouncing up and down on her flattening cleavage.

"What is the minimum monthly allowance for a student, anyway?" Juliet asked the girls. She needed to know before she ripped open her envelope, and was wheezing at a number that made zero sense to her.

"Two hundred dollars," said Nala, lathering up on SPF.

"And if your parents can't afford two hundred a month, then the school takes out a loan in your name," Tess replied coolly.

"And you have to pay them back—plus interest—which is always like . . . a zillion bucks."

The way Tess saw it, there was no possible way she came from some shack-of-a-home with canned meat and coupons. That silky black hair and flawless, velvety skin had to come from the totally expensive prenatal vitamins her mom had taken when she was pregnant with Tess. Fortune was in her money-green blood.

"So, how much do you think Ginger will owe?" asked Juliet, watching as the poor girl wrapped her pasty arms around her shoulders while her heavy-set friend tried to calm her down with an eerie lullaby. All five girls observed.

Couldn't hippo keep the horror-film cradlesong away from the public assembly, Tess thought harshly, blowing at her bangs. "Hmm. After Primary boarding, food, cellphone bills, clothing, toiletries, and recreational crap, Ginger is looking at about . . . I'd say . . . thirty-five large from Bluffdale Prep alone. Maybe more."

"It's kind of weird, isn't it?" Sosie interrupted. "Receiving money from people we've never met? The first thing we'll ever know about our parents is the size of daddy's wallet."

Daddy's Casio Castillo wallet, Tess hoped. "It's only weird if you make it weird."

Juliet scratched her waffly skin, which had started to break out in a miserable, heat-inspired eczema rash. "I hear it's more difficult to find a boyfriend," she said, watching the flakes of dead flesh shrivel up and float away in the wind. "If you rack up student loans, I mean."

"Well, it's not like you have to tell anyone." Sosie shrugged. She played with the ends of Nala's pecan-colored hair and started to braid. Even though she was acting super relaxed, the idea of mooching off of Nala for the next four years—which would only work if Nala wasn't dirt poor, too—was mildly depressing. Sure, Sosie was the least greedy of the money-gobblers, and was convinced she could survive off of microwavable pizzas and flea market parkas forever, but that didn't mean she wouldn't rather be really, really rich.

Time flew, and Miss Marilyn, twenty-something envelopes in, lifted another envelope and smacked her shrunken lips against the microphone. "Tessa Van der Pool, room 715."

"Something tells me I'm one wrinkly midget away from purchasing my wrapped-bodice, sequined dream gown for the winter ball at the end of the semester," she cooed as she wiggled onto her baby-blue flats and snobbishly walked for the steps. Her loose, glistening locks floated behind her as she popped up the stairs. "Hello, Miss Marilyn. Love the brooch! Is that new?"

Miss Marilyn barely budged. Her forehead wrinkles and her snubbed, sour pout were so motionless that the woman looked like a wax model. "Old as dirt, actually," Marilyn cracked huskily, shoving the enveloped against Tess's cleavage.

"Just like you," Tess winked, snatching up the envelope by her fingers and squirming away. Back near her friends, she dropped to her knees gracefully and pinched the envelope open slowly to add suspense. Of course, it didn't really matter whether she was already private jet, bottle service, and paparazzi-super rich or would have to scout out a billionaire's playboy son to seduce-dirt poor—she *would* be shacking up with champagne diamonds either way. No one would have to know whether she received her pails of cash from her parents or from her lover.

The letter slipped out of the envelope and feathered into her lap. She took a peek, and started to smile voraciously. "I'm rich, bitches!" she giggled.

From her envelope, she then retrieved a golden spending card with "Tessa Van der Pool" embroidered in black letters across it. "And look! A card in my absolute favorite color!"

A few names were called, a few other girls raced to receive their letters, and the tension of the crowd exploded. Marilyn browsed through the next few envelopes, each girl sitting on fire-walking coals. "Sosie Hinkhouse, room 779," she called into the microphone. Sosie jumped.

"Go find out if you qualify to be my new shopping buddy," Tess nudged her arm.

Ew. I'd rather live in a ditch and eat worms . . . or microwavable pizzas. Do they have microwavable pizzas in ditches?

Sosie bounced up and headed for Miss Marilyn, who was twisting her koala-bear brooch on the backdrop of her nasty, puke-green blazer. "Tell me, Susie. What do you think the odds are that you start collecting coupons after this?" Marilyn taunted as she waved the envelope in Sosie's face. Why did she have to be such a miserable witch all of the time?

"Umm . . . it's Sosie first of all, Merlys. And if said coupons can save me a few bucks on microwavable pizzas, I think there's a good chance regardless," Sosie replied carefully. "What can I say? I like cheese."

Marilyn narrowed her thin, over plucked eyebrows. Her eyeballs were yellowish and harsh as they peeked over the podium. "It's Miss Marilyn, Susie. And the answer is twenty-five percent. There's a twenty-five percent chance you'll be collecting coupons, as you'll be so ridiculously in debt you can barely afford to wipe your own butt with the soft stuff." Miss Marilyn yanked off her brooch and shoved it into her jacket pocket. "Happy luck!"

Sosie walked off with her envelope, trying to thrust Miss Marilyn's wheezy voice out of her mind by stomping her boots extra loud. What was the big deal? Debt, or no debt, Sosie would work her ass off to pay for everything she needed — wanted — whatever. And she certainly wouldn't marry some freeloading jerk, either. Everything was going to be ok. Life was not about money.

Sosie was feeling peaceful by the time she ripped open her letter for review. The first paragraph was a bunch of mumbo-jumbo about applying for credit cards and checking balance statements.

Then — finally — there it was at the bottom of the page. Her eyes read over it a few times before she understood. *Parents' donation: $10,000 granted per month for life. Current savings: $1,109,005.98. Current debt: $0. Provided with pleasure by Members of The Elite.*

Holy guacamole! She was rich.

"Elite" was a word she had overheard once or twice when she had caught Miss Iris gabbing away on her cellphone to her sister, Ruby, usually outside the teacher's lounge. Whoever the Elite were — probably some old, perfumed-breath alumni who sipped whiskey sours and mint juleps while they cruised around golf courses on their handy-capable scooters — they deserved one hell of a thank you note.

"Well?" Juliet meddled as Sosie shoved her letter — and her flashy, gold debit card — into her cardigan pocket and perused the lawn, acting nonchalant. "Aren't you going to tell us?"

Sosie watched Tess shave down her nail tips while humming conceitedly, "I'm rich, I'm rich" in an annoying, little voice. *Shut up, or I'll slap you with my giant trust fund,* thought Sosie, visualizing it: a lump of green paper, the impact on Tess' cheek, the fresh, purple welt. Could it be as monumentally hilarious in person as she pictured it in her head? "Like I said, I'm keeping my personal life personal."

"That's exactly what a poor person would say," Tess blurted out, dropping her nail buffer onto the soggy grass and admiring her flat, polished fingers. Now, she'd need to reapply a new layer of coral for the hundredth time.

"Or, a poor person would lie and say she's rich." Nala winked at Sosie while Tess's mouth dropped. It wasn't like Nala to say anything, but Sosie knew that she would do anything for her best friend.

Then, just as Sosie felt the plastic of her new card slip from her fingers, Miss Marilyn's voice crowed over the microphone again. "Nala Middleton, room 779."

Oh god.

As if Nala wasn't already nerve-wracked over the trust fund thing, Tess's snobby smirk left her feeling nauseous as she stood on her fiery snakeskin slippers, wobbled toward the podium, and waited for Miss Marilyn to drop her envelope into her shaking hands. "Guard this with your life, dearie," Marilyn breathed, exhaling a sickly sweet, fruit-scented breath. *Had Miss Marilyn snuck peaks at her financial statement?* It certainly seemed as if Momma hen had been rummaging through the BU wine cellar, and maybe also the bank account information of her baby chicklets.

Nala tore her envelope open and ripped out the letter. Her eyes swooped to the bottom of the page as she walked.

Parents' donation: $200 granted per month for life. Current savings: $0. Current debt: $24,017.89. Provided with pleasure by Members of The Elite.

Provided with pleasure? Really? Couldn't it have said, "with remorse and pity"? And who the hell were The Elite, anyway?

Suddenly, all of those Jon Matinee evening gowns and Laurent Le Blanc mink fur vests packed in her closet, still adorned with price tags, seemed totally insane. Why had she been such a fool? She'd killed herself with a gluttony for fashion. *Mmm, sheer silk chiffon. Gobble, gobble.*

Nala swallowed harshly, designer totes dancing around in her mind. Why did she so love the smell of brand new, calfskin leather? And why couldn't she love microwaveable pizzas the same way Sosie did?

She Who Loves Him, Who Loves Her

"How many calories in these?" Juliet Bigsby scooped two helpings of waffle fries onto her plate and spritzed a dash of salt on top. What was it about French fries and tater-tots that made them so easy to love, even though each plate seemed to pack three extra pounds onto her already corpulent caboose?

"About five-forty," Milly calculated, peeking over her frameless reading glasses at the pile of greasy potatoes.

Ever since breakfast, when Tess started to chant "Julie-eater" while Juliet vacuumed down an entire plate of triple-stack, almond-buttered hotcakes, she had this urge to get supremely skinny before bikini season was over. Sure, her huge chest distracted from her flabby stomach and cottage-cheese thighs most of the time, but who said she couldn't rock a flat belly, too? And who knew? Maybe one day she could get away with a strappy thong suit and a flirty, seashell triangle brassiere.

Well, let's not go overboard.

540 calories? That was like . . . half a medium pizza. Juliet shuddered, glancing down on her plate. "Yeah, but I think the salt, like, evaporates a bunch of the calories," she yapped unsurely. "There was a whole article about it in *Food & Fit to Fit* last month. I'll try and find it for you."

Even though there was no article in the *Food & Fit to Fit* lifestyle magazine about salt, French fries, and calories that ended well, Juliet had to make an excuse for the enormous, greasy plate, somehow. Milly pressed her reading glasses up her wiry nose and fought her instinct to ask Juliet for more details. If salt did help taper off calories—which it totally didn't—why wasn't she a slim-fit in Michel St Pierre's oxford button-up after all those pressed salami sandwiches?

Realizing Milly was fixated on the salt thing, Juliet slid her tray toward the sandwich meat and forked up a few slices of bologna. "There's a guy in French I kind of like," she said, rolling her sleeves down her arms. "He's totally rich, and drives some spruced-up truck, which is kind of funny because he's such a total sports car guy." Juliet pinned her curly bangs behind her ears. "But whatever. At least he can drive."

Milly boredly plopped a serving of scallops on her dinner plate. She didn't really care about boys yet. All she needed was a good science fiction book and a bucket of popcorn . . . with extra salt, just in case Juliet wasn't totally full of crap.

Juliet looked around the cafeteria to scout out Nala and Sosie. Outside on the patio, a few summer-dressed seniors sipped iced tea, virgin cosmos, and fresh melon quenchers, chewed pineapple polenta squares and snapped artsy pictures of their boyfriends with their camera phones. One day, Juliet imagined herself on that patio wearing sexy, pocket-less denims, a studded, velvet tank, and rust oxfords, eating prosciutto-basil crostini with her dreamboat beau, kissing each other after every bite. Sometimes Juliet felt like she could die waiting for senior year.

Juliet began to search the cafeteria. The walls were decorated in big, golden curtains that swooped across the ceiling. Nearby, a banister of Sweet Chestnut trailed the double ivory staircase. Scalloped black lacquer accents flourished beneath the dark lighting. It looked like one of those French country clubs she had spotted in *Earthly Nirvana* last month—totally perfect for hunting out gorgeous athletes after football practice; still sweaty, still bulging with muscle. *I love this place*, Juliet thought.

Milly plopped a huge goblet of creamed corn into a bowl. "Do you really think it's such a good idea to get involved with someone just a few weeks into school? I mean, honestly. How much do you really know about this guy?"

Juliet slapped her bangs away to reveal her thin, furrowing, yellow eyebrows. Why did Milly insist on being such a lame-o? This is why she had no friends. Because she asked stupid questions and always had a stick up her ass. And what could she possibly know about getting involved? She wore socks with sandals, for goodness sake! In fact, a low-budget indie film was about the closest thing Milly had come to "getting involved" with anything. She had considered pursuing acting back in Bluffdale once or twice, but she was far too much of a control freak to stand the demands of her super radical—and slightly lesbonic—director.

Juliet noticed the perfect flow of Nala's brown, silky locks, and began to walk. "You kidding? I hear that if you're not involved with someone by sophomore year, there's really no hope for you." She shrugged at Milly, chewing on a French fry with her small, gapped teeth, ready to hang with the cooler girls. "So let's pray that Knox Ritchie likes me back."

Knox Ritchie? As in . . . the president of Nala's fan club? Yeah. Right.

Knox Ritchie was across the dining hall, sitting with his buddies and complaining about the overcooked roast that looked, and smelled, like minced meat. Juliet spotted him and melted. His gorgeous, sand-colored hair was uncombed, but styled, and his lips were curled into a charming smirk. *No wonder Juliet isn't willing to wait a few months to get involved,* Milly thought when Juliet pointed him out. Knox Ritchie wouldn't be on the market for long.

Juliet led the way to Nala's table and hammered into an empty seat. "Hope you girls don't mind if Milly joins us," she said. *I hope I don't mind if Milly joins us.*

Sosie nodded to show she approved — or didn't care — and popped a ketchup-smothered tater tot into her mouth. "This food is so gross, it's good. Or is it so good, it's gross?"

"It's just gross." Tess rolled her eyes.

No one was too thrilled about Tess finding peace at their new spot in the dining hall. And just because she had tagged along with their group back at Bluffdale Preparatory by providing luxurious scalp treatments and avocado facemasks here and there, that didn't mean she had to show off her half-empty salad plate and make pretentious faces while the others enjoyed hot dogs and cheesecake bites.

Juliet felt Tess watching her as she indulged in a lumpy pudding. Tess's eyes screamed: *That's going straight to your hips, honey.* But weren't hips the newest trend?

"Pretty outside," Juliet piped up, just in time to distract herself from Tess's glare lurking from behind a rhinestone chalice of raspberry spritzer.

"Wish it would cool down, already," Milly added.

Suddenly, across the room, Knox Ritchie jumped out of his dining chair and stomped his chocolate brown, yacht club loafers across the floor, heading for their table. Juliet noticed a provoking smirk crawling up his face as he neared. The boys left behind—Gino Blackthorn, Rocko Borai, Brains Fink, and Max Umminger—all scooped up bites of food and hid behind their transparent water cups and watched. Only Gino genuinely couldn't have cared less about whatever it was that Knox was doing. He took one last bite of his bread roll and then started to nod off beneath his hoodie.

"Excuse me," Knox's voice interrupted as he shoveled his dirty-blonde hair from his eyes and grinned cheesily. He was so put together, he looked like a senior after senior skip day; the deep, shimmering tan on his cheeks glowing like he had been out on a yacht all afternoon, getting high and wake-boarding. He blinked down on Nala, who was peeking up at him from behind her salad fork. "Can I ask you girls a question?"

Juliet nodded. She turned milky as his momentary glance at her lingered on her chest. She played with her curly, yellow hair, hoping that she looked hot and relaxed as she waited. "Sure you can," she managed to mumble, only her voice sounded shaky, and no one was sure what she had said. *Shit!* How was she supposed to nab the gorgeous rowing captain if he couldn't even hear her?

Knox rolled up his sleeves. "Any of you thinking about trying out for cheerleading next semester?"

Tess took a drink to wash down the spinach leaves wedged in her throat. Who the hell had run their blabbering mouth to some wannabe male model that looked like he just stepped out of a low-budget European cigarette ad? No one was supposed to know she was considering cheerleading. The girls of Hip Hop Alliance were after her for Freshman Captain, and she hadn't made up her mind yet about which she wanted to do more. If word got out, Hip Hop Alliance would forget all about her, and she'd have to kill that sandy-haired pretty boy. "Maybe we are, maybe we aren't," she said with her small, angry eyes hunkering down on his preppy, waved hair. "Why the hell do you care?"

"Well, since the senior cheerleading captain holds open try-outs, I just wanted to let you all know that . . . if you choose to try out, you have the team vote," he shrugged, ripping out an empty seat from a nearby table and straddling it so that his big, husky, rowing shoulders rested on the back. "Everyone wants to know about you girls."

Well, at least four of the five girls. Knox smiled, and again glanced at Nala. He was being a little obvious, but he didn't care. She looked so damn beautiful sitting there with her naïve, dreamy eyes on him and her mature lips softly slurping apple juice through a straw. He wished he could hear her speak, just for a second, just to know what she'd sound like.

"Then I guess if we do try out, we'll let you know," Tess replied coolly as she wound her pointy nails around her fork and took another bite of spinach salad.

"Cool," Knox said.

Juliet played with her lacquered heart necklace and tried to look sexy by crossing her legs. There was obvious tension between her and Knox, and everyone could totally tell. *Right?* In French, he had used one of her yellow, frizzy curls to catapult a pencil into Brains' lap. After class, he had waved goodbye to her on the quad, a flicker in his eyes that screamed, "Au-revoir my little soufflé!" And now — in the middle of lunch — he had walked over, looking extra-hunkish in his slim-fit button down, and made up some hilarious reason to talk to her. It was *so* obvious!

"So," Knox said, folding his arms over his chest and scanning the group. None of the girls were terrible looking, except for the one with the horrible pigtails and the thick, square glasses that focused solely on a bowl of creamed corn. The blonde, frizzy one was familiar . . . from class probably. Kissing 101? Or maybe French. "Anyone have Professor Leatherwood?"

"Professor Leatherwood? You mean, Sexypants Leatherwood?" Sosie screeched, nibbling on the fried crisps of a tater tot. "First period! I totally feel bad for any girl who doesn't get to stare at that masterpiece, and watch his big, beautiful lips while he talks about lips." Sosie glanced across the cafeteria at the professor, who was humbly eating a homemade turkey sandwich and listening to the baking instructor, Miss Hart, criticize an overly stale biscotti. His big, beautiful lips slurped coffee from a mug. She could watch him eat all day.

"I have him first period, too," Knox said. "And what about you?" he asked Nala. "Same class?"

Nala nodded shyly. Knox was pretty good looking. He wore his burgundy, button down that showed off his unnaturally white teeth, and had a nice summer tan. She could understand why all of the nearby girls were staring at him.

Knox smiled. "Good. Guess that gives me a reason to go, then."

Tess whirled her cup in circles as if it held expensive wine. "Are you honestly hitting on Nala in front of all of us?" she hissed, grabbing her long, black braid. Why couldn't she spool in some hunk with unflawed, beachy skin from across the cafeteria? What was it about Nala that was so captivating, anyway? It couldn't be her long, almond hair, or her golden eyes, or her beautiful, wide smile, or her flirty, long eyelashes, could it?

Knox threw his eyes back and forth between Tess and Nala. "So, your name's Nala, then?"

He smiled as if it was all he had ever wanted to know.

"Mmhmm," she mumbled, rocking her head up and down. Knox brushed off his freshly dry-cleaned shirt and tried to lean in closer to her. Nala pulled her eyes away nervously and glanced down at her meal: spinach, feta, olives, and balsamic vinaigrette all piled into a bowl. Her appetite had sort of dissolved away since Knox showed up. She felt weird eating in front of him, maybe because he was so pretty.

"Suits you," he grinned, totally captivated.

Suddenly, the table was still. Juliet felt her throat clamp shut. Didn't Knox recognize her from French? Wasn't she the reason he had walked over in the first place? On his disgusting loafers? Pathetic and sad? In need of some attention? Wasn't he tragically in awe of her? Didn't he want to run his stubby fingers through her thick, bouncy curls, get her drunk off of obnoxiously priced merlot, and make out with her in the hallways? And what the hell would Milly think, now that she knew that Juliet liked Knox, who liked Nala, who liked no one, and they were all trapped at some table in the dining hall, some looking pitiful, others thrilled, but all of them puzzled in questionable khaki.

Nala grabbed her empty juice box between both hands and played with it. "Thanks."

The table remained quiet.

"So, this weekend," Knox said, glancing back at his group of friends. If he didn't know any better, he'd guess they were all wasted off of peppermint schnapps by the way they were binging on jumbo pretzel hot dogs and cackling about some perverted joke. "I think we should go out," he said, gesturing toward Nala. "On a date. If you want."

A date?

"I know of a nice steakhouse," he added, picturing Nala in a long-sleeved, sequined sheath dress, sipping on Shiraz and plucking the fried crumbs off of calamari as she opened up to him about her childhood. "Meeting a hunky rowing captain has always been a dream of mine," she'd pipe, breathless.

Nala squeezed the plastic of the box, squirting a little juice up through the straw. "Just you and me?"

Alone?

"Or, a group of us," he offered, as if he had read her mind. "It's up to you." *Anything for you.*

Nala noticed her friends all lifelessly picking at their lunches. Why was the mood so weird and sad when she had just been asked on her very first date? Why weren't her friends saying anything? Why weren't they happy for her? Were they jealous, or did they just want their own dates, too?

"Mind if we . . . make it a group thing?" Nala finally asked. "Your friends and my friends."

Knox nodded, and glanced back at his totally uncivilized group of friends. Football-playing potheads. All of them . . . except Brains, who was just as easily embarrassing because he was such a geek. How would he bring them around Nala? What would she think of him? He turned back to see her big, hopeful eyes. If she wanted it to be a group thing, he'd make it a group thing. For her.

Besides, why should he care if he didn't have Nala all to himself? What would he really be missing out on? A romantic, nineteenth century Parisian restaurant, spoon-feeding her apricot-almond clafouti? A little one-on-one time? There was always next week. And the week after that. And this way, the other boys would shit themselves when they saw her in a dress. He probably would, too.

Knox smiled and slipped onto his feet. "How's Saturday?"

"Great!" she said chipperly.

"Great," and he headed back to his friends.

Nala glanced around the cafeteria, already a little freaked out about Saturday. Knox winked at her from his seat, and then turned to grab a cheese-stick from Max Umminger's plate. Elle Moody, the most gorgeous senior in the whole school, snuck inside from the patio and grabbed a few baby carrots from the salad bar, nibbling on them on her way back outside. And then, off in the corner, Professor Leatherwood. His hazel eyes glistened back at Nala as sunlight dripped through the windows He looked so sad. How long had he been watching her? Long enough to see Knox Ritchie planning their date? Was that such a bad thing?

Soon, the professor's eyes fell and he pretended to listen in on Miss Hart's tirade on the dangers of electric coil stovetops. Nala took a bite of her cold spinach leaves, but realized that she wasn't very hungry and dropped her fork.

Had she made a huge mistake saying yes to Knox Ritchie? Or, was she just regretful because her hot instructor, Professor L, appeared a tad bit . . . jealous?

We're Dating

D ressed in a chunky cable cardigan and double pinstripe, Dutch cocoa-colored, boot cut pants, Knox chewed on an organic, chocolate fudge protein bar and blew into his hands between bites. The fall chill had turned his cheeks a shade of pink, and with the wind blowing sandy hair over his face, he looked like a stand-in for some urbane winter catalog shoot.

Crashing onto the staircase just outside the Kissing 101 classroom, Knox peered across the courtyard and kicked out the driving shoes his mom had sent him for Valentines Day. *Thought these shoes looked like you,* the card read, which was weird—he always thought—since she hadn't seen him in person since he was a baby. He checked his watch. He was fifteen minutes early to class—just like he had planned. His study-buddy, the ever-brilliant Brains Fink, was trotting around the lawn in a bluesy sort of way, searching the ground like he had lost something. Coins probably. Collectors' coins. Whatever. Knox had too much on his mind to worry about Brain's little, pathetic adventures.

Professor Leatherwood sat inside his stale, white-walled classroom, chewing the last bites of a granola bowl he'd scooped from the breakfast buffet line, smothered in tart yogurt and banana. He hated chunky dairy and bruised fruit, but it was better than raisin oatmeal, he guessed. Suddenly, Knox barreled inside his office—driving shoes, and all—smelling like aftershave and mint. A big dollop of yogurt slipped from the professor's spoon and smacked onto his newspaper. "Shit!" He flicked the yogurt into the trash bin. There goes Thursday's editorial: "Women Whip Waffles for Warm Welcome."

What a tragic article to miss out on.

Not.

"Morning, Knox." Mr. Leatherwood retired from his breakfast—hardly a difficult loss, to say the least—and dropped back into his office chair. Add a cigarette and whiskey on the rocks, and he'd make the perfect 1950s "Mad Man"—sexy chin, and all. "Glad to see you're so eager to get to class. Lesson doesn't start for another fifteen, though."

"I know." Knox said, suddenly wishing he had partaken in Rocko's 8 a.m. Bloody Mary binge. Although Knox knew that if he had, he'd likely be shoveling through the boondocks of BU in search of some highly potent weed, flirting with some desperate junior girls in the cafeteria, or passed out beneath his California King bedspread while class pushed on without him. Fortunately for his future, he had other things—or other people—on his mind.

The professor narrowed his round, hazel eyes. What business did Knox Ritchie have at 8:45 a.m. on a Thursday morning? Not that Leatherwood minded. The classroom felt lonely with all the students gone. All those empty chairs were . . . creepy.

"Something I can help you with?" he asked in his just-one-of-the-guys voice.

"I think so."

Knox waited for Leatherwood to jump in and mumble something about being pleasantly surprised by Knox's sudden interest in class or to make a joke of it with some witty comment about the early bird getting the worm. But Leatherwood just slipped back into his chair and waited. Knox could have really used that Bloody Mary, at this point. "I'm taking a girl out this weekend." He said, rolling up his cardigan sleeves. "To some steakhouse, I think."

"Very cool," Professor Leatherwood said. "You'll always remember your first date. You'll have fun."

"Thanks." Knox scratched his recently shaved cheek. "She's in this class, actually. Nala. I don't know if you know who she is, yet, but she sits at the front. Really great."

Professor Leatherwood winced. "I know her."

He remembered Nala mouthing "Great" to Knox in the cafeteria the other afternoon, just before Knox strolled back to his dinner table so smugly, like he had won the lottery and was planning on spending every dime on some vacation to Bermuda. Not that it mattered, but Professor Leatherwood thought Knox Ritchie was too much of a shmuck for Nala, and the idea of her wasting an hour of her life eating under-cooked steak while Knox blathered about rudders and main halyards made him a little sad.

"Cool. She's the reason I'm here."

Knox was already really excited to see Nala in class. In ten minutes she'd show up, reapply her lip gloss, and flirt with his reflection in her pocket mirror, and he'd love every second of it. Knox pined, thinking of her. "Since we're dating now," or *will* be dating, "I thought you could pair us up for dating tutorials, or whatever."

Professor Leatherwood cleared his throat. "You do realize, Knox, if every male student of mine had a say in it, Nala would have a lot of people to kiss."

"Yeah, but it's sort of different . . . since we have a date," Knox argued, rolling his eyes. Was the professor hard of hearing? Knox and Nala were *dating*. They'd probably make out all weekend long. First at the restaurant, where they could appear super mature and heavily in love, sharing *Beef Daube Provençal* and getting drunk off Riesling. Here they'd kiss for the first time. Then, they'd search for a dessert place nearby, probably at some martini lounge with dim lighting and cocoa *mille-feuille*, where they could whisper and French kiss until their lips turned purple. He'd walk her home. They'd kiss. She'd be wearing his sports coat, looking rather suggestive, as if she were naked underneath. They'd kiss. She's say goodnight. They'd kiss. He'd say sweet dreams. Then he'd kiss her forehead — even though he'd want more, even though it would pain him to walk away — so she could know that she meant more to him than one night. All of it sounded perfect, except for the fact that their romantic one-on-one date would be, in reality, a group of ten, and making out with Nala in front of a crowd just seemed tacky.

Professor Leatherwood's brows furrowed. "Sorry, Knox, I partnered everyone up a few days ago. The list has been finalized."

"Can't you finalize it again? I mean . . . wouldn't it be easy to, like, change?"

Professor Leatherwood trashed his breakfast bowl and folded his arms over his chest, falling back into his seat again. No matter what Knox bargained with — no matter how much he begged, pleaded, threatened, or offered to pay — that list would remain exactly as it was.

"Look, Knox, I want to be your friend. But, I *need* to be your teacher. I'm here to help you, not coddle you. Agree with me, don't agree with me — do what you need to do — but that list isn't changing."

Professor Leatherwood stood on his wingtip oxfords and began to organize his desk. The door opened as if right on cue, and a few mopey students with double-shot espressos crawled for their spots, ready to learn — or sleep open-eyed.

Knox walked away and dropped into his seat. The thought of Nala being partnered up with some other dude made him want to smash in a bunch of valuables — Professor Leatherwood's valuables, particularly, like his eco-friendly sedan or his autographed baseball collection.

No One Likes Kiki

N ala and Sosie tiptoed into the classroom a minute late
with cinnamon dolce cappuccinos and sausage and
cheddar artisan breakfast sandwiches stuffed in a to-go
bag. The breakfast boutique and lunch hotspot Cloud Nine was
crazy packed that morning, with a line straight out the door, but
they were too stubborn and hungry to leave without brain-food.

Nala pulled her silky, brown hair out of her face and broke
into the baggie. Professor Leatherwood was looking perfect in
a carbon, slim-fit button up and a dusting of yesterday's five
o'clock shadow. *How very just-a-man-and-my-thoughts of him.* She

wondered if he was still feeling weirdly sad about her and Knox's date . . . or had she made that up in her head?

Sosie ripped her sandwich out. "If Mr. L was younger, I would donate my body to bear his children," Sosie whispered, elbowing Nala in her side. "I'd sacrifice my innie for an outtie. Seriously."

"Not your *innieeeee!*" Nala gasped. She slipped down in her seat and started to pick the burnt crisps from her sandwich, watching the professor paw through a stack of papers.

"How old do you think he is, anyway?" Sosie asked.

Nala shrugged, and gulped her cappuccino. "Twenty-five, tops."

"No way! Twenty-four, *maybe*, but twenty-five? No freaking way."

The professor stood, patting down his creased pants. He did look a little young. James Dean young. "Is everyone here?" he dared to ask. No one replied. "'Cause I have the list you've all been waiting for . . . ."

Crickets.

"Come on! Seriously? Don't you want to know who you're partnered with?"

More crickets. What was wrong with everyone?

"Guess not," he said, a little disheartened. "Then I guess you can just stand when I call your name, and try not to fall asleep." He yanked open his yellow-paged notepad and flipped through it. "Hmm . . . who to call on first? Let's go with . . . mmmmmm . . . Kiki Weames."

Kiki Weames popped up just behind Nala and Sosie, picking her acne with her chipped, unpolished fingernails. Her mousy, brown hair tangled down her back as she flashed her yellow, hamster teeth. Nala remembered her from Bluffdale Preparatory as the girl who'd always harassed the cheerleaders about the dangers of excessive teeth whitening just before painting her naked body blood red and shouting through the square, "Meat-eaters are animal-killers!"

Professor Leatherwood smiled at Kiki as she stood "Hope you don't mind being my guinea pig." Why would she? Humans are to be one with the animals, right? She wrapped her lips around her teeth and stuffed her yellow nails into her loose-fitting, pleated skirt. "All right, Kiki. You've been paired with . . . Knox Ritchie."

Knox Ritchie? Rowing captain, Knox Ritchie? Quarterback, Knox Ritchie? Crickets. Kiki Weames glared at Knox's thick, perfect hair from across the aisle, probably wondering if the gel he used to create such wave had ever been tested on animals. *This has to be a joke,* Knox thought as the peace-and-love hippie wet her lips. What did she want from him? Probably to fool around in the backseat of his truck to the sound of some acid-trip, rock and roll record. Weather Underground type stuff. Better make it a van.

"Knox and Kiki?" Meg Riggle — a potential member of Hip Hop Alliance — whined loudly. "But we aren't even convinced Kiki is . . . a girl," she whispered audibly to her neighbor.

Kiki blinked blankly at no one in particular.

"How about you stand up, Knox?" Professor L suggested.

Knox grunted. He imagined barreling through the tables and tackling Professor Leatherwood — pounding three fists into his skull while screaming, "You did this on purpose, you ass, ass, ass!" He stood finally, and flicked his eyes at Kiki, whose crooked, stoned grin exploded from her face. He waved to her out of sheer pity. "Hi, Kiki."

"Knox, man, we're gonna have fun," she wheezed.

Fun. Right.

Knox wasn't into smoking hookah, or tree-squatting, or protesting mooing filets, or meditating on Tibetan tiger rugs. Naturally, he doubted that they were going to have fun. Although, perhaps if he was a rotten-egg-reeking hippie, Kiki wouldn't be so bad. She could score him some super potent weed, and they could get baked and make out, and he'd be so high and out of it he wouldn't have to remember that her tongue tasted like black pepper and corn flakes. But, Knox was too ambitious to be so stupid and blithe about drugs and his future. In fact, he didn't care to smoke at all unless he was wasted and feeling spontaneous. And since he met Nala, he didn't really care to smoke ever again.

Knox collapsed into his chair and pulled his eyes shut. *Damn Professor Leatherwood. Damn him, damn him, damn him.*

The next four partnerships were pretty harmless. One girl with orange-sherbet hair and choppy bangs was paired with a stumpy boy with gummy cheeks, and both appeared oddly turned on by it. After that, Meg Riggle hooked up with Rusty Tilk, a total meathead with butter-yellow hair and a peach-fuzz beard.

Sosie dreamed boredly and doodled on her notepad until Professor Leatherwood called out Gino's name. He lazily tugged his hood from his eyes and stretched his legs. Shouldn't he be off somewhere eating cold pizza or watching Super Bowl replays? Wasn't kissing class a complete waste of time?

Professor Leatherwood ran his eyes down the list. "All right Gino, you ready?"

"Guess so." He shrugged carelessly. *And by ready, do you mean excited? Because if so, I'm definitely not,* he thought.

The professor hummed his way down the page, and Sosie scanned the crowd, curious which poor soul would wind up with the ass. Maybe Kirsten Woo, or the weird girl with the purple braces, or poor, poor Nala. God, she hoped it wasn't Nala. Leatherwood clasped the notepad tightly beneath his hands. "Looks like you've been paired with . . . Sosie."

Come again?

Sosie shoved her half-devoured breakfast sandwich away from her face. This wasn't happening. No. No. No. No. No. Did it *have* to be Gino? After she'd sworn to ignore him for the rest of time? She looked at him, standing there so oblivious with his hands stuffed in his pockets and his squinty, tired eyes slipping off to LaLa Land. Did he even know where he was? She bounced up quickly, with a let's-get-this-over-with look in her eyes and wiggled her fingers, wishing she could flip him the bird without Leatherwood noticing. Gino looked at her for a second, staring peculiarly down at her hands. Had he seen her do that before? Wiggle her fingers like that? Why did she always resort to that weird wiggle-finger thing? His brows furrowed. They both collapsed into their seats.

Sosie muttered something beneath her breath, and began to eat angrily. Not only was she stuck with the school jerk, but Nala's name hadn't even been called yet, and all of the decent boys were already matched up. Nala watched as Professor L zoomed down the list. One gangly, dark-skinned hottie was paired with a mousy, butternut squash-colored blob; Veronica "big lips" Horn was set up with Harry Hutchinson III. Eventually, everyone was sitting pretty and pleased (well, mostly pleased), while Nala picked her cuticles and watched nervously. If she wasn't assigned a partner, did that mean she'd just have to practice dating Professor Leatherwood?

Well, she figured, worse things had happened.

Sometime or Every Time

Class was nearly over when Professor L called out Nala's name, her mind still fogged with the unpleasant fact that she had never been assigned a partner. Had Professor Leatherwood totally forgotten about her? Was this about what happened in the cafeteria the other day?

As she had rehearsed silently, she jumped up and pretended not to be throwing the worlds wildest pity party in her head; pinwheels, streamers, glow sticks, noisemakers, all thrashing to the beat of her very own piteous soundtrack. Brightly colored Hawaiian leis were afloat in her pity pool.

"So, Nala," Leatherwood began in a hesitant voice. Nala imagined Kiki Weames piping up from the back, stoned and empathetic as always, "Out with it, man," as she rolled her fingers back through her knotted, crimpy hair. "How are you doing today?" he asked.

"Fine," she replied. Leatherwood smiled and glanced down at the paper again. Even though he had made her sit around for an hour slurping coffee while the other students were all linked in pairs, it was kind of adorable that he minded to ask her how she was doing. Then again, it was sort of the least he could do . . . .

"Good," he finally said, scanning the list more intensely. Nala scrunched her toes nervously. "Okay, so looks like . . . you've been partnered with Edward Pote."

Edward Pote? Who the hell was Edward Pote?

"Do you know Ed?"

"I don't think so."

"He's a nice kid," Professor Leatherwood assured. Nala nodded, taking a breath for the first time in what felt like half-an-hour. "As you can tell, he's not here. Down at the nurse's office. Nothing to worry about, though. Had a mild asthma attack, so he couldn't make it to class, but should be fine."

Asthma? The clinic? Was he that always-contagious guy? Would he infect her with mono, or strep throat, or—dare she think—tonsillitis? Maybe she should run to the drugstore after class, pick up some multi-vitamins, some C, some E, fish oil for kicks. However diseased Eddie was, she'd be ready with a Z-pack and a kick-ass immune system.

She just hoped it wouldn't cost her whole monthly stipend.

Suddenly, the door creaked open. "Look at that! Just on time," Professor L said. Through it walked Edward Pote, wearing a bottom-hemmed ruby cardigan with wrinkle-free twills. He strolled in on striped socks and cappuccino-brown slippers, holding his stomach while he waddled for his seat. His body appeared fragile, as he still grasped at his inhaler. He was five-foot-four, with smoky black hair and pasty, milk-skin. He tossed his khaki hunting backpack onto the open desk and poured out a collection of retractable ballpoint pens from a loose pocket.

"Hey Ed! How ya doin'?" Professor L said.

"Fine."

"Glad you could make it back!"

"Mmhmm."

Edward began to organize his collection of writing utensils, adding a sparkly carat gold fountain pen to the mix. Expensive. Stupidly expensive. The pens filed into a straight line. All of it was weird, considering class was practically over. Actually, it was weird regardless. "We were just going over classroom partners," Leatherwood said. "And you've been paired with Nala."

Nala waved to Ed from across the room. His pimples glinted below the florescent lighting. He stopped his categorizing momentarily and gave Nala a charged wave, then threw his black eyes back down onto his desk.

The school bell sounded and students barreled for the exit doors, the room exploding with noise.

Sosie started to giggle. "Damn, La! You really won the how-much-can-my-life-suck lottery, didn't cha?" Sosie watched Edward Pote play with his fountain pens like action figures. He was no Mick Jagger, but who was she to judge? Her own life seemed to suck pretty bad too, right about then. She packed the rest of her stuff into her fuchsia-domed buckle bag. Just beyond Ed, she could see Gino beginning to make his way for the front doors. His soulless eyes leaked black energy. He was heading toward her, not on purpose. Her lungs tightened. "Gotta get out of here. Grab a slice of pizza, or a freaking shot of something. You coming?"

"It's 10:30 in the morning . . . ."

"So?" Sosie threw on her bag.

"You don't drink." Nala folded her arms stubbornly.

"Coming, or not?"

"Not," Nala said. "Go ahead."

Sosie slipped by Nala and kissed her cheek. "Thanks, I owe you bunches." Her cute army boots were eventually taken with the crowd.

Nala took in a deep breath, feeling her body loosen into one of her favorite yoga poses. *Pranayama.* Maybe it was a sign. She needed to relax, to channel Zen, like, now. Her eyes slowly started to drift shut when . . . *SMACKKK!* Knox Ritchie stood, hands implanted on Nala's desk, smiling bleached white teeth at her. "Hey." His teeth glistened in a distractingly vibrant row. "Noticed we both got sort of gypped on partners," he said.

"Uh-huh," Nala mumbled, waking up to reality. And Knox wasn't a half-bad reality to wake up to.

"Sounds a little foolish, but I actually thought Mr. L was gonna put us together, because . . . I don't know . . . we make sense? And I am—or was—having a lucky streak. And I wanted it so bad I thought it would just . . . happen."

Nala gathered up the half devoured sandwich that Sosie had left behind in her hurry, and sucked up the rest of her cappuccino, searching for a trash-bin. "Would have been nice," she said finally, mind elsewhere. Was she seriously stuck with that Ed Pote guy? Why would Professor L do that to her?

Pranayama. Zen. Fast. Before my head explodes.

"So . . . you ready for the weekend?" Knox snatched up the trash from Nala's hands and said, "I'll take care of it," grinning sweetly. He was easy to like, she had to admit.

"So excited!" she nodded, imagining some lavish evening, everyone dressed in suits and dresses, getting stuffed off lobster mac and cheese, or something hilarious and weird. At $10 a bite, it should make jokes and do a little jig on the plate, too. "Are *you*?"

"Hell yeah! Haven't really shut up about it," he admitted embarrassedly, running his fingers through his slicked-back quiff. It was totally true, too. During two-a-days, Knox had been really off his game and Coach Mike had sent him in for a psychiatric evaluation while the others played, tackled, lifted. Knox talked about Nala the entire counseling session. "Everyone looks to me to make the game-winning plays," he had complained. "Must forget I have rowing to worry about, and football, and school. I can usually handle it, but recently . . . can't seem to get my mind to focus. This girl . . . she's like, invading it, or something."

"Women do that," the counselor assured. "Make us feel like boys, sometimes. Not in control. Plenty of young men your age begin to experience feelings of anxiety and uncertainty, mostly triggered by the female sex. For future relationships. For physical stamina. For logical capabilities. Women change the game, and we have to adjust. But there are a few games they don't have to change. Make football one of them."

Like he ever played Football, or women for that matter.

Nala yanked her buttercup zip-bag up her shoulder and started for the exit, quietly strumming her hair ends as she walked. "Are your friends excited, too?"

"Most of them." He shrugged.

Not so much Gino. But Rocko Borai had seemed to be focusing more on Sosie after Knox asked Nala out. He scouted her out during cafeteria meals, comparing her body parts to vegetables — mostly celery and carrots. Brains liked Juliet ever since she showed up on the first day of school, skipping into the dining hall with her bouncy, wild curls splashing about. Then, she *had* to reach for the gluten-free pumpkin bread (by accident), and it was love at first bite (even though she immediately spit it up in her napkin afterward and whined about it for a mindboggling hour).

Max Umminger wasn't much of a socialite, and so he didn't seem too pumped. He'd rather be reading some cheesy starships-and-aliens fantasy novel while devouring raw cookie dough and goofing off with the action figures he stashed beneath his bedframe. But yeah—not so much Gino. He hadn't said much about it. He'd tag along for good food and beer, and if a girl threw herself at him, then what the hell, but he definitely wouldn't make any kind of an effort. Gino wasn't good for much more than sleeping and football, and he was okay with that. In fact, he preferred it.

"Truth is, I'm the most excited," Knox said as the classroom emptied out. "A little nervous. Shouldn't be telling you that, though," he sort of laughed. "There's a lot of pressure on me, Nala."

"Oh yeah?"

"Yeah," he said. "Kind of have to be on my A-game. Gonna hope and pray that my lucky streak hasn't run out on me just yet. So I can show you."

"Show me?"

"You know . . . ." he smiled. "That I am *really* this sexy all the time. I know you've been asking around. People talk."

Nala blushed. The classroom had emptied out, and it was just them and Professor Leatherwood. He kept himself busy behind his desk, reading over the course agenda and scratching out the boring stuff. *No, I will not give a two-part lecture on the history of the French kiss.* He'd just show the students a romantic black and white film and give the guys a few pointers on how to make a smooth move in a theater. None of that "counting shoulders" crap. *And don't eat too much popcorn, unless you want your date to start coughing up popcorn hulls.*

Knox got the feeling Professor Leatherwood was looking for some alone time: to cement his eyes shut with polyurethane, to catch a few z's before the next blitz of horny teenagers paraded through the classroom, to zip through a nudie-mag, or to do whatever it was that kept him from going clinically insane in that maddening little university town. "Can I walk you to your next class?" Knox asked Nala, imagining a quick stop by the Village Coffee Shack to load up on espresso before French. Nala looked like an espresso kind of girl.

"That's okay," she said, appearing suddenly distracted as her eyes mowed over the classroom floor. Her head started throbbing with Ed Pote's name again. "I have a question for Mr. Leatherwood, actually. But I'll see you later?"

"Sure," Knox nodded, managing to smile. Seeing Nala later would give him enough momentum to push through French, but he wished he could see more of her then. His eyes turned vacant as he pushed for the exit. "All right. So . . . see you at lunch?"

"Yeah. See you then."

Knox disappeared through the classroom doors, leaving behind two grey handprints stamped on Nala's desktop. Knox was great. He was funny, sweet, beautiful, seemed to say all of the right things. Why did she have to be such a bitch and send him off like that? What would he think of her now?

"You're still here," Professor Leatherwood piped up from his desk, fixing his eyes on a large manual and highlighting nonsense.

Nala swooped near his desk. She could understand why every girl had sized him up to be a total dreamboat. They'd all blathered about him through the shower curtains, in the cafeteria, at the spa. He was Professor Leatherwood, No First Name: the intriguing, twenty-something man with a gorgeous, prickly chin. He fit the bill and wore the pants tremendously.

"Yup." Nala nodded, wondering if it was weird that she hadn't joined the crowd and barreled out of the classroom doors as quickly as her little legs would take her. *I was never much of a crowd-follower, anyway.* "Sorry to hang around." She shrugged, wishing she didn't have coffee-breath. "I just needed a minute."

Professor Leatherwood dumped the mind-numbingly huge classroom manual onto his desk and pounded his fist on it as if he was trying to crush it beneath his strong, manly pummel. "Me too," he insisted. "A minute . . . or a thousand minutes. Life can be pretty hectic." He drove his eyes over hers and smiled cunningly, as if to suggest they run away to some island chain near the coast, live out of a bamboo shack, drink mai tais and piña coladas out of coconut shells, catch rays during the day, skinny dip at night, and doze off in their coastal blue rope hammock.

She got all of *that* from a smile?

"Is this about Edward? Do you mind being partnered up with him?" Professor L asked.

She shook her head, even though the thought of spending that much time with Ed made her cringe. "Not at all. He seems . . . nice." Nala flipped her hair behind her shoulder and giggled at her own unconvincing response. The professor laughed along. Nala just appeared so young and full of life. Watching her reminded him of the last time he had felt decently happy.

Then, the classroom door smacked open and a squinty-eyed girl with a half pixie cut, half shaved head shuffled in on ultramarine flats and rounded for her chair, angry at the world. Buzz kill . . . literally. The professor rolled up his sleeves and gave Nala a look that simply said, "Busted."

Nala blinked, imagining the lunacy taking place beyond the classroom doors. Knox was probably singing "La Marseillaise" in French by then. Sosie was probably sipping her first pineapple upside-down cake shot. The lawn was likely buzzing with zipping backpacks and clomping loafers. She knew she should join the crowd, probably head to class and grab a seat, even though she had three perfectly decent minutes to make the thirty-second walk to Baking before Miss Hart blew a fuse in her charged, beehive hair. But that pointless conversation with Professor Leatherwood had been the highlight of her week. He was just so mature, and . . . charming.

Professor L's eyes glinted gorgeously up at her. Nala gulped. "I guess I should head out," she said. "But thanks for the . . . break."

Professor Leatherwood straightened up and cleared his throat to hide the fact that he wished they had another ten minutes together. "We'll have to do it again, sometime," he said, his heart thumping at her over-the-shoulder smile as she trotted for the door.

Sometime, or every time.

Peach Fuzz and Hangovers

"A dozen red roses delivered to room 779, Alistair Dwelling. Make the card say, 'Nala, looking forward to tonight. All of my love, Knox Ritchie.' Don't forget that last part," Knox Ritchie clucked into his razor-thin, touch-screen cell phone. "Ritchie with an i-e." The phone clicked, and a dial tone drained through. "That bastard just hung up on me," he whined gruffly. "Should I call 'em back?"

"Hell no. He did you a favor," Rocko said. "You were starting to sound like a little, whiny bitch." Rocko readjusted his cordovan, cable stitch hangover beanie over his buzzed head, his headache scourging the confinements of his skull. "Nala has you whipped," he mumbled, yanking his metal rim aviators over his swollen eyes. Why couldn't he take back the eight unswerving hours of Bloody Mary guzzling, puking, and repeating the day before? Ever since he staggered out of bed and crawled—literally on hands and knees—for his water jug and a posse of cerulean capsule pain pills, his throbbing headache had only gotten worse.

Damn you, vodka!

Fried mozzarella orbited the table, and a stash of marinara fell over and soaked everything, which the boys didn't really mind. Cloud Nine served nothing but hangover food— everything was oiled up, with a side of over-salted sweet potato fries, tater tots, hibachi skewers, or crispy green beans (which no one actually ordered, but it was an option) with every meal. The patio had a nice breeze, and gave Rocko plenty of vomiting space.

"An order of loaded potato wedges, jalapeño ranch on the side," the waiter's nasally voice interrupted as he swooped in like a hawk and drove his beady, blue eyes over the group. He had honey blonde hair and frosted eyebrows that were practically invisible. His lips curved into a wide, zippy smile.

Rocko ripped off his sunglasses and caught the waiter's eye.

"Mine," he burped, feeling suddenly nauseous. The aroma of trans-fats crawled into his nose and he started to second-guess his decision to wobble down to Cloud Nine and shove carbs down his throat. "But I ordered honey-mustard, not this jalapeño crap."

"Honey-mustard?" the waiter repeated. *Then why the hell did I write down jalapeño ranch on my mandatory notepad, and circle it, and underline it, and dot it with a stupid Mexican accent?* Rocko sat smugly, looking pissed and in dire need of some honey-freaking-mustard. "Sorry about that. Be right back." The waiter disappeared into Cloud Nine, fighting off the urge to smash in Rocko's bloated, hungover face with a gallon of condiments.

Knox finished off his twice purified lemon water, his non-alcoholic beverage of choice, much like that of a spoiled teenage girl wanting to shed a few pounds before the big dance. He wanted to look his best for Nala, and that required him to be clear eyed and not reeking of alcohol. He pushed his fingers through his sandy hair, and chips of dried gel flaked away and scuttled toward the cement. Damn, he needed to shower . . . for his third time that day. "How long are you going to mess with him?" he asked Rocko as he shoveled a handful of gluten-free kale chips between his teeth. If Brains and Max were going to pick their noses, rubberneck at the passers-by, chew on their lemon wedges, and gnaw on their dirty nails, Knox was going to eat their food.

Rocko shrugged. He was only messing with the waiter because he was feeling grouchy and drunk and didn't like the way the guy's face sat on his egg-shaped head. Also, he had left his wallet in his room. Oh, and he was bored. "As long as it takes to get a free meal," he admitted.

Gino rolled his eyes. "Damn it. Grow up, Borai." He shoveled a monstrous meatball sub into his mouth, flinging sauce all over the teak patio table. He washed it down with a splash of beer.

"Honest-to-God, Blackthorn, clean up that shit before I puke," Rocko snapped.

"You want to clean it up?" Gino asked. Why wasn't Rocko wasting away in his tomato-juice stained bed sheets or sobering up in an icy shower? Why couldn't he stay out of everyone else's business? Gino shoved forward a clump of unused napkins, and mumbled, "By all means," as he ripped another bite from his sandwich and let the mess pile up.

"Cleaning is a woman's job," Rocko growled. He threw the napkins at Knox and blurted, "Well, woman, clean it up."

Knox frowned and vaguely searched his call log. He didn't bother to respond. He had other things on his mind. Nala. That night, the $150 floral arrangement he had sent to her dormitory would pay off when she showed up wearing a saffron peplum dress — her tan, spidery legs peaking out the bottom — and adorable, wine-dark, slingback pumps. He had gotten the girl, and Rocko didn't. Was there a sweeter comeback than that?

The waiter returned with his peach-fuzz cheeks royally flushed, appearing flustered, embarrassed, and in deep loathing of the asshole who made him run around the kitchen like a headless turkey for honey-mustard. "Your condiment, sir," he said in a bogus, here-to-serve voice, shoving a bowl of honey-mustard toward Rocko's still steaming, loaded potato wedges.

"Made fresh?" Rocko terrorized, eyeing the yellow, gooey stuff that had been plopped in the dish like some athlete's foot toe ointment.

"No, sir," peach-fuzz replied. For a struggling sophomore in need of some extra cash, he sure knew how to keep his cool when it came to moody pricks. And Rocko was the moodiest.

"Hmm. Do you keep it in the desert?"

"The desert?" The waiter chuckled, hoping that this idiot was trying to tell a joke. "No, sir. We don't keep it in the desert."

"Then why the hell did it take so long?"

Rocko sneered. He looked proud of how genuinely assholeish he had managed to sound. He folded his arms grandiosely, smirking his thick, plummy lips and rolling his shoulders back, as if to indicate that a deep tissue neck massage was in order. *Could he ask the waiter to work out those knots, too?* Rocko chuckled to himself. God, was he clever. That desert bit was one of his favorites, yet. And on a day when he was withdrawing from liquor overdose . . . clearly, things were looking up.

Bravo, Borai!

The waiter gulped loudly and sort of shrugged. What was he supposed to say? *I could have spit in your food, sir, but I didn't. Doesn't that count for anything?* His hands ballooned like crab claws as he tried to remain professional and calm. "The — the kitchen was backed-up. We have a new chef," he croaked. "The cabinets were completely reorganized."

Gino rolled his bored eyes. "Forget about it, man. The honey-mustard is fine," he said, giving Rocko a make-another-smart-ass-remark-and-I'll-break-your-neck look. He could, and he totally would. "I'll take the check," Gino added.

The waiter passed along the check and tripped for the kitchen doors, his curly, golden hair trailing behind him as he resisted a celebration dance. *Free at last, free at last!*

"Oy! What was that for?" Rocko hissed, dumping the honey-mustard across the table like a splatter-paint display at some hipster art exhibit. He would call it *Sacrifice of Conning* and boast about the inspiration that came to him in a hungover daze. "When you hit rock bottom, and you're sulking in your all-time low, you'll do anything to survive. Even con some pour soul for body fuel," he would exaggerate to win over some blonde New Zealand chick wearing frighteningly tall snakeskin platforms, totally convinced that Mr. Borai was the next big thing in pop culture.

"Another minute of tormenting, and we would have enjoyed a free meal, asshole," Rocko yacked away, feeling randomly sober and cured of his migraine. "Four free meals and five sodas, but who's counting?"

The guys ignored him and tried to figure out the bill. Gino looked especially ticked as he donated a twenty. He burped, finished off his beer, and burped again. There was nothing more frustrating than Rocko showing up half-drunk, angry, broke, doped out on pain pills and wanting to start up a fight with the puniest guy within reach.

"Dude, lighten up, Blackthorn." Rocko kicked his vintage tanker boots out and mocked Gino's expression. "It's a joke! You spared his life. You're an everyday hero. No one is getting fired today!" Rocko threw his muscly arms in the air and pretended to give one-tenth of a shit.

In the near distance, Nala dragged Sosie by her brand new glazed leather tote down the snaking pathway. She was relieved to finally see the glowing indigo emblem advertising "Cloud Nine" that hanged from the polished white stone. Sosie had skipped her only Friday class in order to mow over the upscale boutiques on campus and raid their just-ins. She bought Nala a two hundred dollar thank-you-for-being-such-a-good-friend cherry satchel, and surprised her with it in the courtyard, smothered beneath eight gigantic shopping bags, two double-shot lattes wound beneath her recently manicured fingernails, and brand-new, mirror-lensed aviators. Why not shop until she dropped and splurge on hand massages and facial creams? She was disgustingly rich, after all, and trying to manage a broken heart. Well . . . it wasn't so much a broken heart as it was a broken ego. A totally shattered one, at that.

Sosie just wasn't herself lately. Earlier, she roamed zombie-like around the shops trying to pick out the best all-organic hair treatment. Normally, she'd rather wash her hair with bleach than buy into that all-natural crap. The day before, she hadn't even touched her Fettuccine Alfredo, and she didn't even glance at the dessert cart. Not even once.

Why didn't Gino remember her? Was she really so forgettable? Or did he remember, and just not want to? Was she bat-shit crazy? Had she dreamed the whole thing up?

"Maybe we can get one of those hot fudge sundaes and eat until we can't breathe," Nala piped up. Bloating up hours before the big group date sounded like a complete nightmare, but she'd do it if it would cheer Sosie up. Hell, she had a brand new cherry-red handbag to prove just how much Sosie appreciated her, so she could spare her lean torso for a couple of days to show some love back. Right?

Knox peeked into the blinding sunrays just in time to catch Nala zipping down the sidewalk, appearing intensely stunning as usual in a deep-cut burgundy knit tee, onyx chiffon shorts, leg warmers, and chestnut riding boots. *Wowzers.* She was with her blonde friend. Sophie, or something. God, she looked hot.

"Wanna grab a beer at the bar before we leave?" he nudged Gino, trying to contain his smile. And it must have slipped his mind to add, "And entertain Blondie while I woo Nala with my good looks and impeccable charm? "

A Little Liquid Courage

"How's the Mediterranean Tuna Panini?"

Nala had flagged down a waitress with spangled freckles and an ivory snakeskin vest of questionable authenticity, and was browsing the menu primly. After she ordered a freshly squeezed lemonade for herself and a caramel fudge milkshake for Sosie, she bounced back and forth between the sandwiches and the salads.

"Our tuna's real good. I'm not a fish girl myself, but it doesn't taste real fishy like—I don't know—salmon, or somethin'." The waitress smacked her kiwi-mango bubble gum between her lips and yawned.

"I'll stick with the chickpea salad." Nala passed off her menu. "And she'll have some fries," she added, pointing at Sosie. The waitress danced into the kitchen on her red moccasins to prepare their drinks and flirt with the cute, shaggy-haired busboy that was "testing" the beers on tap for proper carbonation.

"Hear that? Your best friend in the whole entire world ordered you fries! Yay me! You should dip 'em in your milkshake like we used back in Bluffdale," Nala suggested in her upbeat, all-we-need-is-each-other voice.

Sosie's lips frowned. "Mmhmm. Thanks." She wasn't really in the mood to be upbeat. Couldn't they just sit there and be totally miserable together? Why did Nala have to be such an optimist all of the time? Couldn't she depress herself for like, thirty-freaking minutes, and hate the world, too? All Sosie wanted to do was make fun of the waitress' awful vest and eat carbs and not talk.

Right as she was on the verge of hauling ass to the bathroom just to kick something over, Sosie noticed Knox Ritchie breeze inside from the back patio, looking particularly metro with his hair slicked in a dirty blonde wave. His chillingly ice blue eyes settled on Nala like he was prepared to serenade her with some cheesy love ballad.

Sosie's eyes rolled. *Please don't.*

"Hey girls. Great spot, huh? Guess we had the same idea." Knox fell into an empty seat and leaned his elbow on the table so that he practically stooped over Nala. She was gorgeous. Little burgundy knit hugging around her. Scent like raspberries. For a moment, all he could do was stare at her lips. "Or maybe you're just following me," he flirted.

"Guilty," Sosie chimed in, accepting her extra-large milkshake from the freckled waitress and calculatedly rolling her eyes. "We spend all of our free time stalking you, because you're such a fox,

Knox! Knox the fox!" Sosie grumbled noisily and pulled thick milkshake up through her straw.

Knox just smiled at her sarcasm and laughed it off. Was he really that nice, or just conceited enough to accept the fake compliment?

The waitress passed Nala her lemonade and checked out Knox. "Hey there, Handsome! What can I get ya? A beer, maybe? Some fries?"

"I could use a mochaccino," he supposed coolly. "With a little whipped cream, an extra dash of steamed milk, and caramel drizzle. Please. That'd be great." Knox had already grown used to impressing the girls on campus by ordering complicated drinks in his fancy sports coats and expensive driving shoes, but he hadn't yet had the opportunity to show Nala just how seasoned of a coffee snob he really was. "And, ugh, go ahead and put their drinks on my tab." He winked a blue, glistening eye at the waitress.

"And what about their food? You paying for that, too?" The waitress pushed her strawberry-blonde, tangled hair off her chest, revealing her nametag, Bree.

"Anything they want," he said. "I'll take care of it."

Bree nodded, and then stomped for the kitchen. *Anything they want.* Was he the boyfriend of two? Was he twice as much off the market? At least there was always lemon-haired busboy, right? Though he was two sips away from total obliteration and was looking a bit queasy as he rolled around on the countertop and tallied in black marker across his arm the number of liquor bottles stacked across the shelves. But at least he looked cute doing it. In a drunken, can't-tell-his-left-from-his-right sort of way.

"You didn't have to do that," Nala said. Sweet, considerate Knox. She liked that about him. Easy going. Pay for everybody. Give Sosie a much needed break, and accept "Knox the Fox" as a miffing new nickname, if only for the day. Though Nala had the feeling it would stick. All of it was really, really sweet of him.

"What kind of man would let you two pay for *anything*?" Knox asked genuinely.

Sosie cringed. Knox had only just sat down, and she already couldn't stand being in the crossfires of he and Nala's passionate flirt-fest. She knew her milkshake would go down easier if she didn't have to battle the constant loitering of upchuck in her throat. Sandy-haired, pretty-boy upchuck. But where could she sip in peace? The restaurant wasn't packed, but she wasn't about to sit alone at a table, fattening up on malts. The restroom was probably filthy, so she passed on that. But a commotion arose near the bar as freckle-face's lemon-haired love-interest was dragged into the kitchen and chastised for drinking on the job. The bar suddenly appeared like an aura of big, blue, tranquil energy. Totally empty . . . like Sosie's squashed soul.

"I'm gonna go check on my fries. Want anything?" Sosie asked.

"Nope," Nala said.

"I'll just wait for my coffee, thanks. Good luck on those fries!"

Sosie grinned and slipped onto her feet. She was so cunningly brilliant. Alone; depressed maybe, but cunningly brilliant nonetheless. Or, were Knox and Nala the victors for scoring some alone time? Who was conning whom?

Sosie climbed onto a barstool and arranged her sheer, flowing, wine-colored skirt over her legs. The tan she had worked on a couple of weeks earlier had completely vanished. Oh well. It wasn't like she was trying to impress anyone . . . not anymore, at least. The way she saw it, she could now spend her first year at BU eating lasagna and Hot Pockets and watching the entire 2012 Academy Award nominated films list, all of them supposedly filled with sexy, scruffy-chinned actors that The Bluffdale Preparatory School for Girls had forbidden. Then sophomore year, she could hop back on the gives-a-shit train, eyelash extensions and lip venom ready, and go future hubby hunting with

Tess. Everything was going to be okay. Except for the fact that she had somehow finished off her entire milkshake in about three minutes, and it still wasn't enough to fill her hollow heart.

"What can I get you, sweetheart?" a bartender with the nametag reading "Vic" asked in a deep baritone that seemed to sing in her bones. He had blackberry-dark hair and a ratty, untrimmed beard that was almost cute in a homeless-professor sort of way. His eyes were russet brown. And familiar.

"Hit me," she demanded, sliding the empty glass into his hands. "Let's do cookies and cream this time."

"You got it." He swooped her glass up and spun for the kitchen. Was it attractive that she could eat so much and totally get away with it, or was it just plain gross?

As she watched a football replay on the little television set perched near the wine bottles, Sosie felt a body plop into the barstool next to her. A familiar black hoodie panned into her view. Gino Blackthorn took a sip of a foamy draught beer, looking pensive as he focused on the rerun. *Damn it.* Her muscles stiffened like stale sour dough. It was bad enough she had to see him in class, but here, too?

Sosie felt her cheeks turn red as she buried her face in her hands. "Great," she mumbled into the bar. Gino peaked over, and recognized the curve of her cheek. *Of all the places to sit.* He mentally smacked his forehead with the palm of his hand. Then he looked closer. Was she sick or something?

"You okay?" he asked, almost sounding considerate.

"I'm great," she said, popping her head up and milking a big, phony smile. Any minute, Vic would return with her extra-large cookies and cream milkshake, and she'd look just as hopeless and pitiful as she felt. But at least she had chocolate. It had always been a good friend to her.

Gino glued his eyes on the television set, while Sosie remained silently annoyed. Vic, as if right on cue, showed up with her milkshake. "I added extra whipped cream for you," he said in his dreamy voice. *Great! I'll be sure to thank you when it reemerges as fat on my ass*, she thought, but it was hard to be honestly pissed at someone as cute as Vic.

"That will be two fifty, sweetheart," Vic added.

Sosie nodded, and searched through her bag with sweaty fingers, looking for loose change. Vic stomped his sleek, black sneakers behind the bar, waiting. The more he stood there, the more she worried he'd find a way to make her look like an even bigger pig than she already did.

"I bet you'll like this milkshake more than the first one. It's a little sweeter," he added. *Ah, thank you! Just what I needed!*

Sosie started to panic when she couldn't find her freaking gold debit card beneath all of the must-have junk she had purchased on her shopping binge. Thirty-dollar lipliner and Tahitian vanilla massage oils. Pointless stuff like that. But at least she was realizing she was more of a clutch-carrying girl than the satchel type. Her hands emerged in sweat. She considered pouring out all of her crap onto the counter, but that could get messy . . . and embarrassing. And then Gino pushed forward a ten-dollar bill. "Keep the change," he said, with the same bizarre fixation on the football replay.

"Keep your own damn change," Vic replied. "You might need it to bail me out of a jail cell if I get caught liquoring up you and your buddies again."

"I get it. I owe you," Gino replied in perfect smart-ass. "Just take it."

Vic pocketed the bill and left to refill Gino's beer and check the kitchen for any order ups. Taking a large gulp of milkshake—which was totally better than her first, she'd have to agree—Sosie subtly watched Gino. His eyes were fastened on the TV, hand clasping his beer mug, lips barely wedged open. His chocolate hair wound across his forehead in a casual wave. He was so mortifyingly, annoyingly attractive. Like, really.

"You didn't have to do that," Sosie said finally. An Oreo commercial flooded over the screen, and she had the sudden urge to sip more milkshake. "I have my own money." Lots of it, she could have added.

Gino hardly budged as he took another drink of beer. "Don't read into it."

Sosie's eyes rolled inside of her head. *Same, stupid ass.* She spent a few minutes spying on Nala and Knox from her swivel stool, pivoting around and around until she thought she would hurl. And then, around and around she went again. Whirling, she could just barely make out Nala's round, puppy eyes smushed against Knox's crisply shaved jaw while he bragged about renovating the male dormitory lounge, which sounded more like a transport back to some 1972 fraternity house. All that appeared to be missing from that raunchy, retro flat was a burnt-orange shag rug. *Funky.*

"At one point I had to decide between a fiberglass lounger and a charcoal tweed upholstery recliner. Tougher decision than you'd think."

Were they honestly discussing interior design? *Try not to win her over with your knowledge on sculptural pendant lamps,* Sosie teased in her bored, little brain.

The football replay popped back up on the TV just as Gino finished off the first half of his beer. His bronze skin glinted on his hand as he fiddled with the incredibly convincing fake ID pressed into the pocket of his destroyed, blue-wash denims. Honestly, though, did he really need one? He looked like . . . old. Not Wall Street old, but definitely Harvard Law School old.

His beer glass glowed beneath the low, drooping hang lights. Brown and wet. Like mud. Looked disgusting. "What's it like?" Sosie asked him, blinking at it. She wished she could order a prickly pear margarita and tell him about her week from hell:

about how some jerk she had met back in Bluffdale had forgotten her after only a week. About how the mild dent she put in her month's allowance was wasted on exfoliator scrub and horse shampoo. About her teacher, Mr. L, who would look completely gorgeous in swimsuit briefs. And then she'd casually mention that the jerk she met in Bluffdale happened to be listening to her prattle away at that very moment, and he'd connect the dots, compliment her beautiful, sparkling eyes, and offer to buy her a second prickly pear margarita, which she would exchange for a shot of Naked Yellow Bird, because by then she'd sort of need it. He'd feel guilty. Ask her out.

If only she had a fake.

Gino took a swig. "Beer?" he asked. "Refreshing, I guess. Want to try?"

"Mmm, no thanks."

An order of French fries swooped out of the kitchen door with the freckle-faced waitress in charge of delivery. Since her last appearance, she had reapplied her eyeliner and was wearing new, over-drawn, claret-red lipstick. Her blouse was unbuttoned, showing off her saggy, grapefruit-sized boobs and the tattoo above her cleavage. Or was that stovetop residue?

Nala accepted the fries and passed them to Knox. *Phewww.* After watching her down two milkshakes *and* an order of fries, Gino would never see Sosie as more than the fat girl from Cloud Nine. And he certainly wouldn't remember her as the blonde in a bikini from Bluffdale Prep with the smoking-hot yoga body.

Pushing her bangs out of her face, she tried to yawn to shed her sudden nerves. Maybe this would be the perfect time to bring up Bluffdale, again. Gino had been drinking. The environment was relaxed. No teachers were lying around grading papers or rearranging seating charts. They might as well have been back on that beach, totally alone, the sound of white tipped waves splashing against the sand banks as they curiously checked each other out.

The football replay roared on screen, a crowd of face-paint and foam hands thrashing in their little, two-dimensional box, and Sosie felt her heart leap with anxiety at what she was about to do. She glanced around. Across the room, Knox felt at Nala's deeply bronzed knee where an Africa-shaped burn had appeared after Tess dropped a tray of freshly baked scones into Nala's lap by "accident" during Baking on Tuesday. Bree, the waitress, pursued another batch of freshman hotties who'd all ordered Sex on the Beach and giggled through their little-boy whiskers. Gino's mug of beer dribbled sweat as it flattened nearby. Sosie felt so out of her element. She needed to calm down. Fast. And then her eyes synced with foaming liquid courage.

Suddenly, Sosie snatched up Gino's beer mug and tossed her neck back. Her mouth filled with the flavor of wheat and pistachio. The liquid swished around between her cheeks, until she finally swallowed. *Nasssssssty!*

"Well, that's one way to treat yourself," Gino said as Sosie gulped again.

I wouldn't exactly call it a treat, she thought. The draught beer soured down her throat. Her nose scrunched up as she fought the urge to gag. When she set the mug down on the bar, the taste lingered, tongue like sandpaper. But at least now she was feeling powerful and spontaneous. Was she drunk already?

"Do you honestly not remember me at all?" the words sort off just fell off of her lips. She closed her eyes tight and then cracked them open a slit to see Gino zinging his hands through the air and cussing at the television screen. Hadn't he seen that replay like, ten thousand times already?

His voice trailed off as he snatched his glass back and took a swig. "What are you talkin' about? Who could forget the girl who polished off two milkshakes in fifteen minutes?" He grinned crookedly. "That has to be some kind of record — let me ask Vic."

"No! Look . . . you don't get it," Sosie whined. "That's not even what I meant." She played with the soft, champagne-colored cuffs on her sweater and pouted. Couldn't he just spare her one, nod his big, beautiful head, and admit that he hadn't stopped thinking about her since they'd met in Bluffdale? Did she have to come out and ask him *again*?

Apparently.

"Back in Bluffdale, remember? We. . . ."

Gino's eyes widened at her. Did he care what she had to say, or was he just bored by the toothpaste commercial occupying the TV? He sunk inside his long-sleeved Henley shirt, his hoodie weighing down across his shoulders, and watched as Sosie's lips thinned with stress.

"Back in Bluffdale, we what?"

"We. . . ." She ping-ponged her eyes between Gino and the recently re-emerged Vic, who had appeared with a basket of deep fried zucchini and creamy garlic dip and was counting out the tip jar. Would he mind whipping together an extra strong white sangria and letting her have a sip, or five, just to take the edge off?

She cleared her throat. Her fingers suddenly felt tingly. Her body felt light. And — sigh of relief — she felt a little fearless, too. Maybe it was the beer, or the thought of pomegranate and Sauvignon Blanc. Perhaps she was feeling mentally exhausted and was just ready to get it over with so she could go home and try out one of Nala's brilliant beauty secrets, like a baking soda bubble bath or a mayonnaise hair wrap. Or maybe she just wanted an excuse to spend the rest of September locked inside her boring dormitory room, pigging out on almond pecan popcorn and watching soap opera reruns. Either way, even with Gino Blackthorn looking super gorgeous next to her — his prickly chin and thick, black eyebrows raising and sinking with interest—she couldn't keep quiet any longer.

"Dude, back in Bluffdale we hung out on the beach for like . . . a while," she said. "Don't worry; I'm not savoring your used wads of gum and building a creepy shrine in my closet, or anything. I just don't understand why you have to be such an ass about it. You totally remember me!"

Did she just call him *dude?* Did she just call him *ass?*

The tip jar overturned, and Vic slithered back inside the kitchen with coins teeming from the pockets of his dry, straight-legged jeans. Across the restaurant, Nala and Knox stared dreamily into each other's eyes as they discussed dinner reservations and the ever-more impressive limo service he had snapped into existence with his money-green fingertips. It wouldn't be long before King Foxy Knoxy and Queenie Nalinie boarded their white silk cocoon super yacht and sailed through the Leeward Islands drinking Sazeracs and French 75s during the day, and chocolate liquor s'more-shooters at night. "*Je t'aime,*" Knox would whisper in some schmaltzy, French accent while spoon-feeding her chateaubriand beneath a canopy of stars.

Comme c'est romantique!

Sosie clanked her fingernails together as she waited for Gino to say something. Half a minute had passed, and nothing had happened. He was just sitting there, staring blankly, strangely silent. All that moved were his shoulders, lifting and falling with every inhale. Then . . . at last . . . something. He jumped onto his charcoal-gray high-top sneakers and rummaged through his jean pockets, his thick, black stubble casting a shadow as daylight misted through the front windows. Sosie watched the hair curling over his ears as he mumbled something unclear. She leaned in closer and raised her eyebrows to suggest that either he speak up or forever hold his peace. Of course, they both knew by now that it was a peace she would perpetually disturb until she got some kind of answer out of him.

The room seemed to flood with strangers as Gino headed for the exit. Where was he going? Was he just going to leave her there like that, again? The stubbly hairs on his neck stiffened in preparation for the crisp, autumn wind as he approached the doors. Just a few more steps, and he'd be free. But before his hand caught the door, he peeked over his shoulder at Sosie. She sat, skirt swimming over her naked knees, frowning at him. Soulbroken.

Gino's chest tautened. He wished he had just been honest with her from the beginning, even though he still thought she was better off without him and he was better off alone. Maybe if he was a different guy—the kind that thought about a home out in the country, with kids and a few dogs, some flat screens, a fire pit, a barbeque smoker out by the pool, Friday night lights, Sunday morning communion—maybe then they could make something out of it. But Gino knew that he'd do family differently than his parents had. His kids would know their father was a stern asshole instead of guessing that he was a stern asshole while locked up at some testosterone-packed boarding hell. He knew he'd live modestly. Simple home out in the country. A few dogs. Other than that, he didn't really anticipate anything about having a family. And Sosie probably did. Staying away from her . . . he was doing her a favor.

Gino thought about how truly blonde Sosie's thin locks were as they curled down her sleeves. She almost looked sweet sitting there, hopeless and damsel-like, staring back at him as he slipped away, wishing she could stop him. That was obvious. It reminded him of that day back in Bluffdale, when they had met. He could remember how his legs ached as he jogged over that last hill, where he first saw her playing in the waves, barely covered behind a bandeau and ruffled bikini bottoms, her chest fried with freckles and her exposed butt cheeks dusted with sand, her blonde, crimped hair gusting in the salted breeze as she twirled in the blue-green water. He knew it the moment he saw her: she was a free bird, and he was just an automaton following a schedule full of pigskin and mouth guards. He didn't fit in her world, and she didn't fit in his . . . even though a part of him died to make room for her.

Sosie's eyes glinted at him as Gino took a deep breath and shoved his hands back inside of his jean pockets. "You don't want to know me," he said, ripping his eyes off of her and walking through the door.

She sat, her toes dangling from the barstool, as he sprinted to catch up with Rocko Borai, Brains Fink, and Max Umminger. She watched through the windows as the four drifted back toward campus, Gino taking a last glance back at Cloud Nine before vanishing into the haze of orange sky. At least he was right, for once. She definitely didn't want to know him. Not anymore.

Smashed at Sol's

"How's your salad?" Knox whispered ardently as the waiter—a snob with silvery skin and black, beady eyes named Lloyd—dished the appetizer plates around the parchment and tea stain dining set, and roared in his snooty and seriously butchered French accent, "Enjoy."

"It's great," Nala replied sweetly. Her beefsteak tomato and Parmesan wedge sat smothered in Gorgonzola, as she drew squiggles through the dressing with her fork.

Knox snuck his hand beneath the table and gave Nala's knees a teasing squeeze. Man, did she look perfect in purple. Aye-ye-ye! "Did you get the flowers I sent you?"

"Oh." She dropped her fork to her plate, and swallowed quickly. "Gosh, you must think I'm so rude!" said said. "They were Beautiful! Seriously! I wrote you a thank you note, but . . ." she batted her long eyelashes up at him, "I left it back in the room."

"That's okay." His white teeth flashed her a glowing smile. "It just gives me an excuse to stop by, sometime."

Nala envisioned her envelope of perfect calligraphy collecting dust, resting beside the dozen blue irises and cardinal-red tulips that Knox had sent over. After spending the first eighteen years of her life watching Tess and Sosie and Juliet barrel through professionally wrapped birthday and Christmas presents from their folks up in Cargill's Island, Dirk Hill, or some fancy borough of New York or Connecticut, Nala wasn't exactly used to getting gifts. She would occasionally receive a note from her mother or father around the holidays, in which they mostly bragged about how their beautiful daughter didn't need a shower of gifts to know how much she was loved. Maybe they'd throw in a twenty-dollar bill here or there; Dutch chocolate on Valentines Day; a cross necklace on Christmas, but she mostly received cards.

At least this had made receiving flowers from Knox Ritchie totally special.

Knox glanced around the room as his hand slipped from Nala's knees. Sol was an ultra-lux, up-scale steak house with a toffee-nosed waiting staff and two-toned jacquard draperies dangling from the antique crown molding. He felt strangely at peace: the swish Victorian décor, the sparkling water, the gorgeous girl beside him. The two of them belonged there. If only their friends would do more than pick at their Wagyu Beef Carpaccio like a pack of two year olds.

"I think Rocko likes Sosie," Knox whispered in Nala's ear, glancing pointedly at his bigheaded ass-of-a-friend, who taunted Sosie with a glass of Rolle ou Vermentinu and cheered in a drunken sob, "Here's to us, sweetheart," as the wine sloshed around inside of his glass.

Sosie covered her electric blue bustier dress with her fur coat. Rocko was sort of funny with his wasted, muffled voice echoing "sweetheart" as he sucked down another slurp. But truthfully, wine-stained apparel was simply not an option for her, especially if she was trying to show Gino what he was missing out on. She wanted to be a hot miss, not a hot mess.

Across the table, Tess felt her braid wiggle down her spine as she reapplied her Russian-red lipstick, puckering at her reflection in Gino's whiskey glass. She was so annoyed. Rocko's voice vibrated loudly over the breadbasket. Why should she have to sit through this meaningless torture? Sosie was cackling at Rocko's mindless jokes, Knox was kissing Nala's pampered little ass, Gino was mute. But at least Gino still looked hot. Could his rich, brown hair be anymore luscious? Could his prickly, man-chin be any more . . . manly? All Tess wanted was to play grownup and flee with him to some luxury hotel off the coast, decorated with mocha velvet drapes, cross candelabras, and a double sided, marble fireplace. They could undress into velour robes, pour a bath in their seven-jet Jacuzzi tub, and enjoy complimentary organic bath salts as they exchanged neck massages. They could order champagne and white chocolate-covered strawberries, and make out while their toes pruned. He wouldn't have to say a word, unless it was 'perfect', which would totally slip out as she slipped into her silk, baby-doll lingerie. Her favorite word!

Oh, say it again.

Gino sat in his camel-colored, notched-lapel sports coat, sipping a whiskey sour and watching Rocko and Sosie across the table. She hadn't said anything to him since Cloud Nine. Maybe it was his own fault for leaving her like that. Maybe he should have explained himself better. "You don't want to know me," he had grumbled like an asshole before veering out the exit doors. "You don't want to know me because I'm not the kind of guy you deserve," he could have said, but then he would have sounded like a humble hero and she'd probably like him even more. And he certainly couldn't have that.

"They say oysters are an aphrodisiac," Tess purred as she poked one with her tiny fork. It wormed around inside of its shell disturbingly. She had never tasted an oyster before, but they were known to be a delicacy that only the wealthiest and most refined ordered — and Tess would be damned if she didn't appear wealthy and refined. She shoved the half-shell to her lips and took a whiff. The smell of raw fish and sea salt crawled up her nose.

"You do know what aphrodisiacs are, right?"

"Mmhmm. Sure." Gino shrugged, hardly listening. What was wrong with him? Tess, in her gold tulle scoop dress and chunky platform heels, was practically declaring that she'd be hot and horny once the mollusks cleared her plate, and Gino couldn't have cared less.

"Forget it." Tossing her head back, she let the wormy thing — slime and all — slither down her throat. It tasted like lemon juice and cocktail sauce, with a hint of rubber. *Delish*. She tried not to make an embarrassing face as it went down. Then she started to gag. Gross, fishy rubber; there was nothing sexy about it.

Across the table, Rocko clanked his third glass of wine against Sosie's water as the food arrived. Lloyd set Rocko's plate down. His eyes widened at squishy, orange mush. "What the *hellllllll* is that?" He dug his fingers through the soggy twigs plopped together.

"Roasted rainbow carrots, sir," said the prim and proper waiter. *As it said on the menu, as I repeated back to you, as you nodded your head and begged for extra. Moron.*

120

"Do I look like the freaaaaking Eaaaaaster bunny?" Rocko whined.

"No sir, you do not look like the . . . Easter bunny."

"Then bring me some mashed potatoes."

"Right away, sir."

Lloyd trotted off on his sleek, gunmetal driving shoes, hiding his face beneath his crisp, white gloves. *Stupid, spoiled, rich kids.* Knox shook his head, totally mortified. Was Rocko trying to get a free meal . . . again? Brains scoffed into his enamel-striped cufflinks. Umminger's caramelized sea scallop plopped into his khaki lap as he watched. And Sosie let out a small giggle. Why was everyone freaking out? Wasn't Rocko, at the very least, somewhat hilarious? Sure, he was a drunken buffoon with a loud mouth, but wasn't that loud mouth totally offensive and awesome?

Across the table, Gino was resting in his perfect screw-you slump, looking ultra-peeved as he chopped up his crawfish-stuffed filet and gnawed on asparagus. Sosie kind of like him like that. Annoyed. Bored. Maybe having fun with Rocko was making him mad; jealous, even.

A girl can dream, *right?*

Sosie pulled her chair close to Rocko so that her blonde, wispy hair slid over the sleeve of his jacket. He sure did look good, roaming his eyes over her, and then his plate, and then her again, like he wanted her for dessert.

"Come as close as you'd like, Susie-Q," he said, yanking her seat near. Their knees smacked and she nuzzled into his shoulder. Man, did his eyes look buttery up close. Rocko, Gino, Knox. Was there something in the Elkins water? They were all handsome . . . a little too handsome for their own good. "Don't give me any personal space. I don't want it. I seriously don't." His wine-sour breath wrinkled her nose.

"No personal space for you, then," she beamed, wrapping her silvery, sparkling wrists around his neck and randomly planting a wet kiss on his cheek.

Gino glared over the bread. Sosie's puckering lips, Rocko's horny chuckle, their aggravating joy as her kiss lingered on his cheek—all of it seemed explicitly designed to make his head explode. But was he even allowed to be pissed? He had sort of denied Sosie . . . twice. But Rocko was like, the biggest ass in the world, and Sosie . . . Sosie was his . . . his something first!

Gino's stare stiffened. What could she possibly see in that guy? The same guy who out of sheer boredom had stolen his suitemate's toothbrush, peed on it, and then recorded him puking in the sink at the taste of urine. Even posted it on the web, and it went viral in a few hours. Another time, he stole an ant-farm from the science lab and—just because—let the little critters loose on Brain's Egyptian-cotton bed sheets. He was allergic, of course. And on Christmas Eve three years before, he had covered himself in ivy-green paint and set the Windsor's prized pine ablaze just to shout the phrase, "Mean, green, wood-burning machine!" Everything about him was so worthless, and yet Sosie couldn't keep her naïve, little hands off of him.

Nala shifted in her seat as she danced her naked feet across the black and vanilla soumak rug. She breathed a sigh of relief. Her pyramid studded, round-toe pumps had been so uncomfortable—gorgeous, but uncomfortable—and now without them, she could finally flaunt her brand-new, whipped papaya toenail polish to all of the dropped crumbs.

"Want dessert?" Knox asked, rubbing his full stomach. Perhaps the extra side of creamed spinach he had ordered was a bad idea, after all.

"No thanks." She shrugged. Her appetite had gone south when she saw Rocko's hand going south down Sosie's back.

Nala picked a strand of shining bronze hair out of her lip gloss. Knox watched. Why did she want a group date? Couldn't she tell he was only suggesting it to be nice? They could be strolling down fifth with gelato-filled waffle cones, talking about their love for snowstorms while she cozied up beneath his sports jacket and he kissed the tip of her cold, pinkish nose. But instead, Rocko Borai was grunting nearby, holding Sosie against him as they made fun of Tess's rhinestone-studded eyeliner. It should be Nala's warm breath . . . on Knox's neck . . . and their pretentious, silver-haired waiter's rhinestone-studded eyeliner. Although he'd also be fine if no one was wearing rhinestones. The important thing was that Nala hadn't so much as grazed Knox's shoulder once. Not even by accident.

Cheers to me, and my forever-alone ass! Boo-hoo!

"Look, I had a lot of fun tonight," Knox said. He swallowed the nervous lump in his throat. Nala peaked up from behind her smoky, black lashes and smiled. Did she have to tease him like that when he was trying to make a point? "Maybe next time we can hang out, you know, just the two of us."

"You read my mind." She scooted closer and pressed her lips against his ear. "This is getting *so* weird."

Knox shuddered at the sensation of her warm breath. He had read her mind! And her lips had totally made out with his ear! Or brushed it. Or whatever. Did it matter? They were going on a second date, and next time he wouldn't be caught dead overloading on creamed spinach. He'd need his sculpted abs to be in flexing condition just in case his shirt, somehow . . . you know . . . slipped off.

Clothing Optional

T ess smacked her red-stained lips together and wrapped her boney arm through Gino's as they pulled for the front door. A few dope-eyed seniors were taking shots at the bar, and turned to notice the two glued together like a loaf of pull-apart bread. Tess jammed her nose into the air of cigar smoke. Her classically contoured zip satchel smacked against her hip as she walked. "You should be like, a male model or something." she blurted to Gino. Her messy, black braid whipped between her shoulder blades. "I'll probably model once I graduate, even after I get married."

Gino pushed through the restaurant door and filled his lungs with cold air. Winter meant snowboarding, snow-cats, ski-lifts, and mid-blizzard lounging in a cottage up in the mountains—preferably one with a Jacuzzi, where he could be alone with his thoughts, a twelve-pack, and a blunt. He could feel the ice thawing from his lips already.

"Maybe one day we can do a spread together," she gushed, pulling a stray, black tendril away from her eye. *And we can get married, and tell our children about the time Mommy and Daddy were fitted in nothing-but-hipster wardrobe—floral, lace-up combats and a printed, five-panel cap—making love to the camera, kissing between takes, sharing our chemistry with the world.* And the rest would be history.

"Nah, it's not really . . . me," said Gino, rocking inside of his loafers, cold air sucking at his skin. Even though he had left his pot plant, Doobie, on some junior's windowsill, unwrapped, exposed, he wished he could have one more smoke. If he were stoned, Tess's voice would melt to static, he would pass out on the drive back to campus, and he wouldn't have to cringe every time Sosie declared Rocko to be some kind of comic prodigy.

If only.

The limousine pulled up and the group piled inside. "Next time, you'll just drive," Tess whispered to Gino as she nuzzled into him. "So we can be alone."

Next time?

The door shut, and the limo began to pull forward. Rocko lost his drunken-rage as he dwindled down to earth and recessed into second-buzz (which was never as enjoyable as first-buzz). *Maybe I should puke and get it over with,* he considered. The ice bucket was nearby, and had definitely been used in that way before. It was a college town, after all.

"Try to sleep," Sosie said, dancing her nails down his neck. "We'll be home soon."

Rocko's buttery eyes glimpsed up at her through his slit, red lids. He held in his breath, suddenly seeming so helpless. His lips half-smiled as he whispered, "Thanks, sweetheart."

Sosie tickled her fingertips across Rocko's buzz cut, and stared out the window. Maybe Gino Blackthorn was just a boy, after all. And maybe this Rocko Borai guy was better. He was funny and hot, and — this was the kicker — actually seemed to *like* her. She imagined spending the winter with him, snuggled up beneath his pima cotton bed sheets and watching romantic comedies as they pigged out on chocolate Chex and pecan praline popcorn. At football games, she'd flaunt his letterman jacket and howl his number over the roaring crowd. It would be just her and her big, sexy, football-playing boyfriend.

"Wouldn't you hate to be him right now?" Tess breathed as she pinned her eyes on Rocko's wasted body, lethargic across Sosie's thighs. Gino pulled his eyes shut. He didn't care if Rocko was unconscious and tasting the hint of vomit at the back of his throat. He didn't care if Sosie was founding the Rocko Borai Fan Club in that strawberry-shaped head of hers. He didn't even care if Tess jumped out of the limousine as it wrapped around the highway curve at sixty miles per hour. In fact, he'd probably prefer it. All he wanted was peace and quiet. And for the love bugs in the back to get a freaking room!

Except, please don't, a part of him whispered.

The limousine finally pulled off the highway and slowed to a stop in front of Alistair Dwelling. The fiber optic lighting flickered on as the limo idled. Rocko lifted his heavy head and tried to hold himself up. Was he spinning, or was it the limo?

"You have a very comfortable lap, sweetheart," he said between hiccups, massaging his aching temples. Was he trying to be charming? "Maybe I should just lie back down on your lap for a minute. I'm starting to feel nauseous again."

No. Not charming. *Gross. Definitely gross.*

"Uh-uh! No way!" Sosie shoved him off playfully and flattened her gathered dress over her knees. Rocko cracked his neck and peeled his eyes open. "Think you'll be able to make it home all right?"

"If I say no, do I get to shack up with you?" He smirked.

Shack up? Like a sleepover?

Sosie could picture Rocko's muscly arms holding her. She could feel his chin resting strong and heavy on her head as they drifted to sleep. She imagined feeling his soft kisses on her eyelids during the night. Then, when they miraculously woke up at exactly the same second, their eyes would dance across the room in a wonderstruck haze and they would see . . . Nala, curled up on the far end of her mattress, sleep-deprived and furious. *No, that wasn't going to work.*

"If you say no, I'll keep you company until you aren't such a drunk moron. How's that?"

Rocko nodded his black buzz cut and chuckled. "Fair enough, sweetheart."

Just then, Max Umminger kicked the limousine door open with his taupe, lace-up boot — which was hardly the attire for Sol's Steakhouse — and grumbled as he pigeon-toed toward the sidewalk. Milly, his date, was wearing a denim-tulle sweetheart dress and rose gold sling backs that had stabbed him in the ankle throughout the whole drive home. He could have mentioned that her pitchfork heel was carving a hollow in his foot, but that would require him to speak . . . to a girl . . . with baseball cleavage bubbling out of her dress. And there was no way in hell that was about to happen.

The rest of the group poured after him and they all bee-lined for the footpath. They walked in a drunk and nervous stupor. Had their group date been an absolute flop? Knox had felt tortured by Nala's haunting good looks all evening long, Gino's head was fogged by Tess's infuriating, nasally whine, and Rocko was sloshed out of his skull and drooling all over Sosie's electric blue cocktail dress on the limo ride home. Max had a small, round gash in his foot and Juliet's hair had blown up like an electrical socket toasted her dry. Nala had best described the night as "getting *so* weird" while smacking a wet, accidental kiss on Knox's ear.

Gino grimaced. Had they no shame?

He shoved his hands in his pockets, kicking at the gravel. "I'm heading back," he declared, wishing he could smoke a cigarette alone and enjoy a view of the mountaintops ripening with snow. He couldn't wait to try out the brand new free ride board Knox had given him for his half-birthday in July. What a thoughtful and completely arrogant thing for his friend to do. Half-birthday. *Phhhh.* "Anyone else?"

"Give me a minute," Knox said. He grabbed Nala by her hands and pulled her with him beneath the stoop of the dormitory arch. The arch's shadow swallowed their faces and its thick walls drowned out the sound of their friends' voices.

"So next weekend," he said, clearing his throat. How could she still look so perfect? Her beachy, brown hair curled down her shoulders. She must know exactly how beautiful she is. And yet, Knox could hardly believe it himself. His breath stalled. "Maybe we can see a black and white film at that vintage theater off fifth."

Nala's lips smiled at him shyly. She had never seen a movie before: not one with male actors, at least, as these were banned from Bluffdale Prep. She imagined some golden-haired hunk on screen, sacrificing his last breath of sweet life to save the girl he loved. And Knox would be the perfect person to share that moment with. He was somewhat of a golden-haired hunk himself. "Pleaaaase! We haaaave to! I've been wanting to go there since, like, the first day I ever heard about it! In eighth grade, I think."

"Then we will," he promised. "We'll go. Whatever you want."

Gino's voice boomed into the small space, suddenly. "Dude, come on!" he yelled in a hurry-up-before-I-lose-my-shit kind of way. Knox frowned. He had almost forgotten they weren't alone. Why couldn't they be alone? He wrapped his arms around Nala's delicate, beautiful body and planted a kiss on her forehead. The scent of cherry-mango shampoo flew up to him as his lips lingered against her skin. "Goodnight, Nala. Sweet dreams."

Sweet dreams of you and me, basking in the winter sun on our professionally crewed yacht. Another sparkling champagne, mademoiselle?

"Sweet dreams, Knox," she breathed back.

Nala waved goodbye to the group and gave Knox a wink at the door. And then, she disappeared. Surely she knew that they were destined to be together, right? They would buy some rustic castle in the states, invest in racehorses, and hop around on their private jet to equestrian tournaments around the world. He pictured her gambling at his side while they drank white wine spritzers. They would lie around in their bathrobes in the finest penthouses, ordering room service and couples massages. Couldn't they skip all of the foreplay, and just walk down the aisle, already?

Gino applauded as Knox frisked down the dormitory steps. "Did our little boy just become a man?"

Knox managed to smile and threw a few, lighthearted punches at Gino. They performed a little boxing dance—Gino tossed a fist, Knox tossed a fist, one ducked as the other plunged—until Gino nearly clipped Knox in the jaw and their little game quickly became a threat to his beautifully chiseled face. "Hey, hey! Watch the moneymaker," he joked, his hands in the air.

Unless Nala had a thing for blood and bruises. . . .

"Ready to go, Borai?" Brains Fink asked, his lemon-green eyes tracing Juliet as she flounced up the staircase and slipped inside Alistair while he contemplated a final, *"au revoir"* to appear extra-refined. But she had already bolted and he had chickened out.

Rocko held Sosie's delicate hand in his and looked down at her blushing face. Maybe being drunk and alone with her wasn't such an awful idea. After all, the typical stumble back to Marlborough Hall to order late night pizza, pop in a DVD of last year's football highlights, and pass out with piecrust in his mouth was too damn predictable. He was ready for some excitement.

"I think me and Susie-Q are gonna hang out for a bit," he said, drawing Sosie near. The aroma of fermented white grapes made her eyes swell up with tears. "Alone," he added, already feeling a little horny. Sosie blinked naïvely up at him.

It's a party!

Attendees: Rocko and Sosie.

Clothing optional.

Peeping Rocko

"Everyone must think I'm such a prick." Rocko staggered down the footpath, feeling his gelatin legs wobble to the clunk of his massively huge shoes. He rubbed his fingers through his stubby hair, night air being sucked into his scalp. Sosie was latched onto his side, tracing puddles of rainwater with her leopard platforms. Man, could she wear a dress! "Was I so bad tonight?" he asked, trying not to appear so mesmerized by the way her hips shifted beneath swaths of electric blue.

"No?" she said. Her espresso-colored, patent leather clutch snapped open as she searched for breath mints beneath a pool of gum wrappers and receipts. She popped a seasonal, snowflake shaped mint on her tongue. Just in case. "Maybe we should sit."

They relaxed on a street curb overlooking the crisp, charcoal-dyed dormers of the female living corridor. Up close, the lawn was profoundly green. The willows were twining in the breeze, and the golden-flaked sidewalks glistened in the moonlight. No one was around. The place was totally empty, and they were seeing it that way for the first time. No straggling sunbathers. No mob of poetry snobs. Blairstown was so beautiful and still . . . and so was Rocko.

"That's my room." Sosie pointed to the window at the top left of Alistair Dwelling Place. Light poured through the sheer, silver curtains. *Nala must be up, still.*

"We could've been asleep by now, Susie-Q," Rocko said, warping his lips as he stared up at her room, imagining all of the things that went on in there. Leg shaving parties. Pillow fights. "We could've been asleep *together*, but you just had to turn me down."

Rocko still couldn't believe Sosie had turned him down. Hadn't she dreamed of the day she could play little spoon to a much larger, stronger, manlier spoon—a spoon like Rocko? Was it perhaps the image of a third wheel blinking at them through a torrent of darkness that had turned her off? Because it so turned him on . . . .

The wind picked up, and Sosie buried herself against Rocko's chest. "Think of it as more of a rain check."

Rocko nodded, wrapping his arms around her, squeezing her teasingly beneath his hands.

Sosie began to wonder how a first kiss was supposed to go. Would he dance his fingers through her hair, stare despairingly into her emerald-green eyes, whisper something charming and sexy, and then plunge in mouth first, ramming his tongue between her thin lips until she surrendered for a breath of air and a second snowflake mint? Could it be that simple?

Rocko's drunk, tired eyes perused the lawn. "You and I can have a lot of fun together," he said. "Imagine what we could accomplish with a bottle of vodka." An entire bottle of vodka? *Um . . . death?* "Imagine what trouble we could get into," he enticed.

"Too much," Sosie said a little fearfully.

Back at Bluffdale Prep, Sosie had been punished every now and then for un-lady-like behavior: skinny-dipping in Lake Seraphina, swearing during Sunday brunch toasts at the country club, stuffing her push-up bra and going by her alter-ego — Betty Big Boobs — in Etiquette Class. Blairstown had always represented a fresh start for her: no more naked cannonballs, no more pirate talk, no more Betty Big Boobs. She had made a promise to herself, and she had every intention of keeping it. She imagined that drinking an entire bottle of vodka would violate that promise.

Why did obeying the rules have to be so boring?

Rocko pulled Sosie back in and gave her a passionate hug. She relaxed her head on the shoulder of his sports coat and pulled her eyes shut. Couldn't they pretend to be boring, humdrum, obey-all-the-freaking-rules rich kids for once? It would be interesting. Sosie could complain about the insignificance of recycle bins, while Rocko kissed her botoxed forehead and promised that, in their renaissance-inspired mansion, they wouldn't own a single recycling bin. "Our butler Phipps will take care of the trash, darling," he'd whisper into her argan oil treated hair. "Now go change into your sleeveless polo and cerise pique skort. We have tennis in ten with Brock DuPont and his fiancé, Vivian."

It would be interesting, all right: interesting, mind numbing, and lacking so much as a fragment of joy. She'd spend her day competing with Ms. DuPont-to-be, shuffling on her herringbone tread patterned, snow-white tennis shoes as her butterfly shades bounced around her plastic face. It sounded truly awful. Even pretending was truly awful.

The two sat in silence as Rocko slipped his fingers up and down Sosie's pale, freckled arm, sneaking peeks down her neckline.

"Very sexy dress, sweetheart," Rocko said as his fingers lingered on her spaghetti straps. "Really sticks to your body in all the right places."

"Thanks." She shrugged. "Nala picked it out."

"Oh, Nala." Rocko's voice stuck as he remembered how she looked at dinner, licking the gorgonzola dressing from her sweet, strawberry lips, playing with the purple lace detailing over her neck, smiling at Knox's unfunny jokes. Why did Knox Ritchie get to take Nala out when Rocko had been the first one to notice her, cradling an apple juice-box beneath her delicate fingers in the dining hall? Just thinking about it made him angry. "So are you two, like, pretty close?"

"Pretty close?" Sosie giggled, remembering when she and Nala, just shy of eleven, had floated around their boarding room in ballerina tutus and primrose satin slippers. Sosie would pirouette and side leap as Nala performed *fouetté en tournant*, and the two had curtsied to an audience of curly blonde dolls. "We're practically sisters."

She rolled her head against Rocko's big, manly shoulder to stare up at his lips. Why hadn't he kissed her yet? What was taking him so long? Did her breath still reek of fried calamari? She popped another breath mint.

"Sisters? That's cool." He shrugged, which jounced Sosie's head from its perch. "She didn't seem too interested in Knox at dinner," he added, almost trying to convince himself. He swayed and fell backwards onto his palms. His second buzz was dwindling down, and he dreamed of a forty of malt liquor to delay his corner-rounding sobriety.

"No, she's totally into him," Sosie said. "You'd have to *know* Nala to notice it. She's probably in bed right now surfing the web for wedding dresses. That's just how she is."

Wedding dresses?

Rocko tossed his head back and stared up at the night sky. Burning clusters of stars winked down on him. Nala, browsing for wedding dresses all because of Knox? Knox Ritchie? Preppy, little pretty boy? But Nala was supposed to be his. Ever since he had first noticed her, he knew—he could feel it deep in his bones—that he absolutely had to have her. Would-never-be-satisfied-until-he-did, had to have her. Eventually she'd get bored of Knox, he hoped, and then he could swoop in. In the meantime, he could have fun with Sosie. They could skip class, throw parties in their underwear, and listen to indie records as they made-out and shared corn guacamole. He could tell that she was a chill party girl. But truth was he would never feel truly satisfied with Sosie, because Nala was the one that he wanted. And Nala was the one he was going to get.

Just then, something perched up the female dormitory walls caught his eye. His body felt breathless and stiff at the sight. His heart pounded beneath his dress shirt. It was the shadow of a poised, trim figure weaseling out of a cocktail dress—her long, spidery legs tiptoeing beyond the silvery curtain. Rocko's voice stalled in his throat. Up in the window frame, the silhouette dress pulled loose and willowed to the floor. Nala—beautiful, graceful, totally reserved Nala—was stark naked, prancing around her dormitory room unashamed. Distractingly unashamed. Just beyond that silvery curtain.

"So. . . ." Sosie ran her fingers over Rocko's buzz, her squinty, grassy eyes peaking up at him with desire. "What should we do *now?*"

Rocko's focus bounced between Sosie's thin lips, and the cut-line of Nala's naked body dancing in the window. How could he choose between the cute, available girl, and the girl of his dreams; perfect, unattainable, totally worth breaking a heart or two over? He rolled his head on his sore neck and tried to think. But the more he thought, the more he realized that thinking was entirely overrated. Just like clothing.

He drew Sosie's chin forward with his finger and stared deeply into her green eyes, trying to picture Nala there instead. "Now, we kiss," he said with grain in his voice. Their lips collided in flawless, rhythmic unison. As he shoveled his tongue between her puckered lips, Sosie savored the taste of salt and beer. When he pulled away, she collapsed into his arms, her cheeks blushing with excitement. Kissing was nothing like she had expected. It was better! *So much better!*

"This night has been perfect," she whispered, inhaling the scent of his crisp, rosewood cologne.

Rocko smiled cunningly, welding his eyes shut. He thought with the nude image still stamped in his brain: *It sure has, Nala. It sure has.*

Free the People

Monday morning had rolled around, and Nala was wired on her second blonde roast. The coffee surged through her caffeinated veins until her fingers trembled. Her subtly tinted raspberry lips matched her school cardigan perfectly, and left a luscious, heart-shaped stamp on the lid of her coffee cup. Her hair was pulled from her face for once, with an old, pearlescent headband she had forgotten to toss during her move. It was cheap, but a cure for the common bad-hair day, nonetheless. Of course, Nala's idea of a bad hair day still qualified for a hair show in Vegas.

She whipped her highlighter through a paragraph in her textbook, jotted something down on her worksheet, and then jotted something very similar on Sosie's worksheet while Sosie napped on her desk.

Professor Leatherwood's clear voice rolled over Nala, and her focus jumped immediately to the front of the classroom. He was slumped against the edge of his desk, looking exceptionally chipper.

"Enough busy work," Professor L said. His casual, cotton crew neck hugged his arms perfectly. He pushed his waved, brown hair out of his face and smiled with beautiful marching rows of pearl teeth. For a moment, it appeared he was grinning right at Nala—or maybe just encouraging her to elbow Sosie until she jerked awake. "Time for some fun!" He folded his arms briskly across his chest. "Gentleman . . ." his voice halted. "Can any of you tell me where your hands should go during . . . a first kiss?"

Sosie peeled one sparkling, glazed eye open. Did he just say "kiss"? Her mind raced to Saturday night; the short-lived midnight Frenchie with Rocko Borai outside of the female dorm. It was *sooooo* hot! No wonder everyone made such a big freaking deal about making out. It was awesome! "What'd I miss?" she slurred.

"Nothing much," Nala shrugged, tapping Sosie's assignment. Her flawless, girly handwriting was scribbled all over it.

"God, you're perfect! They should give you a Holiday." Sosie peaked toward the front of the classroom. "*Oooh!* Doesn't Sexypants Leatherwood look particularly dreamy today? I could just listen to him talk for hours," she murmured. "Think he has a six-pack, or is he one of those freaks that has an extra row? I bet he has like . . . ten!"

Nala's eyebrows thinned. Sosie was right. There was something different about the professor today; something even better than usual. He just looked so boy-next-door: so lawn-mowing, slam-dunking, undressing-near-the-window-before-hopping-in-the-shower boy next door. *If only my window overlooked his*, she thought.

From the back of the room, Knox Ritchie popped his soft, white hand into the air and flagged the Professor's attention. His blue eyes avalanched over the room and pinpointed Nala. She was like a vacuum that sucked him right in. A very pretty vacuum.

"Knox?" Professor L called.

Knox's hand fell. He may have been a country-club regular, fed by a platinum gold spoon and patted on the ass every time he took in a fresh breath of air—you take in mighty fine air, boy," he could imagine an old, cigar-smoking golf caddie complimenting – but he was motivated. Driven. Hard-working. He had ambition pumping through his money-green veins, and Leatherwood liked that about him. He studied the material. He actually cared.

The students turned to Knox as he soared out of his chair and onto his moccasin-toed chukka boots. Nala watched, too. She admired the crispness of his shirt, and the maroonish-brown tie hanging from it, happy to finally see him after texting none-stop since their date on Saturday. Knox's gritty, salt-water hair suggested he had spent Sunday afternoon on a cabin cruiser: sun-baking on the open water, diving from the silk-cotton plywood deck, eating tuna sashimi as the sun poured over the waves. At least, that was how Nala pictured it. That was how he had made it appear in all of those messages. . . . But really, he and Gino had just taken turns wakeboarding in the near-freezing lake, dressed in neoprene wetsuits as the motorboat speakers blared progressive reggae, sipping beer and chewing nicotine gum.

Knox shoved his hands into the pockets of his expedition khakis and flipped the loose change between his fingers. From across the room, he could feel Nala's eyes glued to him. Her intensely tanned arms were bare, pinned still. He wanted to kiss every inch of them.

Professor Leatherwood cleared his throat. Knox's eyes widened. Suddenly, he remembered that he was standing amongst others, supposed to be saying something, but he couldn't remember what. He tried not to freak out. Briefly, he considered picturing everyone in their briefs and thong panties — but imagining Nala in a cool mint push-up and garter skirt would only make things worse. He gulped. What was the question again? Something about hands and kissing? Couldn't Nala stop being so distracting for one freaking second?

He cleared his throat. "Just go with it," he shrugged. "Right? I mean . . . people should just stop thinking and start doing." He plummeted back into his chair, searching the classroom for any other takers. *Please. Someone.*

Leatherwood rocked onto his toes. For such an ambitious, caring student, Knox Ritchie was pretty freaking cavalier all of a sudden. Stop thinking and start doing? Had Knox been hanging around the pervert in last period? It sounded like something that Borai kid would say. "Well, that was a — a good effort?" the professor said, disappointment leaking through his voice. "Not exactly what it says in the book, though. Anyone else?"

Kiki Weames coughed intentionally. She stomped onto her artisan leather ankle boots and adjusted her headband over her bangs. Where was her required ruby cardigan, or short-sleeve, frosted button-up, or plaid or khaki skirt? Why the organic hemp tunic and smoky trapeze dress? Had she totally lost all respect for the system? Was baggy boho-wear the ultimate revolt?

"Do you have something to say, Kiki?" The professor asked, pulling a strand of brown hair from his eyes.

Kiki's blazed, black stare floated around the room. "Yeah, man," she said, her wishbone earrings dripping into her hair. "Are you like, even a *real* teacher? I mean, Leatherwood, dude, you're like, seventeen. Is this some jurisdictive power trip? Is the government forcing you to do this, man? Because there *are* child labor laws against the employment of minors. Free the people, you know?"

Free the people? Leatherwood's lips curled gradually at the subconscious excitement that he could still pass for some kid at The Academy of Windsor, shy of his eighteenth birthday. Kiki fell into her seat, stroking the crimped trim that lined her tunic.

"Thanks Kiki," he said, "but I'm just some boring, twenty-three-year-old teacher. No jurisdictive power-trip here."

They smiled at each other. Professor L wasn't bothered by the fact that she was stoned, nor did he care about her beatnik, flower-child outfit, or her rage-against-regulation verbal diarrhea. Somehow, he accepted her exactly as she was: passionate, baked, free.

"Just looking out for you, man," Kiki mumbled underneath her all-natural hookah breath, about ready for a nap as she yawned, mouth uncovered, snaggletooth wedged into her swollen gums. Thank goodness for teachers like Professor Leatherwood. If he wasn't such a good sport, she'd probably be locked up in a psych ward, entwined in a straitjacket.

Professor L hunted for more takers. No one had yet answered his question reasonably and, thinking about it, he wasn't sure he was up to explaining. "Why don't you guys talk amongst your-selves for a sec?" he said, slipping behind his desk and fumbling for a collection of instructional DVDs thrown into a box. Maybe he was a bright, twenty-three-year-old instructor employed at one of the finest Kissing School campuses across the country, but he was completely unprepared for the clueless, pothead zombies running circles around his teaching philosophy.

The DVD cases cascaded onto the floor as he rummaged through the final few: *Managing Public Displays of Affection*, *First Date Terrors*, and *Mistletoe: Friend or Foe?* No tutorial on hand placement, which he probably should have known.

"Well, it looks like I've misplaced the DVD," he grunted, his waved hair popping up behind his desk. "So that's out of the question." He stuffed his hands through his short, thick trim and thought pensively for a minute. "What if I just show you guys? Cool?"

"Cool," someone said.

He smiled embarrassedly. For a college professor, he was pretty freaking unorganized. But there was something slightly charming about it. His sweat spangled hair-ends clung to his embarrassed, blushing temple. He looked like a lost puppy, searching for a warm home, some biscuits, maybe someone to scratch his filthy, pink puppy-tummy. Nala watched as Leatherwood seated himself on the edge of his desk and flipped through a notepad of yellow papers. The green in his eyes flickered as he scanned his own chicken scratch.

"Okay . . . so . . . anyone want to volunteer?" he asked plainly.

Nala twisted her bronze cross bracelet around and around on her wrist. Professor Leatherwood had always been totally attractive, but she had never seen him look so *normal* before, butchering his lesson plan like an amateur. Maybe it was because she had just found out he was only twenty-three. Maybe it was because he was acting merely human, with mistake after stupid mistake. Perhaps the rumors circulating about him being a vampire, or the son of Zeus, or an actor in some hidden-camera television show didn't help the perception that he was somewhat more than ordinary. But now she knew the truth. He was both hot and flawed . . . and more importantly, hot.

And did she mention hot?

Then, suddenly, Leatherwood's eyes caught Nala's. His pink, moist lips grinned brilliantly. "Okay, sure," he chimed. "Thanks for volunteering."

Was he talking to *her?* She scrunched her toes up inside of her ballet flats and peaked behind her shoulder. Kiki was hunched over, open-mouthed in a puddle of drool. She snored until she choked on her own spit, sat up abruptly, and then passed out again. Well, she certainly wasn't volunteering. "Nala?" he laughed cutely as she searched behind her for raised hands. "Want to join me?"

Oh crap. He's talking to me!

"Okay," she mumbled. She glanced up to find her arm shoved into the air, fingers dangling loosely above her headband. *When had she volunteered?*

"Just warning you all, I'm a bit rusty," Leatherwood chimed, his voice cracking with anxiety. But he sounded a tinge excited, too. Nala slipped across the room, her chocolate-brown locks scooping down her back. What had she gotten herself into?

"You nervous?" he whispered when Nala caught up to him.

"A little."

"Well, don't be." He flashed his big, perfect teeth. "You'll be great." Nala nodded, watching him watch her. "Ready?"

"Sure."

"Okay everyone, pay attention. Guys, watch my hands."

Leatherwood breathed a sigh of relief. What if it had been Kiki who had volunteered, blowing her smoker's breath into his mouth accidentally? Then again, wasn't volunteering to participate in a university class somehow against the hippie handbook? Thank God for Nala: sweet, helpful Nala. Nala whose lips were plump like strawberries, he was suddenly noticing, and whose bright eyes were flickering, and who's gleaming white teeth radiated below the florescent lights. Nala with her loose, curled, almond hair, with her thick, manicured eyebrows.

Shit. Focus.

Professor L shook away his thoughts and attempted to begin the demonstration. His hands slipped loose from his pockets long enough to feel the classroom breeze crawl beneath his fingernails, and then he shoved them back into hiding. A sudden lump the size of a grape crawled into his throat. What was the big deal? He'd kissed plenty of girls before. And this wasn't even a kiss. It was a demonstration. A freaking hand demonstration. It was nothing. He'd trained for this stuff.

Nala's big eyes searched him desperately, wishing he'd hurry up and start so she could escape all of the boys blinking grossly at her once unbuttoned cardigan. Being the center of attention *so* wasn't her thing. Why wasn't Professor L doing anything? Was something wrong? Was it her?

Tension bounced thickly between their bodies. God, Leatherwood hated feeling powerless . . . especially to a girl. A minute earlier, he had praised his supposed father Zeus just knowing that Kiki's hookah breath would be nowhere near him, but suddenly, all he wanted was safe Kiki as a volunteer; undesired, stoned, sleepy Kiki, who would doze off as she swayed inside her little, hippie, mud-splattered booties. All he'd have to do was play puppeteer; move her hands around with his a little. But it was a little too late for that.

Finally, Leatherwood was holding Nala's soft cheek in his hand, not knowing how or when he had moved to her. "Put your left hand here," he displayed to the classroom, clearing his throat. There was no way in hell he was going to lose his cool in front of that crowd, with that girl, and that hand *there*. Totally, inappropriately, enjoyably *there*. "And then, your right hand." Slipping his other down the curve of her jacket, he imagined them alone, somewhere private, eating Pad Thai with chopsticks out of half-pint Chinese take-out boxes, laughing at her sauce-splattered cheek. They'd sit on his apartment floor, talking about their mistakes and dreams. She'd laugh when he told his only joke. And then, at some point, he'd kiss her.

Shit! Focus!

Nala's throat thickened. Professor Leatherwood's fingers dipped into her bluntly cut hair as cologne seeped from his button-down. It smelled like oak moss and sandalwood and something else. She wished she could rip the shirt from his body and fall asleep in it every night . . . maybe count his abs for Sosie. Of course, sleeping *next* to him would be a more practical option. Practical and illegal, she had to remind herself.

Suddenly, Professor L ripped her in. She fell against his body. His lips were so close to hers that all it would take was one slip. "Put your hand on my chest," he whispered into her ear. His shirt felt like cool butter beneath her warm hand.

And then suddenly, from the back of the room, Knox Ritchie stood and clapped his hands obnoxiously, giving the professor the get-your-hands-off-my-girl stare down. The others joined him in earsplitting clapping and howling, and then the classroom bell rang, and the sound of bags zipping and shoe-stomping took over the room. Nala's hands slipped away from him first. She blinked her long, black eyelashes up at him.

Could she tell how beautiful he thought she was? Could she feel a connection, too?

"Thanks for the help," he breathed, his trembling hands slipping inside of his pockets again. "Thanks for volunteering in the first place," he added awkwardly.

Why was he acting so weird? He was almost like a boy with a crush.

Nala nodded, and slipped back to her desk as Leatherwood watched her pack her bag. Nothing felt normal. His mind was crammed with thoughts. Thoughts about her. Was it just that he found Nala beautiful, or had he actually started to fall for her? His student . . . .

Either way, Papa Zeus would be so disappointed. . . .

Anything for You

"Thanks again for your help," Professor Leatherwood called as Nala hoisted her bag over her shoulder. She shuffled her cinnamon, facet-beaded sandals toward the front of the room. "You're welcome. Hope I did okay."

A few students crowded by on their way to the exit. Knox Ritchie interrupted. He stuffed his fingers through his slick, sandy hair. Nala and Leatherwood had looked so completely in love during the demonstration—her body melting against his, his hands in her hair, their eyes locked—and now, they were smiling hopelessly at each other like they never wanted that demonstration to end. This was like his worst nightmare: an older, taller, debatably better-looking version of himself contending for Nala's love. But usually, his nightmares ended with him waking up in sweat-soaked Egyptian cotton. This time, the horror show just kept rolling

"Hey, beautiful," Knox interrupted, cheesy, over-bleached smile flared. "Ready to go?"

Nala twisted her necklace beneath her fingers. Sure, she was ready to go, but she wasn't sure she *wanted* to. Her eyes flew back and forth between Knox and Professor L. The totally hot, book savvy, boating connoisseur Knox Ritchie stood, the corner of his lip twitching with impatience at her. He was so sweet to walk her to class. She loved that about him; always so thoughtful. And on her other side, the unquestionably gorgeous, woo her with his deep, dreamy, hazel eyes, twenty-three-year-old, completely off-limits Professor L swallowed loudly, creamy eyes glossing over like he was hiding a secret. She wanted to know the secret.

Ughhhh. Nala combed through her hair ends anxiously. She just wanted to escape to some spa in the city for a week. She wanted to be utterly alone to mull things over. A hot stone massage and cucumber facial would free her from her little crush on the teacher, and she could get back to solely focusing on Knox. No distractions. But did really she want to be freed?

She'd better make it two weeks.

She rested her finger across her wet lips and nodded at Knox. "Ready." Her eyes blinked at the professor as she moved for the door, Knox dragging her by her cardigan sleeve like a real yacht captain. *Blue water sailing, from here forth.*

Professor Leatherwood cleared his throat, suddenly scratchy and dry. Was it just him, or did Nala actually look like she wanted to stay with him? Her haunting, round eyes appeared to beg, "Save me!" as she was pulled. Knox kicked the door open and whispered, "After you."

The professor's heart thumped in his ears. "Actually," he choked out, "Nala . . . if you could . . . I need you to stay after." Nala and Knox spun around. He rummaged through some old papers on his desk. "Just some things I need to work out with your last assignment," he added.

Nala gulped. Was this about Sosie's paper? Because she was just trying to be a good friend. "Umm . . . okay." She glanced back at Knox, whose eyes were calmly swooping over her.

"Don't worry. I'm sure it's nothing. I'll see you at lunch, okay?" he said, kissing his lips against her cheek.

Nala smiled weakly. "Okay. Bye."

Knox trotted down the steps and onto the beautiful pistachio-green color of short trimmed lawn. His shoes pummeled at days worth of mowing, his veins boiling up with anger. The last thing he wanted to do was walk by himself, but it wasn't just that. The thought of Nala up there with Leatherwood alone . . . it drove him nuts. She should've been walking next to him: all of the beat-niks on the quad turning to stare at the two together, just like they were meant to be.

Nala watched from the classroom window as the last of her classmates slipped out of the exit doors, their archetypal trims blowing harmoniously in the breeze as they scooped for the dormitory. Professor Leatherwood guzzled down half a bottle of water, his Adam's apple bouncing in his throat.

"I don't think your boyfriend is a fan of mine," he said coolly. His scruffy chin sparkled with spilled spring water. "Maybe he thinks I'm—I don't know—stealing you away?"

Boyfriend? Stealing? Nala blushed. By boyfriend, did he mean Knox? And by stealing her away, did he mean her time, or . . . her? For a moment, she imagined a romantic vacation to the Caribbean, compliments of her sexy abductor, No-First-Name Leatherwood. They'd sip mojitos, sunbake from their oasis cabana, lather each other's freckled shoulder blades in tanning oil, watch the beachcombers sweep the sand dunes for treasure, swim with the dolphins. She'd wear her zebra-print, beach-ready halter, fold-over bikini bottoms, and Egyptian-blue, open-stitch cover-up all day long. The one she bought on sale from Jon Matinee. And Leatherwood would be gorgeous in his bungalow swim shorts. A young Gene Kelly on the beach, totally sweaty as he plunged into the waves. At night, they'd find a candle-lit, ocean side restaurant and order seared ahi tuna and king crab legs with chardonnay. Eventually, he'd wisp her beach-blown hair from her eyes, grin at the grains of sand frothed in her eyelashes, and mouth, "I love you," just before dinner arrived.

Oh, and wouldn't she love him back.

Nala tossed her hip against the professor's desk, trying to forget the image of his board shorts and ten abs. "He's not my boyfriend," she said. *He just kisses me on the cheek, and sends me flowers, and buys me dinner.*

"Well, he certainly wants to be," Leatherwood added, a hint of jealousy in his voice.

Nala stroked her mile-long hair over her cardigan. "Really? You think?"

Her shoulders slumped at the sound of her own voice. Talking to Professor Leatherwood made her feel so childish. Or teenish; like early teenish, when her life was all sleepovers, braces, puberty, and wondering about boys. Everything he said was so brilliant, saturated with five years worth of extra knowledge, and everything she said was so naïve and stupid. How would he ever see her as some stunning, mature woman when she just seemed so . . . innocent?

She focused on the faded imprint of his name splashed across the chalkboard. It was a few weeks old, hardly readable anymore. At least he had the handwriting of an eight-year-old. Thank goodness for that.

Professor L cleared his throat while his eyes circled across her beautiful, blemish-free skin. "Look, Nala, you're going to meet a lot of guys over the next four years, plenty of them just like Knox Ritchie. Say the right things. Take you out on nice dates. But don't feel like you need to settle down right away. You just got here."

"I *did* just get here," she said to herself. Her tense body started to relax, and her once caffeinated veins cooled. She felt better already. "And I *don't* need to settle down right away," she nodded. "Why hasn't anyone *ever* been this blunt with me before?"

"Because." Professor Leatherwood took another gulp of water. His lips were moist as they slipped from the bottle lid. He gazed steadily at it as though speculating another sip. But Nala had the feeling that was not on his mind, at all. "Want me to be honest?"

"Honest. Please."

"Okay." He shoved messy locks of hair from his sharp eyebrows and fell against the deep, purply-red leather of his chair; dashing and wealthy-looking, like a New York Times best selling crime novelist vacationing in the Hamptons. "Honestly, you're the competition. Every other girl in this school is competing with you."

"With me?" she rasped. "What do you mean?"

Leatherwood chuckled. Was she really so naïve, or just fishing? The silence felt agonizingly stiff as he tried to find the right words. Any minute, a horde of readily-bored, impatient, pothead boys and bitchy, hypercritical, overly-sensitive stuck-up girls would come crawling through the entry, hunting for their seats. He knew had to be careful about what he said; how honest he was.

The tick of the metal gear wall clock buzzed through his brain. Three minutes. He took a deep breath and peered into the big, round whirlpools of curiosity watching him back. "Nala, come on. You know how gorgeous you are," he blurted out. "Girls want you off the market, and boys want you to themselves. You're the competition, *and* the prize. Get it?"

Nala's thick, Audrey Hepburn eyebrows narrowed on him. Gorgeous? The competition? The prize? Nodding, she played with the loose fringe on her sleeves. Pressure weighed down on her.

"It's frustrating, isn't it? How no one's looking out for you," the professor added, suspiciously serious.

Nala ate a little of the tangerine lip gloss nervously from her lips and gave the professor a forced smile. "Except for you."

"Yeah," he confessed timidly. "Except for me."

Just then, Milly Hodge slithered through the doorway, her honey-yellow braid swinging forcefully between her pale-salmon tinted shoulder blades and her tortoiseshell bifocals pressed into her cheeks. "Early as usual," she announced, thwacking boyishly down the aisle. Her beady mouse eyes hunkered down on Nala as she wound for her desktop. "Hey, friend," she muttered, "transferring into the *cool* class?"

Nala wrapped her arms around Milly's neck and gave her a perky squeeze. Even though Milly couldn't have shown up at a worse time, and even though she was totally awkward and kind of inconsiderate, it was always good to see a familiar face wandering around BU. New schools could be so lonely. "Nah, still in first period." Nala felt Milly's skinny limbs slip from her hug.

"Why you here, then? Interested in the assistant position, too?" Milly's voice cracked frantically. She threw her burnt orange, cross-body satchel against the swirling tile floors. "I was just about to apply." She slouched into her chair with a loud thud.

Professor Leatherwood threw his eyes between Nala and Milly. Being alone with Milly a few hours a week in that box of a classroom, her shrill, nasally voice harassing him to grade with a red fountain rather than a red ballpoint, sounded downright nightmarish. He stretched his toes in his classic, 1950s inspired shoes.

"Sorry Milly," he shrugged. "Nala just got the position." He jumped up and rifled through the mound of paperwork on his desk. "That is, if she still wants it?" he added, peeking up into her eyes. *Wink.*

Milly watched Nala jealously. What did Milly want with some lousy, TA position, anyway? It was a few late nights a week with Professor L . . . alone. The twilit moon would spook through the frosted windows as they clacked chopsticks through take-out boxes and sipped hot cocoa, whips of melted, chocolaty marshmallow gleaming off of Leatherwood's perfect, white teeth. They'd breeze through assignments, but probably spend most of the time talking. Getting to know each other on a deeper level.

Nala's skin began to thaw beneath the thrashing, white light bulbs. What if she took the TA position? She could score some extra cash for tuition. And she could finally prove to him that she was just some innocent, little girl.

Milly felt sick as she waited for Nala to say something. "Well . . . ?"

Nala shuttered back into reality. "I would, um — love to."

Milly dropped to her desk, and stuffed her headphones in her ears, blasting classical music as she read and re-read the week's agenda. Her eyes flooded with tears. All Milly ever seemed to do was pout.

Boo-hoo me!

"Thanks for that," Professor Leatherwood breathed when he could tell that Milly wasn't listening. "If you're not up for it, I can find someone — "

"No!" she butted in. "I meant it. I'd love to."

The classroom started to fill up, and Nala — who had been suddenly bombarded by muscly, drooling rowers in raglan sleeve zip jackets — waved goodbye and rounded for the exit, her waving, chocolate locks dripping down her spine in gorgeous layers.

"Wait," Leatherwood's deep, scratchy voice called after her. She skipped closer, smiling indiscreetly. "Since we're going to be working together," he scratched his stubbly beard, and whispered "maybe you should call me by my first name . . . Graham. If you can keep it to yourself."

Graham. Nala's eyes lit up. He looked like a Graham. *Gorgeous Graham.* Her heart throbbed, harmonizing with the sound of the late bell.

"Don't worry. I'll write you a note," he said so casually. "Mind starting early? Like . . . next week?"

"Not at all."

"Cool." He smiled. "I owe you big time, Nala."

"Don't worry about it, Graham," she wanted to say. "Anything for you."

All Eyes on Nala

Nala hiked across the moonlit quad, her dress train flowing shortly after her. It was her first evening working as Graham's TA, and she couldn't tell if her body was humming because of nerves or the double-shot macchiato she had chugged for energy an hour earlier—which, she realized, was probably a dumb idea. She could already feel her mixed-berry deodorant hard at work beneath her armpits. *Crap*.

Light poured onto the lawn from Professor L's building windows. Not Professor L. Graham. Gorgeous Graham. The seven p.m. class was just winding down as she climbed the stairs, and Graham's husky, baritone voice slipped through the door cracks.

"In chapter seven, the narrator actually compares his first date to a carnival," he said, his voice somewhat muffled. "But then, when he took out Odette from camp, he described their 'spark' as 'lackluster, at best.' Are you sensing a theme?"

Nala peeked through the window in the classroom door. Graham stood in a limestone, linen-blend button-down, folding his deeply tanned arms across his chest. He smiled cheesily down at the pages. She had never seen him look so . . . happy before. Her eyes stretched over the audience, which consisted mostly of a few obnoxious jocks, perpetually love-struck girls staring sickeningly at the professor, and some snorers. Standard. So why was he so happy? Suddenly, she tripped into the door and it popped open. Everyone stared. Her sheath of rose pink clung with static to her skin. Her feet began to sweat. Her matted, windblown curls perfectly framed her embarrassed face.

"Come on in, Nala," Graham invited. His hair fell in waves over his ears, giving him that coveted starving-artist look. Was she to be his muse, or was she there for his amusement?

Nala slipped inside and waved faintly. Her leather cuff shifted slightly on her wrist. The minor uproar of the class that followed her appearance dwindled down quickly, until it was just one boy with strawberry-blonde hair and peach fuzz named Henry Woods, who whispered something to his friend, John Crasp. They both smirked and licked their pale, thin lips as they watched her move.

"Why don't you have a seat in the back?" Graham said, a happy-to-see-you grin crawling up his face. She smiled. *Happy to see you, back.*

Moving down the aisle, Nala passed Henry. His strawberry blonde, scraggly top fop dipped into his eyes, still visibly admiring her. "Where've you been hiding?" he piped up. A rolled cigarette stuck out from behind his freckled ears. His cheeks were swollen like cherries and his eyes were ice blue. Nala ignored him and slipped toward an empty seat. She hated when boys were over-confident. As if he had a chance.

Perv.

Scooting by, her body suddenly cringed. Henry Woods, totally out of nowhere, reached up, grabbed her, and gave her butt a horny squeeze—though, if she really thought about it, she probably should have seen it coming. John Crasp chuckled piggishly nearby as the two high-fived beneath the table and mumbled grossly under their breaths.

Ewwwww! Nala felt her cheeks scald with embarrassment as her feet took her deep into the classroom, the lingering feel of her lace-trimmed boy short panties being clasped beneath a ginormously huge link of fingers.

"Mr. Woods!" Graham's voice rattled. Nala slipped into a seat and grabbed her face in her hands. She was so ashamed! No, she was mortified! Ashamed, and mortified, and angry, and uncomfortable. All of it.

Graham stared heavily at the guy. "Get the hell out of my class."

"But I was just having fun . . . . "

"Fun? What . . . Xbox and pizza aren't enough for you, anymore? Have to go around grabbing women inappropriately? Like to make them feel helpless and uncomfortable?"

"Come on, Mr. L. We were just screwin' with her."

Graham's voice deepened. "No . . . 'screwin'' with someone would be like me telling you that it wasn't a big deal and not to worry about it right before I kicked you out of my class."

"Leatherwood, Dude, it was a joke! Just a joke!"

"Well, for your sake I hope that Principal Dotie finds it funny as hell." His eyes zoomed to Nala who was peeking back at him through her slit fingers. He hated how she must have felt—so

159

completely alone. Poked at like steak. If only he could scoop her up and hold her until she felt better. Or kick the shit out of Henry Wood's disturbed soul. Either one.

Graham found Henry picking the thick, oozing puss from his once popped, but still totally infected forehead pimple. Maybe if he wasn't a teacher, the faint sounds of a siren would already be bustling through the front gates, striping blue and red across the hickory-strewn court. Ambulance, EMTs all rushing to the scene. Or maybe, four Italian-leather suits marching on sleek, black oxfords would show — casket in hand — followed by a preacher, a cop, and a set of shiny handcuffs. *No.* He wasn't a killer. He was just a guy who wanted to kill someone at the moment.

Totally different.

The boy stomped his kiltie wingtips and threw on his backpack. All he could think about was his upcoming football game. Would Leatherwood have him benched, suspended, downgraded to the practice team, double-downgraded to water-boy, triple downgraded to mascot? He peeked over a shoulder at the class, which was festering with whispers. Nala's teary, swollen eyes glowed from behind her fingers.

Graham propped the door open with his derby shoe and invited Henry to step outside. The wind was blistering cold. He yanked his zipper up to his neck and readjusted his slim, backpack straps. "Mr. Leatherwood, I swear I won't do it again."

Graham pulled the door shut. His fists clenched at his sides.

"Didn't you hear me? I said I'll stop," Henry whined.

Graham's voice stalled, hypnotized by Henry's cringing apathy. "I'll have you transferred out of my class tomorrow."

"But Leatherwood, *dude*, coommme oonnn! You know I was just screwin' around, right? Please! You can't tell anyone! They'll kick me off the football team!"

"Henry," Graham said. "Don't even look at her again."

Graham slipped back inside and dismissed the class, which had blabbed unceasingly about what was going down beyond the classroom door. Geo-printed canvas bags and skateboards began to clear the room. Henry was long gone by then, clear across campus. Nala could feel safe, he hoped. He'd keep her safe.

"See ya in athletics, Mr. L," Luke Ferguson waved, his thick, lumberjack beard wobbling in the gust of autumn wind as the door flew open.

Graham rummaged through his desk drawer. "Remember to fill up that water bottle next time, and . . ." he ripped out a coffee-stained napkin and passed it to Luke. A few catchers' tips were scribbled across it in blue ink. "Study this. Know it like the guards on your helmet."

Nala searched through her bag it for some gum, totally humiliated by the way everyone kept pointing at her. She wanted to forget about what had just happened, but she couldn't . . . not when everyone kept staring. She blinked down at her packet of gum and tried to forget about Henry. Before long, it would be just her and Graham — totally alone. No gawkers. No butt-grabbers.

Her safe haven.

Suddenly a strong, hulking grip grabbed her by the shoulder. Nala jumped. "It's true what they say," some familiar voice rattled from behind. "Pretty in pink, I mean." Nala peaked up, and her eyes cowered over a handsome, chiseled, dark-featured face. Rocko Borai straightened out the hem of his crew neck, smiling with thick, pearlescent teeth. "Aren't you a little late for class?" he said, leaning his hands into her desk.

Nala chewed her gum. "Actually, I'm Professor Leatherwood's new TA," she said.

"TA, huh?"

Rocko had cleaned up since the weekend, when — if Nala remembered correctly — he'd harassed a waiter about rainbow carrots and polished off an entire bottle of wine himself. He was actually totally cute in his slick, cornflower blue oxfords, and pleated khaki pants. But all she could think about when she looked at him was Sosie . . . he and Sosie making out. Her best friend she had known for like, ever, and . . . this guy. This guy she barely knew.

Weird.

"You coming to the game on Friday?" he asked, picturing her bundled up in the stands beneath a frosted-tulip parka, his number stamped across her cheek.

"Uh-huh." Nala balled up her gum wrapper and buried it among the lipstick tubes in her bag. "Knox invited me. Get to wear his letterman, I guess! Whatever that is."

Rocko rolled a finger over his prickly chin, hating Knox a little more than usual. Since the group date, he hadn't been able to stop thinking about Nala. The outline of her little ballerina body frolicking around in naked bliss was forever impressed in his mind.

Rocko stared down Nala's dress, catching a vague glimpse of her cleavage. "That's a shame," he said, winking a sparkling brown eye and kicking onto his oxfords. His lips curled devilishly. "You'd look *so* good with BORAI on your back."

How Close is Too Close?

Nala and Graham were finally alone. Moonlight dribbled in from the classroom windows. It was difficult not to feel a romantic pull with the dim lighting, the cold weather, and the smell of hazelnut coffee seething from Graham's breakfast mug—as if they had spent all night together rolling around in silk bed covers, counting down the seconds to sunrise and omelets. He peeked up at Nala through the poorly lit room.

Enchanté, mademoiselle.

"Sorry about Henry," he said from behind his desk. A single lock of golden-flecked hair swooped across his forehead. "You okay?"

"Sure." Nala nodded. Honestly, though, she could still feel Henry's gross, cracked fingers crawling up her butt, squeezing it like a lemon wedge. It was so vile she thought she could faint, or puke, or waste ten years of her life sprawled out across some psychiatrist's canary-colored chaise longue, over sharing every tick of Henry's horny grab: his plunging fingers, his vigorous honk, even the curl of his wiry, perverted lips as he did it; smiling like the freaking "It" clown. None of this she'd actually admit, though. She was a mature, sophisticated adult. She was a twenty-three-year-old stuck in an eighteen-year-old's body. She didn't let such trivial things bother her. She could deal. Boys will be boys, right?

"I could have guessed he'd try something with you." Graham jumped onto feet. *Because Henry's an ass, and because you're so pretty.* "He has a thing for brunettes," he added. Graham searched through a crammed drawer of assignments and transcripts.

"Boys like him don't faze me." She shrugged her slender shoulders. They were like two grown adults, chatting at a bar. She could picture herself sipping a dirty martini at some lounge boutique downtown, her long, spidery legs peeking out of a slip dress, a shade of coral-red slathered across her lips. Graham would slip through the front doors wearing a flawlessly fitted suit, his golden-chocolate hair waved beneath a vintage fedora. He'd take a seat next to her, order a whiskey on the rocks, and mumble to the bartender, "Whatever she wants, put it on my tab." He'd wink, and she'd mouth "Thank you" as her fingers snatched up her martini glass for another sip. And they'd spend the entire night talking. Falling in love.

Graham popped his head up, amazed by how casually she was taking everything. She had just been fondled! She should have been pissed. She should have been throwing things, or crying. Had her mind been erased? Was she really that put together? That mature? "You seem to have it all figured out," he noticed.

"Well . . . ." Her voice caught in her throat. "He's a freshman boy. Can't say I'm surprised."

Their eyes locked for a split second, and Graham had to remind himself that she was also a freshman . . . a freshman student . . . his student. Still, something felt strangely comfortable about being alone with each other, and the sound of their breathing. "So," his voice cracked. "I didn't know what color you'd like." He ripped out a twenty-something pack of grading pens from a drawer. "So I just—bought the whole thing." He began to read the back. "We have peach, primrose, iris mauve, banana, olive drab, turquoise, cobalt blue . . . . Any of these real colors?"

"Someone said so," she giggled. It was kind of cute how he read the options out loud, his lips frowning at every ridiculous shade of pink. Had he really hunted for a bunch of silly markers somewhere between the super tampons and eyelash growth serum just for her? How totally sweet.

Graham sighed. "Please tell me you like at least *one*."

"I like them all, but primrose the most."

Graham lobbed the pen into Nala's cupped hands in a perfect arc. "So . . . ." His mind flooded with blankness. Even though the school allowed him a TA, his curriculum had barely taken off. There was hardly any work to be done. He supposed he had gotten a little ahead of himself, but at least he wasn't stuck with Milly Hodge. "Seen any good movies lately?"

"Never seen one, actually," she shrugged, tugging on the ends of her jacket. "Not a real one, anyways. They were illegal back in Bluffdale. Couldn't see a man's bushy eyebrows. Couldn't hear some guy's voice. Nothing. We had this zero testosterone policy. That's what they called it." Graham's mouth fell open. He had grown up in Elkins, had the same stupid rule about women, but his buddies still managed to smuggle in a few movies. PG-13 stuff. "I mean . . . *goodness,* I'm not a recluse. I've seen movies with women before. I know what a commercial is, I'm not an alien. Just none with men . . . which is, like, all of the good ones I hear."

He sat on the end of his desk and admired the long, sleek projector screen near the back. "Well, we're just going to have to change that."

Ten minutes later, Ford Nickleby, a man with a buttery blonde frat-boy cut, popped onto the screen, his silvery eyes smoldering with pain. He kissed the rocker-waved bangs of some chick whose zebra-print bikini straps peaked from the folds of her olive, grunge shift dress. They rocked on a porch swing overlooking a lake. "We could've been bandits or bank robbers, her and I," Ford's voice whispered. His squinty, blue eyes examined the distant boardwalk where a couple was stripping down to their underwear and plunging into the waves. "Jessie was a free bird, and I was an outsider. We'd get stoned, listen to garage-band heavy metal, make-out on the dinghy. Mom hated Jessie for puking on her favorite dhurrie rug, but Jessie was the best bad decision I ever made."

Graham and Nala lay flat on the tile, their heads thrown next to each other on seat cushions. They were so close that they could barely pay attention. One would shift, and the other would feel a warm brush of skin, and they'd suddenly remember what they were to each other: a teacher and a student; wrong by most accounts. When the movie was almost over, Nala felt Graham's shoulder bump against hers. "Sorry," he whispered. His big, hazel eyes blinked at her through the black room and — was that an I'm-so-happy-you're-here smile? Their heads nearly knocked as she twisted to say, "That's okay."

Music swelled suddenly as Ford Nickleby grabbed the face of wavy-bang girl and smacked his lips on hers. Nala felt her stomach churn. *A kiss.* The first one she'd ever seen, which was kind of sad. She expected it to be different, somehow. Fireworks, or lightning bolts shooting off in the background. Something big.

Like what? High-fiving lips?

The screen went black just before credits began to roll down the screen, glowing white words the only light in the night-dark room. Graham rolled his head on the cushion and looked Nala in the eyes. "What'd you think?"

What did she think? She couldn't really remember much, except that Ford and Graham kind of looked alike. Ford was blonde, but had the same square jaw, hazel eyes, and sexy, stubbly beard. The acting was sort of lame, and the story was slow, She tried to remember something about the movie she had liked, or didn't like—just something she could remember—something other than the kissing. "That part when Jessie moved away was really depressing," she final said, recalling the scene where Ford's washboard abs appeared as he and Jessie packed boxes and hauled them out to a truck.

"Yeah," Graham nodded. "I kind of . . . ." His voice stalled. "I kind of hated it."

"Hated it?"

"Yeah." He pinned his eyes on the ceiling and laughed. The backdrop projection faded and the room went startlingly black. Nala rolled on her hip and faced Graham. She could barely see the gleam of moonlight reflecting from the whites of his eyes.

"Good, because I think . . . I hated it too."

"Did you?" Graham lit up like he was dying to know more. It was like he thought she were some pretentious movie critic with silver-streaked skunk hair and a ski-slope nose job who was paid to write reviews. "Thankfully, in Extraterrestrial War Games part III, the Earth was spared from total obliteration. However, the minds of the poor, tortured viewers were not," Nala would say in a snobby whine. But playing bitch *soooo* wasn't her thing.

"Next time, I'll bring something special for you," Graham said. "Something you'll like."

"Like what?"

"Like . . . one of the best movies of all time."

Nala nodded, clenching the tiny bones of her fingers as the ventilators suddenly spurted wafts of cold air.

"That is, in my opinion," he added. "Something about it reminds me of you."

Me?

Silence hung as Graham finally crawled to his feet and helped Nala stand. They hovered near the exit. The window dimly showed a murky, dark night. Wind howled outside, stripping the sugar maples of their leaves. Nala zipped her denim anorak up to her neck and breathed a noisy sigh. She didn't want to leave. She wanted to stay with him. She wanted to feel the kiss she had seen on screen from Graham's lips.

"So, same time next week?" He asked, grating the scruff on his cheeks.

"Sure," Nala said.

Graham yanked the door open and Nala slipped outside, burying her cheeks in the collar of her jacket as she jogged down the steps. She peeked back at him and waved. Her hair flooded over her lips and eyes with a sudden gust of wind. "Night, Graham," she said as he watched her wander across the lawn and disappear into the deeply blackened night sky.

And immediately, he wished he had picked a longer movie.

Football Flirting

The stadium lights were blindingly bright. Nala blew at her deeply conditioned wisps of brown hair as she scanned the football field. She was wearing a sequined dolman tee, Knox's letterman, and a pair of bleached out skinny jeans that hugged down her extremely narrow thighs. Sosie called them Starbucks straws because they were long and thin and green.

On the field, Rocko Borai took a break from punt-practice and wiped his forehead with his jersey. His abs barely peeked from beneath the hem. He found Sosie and Nala in the third row, blinking over the arena in naïve bliss. God, Nala looked good.

Even from far away. Even in Knox's stupid, stumpy letterman jacket. He waved his bulky helmet through the air and winked directly at her.

Nala and Sosie waved down. "He hasn't talked to me, you know," Sosie said, stuffing the sleeves of her floral crop-top up her elbows. Rocko popped his helmet back on and ran on field. "Isn't it some cardinal rule? You talk to the people whose teeth you suck on."

"Okay, I probably could've gone without that visual," Nala said. "Look . . . you probably just make him nervous."

"Make him nervous? Nala, I'm an angel."

Nala rolled her eyes. "He's probably just nervous."

"Oooh, boo-hoo! Whatever! Rocko Borai doesn't get nervous. He's probably allergic to it, somehow, like he's allergic to carbs and water." Sosie's bullet necklace bounced up and down on her freckly chest as she wiggled to get warm.

"He told you that?"

"Don't look at me funny. It's not like I believed it."

Nala giggled softly. Sosie probably did believe it, and had to search the web to see if it was even humanly possible.

The smell of Knox's cologne crawled up Nala's nose as she fidgeted beneath his jacket sleeves. When would the game actually start? She was starting to get bored, and a little hungry. And she had to pee. Her eyes wheeled the stadium vacantly. A few rows down she noticed Graham Leatherwood standing in a cosmic blue, soft shell jacket, his full, wavy hair inching down his neck. Miss Hart, the baking instructor, was latched onto his side. Her recently trimmed, yellow highlights were wound into little braids and her lips were laughably enlarged by lip liner. Clown-red lip liner.

Were they on, like, some kind of a . . . date?

"Well, well, well . . . lookie what we have here! Miss Nala No-One's-Ever-Good-Enough is crushing on Sexypants! Knew you had a thing for grey chest hair," Sosie blurted. Nala ripped her eyes from Graham. "Bet he'd let you shave it!"

"Could you *not* go there?" Nala stuffed her hair behind her cross studs and cringed as Miss Hart nuzzled her pointy chin into Graham's shoulder. "I'm not in the mood." She wasn't *crushing,* she was simply *noticing.* And noticing Miss Hart nuzzling into Graham's shoulder just happened to make her cringe.

"Let me just ask you this," Sosie persisted. "If Leatherwood and all of his muscly body parts asked you on a date—you know, if we weren't all pledged to this lame cult boarding school—what would you say? Yes? Hell yes? Am I getting warmer?"

Nala grinned, thinking about it. Would she go on a date with Graham Leatherwood? Different world, different place kind of thing? What kind of moronic question was that? It was like asking if she wanted garlic and butter on her mashed potatoes, if she wanted a free knit to go with her brand new Mikado yellow, ombre jeans. Of course she'd say yes!

Yes! Yes! Yes!

But as Miss Hart continued to stroke Graham's stubbly neck, Nala denied herself the option of going there . . . of thinking about what it would be like to actually date Graham; to kiss him; to drag his hand through the MoMA; to fill his fridge with celery and orange juice while he jogged around the park. It was just so stupid to want what she couldn't have. Just like waiting for her boobs to grow a cup size. Probably not going to happen. "Graham's just not my type." She shrugged, and her thin shoulders poked up underneath the thick leather of Knox's coat.

"Uh-huh." Sosie nodded suspiciously. "And by *Graham,* you mean Professor L?" *Oops.* Nala grabbed her mouth. She had done exactly what Graham had asked her not to do. Slip. Sosie's lips curled deviously. "Graham Leatherwood. *Geeeeeeze.* It's like all the hotties of Hollywood and South American football got together and birthed the perfect human being! Just stirred him up in a big pot of thick hair and tanness, and poured him out and let him cool. And somewhere along those beautifully chiseled lines, they decided to name him Graham . . . because he was as delicious as a graham cracker!" Sosie chewed on her sticky lips. "By the way, kudos on finding out his first name. What'd you have to do for it? Sharpen his pencils with your teeth?"

"Sometimes I just want to crawl into your brain, and see how it works," Nala said.

Sosie snapped her eyes back and forth between Nala and Graham, shaking with excitement. "Come on! What do you two do in that classroom all night, anyways?"

Nala peered down at Graham again. His hair was pushed out of his eyes, and he whispered something into Miss Hart's ear, something so funny it made her snort. Hart jammed her hands over her mouth to shut herself up. The two almost looked like a couple. But, just before Nala looked away, Graham noticed her in the crowd. Their stares collided. Graham's lips mouthed "Hi" as he smiled discreetly. Nala mirrored him and mouthed "Hi" back.

"We hang out," Nala shrugged. "Harmless, PG stuff."

Though she *soooo* wished it was PG-13 stuff . . . .

Out on the field, Knox Ritchie jogged toward the crisp, white thirty painted near the sideline, stomping on his talon elite football cleats, his apple butt flexing as he stretched his calves. A pack of girls in the nosebleeds squealed, "We love you, Knox!" Their giggles reverberated through the stands.

Nala observed the field once the cheering had died down. "Knox is growing on me," she whispered.

"Yeah?" Sosie hummed. "Well, at least he's growing in *some* way."

Suddenly, a voice buzzed through the intercom speakers. "Welcome, ladies and gentlemen, to the first football game of the season." Principal Dotie's voice rattled in their ears. He was this chubby, Chinese buffet kind of guy with a slick, silver mustache that always reeked of nutmeg coffee. He had a deep, rumbling voice and wore the same nasty, eggplant-colored, corduroy button-down every day. During games, he usually remained tucked away in the announcer's suite, plucking pistachio shells and guzzling pints of soda. Sosie was pretty sure he was gay, because he spent a lot of unnecessary time in the boys' locker room. "So put your hands together for the Second-Year Jaguaaaars!" Dotie howled.

The crowd roared as the Jaguars swooped over the field, their ebony helmets gleaming beneath the stadium lights, pounding fists angrily against their jerseys.

"And the competition, playing a uniformed game for the first time on Blairstown soil, please welcome the First-Year Hammerhead Shaaaarks!" Dotie's salt-cracked lips smacked against the microphone, and the audience grabbed their ears.

First-years would play second-years and third-years would play fourth-years in football until the season officially started. Then, whoever made the Blairstown football team roster would play other kissing schools, like Milford University, Norwich University, and—their biggest rival—Emporia University. Screw you, EU! Sosie and Nala couldn't wait to draw "BU" on their cheeks like all of the senior girls in the Blairstown brochures they'd received back at Bluffdale Prep. Maybe they'd even rhinestone their BU facepaint! Glam it up a bit.

Knox Ritchie, Rocko Borai, and Gino Blackthorn jogged on field, their uniforms clinging tight like skin. Knox peeked through the crowd of leather jackets and peanut bags at Nala, and waved through the air. *God.* She looked so perfect up there. Her eyes glowed. Her long neck stretched beyond a raspberry infinity scarf. Her teeth shimmered in perfectly straight stacks of white. She smashed her lips to her fingers, and blew him a kiss. *Muuaaahh!* Knox's heart rattled inside of him. They were so perfect for each other. She *had* to know that.

"Hey there!" Brains Fink wheezed from behind Sosie and Nala, stuffing his gnawed-down nails through his curly top fop, his burned henna, twill boat shirt billowing with every small movement. He held three roses in his hands.

"Oh, hi." Nala smiled, trying to remember his name. It was something obvious; a nerdy sci-fi reference, or a body part. Spock, or Forehead, or Four-Eyes, or something. But all she could remember was the ridiculous atomic-tangerine sports coat he'd worn at Sol's with a barrel-cuff paisley shirt and fandango-purple tie. Juliet had never been a braver soul than the night she sat next to *that*. "Nice flowers," Nala added.

"They're for you two," he said, handing them each a rose. "From Knox and Rocko . . . and one for Juliet. Seen her around?"

Brains searched the crowd. Juliet had been so oddly pleasant at Sol's Steakhouse, and he hadn't really stopped thinking about her. Everything about that night had been perfect; her bouncy, unsophisticated curls whipping into his water; her massive breasts bubbling out of her lemon-yellow, chiffon peplum every time she reached for the bread basket; her voice blandly requesting another Shirley Temple. She was so disastrous and intriguing at the exact same time, just like a train wreck. Such a catastrophic, mesmerizing mess.

"She's with Tess," Sosie said, hugging her rose with adoration. Maybe Rocko had been thinking about her after all. Maybe that kiss had been as monumentally life-changing to him as it had been to her. "Off waxing each other's eyebrows, or shaving each other's legs, or clipping each other's toenails. But don't get your little anime boxers in a twist. They're meeting us after the game."

Nala re-applied her lip gloss and peeked over her shoulder at Brains. "So, why aren't you down there playing?"

"Injury." He kicked up his moccasin boot and showed off his wrapped ankle, which swelled like bread dough beneath a band.

He cleared his throat and flexed his scrawny leg so that the calf muscle nearly bulged. "Bliss! Bliss! Injury and bliss! The life lesson of which others will be measured against! Hail to the breaker of bones, the crusher of souls, the inventor of pain and bliss."

Umm . . . what? Sosie caught her mouth in her hands and started to laugh.

"Haven't you heard of Sir Patrick Rice III, the greatest poet of the seventeenth century? Winner of nine Lost Empire Lyrical Virtuoso Prizes? *City on Tornado Hill? Obliteration Valley? 13 Squires of Cicero?*"

Sosie's eyes widened. "What the *hell* is coming out of your mouth, Pegleg?"

"It's not important," he whined, stuffing his box glasses up his nose. *It's never important.*

Down in the stands, Graham Leatherwood swigged the rest of his beer, breathing a sigh of relief when Estelle Hart complained of her fuchsia, t-strap platform-sandals that were skinning her toes, and clunked onto a bleacher. All day she had been talking about caramelized banana pudding, praline pull-apart bread, rustic plum tart, amaretto-almond pound cake, and chunky chocolate gobs, as if Graham cared. Truth was, he was relieved when she finally took a break. Her braids had ripped loose with every collision of her massive head with his shoulder, forming a halo of frizz, and all she seemed to talk about was food and dying. As if her shoes could really kill her. Graham placed his empty bottle on the bleachers, skimming the crowd. He'd prefer it if no one assumed they were like . . . officially together.

Nala panned into Graham's view again: deeply tanned cheeks; long, green skinny jeans; boiled wool and leather clasping her tight. He couldn't really help it . . . he was drawn to her. She was totally magnetic. His head seemed to twist without his consent. It was all mechanical. Long locks of almond hair swam down Nala's back as her eyes blazed up at Brains. He must have been telling one of his stories. "I'll be back," Graham whispered to Estelle. He couldn't help it. Mechanical.

"Where ya goin'?"

"Gonna check on one of the guys. Twisted his ankle last night."

"Mind grabbing me some kettle corn if you get a chance?"

"Sure," Graham said. "Might be a while." Don't hold your breath. *Or do.*

Sosie and Nala were comparing roses when Graham Leatherwood's thick, wind-blown, James Franco hairdo popped up through the crowd. Nala gasped, and swung her head toward the field. What was he *doing*? Why wasn't he down there with Miss Hart? And was Sosie going to do something stupid, like call him by his first name? *Oh, the agony!*

"Evening Emmitt . . . Sosie." Graham nodded. "Nala." She blinked her eyes over a shoulder, and gave him a casual grin.

"Hey, Mr. L," Sosie flirted, smacking her sticky lips together. "Hot jacket! You here for business, or pleasure?"

"A little bit of both." Graham laughed, stuffing his hands through his hair, looking out across the powerfully lit field. He elbowed Brains, and they spoke football stats for a minute. Sosie nudged Nala. *Time to start gnawing on the pencils.* Then, during a long moment of silence, Graham cleared his throat. "Nala, think I can steal you away for a minute?"

Steal? As in . . . alone? "Okay," she mumbled, admiring the barely-there pores in Graham's smooth, creamy skin. The stadium lights fell on him perfectly, like he was a super model in an all-organic, hemp clothing catalogue. He was just scruffy enough to pull off retro-hippie.

"You ready?"

Nala followed Graham into a mine of smelly, obnoxiously swollen, beer-bellies: mostly shirtless boys with paint and sweat smeared across their flabby excuses for chests. They all leered down at Nala as she weaved through. "Sexy Mamacita! Papi likey!" one called, while a few others whistled. Graham finally slipped down the stadium stairs, and Nala tumbled quickly after him. A few students flew by with popcorn spilling from greasy, red and white-striped buckets, and jogged up the steps. Nala and Graham were alone, roaming the concessions, whiffing the jumbo pretzel-infused air.

"Having fun so far?" Graham asked. Nala pranced on her toes so that the taupe fringe swayed rhythmically from her boots. They walked side by side, their feet dragging together.

"Um . . . kind of? I still don't really get it. Football."

Graham snuck his hands into his shoot-from-the-hip denims and counted the globs of black gum entrenched in the concrete like tar. Alone with Nala again . . . at last. It felt as good as a caffeine fix after partying all night at some rap concert, which had actually happened once back in school. He wished he were back in school . . . with her. Their story would be simple and raw; Caanes International Film Festival material. They'd call it The Missing Freshmen or Young Love. Or maybe they'd get really artsy and name it something that made no sense at all. One word, of course, like all of the Sundance nominees. *Ketchup* or *Horsefly* or *dip* . . . with a lowercase 'd' for no reason.

"Football must be so weird for you," he said, casually peering down on her.

"Definitely," she nodded. "It's different."

Nala drew in a long breath. Something felt wrong about walking with Graham out in the open, like she was doing something illegal, like having a crush on an older man was a punishable offense. All she could think about was the other night, when his hair had barely tickled her cheek, his eyes had blinked at her through shadowy, gray air, their bodies had sprawled out across the cold floor, so close she could hear his heartbeat. Or was that hers? *Ugh,* she wished he had kissed her! Why didn't he kiss her? Besides all the obvious reasons . . . .

"So, I bought this new movie," Graham said. Nala watched his lips, wondering what they would taste like. Probably like wintergreen or cinnamon. "Well, actually it's an old movie. The cast is great, though. Won a few awards. You'll like it." He massaged his fingers in his pockets, feeling the cool sterling silver of his money clip. "When I was your age, I wanted to be an actor, actually."

"Really?" she asked, imagining his name pour down the credit list after his first big blockbuster hit. They'd be at Ziegfeld Theatre in New York City to watch the premier. The room would be packed; friends, family, actors, and directors all there to watch Graham's work. Nala and Graham would holds hands, whisper, kiss between scenes. A throng of fans would chant his name just beyond the sumptuous gold-trimmed curtains. They'd sneak out the back into a sexy stretch limo and their muscly bodyguards would shield them from uber-fans with paparazzi cameras. Graham would gently kiss her fingertips. *I'm so glad you're here.* Mr. and Mrs. Graham Leatherwood: dreamboat movie star and fashion icon. The perfect couple.

Graham flicked his hair out of his face and looked down at Nala. Her freezing lips grinned adorably up at him like she could listen to him speak for hours. "It was a stupid dream. I was young."

"No dream is stupid," she said. "And I'm young."

"Yeah, of course you are. Young and smart." *And beautiful.* Graham swept toward a little concession stand, and Nala kept beside him. His skin glowed through his prickly beard. That night, for some reason, he looked a little older; a little sexier. Maybe it was because he had just mentioned his old dream of being on camera. She had always wanted to be in the spotlight, too. They were so alike.

"Some people might say that you're young and smart," Nala piped up, hugging her arms as she approached a large sign with little cartoon popcorn men dancing around on it.

"Some people," he laughed. "Like my mom." Graham blew into his hands, smelling sweet, melted butter. "I say you're smart because you are, not because I'm your teacher, okay?"

"Okay," she said.

"Because you are . . . smart. You're not like the other freshmen. You drink coffee to keep you awake and mindful, and not because it gives you an excuse to eat whipped cream. At least that's what I've noticed. And you read classic novels. You're not really into vampires or werewolves. You don't have anything against them, but they're just not your thing." He smiled proudly. "Kind of have you pegged?"

"Kind of," she admitted, a little scared, a little in awe. Had he spotted her on the lawn reading Jane Austen? Was that what this was about?

Graham slipped up to a counter filled with 99-cent peanut bags and ordered two hazelnut hot cocoas from the sweet, balding eighty-something-year-old named Bobby who manned the first concession stand. His powder blue gaze searched Nala and Graham as he handed over the drinks. "How long have you two been going steady?" he wheezed.

Graham and her? Was the kind, old thing delusional or just blind? Or could he see it, too? That something was there between them. Bobby slurped his club-member only, "Sports Fanatic" half-gallon jug of soda through a jasmine-yellow plastic straw and gave Nala a little grandpa wink. *Woohoo!* She looked mature enough to pass as some BU junior with a totally gorgeous senior boyfriend! A boyfriend whom she could kiss casually, through whose arm she could wrap her turquoise toggle-garbed wrist in crowds, who would take her on long, curvy drives through the mountains in his sexy, beautifully-lined roadster. All she needed was a gift—something like his favorite watch, or a Tiffany's necklace—to tell all of those gross, flabby chested boys upstairs that she was taken.

Taken by Graham. Who was not a senior. Who was a teacher. Her teacher.

Bobby's words hung in the air as the so-called couple rocked inside of their winter boots and tried to think of something less awkward to say than, "Yeah . . . she's my student, he's my teacher."

"No, no! Let me guess," Bobby interrupted, feeling extra confident as his old-fart energy pills kicked in. "Six months?"

Graham laughed under his breath. Bobby's wrinkly cheeks sagged like the jowls of an Aussie bulldog as he waited. If he tossed Bobby a treat, would he wag his tail and play dead too? Graham sighed, figuring it probably wouldn't be genius for an old man to play dead. His eyes stared at Nala with a relentless mischief. *Uh-oh.*

"Well," Graham mumbled, pinching at the plastic of the displayed dollar peanut bags. "Seven months in October, right?" His eyes gazed down on her adoringly as she dragged her tongue over the white fluff of whipped cream on her lips.

"Hoo-rah!" Bobby screeched, his jacket sleeves shoved in the air as he did some sort of celebration dance. When he came to a stop, he grinned and pulled a shining flask from his pocket. "Think she's the one?" he wheezed, splashing something liquid and dark into his drink; something that smelt like moonshine. It probably was moonshine.

Graham sort of smiled, taking his first sip of hot chocolate. Then he leaned over the bar and whispered, "Wouldn't you?"

Lucky to Have You

Just as Graham had suspected, there were a few empty seats near the concession stands. Nala settled onto the farmed-teak bench Indian style and sipped on her creamy hot cocoa. The stadium roared furiously as Principal Dotie's pretentious yelp poured through the speakers: "Touchdown Sharks!"

Nala stuffed her polished fingernails through her hair and took another gulp of cocoa. Being alone with Graham made her feel so mature and developed, like she was that early bloomer who was dating boys while all her friends were still waiting around for their bras to fill out and their periods to start.

"I guess we're winning," Nala piped up, playing with the fringe on her boots, feeling heavy eyes watching her. She wasn't exactly sure why Graham had dragged her away from her totally enjoyable view of the field; she'd been close enough to see all of the muscles in Rocko's flexing six-pack as he yanked his jersey back and danced conceitedly across the twenty during warm-ups. But she was happy he did.

"Did you want to go back? So you can watch the game?"

"No way," she blurted. Graham plopped down next to her. He stuffed his hand into his denim pocket and ripped out his cell phone, clicking through a few messages. "Unless you need to go back," Nala added as Graham typed his fingers against the phone keyboard.

Miss Hart was probably sulking around in her watercolor frock and mint-green, dragonfly blazer, pulling at her fried, yellow split ends and blowing up Graham's phone with texts like a psychotic ex. *Was she an ex? Or worse . . . a girlfriend?* Was Graham in such a desperate need to text her—or someone else? His cell phone slipped back into his pocket, and he began to groom his stubbly chin hairs. "Can we pretend you're just a friend for a minute?" Graham asked. His cellphone vibrated loudly in his pocket. "I mean, you are a friend, but . . . can we forget that you're a student for a minute?"

Nala's eyes searched up and down Graham's face. He looked flustered. Nervous. She nodded vacantly and bit into her bottom lip. Worried. Guilty. She took a giant gulp of hot chocolate. "Sure."

The crowd cheered wildly in the background. Graham stared into his lap where his hands were clasped tightly together. He wished they were back in the classroom—alone—hidden by darkness, silence ringing in their ears and the smell of rocky ledge bars, hazelnut-flavored coffee beans and chalk swiveling over the desks. At least there he wouldn't have to worry about being seen with Nala. He wouldn't have to stress about what that might look like to a fresh pair of eyes, because in that classroom, she was his TA. Plain and simple. Their relationship was totally platonic, totally professional. But here . . . .

Bobby, the concession stand man, stacked plastic cups in the distance. He was harmless, thank God, but Graham was still worried about everyone else. He was worried about Sosie kicking her size seven, mid-rise ankle boots around the stadium in search of her best friend, or Miss Hart organizing a search party to bring Graham back, dead or alive. She seemed like the type to preserve her passed-lover's rotting corpse in her basement, where she would spoon-feed him mashed carrots, give him organic lavender bubble baths, and kiss his shriveled lips.

Graham checked out Nala, stunned at how beautiful she looked in some other guy's jacket, her brown waves of hair trundling over the sleeves, sleek and shiny. "Is Knox your boyfriend?" he asked. "The jacket, and all . . . I'm just wondering."

"Not really," she shrugged. "We've gone out a few times, but we aren't exclusive, or anything. A friend told me he got in trouble during football practice, so I think he has other things on his mind. Besides, it's still pretty new. I haven't really thought about it."

Yeah, right . . . .

Knox Ritchie already had quite a reputation whirring around Alistair Dwelling. Even Graham had heard about it, a little. His dreamy blue eyes were the butter to every honey-blonde, pixie cut freshman girl's bread. His IQ was borderline genius, which all the sophomores talked about. *Books equal Ferraris,* they'd all chant in the showers, so consistently that Nala wondered if they were in some green-grappling cult. And every girl loved that fact that he was starting QB for the freshman team. Nala was totally lying when she said that she hadn't really thought about it. There was a sense that if she turned Knox down, he'd quickly be swooped up and out of reach. But when all was said and done, her mind was more often occupied by something — or rather someone — else.

"Ok." Graham ripped out his cell again, flipping it between his fingers. He was in sudden need of the lip balm he had stashed away in his sedan. "Pretend you and Knox are a thing for a minute," he said, folding his arms over his chest. Was he forgetting that Nala and Knox were — kind of — already a thing? "And your relationship is just . . . not where you want it to be. Or, not where he wants it to be, I guess. So, he decides to end it — not because of you, but because of him — because he isn't completely committed. His head is somewhere else . . . like football."

"Okay . . . ." She nodded, trying to imagine it all — though by the way Knox treated her, it was a little hard to believe he'd be anything but faithfully hers.

"He just thinks that you would be happier, and he would happier, if the both of you . . . just kind of . . . took a break."

"Uh-huh." She nodded. "I mean, that would definitely make sense."

"Definitely, right?" Graham's mouth curled into a you-totally-get-me smile, and Nala felt her stomach do flips inside of her. He just had this way about him. Like Humphrey Bogart.

Graham shifted to the edge of the bench. "I've kind of been seeing Estelle Hart for a few weeks. Nothing serious, we've just gone out for dinner and drinks once or twice, and on a weird horse and buggy ride around the city she set up last Friday." He chuckled at the image of Estelle popping open a bottle of cheap Moscato and insisting that they "cheers" to the soft plop of Icelandic pony droppings. Talk about off the wagon, on the wagon. "And up until recently, she was just a friend I said morning' to when we were in the teacher's lounge preparing for first period." He rubbed his eyes harshly. "It just gets lonely here."

"Yeah?" Nala gulped. Even if Graham was lonely, did he really need to hang out with Miss Hart? Couldn't he just rent movies, play Xbox, or buy a dog? He seemed the Golden Retriever type. She began a thorough search in her jacket pocket for a stick of strawberry gum that she had squirreled away. "So you decided to hang out with her to pass the time?"

"Exactly." He shrugged. "But when her feelings became clear to me last night, I realized I have to end it. Not because of her, but because—like I said before—I'm not completely committed. My head is . . . somewhere else."

Graham's eyes darted to Nala, who was cluelessly playing with her gum wrapper. All he had wanted since they watched that movie together was to tell her the honest truth: how he hadn't stopped thinking about her in that long, pink dress. How he had all of these feelings . . . serious feelings . . . feelings he couldn't control. How he felt a weird connection with her . . . unexplainable, like nothing else before. Did she feel the same way? Did she feel the connection, too? His lips frowned as he hurdled onto his shoes and stretched out his long, beautiful arm to hoist her off the bench. He couldn't tell her the truth. Not then. Maybe not ever. "Let's get you back," he breathed, sounding a little overwhelmed. Being honest with himself was exhausting.

"But you . . . ."

"Yeah, don't worry about me. I'll figure it out. And, umm . . . thanks . . . for listening. You're really . . . great."

Nala shuddered, not wanting to leave. She felt like they were just getting started. She hadn't even finished her hot chocolate, yet. Graham led the way back after grabbing some kettle corn, climbing the stairs just in time to catch Knox Ritchie chuck the football into the end zone to his buddy Chandler Vanderkrump. Chandler threw the ball to the ground and slammed his inflated chest against that of some gangly kid nearby.

"Where have you been, you little skeez?" Sosie snatched Nala up in her arms, holding her in a bundle of floral-printed cloth. "You missed Rocko kick the bajeebers out of someone!

He got flagged and everything! It was so hot, I could have melted." Sosie ripped into a small hangnail and watched Professor Leatherwood's back fade into the crowd. "So . . . dish!" She squeezed Nala, her eyes burning with excitement. "What kind of trouble did you and Sexypants get into?"

"Trouble? Forget who you're talking to?"

"I know . . . you're such an angel. Blah, blah, blah!"

Nala stared into the crisp, autumn night flooded with stadium lights and face paint. Truthfully, her and Graham hadn't gotten into any trouble, but that didn't mean she didn't want to. Far beyond the naked-chested mob of chubby, sport-obsessed sophomore and junior boys, the back of Graham's head followed Knox's zipping body as it spun around on field. Did angels wish to be whisked away by hot teachers? Or had she entered the dark side of barely-moralistic push-up bras and unlawful flings? It seemed her innocent reputation would soon dissolve away if she let her feelings for Graham unravel beyond that night.

"Oh, come on, entertain me!" Sosie piped up as the wooing of the audience faded. "That loser Brains talked my ear off with enginerding crap for half-an-hour. Like — who cares about space shuttles? There are more important things . . . like seashells and French fries. Drive a freaking beach-friendly, cheeseburger hovercraft, and then we'll talk."

Nala peeked through the crowd, discovering Miss Hart standing beside Graham, her spider-long arm wrapped around his cotton twill collar as she chewed kettle corn with her exaggeratedly vermilion lips. "Nothing exciting happened," Nala shrugged. "We just went over the syllabus and grabbed hot chocolate."

"Yawn!" Sosie rolled her eyes. "No offense, but I'd rather pick gum off these rusty benches than become a TA."

"Yeah." Nala shrugged, not really wanting to remind Sosie that she needed the money. Instead, she stole another glimpse at Graham. He had been watching her already. Hopeless, hazel eyes peered through her, seemingly regretful of something. Not saying everything that he had wanted to say, perhaps. Or feeling something that he shouldn't have felt. Estelle dug her braids into his chin and pulled him against her watermelon boobs.

"Sexypants is lucky to have you, you know," Sosie said, jiggling her necklace and watching the field pensively. "Even if you are the only girl in this bubble of pigskin and fondant who doesn't want to floss your teeth with his tongue."

Well, Nala thought, *I wouldn't say that . . . .*

Second Base

"Nice ride, Ritchie Rich!" Tess tugged her charcoal-gray, lambskin drape jacket over her cleavage and stroked the chestnut-colored, premium leather seat that cushioned her ass; her suddenly toasty ass. Seat warmers in the back row . . . not too shabby! Sitting in that truck, whiffing the beautiful leather, all Tess could think about was marrying Knox Ritchie, pre-ordering the newest Laurent Le Blanc cutaway bikini, and taking a yearlong honeymoon with her rich hubby to some all-inclusive tropical resort. Somewhere lux.

"May I refill your mojito, Miss?" the thong-adorned cabana boy would insist.

Unfortunately, Knox Ritchie was far too infatuated with perfect, little Nala to even notice that Tess's butt cheeks were practically heaving out of her tribal print skirt. And it wasn't by accident. But at least Gino looked beautiful in his post-football sweats. And who knew? Maybe he would inherit an estate in Dirk Hill and a cute, little sports car. Maybe he was already rich, but was just the frugal type. "Where are we going, anyway?" Tess whined, picking at her neon pink fingernail polish. "Because if I have to track through mud in my new flats, I'm going to kill someone with them."

"Relax, sweetheart." Gino yanked his eyes shut to block out the noise of Tess's incessant whining and stuffed his fingers through his recently washed hair. "You'll survive."

Knox parked his truck next to Brains's hideous 1989, egg-plant-purple minivan. "All right, ladies. We're here!"

Tess slammed her ski-slope nose against the back window. Just as she thought — it was in the middle of freaking nowhere! She slipped her hands into a pair of shearling flip mittens and kicked open the door.

The group trotted down a mudslide, snaking toward a little fire pit. Rocko Borai carried a duffel bag, while Brains Fink and Knox Ritchie supported a stainless steel keg between them. Gino fiddled with the joint in his pocket, which he had traded some senior for with a money clip, and debated sneaking off somewhere to smoke it alone. Nala grabbed Sosie's hand, and the two bobbed down the mudslide together, giggling about the suspected beer sloshing against the insides of the keg. Tessa cried about her already-ruined flats, as Juliet stared longingly at the back of Knox's head.

If only he loved the back of her head the way she loved his.

Ten minutes later, the fire was going. Nala and Knox plopped down on a tree trunk together and thrust out their hands toward the flame. "So, what'd you think of the game?" Knox asked eagerly. Had she noticed him dancing out of the pocket? Or seen his fifty-three yard pass to Chandler Vanderkrump? Did she approve of his seven-step drop?

Nala gulped, feeling like she just swallowed a crab cake. What did she think of the game? Well, for an entire quarter, she had been curled up on a teak block bench at the back of the stadium, sipping hot cocoa and admiring Graham Leatherwood's perfectly toned arms. And for the rest of it, she had wished she was curled up on a teak block bench, sipping hot cocoa and admiring Graham Leatherwood's perfectly toned arms. "Ummm." Her voice cracked as she tugged the letterman sleeves over her freezing hands. "Everyone kept cheering your name. They were saying you're a prodigy. I had no idea how good you are."

That would work.

Rocko Borai approached, passing Knox and Nala two plastic cups of vodka-spiked punch, which he had craftily filled the keg with earlier that day. It was easy, really. Along with Knox's help, he pried out the slide piece of the keg with a flat head screwdriver and dumped handles of vodka inside, some orange juice and tropical punch, and anything else he could scavenge. Coconut oil. Almond milk. And he called his creation 'stupid sauce.' "It's strong, ladies," he warned.

As Rocko stomped off to grab his own, Knox ran his thumb over the brim of his cup. A prodigy? He took a sip of stupid sauce, his eyes glowering over the lip of the cup. "Says the girl who has her own fan club," he replied, smiling behind his drink coolly.

"Everyone have a drink?" Rocko sloshed his liquor around the cup like a whirlpool, taking a whiff. It smelled like rubbing alcohol, plus a hint of eucalyptus. He moved over to the keg, and tipped himself some more. His camel-brown chukka boots stomped through a high stack of leaves. "Welcome to Second Base, girls," he roared, his calfskin leather jacket limp on his shoulders as he showed off the surrounding woods. "No one's leaving here until one of us gets naked. My money's on you, Blondie."

Juliet shoveled her floppy, damp curls out of her eyes just in time to see Rocko Borai pointing a boney, stubborn finger directly at her forehead. "Me?"

"You look like you know how to get down."

Get down? She twirled a strand of hair around on her ring finger, feeling Brains's hot breath on her neck nearby. "Just ignore him," Brains whispered. But she couldn't. Rocko was such a hottie. His eyes were like caramel and his large, luscious, intensely red lips were leering down on her like Twizzlers. She didn't want to ignore him. All she wanted was to feel beautiful like Nala and Sosie and Tess, and Rocko Borai knew how to appreciate beauty.

"So, what's in this drink, anyway?" Her nasally voice cracked as she peeled off her lemon yellow, ruche-sleeved coat, forcing her freckled cleavage to sally forth. Her big, bubbly boobs bounced inside of her bustier like Jello.

"Ummm," Rocko coughed as Juliet jiggled restlessly, kicking her pointy cheetah flats in the dirt. "Let's see. There's . . . some orange shit, some peach shit. A hint of grape shit. Some vodka. It tastes like sherbet. You'll like it."

"Then bottoms up, I guess." She locked eyes with him and grinned. Maybe they'd sneak off later. Maybe she'd taste those Twizzler lips. Then she pinched her eyes shut and took a giant gulp. The vodka burned her throat the whole way down, and she resisted the urge to spew it all over Brains's already puke-colored crewneck t-shirt. "Whew!" Her liquor-reeking breath drifted sickeningly into her nostrils. "Am I drunk?"

"Not yet, party girl." Rocko licked his lips hungrily. "But when I'm through with you, you won't know which way's up."

Charming.

Back in Bluffdale, the girls had once been allowed a sip of merlot with a tea biscuit during etiquette class. Miss Iris had even offered Nala an iced Frangelico at some hole-in-the-wall Italian bistro on her sweet sixteen, but liqueur was like, one thousand calories, so Nala had respectfully declined. Except for Sosie's random chug of beer at Cloud Nine, none of them had really partied.

But there was a first time for everything, right?

"This won't kill us, will it?" Juliet piped up, blinking nervously at the punch.

"There's probably a ninety-nine-point-seven percent chance it won't," Brains mumbled. His European short-chop-do dipped down into his eyes. "Unless your stomach's a bottomless pit." His fingers tickled Juliet's belly awkwardly and she slapped them away. "Like the Bermuda Triangle. Well, that's my theory, at least."

Well then could you like, jump in it?

By the time everyone had tried the stupid sauce, Juliet was finishing off her second cup. Pale, milky flubber bounced out of her shirt as she relived her fifth grade dance competition routine. "Nala had the only solo," she remembered jealously, stumbling back to the downed pine trunk on her wobbly legs after she had demonstrated the infamous pelvis swoop. "Because she's perfect at everything." She rolled her eyes and ordered Rocko to fill her up. He agreed, although he much would have preferred to feel her up. It wasn't his fault. Those boobs were aggressive.

"No offense, Jules, but you never really had the body for dancing," Tess said as her lips cautiously slurped up her drink. She wiggled on her bones, tormented. Gino was lying next to her being about as interesting as Plymouth rock, and all she wanted to do was go home. She smacked a mosquito with her free hand and complained, "This is honest-to-God the grossest place on the whole freaking planet!" Juliet ignored Tess, continuing to jiggle drunkenly in front of her. "And the view from down here is nauseating."

Juliet turned red as she refilled her cup for the third time and Tess continued to point to the cellulite stacked on her thighs like cottage cheese. Juliet stared at Rocko, but couldn't be sure if he was listening to Tess, or just musing in his own blurry mind. Maybe her body wasn't perfect, and maybe she wasn't as pretty or as cool as the other girls, and maybe she was just feeling upset because she was a little drunk, but she was a nice person and she meant well. *Didn't that count for something?*

Nala felt Knox sweep her thick, brown hair across the sleeves of her jacket. "Don't feel like you need to drink that," he said, pointing to her slowly draining cup. "If you want to sit this one out, I'll bench warm with you. We can just talk. Hang out. Or — you know — if you want to go home, I'll drive you. Whatever you want."

Nala's body softened. Sweet, considerate Knox. "I'm having fun," she said, feeling a little loopy from the drink. "*You're* fun!"

"Thanks," he chuckled, noticing that Rocko was now up on his feet, trying to tango with Sosie, who tipsily tossed her thin, streaky hair in his face. All Knox wanted was to take Nala somewhere where they could be alone and lie in each other's arms. They would talk about their childhood dreams under the stars. How many children they wanted. What kind of puppies they'd buy. But he wasn't sure that she was up for it. After all, she had requested that her four girlfriends crash their first date . . . .

"Hey! So, I wanted to tell you . . . ." Nala raised an eyebrow. "Since I'm assisting Professor Leatherwood now, I think I could convince him to make us partners in class."

Knox shot up. "Really? You think so?"

Partners? What was next . . . marriage? He'd buy her a mansion with Victorian turrets, or a colonial home with a wrap-around porch, or a stone-cliff cabin on Cargill's Island. Whatever she wanted. They'd get married at some wine vineyard with show-ered wisteria teahouses, reading off traditional vows because, of course, Nala was a girl who cherished tradition. Sosie would be the Maid of Honor. Gino would be the best man. Being partnered up in class was just the beginning . . . .

Knox finished off his cup, and motioned Rocko to top him off. "Nala, that would be . . . awesome."

"I know." She beamed excitedly, bouncing up and down like she was sitting on a stability ball. "Wouldn't we make a good team?"

Rocko marched over, exaggerating his broad shoulders as he stepped between them. He shoved a filled cup against Knox's silver, trim fit tee. "Here ya go, princess," he mocked, plucking a cigarette from behind his ear and clamping it between his teeth. "Think you could spare an old, worthless friend a light?"

"You know I quit." Knox stuffed his shirtsleeves up his arms and waited for Rocko to move along, hoping the fact that he used to smoke cigarettes wouldn't be a turn-off. Would it help if he mentioned that he had quit just for Nala? Rocko stared down on him, annoyed. Even though that black, buzzed head had been a part of the gang since fifth grade, Knox had never liked him much. He was always such an ass.

"You quit *lighters*?" Rocko chuckled, his tongue running up and down the filter of his cigarette. "Well, you know what they say. Once a quitter, always a quitter." Rocko rolled his eyes and cocked his head in the air conceitedly. "That pretty, little girl-friend of yours should remember that." He trooped away, peek-ing back at Nala hungrily before he showed Juliet how to do a proper jumping jack.

"Sorry about that." Knox took a long drink to try and stay calm. His fists flexed at his sides.

"It's okay," Nala shrugged. Boys were so weird. Always mak-ing fun of each other. Always being jerks. And then, as she tried to stand and stretch, the ground swam under her and she plopped back down onto the log with a thud. Knox's arms snatched her up. Her head felt light and heavy as it bobbled on her neck. She blinked her eyes. Everything was a big, blurry splotch of flailing arms, smoke, and moonlight. *Stupid Sauce.* She looked at Knox, her vision slowly clearing.

"You all right?" he asked, bleached teeth flashing at her like headlights. He was still holding her there, in place.

"Fine," she said.

Knox's hands slipped away carefully. *No. Not yet. Don't let go.* He looked perfect; his hair ruffled and spiked with shower water, and his eyes beautifully kindled in the twilight glow. He was like an everyday guy, only with better bone structure and hundred-dollar sweatpants.

"So," Knox watched as Rocko obnoxiously drilled Juliet on the proper form of the tango, "you think you can talk to Leatherwood?"

"I don't see why not," she breathed, kissing her lips together teasingly. He was so gorgeous. So, so gorgeous. Why hadn't she seen it before?

"Because, honestly, I'm really into you . . . ." he said, slipping his hand up and down her thigh. Nala collapsed, her insides melting like icicles. Rocko's voice echoed in the background. Tess was nearby, yapping on and on about Jon Matinee's street-style grunge line premiering in the spring, and jumped up to brush the filth from her skirt. Brains was throwing leaves at the fire. None of that mattered, though. They didn't even notice. They were like the only two people on the planet.

"Want to take a walk?" Knox asked. Nala checked out the once-lively ambience surrounding her, now fizzling out. Juliet went back to playing leapfrog with Rocko. Nala wondered how much longer until one of her boobs played peek-a-boo with the crowd.

"Yeah, let's walk," Nala said. *Before this gets any weirder* . . . .

Nala hugged herself, thinking about what would happen once the two of them were completely alone. What if he kissed her? Would she be ready? She rolled her little, stud earring between her thumb and forefinger before tossing back the rest of her drink.

A little liquid courage . . . just in case.

Too Perfect

"**W**hich one of you losers wants to go first?" Juliet tugged on her bustier top and took a swig of stupid sauce. Everyone was being so boring since Knox and Nala had disappeared, probably off somewhere complimenting each other's every sneeze. Even though she wasn't thrilled that her crush had scampered off with the most gorgeous girl in school, Juliet couldn't say she was very surprised. Regardless, she was still planning to make memories she'd forget by the morning. "Well?"

"How about you, Blondie?" Rocko juggled his cell phone in his hands loosely, ready to snapshot a stray boob if Juliet toppled over and proved to be as drunk as her frumpy curls — misted with sweat and the cool, damp air — made her seem.

"Seriously? No one?" she whined. "Aw, you guys are no fun," She licked her mouth, suddenly craving cinnamon chips and pineapple salsa. "Where'd Knox run off to, anyway?"

Knox and Nala flew up the mudslide, narrowing in on the parked truck. He turned on the car's satellite radio, and twiddled between channels until The Zombie and the Zs' latest album, Cigarette Smoke, began to boom through the cracked windows. Knox hoisted Nala onto the bed of the trunk. "Have you heard this one?"

Nala shook her head. "Don't make fun of me. I like classics. Oldies. Pretty much anything on a record player. I think it has something to do with the static. Makes me feel like a fifties housewife. The Temptations come on, and I can see myself baking cranberry ambrosia in a peacock plume apron." Nala lay down next to Knox, relieved to find that the world was no longer spinning. Her hair sprawled out like whitecaps rolling in on the beach. Maybe 1950s housewife and turntable static was too deep to discuss on a second date, but she didn't care. *Just call me the ocean — deepity deep deep.*

"I bet you look cute in an apron," Knox said. He stroked Nala's hair with his fingertips, lightly brushing at her forehead. His earnest eyes inspected her for a sign. What did she think about him, anyways? Was this a crush? Was she just passing the time? He popped up on his elbow, and sucked cold, winter air into his lungs. "So, you said you're working with Professor L? How's that going?"

"All right," she said, braiding the ends of her hair. She hadn't really thought about Graham . . . not for a few hours, at least. But now, suddenly, she was. That conversation at the stadium . . .

about Miss Hart, Knox, being emotionally unfaithful . . . that was weird, right?

Knox fidgeted uncomfortably, wishing she'd say more. Anything. Everything. He'd never judge her.

Nala peered into the sky. "There isn't much to do. So far, I've reorganized a bookshelf and trashed the old curriculum with a paper shredder."

"Look at you!" Knox's voice cracked and his hand snatched at hers. "If I didn't have a crush on you before, I do now."

Nala blushed, smelling s'mores and a hint of burning cinnamon lingering in the air. Noise arose near the fire pit. What were they conjuring up down there? She imagined a pool filled with chocolate icebox pies and hazelnut truffle bites floating like sunbathing rafts, a slide of mocha-cappuccino blossoms, a marble sheet cake seesaw, pecan toffee monkey bars, and a white chocolate panna cotta trampoline.

Hmm, someone was drunk and about to start her you-know-what.

Knox's fingers glided between hers, pulling her back down to planet Earth. "I have a confession to make, Nala," he said gruffly. *A big one.* He cleared his throat and lay back, his squinty, blue eyes admiring the North Star. Sparkly and big, like Nala's eyes.

"Yeah?"

"Yeah." His voice rattled as he tried to calm down. All of the liquor surging through his veins made it impossible to lie still. "It's about Leatherwood, actually." He stopped stroking her head for a minute. "You and Leatherwood."

"Me and Leatherwood?" Her heart began to thump against her chest like a broken cuckoo clock. Did Knox know about her crush? Did he know that she and Leatherwood had watched that movie together, sprawled out on the floor like a couple of kids building forts? Did he know that they had snuck off during the football game? Was this about the little, white lie they told the concession stand guy? Celebrating their 7-month anniversary, or whatever?

Or was it six?

Nala shrank into a little, panicked ball. Knox relaxed. His voice breezed through the cool air. "God, I can't believe I'm admitting this." He rolled an old cigarette stub around in his jean pocket. He wished — just for a minute — to take a drag to unwind. Just once. He squashed the stub, and flicked it away. "For some reason, I thought there was something going on between you two. You and Leatherwood," he said. "Isn't that the most ridiculous thing you've ever heard?"

Well, not entirely . . . .

Nala remained silent. The grim, gloomy skyline frowned down on them, and Nala dreamed up a pretentious, jock cloud scowling at her, judging her from his mighty tall field goal post, and whispering, "Guiltyyyyy" beneath his cloudy breath.

"It was so stupid. I don't even know why I told you," Knox confessed sorely. He repositioned himself to toss a thick twig that was stabbing him in the back. "Sometimes, he just looks at you this way . . . the same way I probably look at you. And god, if he likes you the way I like you . . . ."

Nala rubbed her temples, trying to relax. At least Knox knew nothing. He had only imagined something, like she had imagined that weird cloud thing. And even in her hazy, vodka-induced state of mind, she knew she had made that wad of puffy fluff up. "So," Nala dipped farther inside of the jacket sleeves, breathing in Knox's delicious scent. "What are you trying to say, *exactly?*"

Knox rubbed his chin. "I'm trying to say . . . ." He took in a deep breath and slipped his hands up inside the sleeves of the letterman, soothing her goosebumped arms. "That you make me the jealous guy I've never been."

Nala smiled widely. Knox was so irresistible when he said things like that. He made her feel special; wanted; beautiful. A future with him would be a trance of jet planes and escargot, high-waisted bikinis and tropical fruit daiquiris, summers in Barbados and winters in the Swiss Alps. Everywhere they vacationed, he'd be there behind a camera, capturing the most authentic beauty of the world . . . her. He'd love her madly. A life with him would be careless and romantic; even the obligatory charity balls would come with a spa day of deep-tissue massages and skin treatments. He would do anything to make her happy. Anything. She could already tell he was just *that guy*.

Nala hovered near and kissed Knox on the cheek, feeling his jaw clench beneath her lips. It was almost impossible not to like him, not to want more, despite the fact that Graham gave her the tinglies. Knox was just so perfect. But maybe—she worried—a little too perfect.

Feeding the Buffalo

"Egyptian cotton bed sheets, peach bellini herbal tea, pink lotus petal bath scrub, and my favorite Bahama Mama tumbler candle . . . all awaiting my arrival back at the dorms. What I left behind for . . . this. Remind me again what I'm doing in this shit hole?" Tess flicked the mud off of her new, studded-toe ballet flats and rolled her gray eyes. "Gino, be a sweetheart and walk me home." She tugged on his trim-fit, heathered hoodie. "How about I give you three dates? I'll even let you take me to the theater, and sit through one of those boring war movies you boys love so much."

Gino sat against a giant pine tree log, sipping from a beer bottle and flipping the cap between his fingers. Who had convinced him to skip out on his post-game ice bath just to listen to Tess talk about embossed crocodile satchels and perforated totes, whatever those were? He could be stoned already, mowing into a mountain of nachos and watching re-runs of the game with the assistant coach. Instead, he was sitting in the dirt, sipping a cold beer on a cold night and flipping a cap between his fingers, wishing he could flick Tess away so easily.

But at least he was drunk.

"Can't you hear me?" Tess barked, tucking her clutch beneath her armpit. "All right, fine! Make it four dates. But seriously, after that you're going to have to serenade me, or buy me a freaking marching band, or something."

Brains Fink stumbled over, his eyes surveying the fire pit as the flame fizzled out. "Do we have any more liquor?" he announced.

"Aren't you hammered enough, nerd?" Juliet piped up, pulling her soaked, frizzy bangs out of her eyes. At some point, she had passed out on a log. A string of drool had crusted from her lips to her chin. She wiped her face with her coat sleeve, hoping she didn't look sloppy. Though she sped past sloppy three drinks ago . . . .

"It's to stimulate the fire," Brains said, stuffing his square, tortoise glasses up his nose. "I don't drink. So Tess, if you want, I can drive you back. I'm usually the DD, anyway."

Tess shrugged, and checked her purse for her new strawberry lip shine. If Gino Blackthorn wouldn't walk her back, she supposed she'd have to settle for a ride in that pukey 1989 minivan. *Here's hoping I don't get lice.* She wetted her lips and blew Gino a kiss. "Even if you *are* a lazy jerk, I still love ya!" She stuffed her gloss back in her clutch. "Coming, Jules?"

Juliet scavenged up her things: her missing cheetah print flat and her clunky cable chain bracelet, all sprawled out like confetti.

She didn't really want to catch a ride home without saying good-bye to Knox, and she certainly didn't want Brains Fink to get any ideas—especially when he kept looking at her hungrily with those beady eyes. But Tess wasn't someone she could stand to piss off. "Coming," she chimed, jamming her bracelet up her wrist and scampering away.

Sosie sat, clicking through her cellphone, waiting for Rocko to return from what must be a luxurious piss in the woods, rounding on five minutes. Her head ached, her boobs were scre, her throat felt like she had swallowed a brick oven, and now she was just twiddling her cell phone in her lap, waiting for Nala and Knox to quit counting stars or massaging each other's scalps or whatever they were doing, so they could all just go home.

"Can't you turn that thing on silent?" Gino mumbled under his breath, tossing his empty beer bottle near the fire pit.

"I could," Sosie supposed. She'd been looking over some pictures, but decided to press a few extra buttons just to be obnoxious. After all, it wasn't like she was carving a saxophone out of black gum bark and pine needle and playing bluesy jazz to the beat of Gino's swishing and swallowing. "Why don't you go catch a ride with Brains and leave us noisy texters in peace?" She jumped onto her shoes and started to kick stray trash into a pile near the fire.

"Beats having to share a van with your friend Tess . . . ." He threw a few plastic cups into Sosie's stash of garbage, all he could grab without having to stand up or move too much.

"Tess is *not* my friend."

Sosie blinked down at the mound of broken glass, cigarette butts, and plastic. One of two proximate trashcans was completely filled, and the other reeked of spoiled milk and salmon, so Sosie just kicked the trash into a nearby hole. *Party favors for paroled convicts*, she rationalized. She plopped down Indian style near Gino, combing out her split ends with her fingers.

"I thought you girls were like, a tribe?"

"If we're a tribe, than Tess is the first one I'd feed to the buffalo." She started to zip up Knox's duffel bag, figuring that the more ready they were to leave when Knox and Nala got back, the sooner they actually *would* leave. She snatched a pack of breath mints that were bulging out of a side pocket. Her eyes squinted at the label. Mmm . . . mojito mint! "Want one?"

"Umm . . . no thanks."

The can popped open and Sosie tipped two into her mouth. They tasted like kelp and chicory as they dissolved on her tongue. She wrinkled her face.

"Those are nicotine mints, you know," Gino said, slightly laughing.

"'Scuse me?" Sosie spit the mints into the dirt and dragged her tongue all over her sleeves. No wonder they smelled like swamp. "What the hell is nicotine?"

"A chemical in cigarettes. Knox is trying to quit smoking . . . or already did quit, I guess."

"Oh, so now he's addicted to this crappy mint stuff, instead? Sounds like a lose, lose." She stuffed the mint crap back into the bag, and continued to scrub her tongue until it was raw. *No cigarettes for me, thank you!* Gino tried not to laugh again, afraid Sosie would chuck an empty vodka bottle at his head if he did. But, he had to admit she was slightly charming. In a sleep-with-one-eye-open kind of way.

"Did you see where Rocko went?" She plummeted back to the dirt, twirling her ankh knuckle ring around her finger as she searched the backwoods.

"Nope." Gino picked up a twig and dragged it through the topsoil, drawing a lazy figure in the dirt. Man, he was bored. "Is Rocko like, your boyfriend or something?"

"I don't know." She shrugged, hitching up her sea-foam blue metallic skinnies and feeling her stubby calves rasp against her wrists. Whatever. It was winter. She could afford to pass on the razor for a few more days. "Why do you care, anyway? We're not friends, remember? You and I don't even know each other." She clamped her mouth shut to keep from sounding like a broken record: "We never met on the Bluffdale beach, we never flirted in the ocean, I never checked you out in your phthalo blue board shorts. That never happened, right? According to you?" Sosie rolled her eyes, sucking on the inside of her cheeks.

Gino shrugged as loose dirt hardened like clay beneath his fingernails. The stick figure was turning out to be a horse with five legs. "Just curious, I guess," he said, scraping a giant X across the portrait. Maybe he was prying, but Rocko and Sosie couldn't possibly be a *thing*. For starters, Rocko had been doing nothing but fantasizing about Nala's butt harnessed up in yoga pants performing some unspeakably flexible act ever since he first saw her in the cafeteria, nibbling on a blue cheese wedge like a rabbit.

Not to mention that Rocko was an ass, and Sosie was kind of . . . intriguing?

The wind picked up and dust shivered over his disastrous attempt at art. "So, you have a thing for jerks, then?" he accused as he searched for another beer nearby.

"Maybe I do," she supposed, arching one thin, blonde eyebrow at him. "There was a point in time when I thought *you* were kind of great. So, it appears jerks are my cup o' Joe." She pouted her peach lips, wishing she was more athletic so she could just get up and jog to that twenty-four-hour doughnut boutique on campus and splurge on lemon-glazed poppers with coconut frosting, or a pudding filled doughnut *croquembouche*. Something to fill that gaping hole in her ego. Mmmm *doughnuts*. Carrot cake and cinnamon and glazed devil's food! Now she couldn't stop thinking about them. Maybe one day she'd get fat and have to join a gym, but until then . . . bring on the fried flour.

Gino blinked, remembering the image of Sosie dancing around in her strapless, fire-coral bandeau top on the beach, her cherry-red shoulders frying in the sun. But no, she was never meant to be more than a stranger to him. Freshman year was supposed to be about football and academics. Hanging out with the guys. The last thing he needed was some girl distracting him.

And Sosie was the kind of distracting that really stung.

He shook his shabby, brown hair and fell back into the bark. "Look," he said, glazy eyed. "Rocko's not into you." His heathered hoody poked him in the neck as he stretched, and collapsed again. Anything to keep busy during such an awkward moment.

What? Sosie felt her heart plummet into her stomach. She peeked back at the woods, which were thrashing green in the cool breeze. Somewhere back there, Rocko was peeing on a tree, printing his name and someone else's in a urine drawn heart.

"He's got a thing for your friend," Gino added.

"*Friend?* As if I only have one?" Sosie stared blankly at the dirt, feeling like a loser. Wasn't Gino aware that you don't knock a girl down, and then, just as she's brushing off her rather expensive boho-grunge downtown parka, knock her down again? Wasn't there some cardinal rule in the *How Not to Be a Complete Asshole* playbook about that? What were they teaching those boys in Elkins, anyway?

Gino felt bad as he watched Sosie pound at the dirt. "Look, I'm sorry, but it's the truth." He shrugged. "He's been talking about Nala since we got here. Knox just got the jump on him."

Sosie gulped noisily, running her fingers like a rake through the brown earth. It wasn't like she *loved* Rocko or anything, but it was so typical. Every guy on the face of the planet wanted Nala, and Sosie was just that outrageous friend with designer bags and one-liners.

"Maybe you don't believe me, but I really am sorry," Gino rubbed at the short, stubbly hairs on his neck, wishing he hadn't said anything at all. Sosie looked so sad, and it kind of seemed like this was a reoccurring thing for them. He'd say something, and then she'd feel like crap . . . and then he'd feel like crap for making her feel like crap. It was the crappy circle of societal life. Gino flinched. "I just thought you deserved to know."

Sosie peeked up finally, staring back at him through the shadowy air. She looked like she was seconds away from crying, but wouldn't—because she *so* wasn't that girl.

"Thanks," she managed once she had composed herself. Her voice rattled inside of her as she choked back the tears. "But that doesn't make it suck any less."

Gummy Ears

Rocko yanked up his zipper as he jogged up the gravel trail. His body stumbled to a halt near the fire pit where Sosie was sprawled out on the dirt, biting her cuticle beds and Gino was clicking through his cell.

"Look at you two lovebirds!" Rocko said drunkenly, glowering down on them with beady, brown eyes. In the dark, he almost looked like some ax-murderer from a grungy, independent horror flick. All that was missing was a bloody, fingerless hand sticking out of gross, hand-me-down cargo pants. But of course he'd never be caught dead wearing those. Better make him a zombie ax-murderer. Then he *would* be dead.

"What are you guys talking about?"

"Does it look like we're talking?" Sosie snapped, lathering her lips in peach-flavored goo. What did Rocko mean, "lovebirds?" Was he really not into her . . . at all? Not even a little? Was he really not bothered by the fact that she and Gino were sitting near a fire pit together, not talking? Did that kiss really mean nothing to him? Maybe Gino was right. Maybe Rocko was just using her to get closer to Nala. A sour taste rose to her mouth. Now that she thought about it, he had kind of been flirting with Juliet all night. Perhaps he was just a pig who was drawn toward hourglass-shaped estrogen and moodiness.

Rocko clunked to the ground and yanked his eyes closed. All he wanted were painkillers and pizza; preferably, those little blue capsules that made the room do flips and deep-dish anchovy. Add in Nala wearing a bitchin' biker bikini and metallic shades, dancing the *Macarena* on some beach in Rio de Janeiro, and he could die a happy — and totally tanked — man. His mind slipped away into that dream. Margaritas, cabanas, and deep tans.

Sosie stared at him, disgusted, until he started to snore. Drool spilled out of his lips and he kept a firm grip on his crotch.

"So, I guess we can go now," she said to Gino as she glanced at Rocko's drooping body, and hopped up on her ankle boots. "You may have to carry your idiot friend, here."

"He's not really my . . . whatever."

"He's not really your what? Friend?" she gulped, looking down on Rocko's pathetic, drunk ass. For a split second, she could have sworn he was sucking his thumb. "But I thought you guys were like, *a tribe*?"

"Cute, Freckles," Gino flicked dirt off of his sleeves and stood, ripping Knox's asparagus green, polyester duffel up with him. "Just so you know, I'd feed him to the buffalo too."

The gravel trail ran up the mudslide and curved for Knox's parked truck, music still pouring out the opened windows. Gino wasn't wasting any more time on Rocko, and he sure as hell wasn't about to carry him back to the truck. He didn't even care about the $250 keg roasting near the fire pit, probably explosive. All he wanted were blackout shades and toothpaste.

Sosie stomped her fiery, pigeon-toed feet up the hill after him, her bangs thrashing into her eyes as she walked. "Umm . . . where the hell do you think *you're* going? Are you just going to leave him there to freeze?"

"Better to freeze than be buffalo dinner, I'd say." Gino readjusted the duffel strap on his shoulder. When he got back to the dorm, was toothpaste all that necessary? Or could he just swish around some mouthwash and call it a night? Behind him, he could feel Sosie snarling at his head, her mouth pruning with anger. Was this because he made another buffalo joke? "Hey, you're the one who said it in the first place. Not me."

"Okay, fine, that was a bitchy thing for me to say," she admitted, peeking back at Rocko, who had scrunched his body up into a tiny ball. *What a widdle baby.* Asleep, he almost didn't look like a spineless jerk that would make out with someone just to get close to her best friend. Then again, he also didn't exactly look like someone who deserved to die of frostbite, either. His gravestone would read: "Here lies Rocko Borai. Student. Athlete. (Wet) Dreamer. His death was lonely and cold . . . just like his heart."

Sosie jammed her fist into Gino's side until he flinched. "Come on, it's like, thirty degrees out here. And even though I should be taking this opportunity to draw Rocko a pervy, Italian mustache, or pierce one of his nipples, or spit gum in his ear, I still think he deserves to puke in the privacy of his own wastebasket."

"Spit gum in his ear?" Gino chuckled, shaking his head. He wondered if Sosie had always been so annoyingly insistent. He pictured her in boyfriend shorts and a grungy, misfit button-up, waving some obnoxious picketed sign around campus and screaming "Love, not war" in deep rasp. Although, thinking about it, she kind of seemed more the "Onward-the-gun-brigade" type. His eyes flexed on hers. One thing was for sure—Sosie was used to getting what she wanted. "You didn't really think I was going to leave him there, did you Freckles?" he asked.

Sosie blinked blankly. Freckles? Who the *hell* was Freckles? And of course she thought Gino would just leave Rocko there. He had never really seemed like the sympathetic type. In fact, he had never really seemed like the have-any-speck-of-emotion type. Sosie watched as Gino took off, sprinting the rest of the way uphill to drop the bag off near the truck and quickly jogged back down the hummock for Rocko, thrashing brown hair whipping in his face.

He's kind of sweet in a totally jerkface way, she thought, watching. It wasn't so hard to remember what she had liked about him from the start. There was something so mysterious and cool about him, like he was a bourbon-drinking, football-playing Renaissance man from another era. He probably built all of his own furniture out of reclaimed barn wood, and brewed up his own brandy. She wouldn't be surprised if he suddenly whipped out a crushed wool fedora, sparked up a Cuban, and chimed "Fancy seein' you here." Sosie shuddered. Did she still hate him? Because *hate* used to feel a little different . . . .

Sosie could barely see through the darkness as Gino hoisted Rocko over his shoulder. He let out a pained grunt and swiftly worked his way back up the hill. She was a little surprised. Going back for Rocko . . . that was sweet. Sosie groaned, knowing what she had to do. She had to forgive him . . . for everything. Not for him, but for her. So she could move on. So she could stop craving doughnuts at 2 in the morning. And going after Rocko was worthy of an apology; not to mention that the muscles exploding beneath Gino's sleeves looked like those of a Portuguese model she had grown pretty fond of over the years; some guy in a Laurent Le Blanc swimsuit catalogue. But she was pretty sure Gino was Italian. Or Greek. But who the heck cared? Beautiful was beautiful in any country.

Gino caught up to Sosie finally, sopping with sweat, and they strolled quietly toward the truck. He took his final steps with Rocko slumped over his shoulder, his perfectly round eyes glowing in the moonlight. Hot. So hot. Like Portuguese dude, but better. Sosie couldn't admit it until right then, newly grudge-free, as Gino's hair blew back to frame his perfectly angular face. Perhaps it also had something to do with the fact that he had — for the first time ever — displayed characteristics of a real human being.

"The rest of the trash as you requested," he said, as Rocko's lifeless arms stretched for the dirt. "Mind grabbin' the door?" he grunted. His shoulders ached from carrying two hundred pounds of drunken waste.

"Mmhmm," she breathed tensely, her legs buckling up beneath her. "Look, Gino, I think . . . ." She paused, watching Rocko belligerently blow a bubble of spit in his sleep. "I think I owe you an apology."

"K . . . ." he said, nodding at the truck. "What for?"

"Here . . . let me get that." She jumped ahead of him and yanked open the back door. The seats smelled of expensive leather, and she imagined that it was actually the upholstery in some beautiful, foreign convertible that she and Gino were using to swerve down the roads of Amorgos, Greece. Her sweet-honey strands would flip in the breeze, brushing against her lemon polka dot vintage shades, while Gino's expensive watch twisted with the steering wheel. He'd look over, his chocolate eyes peeping out of aviators, and smile a suntanned grin at her. Forget Bluffdale Beach. They were headed to Katapola!

Sosie climbed in, maneuvering around a football playbook, a lateral resister, shoe weights, a half empty bottle of whiskey, and some book on how to get rich. The music blared in her ears until she popped in the front and clicked the radio off. She fell into the back, glaring out the open door at Gino. "Maybe I should have believed you when you said you didn't remember me." Her voice echoed over the empty seats from inside. "Sometimes, I can be a little dramatic."

Gino heaved the two hundred pounds of Rocko's dead weight inside the car; Rocko's basketball-sized head bounced on the leather seats next to Sosie. She stuffed his arms over his chest so that he looked like a mummy. Dead man walking sounded about right, considering that Rocko had used her just to get close to Nala, and she would therefore have to kill him soon . . . . Slimeball. She crawled over Rocko for the door, her shoes accidentally scraping the remnants of Knox's playbook.

"Don't worry about it," Gino said. He grabbed Sosie's hand and helped her hurdle onto the ground. Her shoes hit the dirt with a thud.

Gino felt her skin beneath his fingers. By now, every inch of him regretted lying about the beach thing. It was a stupid thing to do. Either that, or drunkenness was filling him with doubt. But ever since Sosie had apologized, he really felt like a jerk.

"So, are Nala and Knox like, building a stargazing tower out there or what?" Sosie budged toward Gino, staring through the trees in the near distance.

"Not exactly." Gino jerked his head toward the truck bed, and Sosie lifted onto her toes to see over the side. There she saw them. Nala nuzzled her sweet, angelic face deeper into Knox's neck and curled her body against his like a roly-poly.

"They look so . . . happy," Sosie breathed, feeling a little jealous as Knox's hand absently stroked the top of Nala's head, as if they slept like that every night. "Should we wake them up?"

"Let's give them another minute."

Gino seemed quite the romantic by petitioning for truck bed spooning with such certainty and vigor. Let man and woman snuggle in peace! He drifted toward the passenger seat to find something, and Sosie stood plainly, blinking her eyes across the decomposing tire tracks, letting her mind run amuck. This was rarely a good thing. She was happy for Nala, she really was, but she couldn't help but wonder how long it would be before it was her turn to fall asleep next to some sweet guy in a truck bed? Who would this sweet guy be? Anyone but Rocko.

"Here." Gino held out a piece of chewing gum when he returned. "Hope you like fruit."

"Thanks. I do." Although of course she'd prefer strawberry-marsala with chocolate ganache lined tarts, or blueberry brie galette, or puff pastry honeyed pears, or any of those doughnuts to chewing gum. But it was better than veggies, she supposed. Sosie stared through the back door of Knox's truck, watching Rocko flip onto his ribs and—only for a moment—peel his beautiful, brown eyes open before passing out again. "I'm really mad at him for what he did to me," she confessed; smacking the gum between her small, square teeth. "I can't believe I kissed *that*!"

Gino blinked down at her, looking a little bothered. "You two kissed?"

Sosie shrugged. "Only for a minute. It's totally embarrassing now. I definitely regret it," she said.

They both watched as Rocko squirmed around on the row of seats, trying to get comfortable. He was a strangely unsatisfied drunk. Flipping. Groaning in his sleep. Gino recalled a time back in Elkins when Rocko—smashed off of Sazerac—had threatened to file a lawsuit against the Elkins Quarter Country Club if the staff didn't embroider his initials across every heavyweight dinner napkin hem. Rocko had heard a rumor that Willie "The Wolverine" Borai—some legendary professional football star he was convinced was his father—had donated all of the dinnerware to EQCC some time that spring. He felt entitled to an embroidery, at the least. And then, there was that thing at Sol's

. . . the rainbow carrots incident. And when he was hungover at Cloud Nine, and just had to have honey mustard . . . he might have gotten that guy fired if Gino hadn't stepped in.

Rocko was such a prick, sober or drunk. And now, he was a prick who had kissed Sosie.

Gino shook off the image of Rocko's fingers tangling in Sosie's blonde hair as he pressed his lips hard into hers. Why was it bothering him so much? Why did he care? He fiddled with the gum wrapper balled up in his hand, staring through the open truck door at Rocko's muddy, neon-yellow sneakers. "Wanna get him back?" he asked when Rocko's movement finally subsided. They stared down on his motionless body, which had come to rest with his arm trundling over an agility cone. "Remember what you said earlier? The Italian mustache thing?"

"Yeah?" She shrugged.

"Well . . . ." Gino slipped his fingers through his windblown hair. "We don't have a pen, but . . . we do have gum."

What a brilliant, evil mind you are.

Sosie's lips bowed wickedly. She climbed into the truck, carefully slinking near Rocko's dangling head. His eyes were pinched shut and his mouth was wedged open, blowing sour liquor and onion breath. Sosie dipped closer until her lips almost kissed his buzzed head. She breathed in a lungful, wound back, and spit her saliva-drenched, tropical-punch gum into his ear. She flew out of the car, barely missing Gino as she tripped over her feet and lumbered to the ground.

"I can't believe I did that!" she shrieked, bouncing up and brushing off her clothes. "Can you believe I did that?"

Gino smiled genuinely and pulled a strand of golden hair out of her eyes. Their breathing slowed together. "Actually," he whispered, "I can."

Just then, Nala popped her foxlike face up out of the truck. Her hair was matted against her cute, swollen cheeks, and her eyes were huge and startled. "Is everything okay, you guys?" Knox's head appeared over her shoulder, looking especially tired. He rubbed his fingers through a knot in Nala's back and pecked his lips against her bare shoulder. Although Sosie knew they were both total innocents, it would have looked to anyone else like they had spent the evening ripping each other's clothes off.

Sosie and Gino glanced at each other, trying not to laugh. They both figured the gummy-ear thing would be their secret. And they also thought . . . if Nala hadn't woken up, and Knox hadn't woken up, and Sosie and Gino had kept on staring at each other, breathing together, whispering about Sosie being a total, adventurous badass, then there might have been a kiss.

One lingering, beautiful, out-of-this-world kiss.

But they'd never know for sure.

Hangovers and Oolong Tea

"Shh! Let her finish!" Juliet Bigsby squealed, stuffing her garbanzo bean bagel between her teeth and stirring her fork through a bowl of acorn squash. "So, did he kiss you, or not?"

The girls doubled their chunky scarves around their necks as the breeze swept over the patio. The outdoor heating lamps powered up around them.

"Nope." Nala slurped her scorching hot, spiced mandarin tea and grinned thinking about that night. Knox Ritchie. What a *surprise* he'd been. She relived last night, remembering how adorable he was, how safe she had felt held by him, falling asleep beneath the stars, his wet lips kissing her bare shoulder. "But we came close, once or twice," Nala said, smiling cheesily at the ice cubes afloat in Sosie's cream soda.

Juliet ripped a fresh slice of mushroom and Swiss cheese pull-apart bread from the wine-cork lazy Susan, checking out Knox Ritchie and Brains Fink playing shirtless Frisbee in the grass. Weren't they cold? Juliet pouted, watching Knox wind up. Knowing that he liked Nala was worse than Chinese water torture. He was all she had ever wanted. Well, him and another slice of pull-apart bread. "But you two aren't official, right?" her voice rattled nervously.

"Who the hell cares if she's wearing his stupid pin?" Tess popped a green grape between her teeth, squashed it, and stared at Juliet. All she could think about was how Jules needed to lay off the carbs, especially if she wanted to keep her spot at their new patio table. After all, senior guys lurked around that outdoor edifice like milk-deprived stray cats, and she wouldn't be caught dead socializing with a fatty. "Knox has been in love with Nala since, like, before they met, Jules. There's a whole science behind it. Gorgeous people fall in love with other gorgeous people, and make gorgeous money, and create gorgeous babies, and live gorgeous lives in their gorgeous homes." Tess winked a glistening eye at some country club passer-by with a sexy faux-hawk. The patio was a meat market, making Tess reconsider her recently adopted veganism — which turned out to be really lame, anyway. Who knew that low-fat cream came from milk, and milk came from cows? What was she supposed to splash in her coffee?

Juliet buttered the second half of her bagel and debated where to take her first bite. "What science?" she muttered, spinning it in circles on her finger. Every half-minute, she'd steal a glance at Knox. When could he be hers? And how? Then Nala: her floppy-brim, straw hat; her perfect, China-doll posture; her strawberry lips; her slender, tanned arms glued to her little figure. No wonder Knox was in love with her. Everyone was in love with her. She was perfect.

Tess sucked on another grape, trying to make it last longer than the first. The approaching weekend would be her last opportunity to sport her slim torso before the winter season sprung into full blast, and she wanted to make sure it went out in style — without a single extra bite of food on her hips. Bye-bye bi-polar fall. Hello slouch beanies and infinity scarves!

Tess fluttered her eyelashes across the table. She loved being asked questions. It reconfirmed that she was needed. "Okay. For instance: you're a 6, Jules, so you should hook up with that Fink guy with the nerd glasses and curly quiff cut. He's a 5, but the book says you can date up or down a point."

"Book? What book? Who'd ever buy that shit?" Sosie irritably stuffed her new, JM retro-round shades into her scalp, wanting to jam her cocktail ring down Tess's blathering throat. "Don't pay any attention to that crap, Jules. You're a twenty-nine in my book. And my book's a hell a lot better than whatever-it's-called."

"There's no twenty-nine!" Tess snapped.

Then — just in time, it seemed — Knox Ritchie headed toward the brunch bunch. All the girls turned to look as he smeared sweat from his forehead with his bandaged knuckles. "Hey ladies," he breathed, looking particularly chipper, and in shape. "Everybody enjoying their first hangover?"

"Not really." Juliet furrowed her overly plucked brows, feeling woozy.

"How are you functioning?" Sosie whined, stuffing her sunglasses further up her nose to hide from the daylight.

"Just used to it," he shrugged, pinning the Frisbee under his armpit.

"Maybe next time you can, like, make us some Bloody Marys, or something. Common cure for the everyday hangover, right?

Rocko told me you're a cocktail wizard!" Juliet's nose scrunched up as she jammed one color block-patterned platform heel into the other. Since when was "wizard" an acceptable word in polite company? And why was she wearing heels when she was hungover? Oh yeah. To impress the boy she loved. Like he'd ever notice.

"This upcoming weekend I'll pick up some tomato juice, then. How's that?"

"Okay." She batted her thin, blonde eyelashes. "That would be wicked!"

Enough with the wizard references, already!

Knox yanked his marled, mock neck zip-up over his head and pulled up a chair next to Nala, who fidgeted underneath her mint-green, Aztec cardigan anxiously. She was really excited to see him. Her straw hat dipped over one smoky eye as they smiled adoringly at each other, and Juliet felt a handful of garbanzo beans doing flips inside of her gas-inflated tummy. Brains popped onto the patio just then, carrying two pink-orange shakes, and plunged into an empty seat next to Juliet.

"Want a banana?" he piped up quirkily, pulling one out of the pocket of his burnt orange prep sweater. He loved the way Juliet's curls framed her face, as if she slept in sponge rollers and didn't own a reasonable comb.

"I don't really like fruit, but thanks anyways."

"She only eats processed sugar," Tess fussed, chewing on a fingernail. "So don't take it personally."

Knox hammered his fingers on the keyboard of his cell phone and retrieved his protein shake from Brains. Coach Mike had them on a pretty intense diet: fish, raw egg, granola, brown rice, protein shakes. "So, I bet Alistair is festering with gossip about this winter dance thing." He gulped his drink slowly, snatching up the flyer pinched between the breadbasket and the lazy Susan. On it, senior cheerleading captain Elle Moody and her sexy, junior beau Nicky smiled cheesily, their cheeks smashed together like Siamese twins. "'Join us in celebration of the 24th Annual Winter Wonderland Ball: A Blizzard to Remember.' Who writes this stuff?"

"Someone told me Miss Hart's in charge of decorations again. That woman doesn't know the difference between streamers and streakers." Tess scoped out her reflection in her rose gold bracelet watch. She pinpointed a bowing wrinkle on her forehead and scrambled through her mustard-yellow shoulder tote for concealer.

"There are going to be streakers there? Count me in!" someone joked from behind. Gino Blackthorn came out of nowhere on desert boots, chewing on a granola bar. He lazily straddled a backwards chair, dangling his arms over the back. In his vintage leather bomber jacket, he looked very 1950s war hero. "Hey, Freckles," he said, looking right at Sosie. "Have you volunteered?"

"For?" She slurped her cream soda through a bamboo straw. What had taken him so long to show up? She had wanted to see him since she rolled out of bed that morning and rejected a cup of Nala's wild papaya oolong tea. She wouldn't drink that crap no matter how many shots of energy Nala had spiked it with, no matter how well it cured hangovers.

Gino's gunmetal-gray aviators slipped down his nose. "Streaking, of course."

"Uh-huh, I applied," she teased. This was what she liked most about Gino, so far; he was totally dry. Even if she couldn't read him like an open book, she got his humor. "But apparently they're only accepting stupid, skinny guys." She pouted. "So I gave them your name."

Gino smiled wide. *Cute.*

Juliet had bounced up to grab a tray of veggies and dipping sauce for the table and was scavenging for some carrots at the indoor buffet when Rocko Borai waddled through the cafeteria doors, stumbling drunkenly toward her. He had woken up to house music and tangerine mimosas, courtesy of his roommate, Chandler Vanderkrump, and had been through four drinks before he had a sudden hankering for biscuits and southern sausage gravy. "How's my little leapfrog doing this morning?" He laughed, his raccoon eyes hiding behind tortoise-colored, rubberized shades that looked like they belonged to a frat boy. Rocko was a frat boy, minus the frat.

"Fine." Juliet sprinkled some broccoli heads on her tray. "Everyone's out on the patio. Pull up a seat!"

"Yeah, I will." He peeked out the piazza windows, spying on Nala as Knox let her try out his protein shake. "Knox is such an ass, you know?" Rocko said to Juliet. "What does she see in him?"

"I don't know," Juliet shrugged, shoving a white-chocolate strawberry up her sleeve for a post brunch snack she'd likely devour in the privacy of her own atomic-tangerine, Bauhaus quilted canopy bed. There, Tess couldn't make fun of her. "Maybe she finds him charming and sensitive? Maybe his beautiful, bouncy hair gets her hot. Maybe that little, heart-shaped freckle on his neck is so cute she just wants to lick it!"

Oops. Had she said that out loud?

Rocko almost choked on the goat cheese zucchini puff he was gnawing on. His beady eyes stared down on her. "Damn, Blondie! You're in love with Ritchie, too?" he squealed, the fluffy, mantis-green muffin splurging out of his mouth like lava.

"Shut up! Shut up! Shut up!" Juliet wobbled for the patio doors with her veggie tray. The last thing she needed was for scum-of-the-earth-although-quite-gorgeous Rocko Borai to blab his blabbery mouth all over campus about her massive crush on Knox Ritchie, especially when Knox was dating the cheese of BU.

Rocko drunkenly barreled after her. "Wait just one stiletto-stomping minute there, Blondie." His eyes gleamed with mischief. Juliet chewed on a carrot nervously. "What if I told you Knox Ritchie could be all yours?"

"Yeah?" she said, her floppy blunt-cut bouncing on her shoulders. "I'm listening."

Rocko propped the patio door open, blowing his mimosa breath through his teeth. At the table, Sosie was yammering away about the time she and Nala had planned to go skinny-dipping in a pond behind their Bluffdale Prep dormitory.

"Just when I had stripped down into my little flamingo-pink panties—remember those? God. Hideous," she said. "And after I flipped in, Nala chickened out! I spent the whole next day scrubbing my swamp-green hair with a nylon bristle brush while Nala baked puff pastry chicken potpie as some kind of peace offering." She laughed.

"Just so you all know, she ate the whole thing," Nala defended friskily as Knox played with the baby hairs frizzing out of her flop hat and curling down her neck.

"Damn! Look at them," Rocko pointed one dry, bony finger at the happy couple. "That's the problem. They're like two freakin' puppy dogs, and all they want to do is pet each other."

"So . . . ." Juliet blinked, remembering the first day she saw Knox Ritchie funneling into French, his cool, dirty-blonde hair gelled away from his face, his bleached teeth grinning at the creamed julep-colored classroom walls. She had loved him since the very first moment he said, "*Bonjour.*" Her heart raced as she watched him twirl Nala's baby hairs round and round on his finger. Rocko watched beside her angrily. *Ah-ha!* He loved Nala, too—just like every other pair of pecs on campus.

"What are we supposed to do about it?" Juliet panted sadly.

"Well . . ." Rocko mumbled as he snatched up the veggie tray and trundled cockily for the patio. "I think it's time we give those two some new toys to play with. A frizzy, squeaky yellow one and a big, sexy T-bone."

Juliet shivered. "You aren't supposed to give T-bones to dogs. They can splinter in the digestive tract."

Rocko leaned heavily against the door, glowering back at Juliet's haze of blonde curls. "Don't think I know that, Blondie? It's called a metaphor. Look it up."

Juliet observed as Rocko went on to snag a seat from a gang of anorexic redheads and plop down next to Nala. "I brought veggies!" He passed the plate off, murmuring into her ear, "I bet you can understand my advocacy for healthy living. You look like you take care of yourself."

Says the boy hammered off of . . . what was that smell? Tangerine mimosas?

Juliet watched Rocko's effortless flirting. He acted like Knox was nothing more than a stupid little fly with sturdy butt muscles. And even though she was skeptical of Rocko's strategies, she was sick of not getting what she wanted. Tess was constantly bullying her to order salad and sorbet instead of fried calamari and island rum cake, Milly had claimed the extra dormitory closet space for her science fiction book collection rather than allowing space for Juliet's eczema lotions and detangling spray, and Nala had snatched up Knox Ritchie like rabbit eye blueberries before Juliet could scream "cobbler!" For once, she wanted to fight, especially if it meant that Knox Ritchie would soon be tweaking her unruly whorls of baby hair in public.

She skipped over to the patio table and lunged into her seat, feeling suddenly alive. It wouldn't be long before she'd be bragging to her girlfriends about her spit-swap with Knox Ritchie in the bed of his truck. She giggled as Nala forked a few celery sticks onto her plate, unable to stand the excitement of her and Rocko's master plan. Now, all she needed to know was . . . what was the plan, again?

I'm Happy if You're Happy

Juliet Bigsby wisped yellow, wiry frizz from her eye and licked the dribbling *tres leches* gelato from her waffle cone. Her gladiator sandals dangled from the cafeteria stoop as she spied on Knox Ritchie, slumped aboard a far-distant dock. His skin radiated gold as the sun spilled down the pine-strewn mountaintops. His muscles flexed as he determinedly scrubbed the blade of his practice oar with an abrasive. His eyes were calm, like the stillness of the lake. Juliet took a deep breath and jammed her scoop of gelato into the stone before hopping to her feet. Rocko's voice echoed in her head. "It's time we give those two

231

some new toys to play with," he had suggested. It was time for Knox and Nala to aim their disgusting, lovesick eyes elsewhere.

She reeled closer to Knox, staring from behind her gold-rimmed owl shades as sweat frothed his bare chest. *He must be working on his tan,* she admired longingly, and suddenly imagined him serving her a spicy margarita from their bungalow in St. Thomas, their skin as crisp as their beachside tortilla chips. Finally, her sandals grasped the dock and there she was, peering down at him, bizarrely quiet.

Knox seemed focused as his arms juddered over the paddle. "Hey," her voice trilled. He jumped at the sound and glanced up at her, hands still gripping his oar. All he could see was her yellow hair beaming in the sunset, below which he found a ketchup stain splattered on her khaki skirt. His smile grew.

"Hey, Jules. Didn't see you there."

"Sorry." She giggled, thumping closer. She slumped down to sit beside him and massaged her sticky, gelato fingers in her lap as he set the oar to the wood of the dock, and relaxed. "Mind if I join you? I never go to class on Mondays."

"Sure," he said, kicking his legs out. "I could use a break, anyway."

Juliet nodded as Knox's eyes wriggled over the lake. She wished that he would look at her. Just for a second. The view from the dock was spectacular, though, so she could understand why he'd prefer to look out. Calm, green water. Big, fluffy clouds hanging low. Green willows flowing beyond the property. Perhaps this could be their new tradition . . . Mondays at the lakefront. Maybe they were destined to fall in love like this: sunsets and oar buffing.

The evening air slightly darkened the space between them as Knox grabbed his crew neck and slid it over his head. The sky was deep orange, now. Sunset would be over soon. "So, why are you skipping your late class? Does Brains send embarrassing assortments of roses on Mondays, or something?"

"No." She laughed shyly, admiring how the remaining daylight speckled Knox's long eyelashes. "Brains is just a friend."

Knox's hands slipped behind him and he used his palms to prop himself up. Today was the first day he hadn't texted Nala. He was testing her, seeing how much she liked him. Something Coach suggested. It was beginning to drive him crazy, all that waiting. Every three minutes, his fingers would scramble for his cell to check for a text. When her name was tragically invisible, he'd cram it down between the old cigarette and the pack of nicotine gum in his pocket.

He leaned over and pressed his fingers through the cool, green ripples of the lake. "Just a friend?" he asked Juliet. "Does he know that?"

"Obviously not," she said, flipping her hair down her back to cover her neck, which was red and clammy with eczema. "He's just not my type."

"Really?" Knox's voice cracked as his fingers slipped from the water. Even though Juliet wasn't Nala, she was great company. Nice. Easy going. His mind was no longer disarrayed by images of Nala's thick, brown hair cast across his chest and her perfect, tan legs kicking the air at Second Base. Now, she was just someone he'd like to hear from. "Aww, come on! The guy's a catch! I mean . . . he's a little on the nerdy side, but it's just because he was born with an encyclopedia for a brain. And someday, that encyclopedia is going to make him and his wife seriously, seriously rich."

"I don't care if his brain is made out of hundreds of little rocket scientists! I'm not attracted to him," she said matter-of-factly. Why was Knox pestering her about Brains, anyway? Couldn't they just sit, enjoy the view, forget Nala, forget Brains, and be?

Juliet's stomach churned as Knox's hand slipped into his pant pocket and yanked loose a cell phone. What did he keep looking at that for?

"So if you aren't attracted to intelligence or money," Knox said when his eyes fixed on her bright, blue gaze, "what *are* you attracted to?"

What was she attracted to? Wasn't it obvious? She swallowed the urge to shout "you" in his face. It would probably end badly if she did. Karma, and all. An avalanche would like, flood down the hillsides of the Rocky Pines ski resort, and sweep them both away. Then he'd really be out of reach. "Hmm . . . well . . . ." She took a breath and held it. There Knox was next to her, the two of them alone, breathing in the autumn air as it flounced over the lake. His jaw gnashed as the breeze picked up. His muscles flexed. He was all she had ever wanted. Didn't he know that? Did he maybe — deep in the dungeons of his soul — want her back?

"Want me to be perfectly honest?" she asked hesitantly.

"Honesty is the best policy, Jules," he said, his eyebrows wrinkling with the absurdity of the question. "I'll keep your secret, sweetheart," he promised.

Sweetheart. Jules. Surely he wanted her.

"Okay." Juliet's heart walloped loudly in her big, perky chest. Maybe if she let Knox know how she felt — how he was her type down to his very last chin hair — he would start to see her differently. Maybe he would love her, then. "I like short hair," she started. "And blue eyes. I like a guy who's sensitive, but manly. And strong, but funny. I want someone who's honest, but can . . . keep a secret," she confessed. Her eyes glowed with hopefulness. "I don't know, Knox. I mean . . . you're my type."

Knox blinked blankly back at her. "Me? Really?" His lips twitched into a smile. All of that hair gel, all of those chin-ups, all of the time he spent shaving his barely-there scruff was really paying off. He knew some of the other girls noticed, too — but did

Nala? His smile faded. "That's cool, Jules. No girl's ever been so honest with me before. I like that about you," he said. "You just call it like it is." He glanced back at Juliet, wishing that Nala's bleached smile would appear in place of hers. "You're a really good friend," he said. His fingers grasped her neck and massaged her briefly. She ripped away, worried about her rash, and wondered if he had noticed the rough flakes of her skin. *Friend?* Why did she have to be that awkward girl with the rash and the crush? Why couldn't—just for once—she be healthy, and pretty, and normal?

Juliet felt sick to her stomach as Knox's voice echoed in her skull. He'd called her a good friend. He might as well have asked her the size of her penis, that's how obviously unattractive she was to him. *Friend. Friend. Friend.* She couldn't seem to tune out the memory of the word. The lake water suddenly reeked of swamp and septic fish. The sunlight scorched her eyelids. The wood dock splintered her milk-white ass. Was that all that Knox thought of her? Just some androgynous chum who calls it like she sees it? Just a good, honest *friend*?

She painfully stared at Knox's smile. He didn't seem to realize how devastating it was to hear those words. He was stupidly and luckily clueless. "So, what's your type?" she managed, fighting off her urge to puke all over his baby-blue yachting loafers.

"I don't discriminate, Jules. I think all women are beautiful," he said, his voice stifled with doubt. "But I guess if I had to say, I'd just give you a name."

Juliet pulled on a thick, yellow lock of hair and watched him as he thought about someone else. He looked as pitiful and sad as she felt. "Let me guess . . . Nala?"

He smiled, watching the whitecaps of the lake splash against a nearby berth. For a minute, basking in Juliet's admiration, he had almost forgotten about Nala. But Juliet's question had sucked him back toward Nala like a moth to a flame.

"Does she talk about me?" Knox asked Juliet. Her pale eyes narrowed on him sadly. She wasn't just looking at Knox Ritchie: rowing captain, QB, impeccably chiseled human. She was staring into the eyes of someone who had it bad.

"God, listen to me. I should just shut up." Knox grunted, scrubbing at his oar again. Juliet watched and realized for the first time — there on the dock, surrounded by the must of autumn leaves and smooth pinewood — that he would never be hers.

She pinched her eyes together, allowing the tears to dissolve away, praying that when she opened them she would no longer want Knox except as a friend. Her heart pounded in her ears. When his golden hair finally pulled into view, she had to fight the urge to throw her arms around him, hug him, feel his breath on her skin. The stress of it all made her sick. Her crush had somehow morphed into cataclysmic adoration while her eyes were closed.

"To be honest," Juliet started, unsure what to say next. Knox's expression weakened at the sound of her voice. In that second, she knew what Rocko would demand of her. *Just make something up. He'll get over her eventually, and when he does, there you'll be to pick up the pieces.* But she couldn't do that. She couldn't stand to hurt Knox. She just wanted him to be happy. "She'd be crazy not to like you," Juliet said.

And suddenly, Knox was smiling. He was staring at Juliet as if he was seeing her for the first time. His teeth flashed her a glowing, snow-white grin. Was he finally realizing that she was the one he wanted all along? Did he finally see her for the beautifully tragic — but beautiful, nonetheless — woman that she really was? She felt her stomach whip wildly beneath her high-waisted khaki skirt. Was this it? Was he about to confess his love for her?

Then, Knox's eyes slipped away. His hand appeared with a cell clasped firmly beneath trimmed fingernails. He mumbled something quietly to himself, grinning stupidly. "Sorry, Jules," he said, hopping to his feet. "It's Nala. I gotta run." He grabbed his rowing oar and loped down the dock, his sandy hair bobbing wildly on his head. Just before his loafers caught the grass, he turned to face Juliet, his skin perfectly radiant in the tint of purple sky. "Looks like she does think about me after all," he said.

Well good, Juliet thought as he navigated the flurry of khaki pants sprawled about the shore. Strangely, she was a little happy as the flash of Knox's blinding smile balanced in her mind. *I'm happy if you're happy,* she thought, aching.

Although happiness used to feel a lot less like heartbreak, before boys were involved . . . .

I Know What I Want

Nala Middleton arrived at Graham's door wearing an abstracted floral button-up blouse, high-waist, acid-wash denims, and a fishbone collar necklace. The plastic corner of a DVD case poked from her envelope clutch. She had been waiting for alone time with Graham since the football game, and watching him in class that morning was true torture. Truthfully, she still had a little crush on him. Minor. Innocent. Knox was in the picture now more than ever, and Graham was just her teacher. Her friend. Regardless, all she had wanted to do all day was drink hot chocolate with Graham and talk about

Estelle Hart, or 1970s blockbusters, or that cute, old guy from the concession stand who pegged them as a six-month success story. That's what friends did, right? Talk?

Graham's seven p.m. class poured out the classroom doors just as Nala approached, stuffing her thick, unctuous locks behind her shoulders. She had spent two hours getting ready, and wasn't about to arrive with lip gloss in her hair. Getting ready for herself, not for Graham.

Of course not.

"See you guys back at Marlborough!" Rocko Borai waved to Chandler Vanderkrump and Max Umminger before he turned to see a beautiful, dolled-up someone standing at the top of the steps, glowing. He'd know that tight, little figure anywhere. "Hey sweetheart," his voice rang as he marched up to Nala proudly, chest inflated. "Aren't you a vision in blue!"

"Thanks," she said, stroking her messy sock bun. There was always something unnerving about running into Rocko Borai, as though he was always undressing her with one eye. "So, I heard about you and Sosie," Nala said. "Sorry it didn't work out."

"Nah, it's all right. The love gods must have something else in store for me." *Something brunette.* He shrugged inside of his waxed cotton jacket, trying to keep warm. He wasn't completely used to the winter breeze just yet. He especially missed the little beach hotties in spaghetti straps and booty shorts who had once roamed the courtyard, sipping raspberry lemonade in the shade and snaking across the grass in massage trains of glowing, sunkissed skin. At least Nala had skipped out on the long johns and was sporting her very trendy, fringe shorts that evening. Cute, little goose bumps budded down her legs.

"So, I thought you'd be interested to know Professor L kicked Henry Woods out of class *officially.*" Rocko fingered the cigarette in his coat pocket, wondering if she'd mind if he lit up right there. Maybe she'd find it sexy, in a biker and bomber jacket sort of way.

"Um . . . Henry who?"

"That ass-clown who groped you last week!" he said. Rocko's tongue grated the roof of his mouth. Man, he really needed a little smoke. "I would have done something about it myself, you know, but I haven't seen him around campus."

"Sheesh." She wrapped her arms around her shoulders, feeling woozy. The butt-grabbing incident had been embarrassing, sure, but she had nearly forgotten about it. Henry Whatever-His-Name-Was probably hadn't, though, now that he had been kicked out of class.

"Yeah, Leatherwood had him benched and everything. It's a big deal in the locker room. People were throwing shit. It was bad." They both peeked through the classroom window, where Graham was weaseling away behind his desk. He filed through a mess of papers, staring pensively through his full-rimmed, hipster glasses. "Look, don't even worry about it. Henry can't even bench above 150. Most of the guys were happy to see him go."

"Yeah?" She licked the inside of her lip. What was benching, and how was it different from being benched? Would the entire athletics department despise her for getting one of their very own meathead jocks kicked off the team? She clutched at the DVD in her bag and crept toward the classroom. "Well, I probably should get inside." She wrapped her arms around Rocko's neck and hugged him loosely, taking in a whiff of his crisp, jasmine cologne. Smelt like what she imagined a strip club to smell like.

"Yeah. Yeah. Go do your overachiever thing." He felt her slip through his fingers, her skin like butter. "See you around, Miss Na-la."

"See ya!"

Nala quietly opened the classroom door and poked her head inside. Graham was still sitting with his cherry-red fountain pen and paper mound, listening to some indie record blare into his noise-canceling headphones. He flicked a brown hair out of his face and marked another X on a paper. Nala could have pulled up a chair and just watched him scribble away. He had a handsome, rugged face like the old movie stars — he made every boy in her class look like a snub-nosed monkey. Well, everyone but Knox . . . but she was a little biased.

She skimmed along the wall, watching him closely. He was just so damn perfect . . . in a friend sort of way. And then, suddenly, she felt something stab her in the leg.

"OUCH-CH-IEEE!"

Graham ripped his headphones out of his ears, his eyes bouncing between Nala's petrified face and the pencil sharpener dangling slackly from the wall, blood sprinkled on it's sharp edge.

"Nala! What happened, sweetheart?" He swerved around his desk, tripping on a table leg in his rush to help her.

"Ummm . . . ." She gulped. The puncture wound wasn't *that* deep, but as blood dripped onto the floor, she started to feel dizzy, leaving zero time for her to luxuriate in the fact that Professor Sexypants had just called her "sweetheart."

"I didn't even see that . . . thingy . . . sticking there . . . in the wall. I'm really, really, reeeaaally sorry." Nala slumped against the wall, and Graham reached out his arms to catch her.

"No, I'm the one who should be apologizing. That thing's ancient. It's been here since before I was a student. I'm not even sure it works, and apparently it's a safety hazard," he said. "Here, let's get you cleaned up. Put your arms around me." He snatched up her tiny limbs, Nala wrapping her arms around his neck like a boa. Her nose nuzzled into his chin, heart swelling at the sight of her own hair trundling down his oatmeal-colored, crew neck sweater. The way he had demanded, "Put your arms around me" made her seriously dizzy. *Whatever you say, Mr. L.* He sat her on his desk and searched a drawer for the first-aid kit.

"So, I never pegged you as the clumsy type," he joked, rustling around inside the drawer. He returned with some ointment and a few bandages. "This may sting a little."

Graham squirted the ointment over her gash, and Nala winced. It felt like a thousand ants were gnawing on her like she was a piece of shriveled up fruitcake; and Nala *hated* fruitcake. Her eyes watered up as she fanned her hand spastically through the air. "You're right! It does! It really burns!"

"Here, let me." Graham leveled down and blew his warm breath over the goo. His hand grazed her thigh accidentally, and she nearly toppled over from the rush of excitement that tore through her. Just a friend. Just a friend. Just a friend. His eyes peeked up at her, pleading: I'll take care of you forever. Just a friend. Just a friend. Just a friend.

"Better?" he asked instead.

"Thanks. Yeah. Better."

Graham stuffed the first-aid kit back inside of his drawer, assuming he wouldn't see it again until some show-off in second period tried to light his hand on fire. He peeked back at Nala, who picked the withered-up pencil shavings off of her Chelsea boots and flicked them onto the floor.

"So — only if you're feeling okay — I was thinking . . . we should probably watch another movie. Get you a little more experience under your belt. I brought that one I was telling you about."

"Actually," Nala looked up from her wound. "I have a surprise for you."

"Yeah?"

She limped to her envelope clutch and snatched the DVD case out of it. "The guy at the store told me it's a classic." She shrugged, and her clunky, triangle cuff bracelet slid over her wrist as she shoved the movie forward. "When I read about it, it just sounded so much like you." Graham glanced down at the case, appearing slightly mystified and a little amazed. "Uh-oh. You've already seen it, haven't you?"

"No. I mean . . . yes, I've seen it, but . . . ." His hands wrestled over his desk until he grabbed something. A box. A DVD case. It was his copy of the same movie. He flashed it toward her. "Amazing, right? That we'd think of the same thing?" His body slipped closer, clanking the cases together like bread slices. "So . . . who's are we gonna watch?"

As the previews flashed on screen and the classroom lights flickered off, Nala lay flat on the floor, pinching her bandage beneath one hand and supporting her head with the other. Graham's body fell near. He smelled clean and piney, like soap and woodland. Extremely manly and . . . just a friend. Just a friend.

Knox Ritchie popped into mind, suddenly, and Nala wondered how she'd bring the partners thing up to Graham. Truthfully, she wasn't even sure if she wanted that, anymore. It had seemed a great idea after a few swallows of stupid sauce, and every time she was with Knox, she liked him more and more. She knew he'd always take care of her. If he married her, he'd buy her a sporty car she could drive through the city, and make sure she had a country club membership so she and Sosie could die as silver-headed, appletini drinking tennis players who shared mushroom brie soup and peppered salmon Monday through Friday at their very exclusive seniors table overlooking the golf course. He'd massage her feet when she was having a really bad menstrual cycle. He'd even buy her tampons, she bet . . . or send someone else to buy her tampons. Their butler Vladimir, probably. Knox was definitely a *safe* bet, and soooo sweet. But every time she was with Graham, the world seemed to make a little more sense. Or perhaps, she felt that they made sense together, which in reality made the world seem a little less sensible. Especially since he was supposed to be *just a friend, just a friend*. Whatever. Either way, she wasn't sure she wanted to settle down with Knox. She was only halfway through her first semester at Blairstown. She had only been on two dates, though the last one was more of a party than anything. And isn't that what Knox would assume if they became partners? Pledged to each other for life?

Graham plopped down next to her with a blanket, which he lobbed over her bare legs. "Thanks," she whispered as he slipped beneath it, too. Sharing a blanket with Graham made her feel breathless, even though he was still an arm's length away. "So, did you figure out that Miss Hart thing?"

"Yeah." Graham flicked through the screen of his cellphone to silence the ringer, wondering when it would vibrate *again*. "Actually . . . I ended it, which she didn't like. And, she sort of hasn't stopped texting me since." He bowed his arms behind his neck and allowed the DVD menu screen to play over and over, blaring some heroic theme song as an explosion overturned a car and a man's face faded through the flames.

Nala squirmed, pulling the blanket up to her chin. "Aren't you relieved?"

"I am." He nodded. "And I'm not."

I am, and I'm not? What did that mean, exactly? Estelle Hart was a bleak, overly dramatic, elitist-wannabe with fake hand-bags and a bad haircut. All that she and Graham had in common were their teaching certificates and hopefully, but not necessarily, toothpaste. What was there to be *unrelieved* about?

Nala blinked, trying to act unbothered. "So, you maybe still like her?"

"No," he shook his hair out of his face. "It's never been about that. I just thought . . . we're just two people who are stuck here for the next ten years, and I figured we both could use a friend." He cleared his throat, wishing he had a beer. "But I guess that wasn't enough. I don't know where she expected all this to go." He clasped his phone tight as it buzzed in his pocket. "Now I'm the asshole who led her on, I guess," he said.

He looked at the new text message flashing on his screen.

Been going thru our old messages. U asked me 2 save u a seat @ staff meeting. Thought we were happy. Don't understand. Plz txt back, Hon. Xo, Estelle

Graham shoved his phone back into his pocket, wishing he could board some dinky fishing boat and drift off the coast and far away to Golden Mahseer territory, where cell phone range was scarce and Estelle was extinct. Leave it up to her to concoct some wild fantasy about a diminutive staff-meeting text. No, by "save me a seat" he had not meant, "let's elope and get married." He peeked over at Nala. Her massive, golden eyes were fastened on him. Glued. He may have been screwed for the next ten years, but Nala didn't make him feel like a lost cause. She was his glimmer of hope.

Graham propped up on his elbow. "I feel bad, but I just—I just know what I want. Or, whom I want, I guess."

Nala curled into a ball so that her chin nearly rested on her knees. They were like two campers trapped in a tent in the Carolina Hemlocks, sharing a blanket and talking about their pasts to stay awake through the storm filling up South Toe River.

"I'm jealous, you know," Nala piped up, sucking the lip balm off her lips. If anything were to happen—if Graham randomly got the desire to kiss her—the last thing she wanted was a sticky mouth. She rolled onto her hip, staring wistfully up at him. Who was she kidding thinking they could just be friends? Their pull to each other was chemical. "I wish I knew what I wanted the way you know what you want."

"You will," he promised her truly. "Life's too short, you know? Gotta go after what you want. No matter what the sacrifice . . . ."

The Reason

Since the movie ended, Nala and Graham had spent an hour and a half splurging on Milk Duds and white cheddar popcorn and talking about Graham's life.

"Did you have those semi-rimless glasses, too?"

"Oh yeah." Graham popped another Milk Dud and rolled onto his back. The ceiling was ablaze with the reflection of koi pond waves spattering through the back windows, painting the room in a pretty blue. Bleu de France, blue. Honestly, Graham felt like he was in France, at some teaching convention in a fussy, Old World Parisian hotel. And Nala was some beautiful, fearless tourist he had met in a medieval hillside town scoping out the underground shopping precinct for trés chic, vintage scarves and potted honey. And even though Graham was a simple guy, he got excited just thinking about their little sabbatical across the pond.

"And I had acne, and braces, and . . . god, this is the worst. I had a bowl cut until I was twelve."

"Twelve!" Nala squealed, kicking her shoes in the air as she cackled. She wasn't even positive what a bowl cut looked like, but it sounded disastrous. "Well, everyone goes through an awkward phase."

"Awkward phase? Nala, I belonged to the Tatakau Manga Club."

"Tatakau?"

"It's means," he paused embarrassedly, "to fight, or go to battle in Japanese. Don't ask."

Nala ripped into the bag of popcorn, chasing Graham with her eyes. Tatakau Manga Club, or not, he had grown up to be quite a sight. His beautifully tumbled hair, his chiseled face, his dreamy, curling lips could have been drawn for a comic. He was like the rugged, heartthrob intelligence officer from one of those action-packed thrillers Nala had heard about. Nerds make the best heroes, apparently. Just like Clark Kent.

Was she his kryptonite?

Graham shoved his fingers into his scalp, his eyes following the reflected trail of koi pond water dancing on the ceiling. "If it's worth anything, by high school I had shaved my head and joined the football team."

Nala giggled. She didn't care about buzzed hair or football teams — if she did, she'd be dating Rocko. She couldn't stop thinking about one thing in particular. The same thing that had been driving her crazy since the first moment she saw him.

"Graham?" Her voice cracked as she joggled the fringe on her denim shorts. "Can I ask you something?"

"Sure. Whatever you want."

The room turned mind-numbingly still, crisp static imploding in her ears. Nala held her breath, wishing she had never so idiotically requested permission to speak. The words just kind of spilled out of her, and before she knew it . . . silence. Graham's eyes stared in unusual calmness. Nala could have told him that she killed some yuppie cheerleader who was getting on her nerves in French, and needed help disposing of the body, and he'd probably reply calmly, "Don't worry, we'll figure this thing out together."

You grab the arms, I'll grab the legs.

Nala blotted her lips with her finger and breathed noisily. "Why'd you never get married?" She blinked up at him, hoping to look a little less pestering and a little more doe-eyed. Sweet. Curious. "Sorry if I'm meddling. You're just a really great guy . . . the last guy on the planet I'd ever expect to be stuck here . . . anime club, or not."

Graham chuckled, tracing the box screen on his cellphone over and over again with his fingertip. It had been hours since the last text. Perhaps Estelle had gotten smashed off of white wine spritzers and passed out on her newly imported Milanese chocolate sofa . . . again. Unfortunately for her, puke wasn't the easiest thing to scrub off of leather, but if anyone could brew up a fantastic furniture polish, it would be the same woman who had developed her own cherry veneer acrylic for nineteenth century Edwardian vanities, just in case someone forgot to use a coaster.

Graham could feel Nala observing, demanding some kind of an answer.

"Why'd I never get married?" he repeated warily, as if he'd always known that by twenty-three he'd be sitting in some stuffy, supercilious classroom with vintage medallions and African iroko wood-refurbished tabletops, rambling about relationships to his beautiful, barely-legal student assistant. He propped up and took a drink from his water bottle, stalling. "I almost did get married once," he finally said.

Nala sat up, tugging at the blanket. "Really? Who to?"

Graham grabbed some more Milk Duds. "Her name was Jayda." The water bottle dangled totteringly in Graham's grip as he considered taking another drink. He wished it were whiskey or bourbon or something strong to take the edge off. Talking about his ex was never easy. "It's kind of a funny story. Jayda was dating my roommate, who dumped her for this Australian girl named Carly or Cali . . . someone on the dance team."

Nala nodded, listening. It had only been two-and-a-half months since Graham Leatherwood strolled into the classroom with his remarkably wide smile and windblown hair, scribbling chicken scratch across the chalkboard and clapping his hands against his steam-pressed slacks like a slob. Only, he wasn't just a slob. He was the hottest guy she had ever laid her eyes on. Sloppy and hot, but more than that . . . . A guy with a past. A guy who had been in love before. There was a girl somewhere in the world, New York or L.A. or London, who at one point had heard him say it out loud. *I love you. I love you more than anything.* Nala's bones sank inside her chest. What would it feel like to watch him say it? To hear his voice put it together? *I love you.* She wanted it so badly, she felt like she could die.

"So, how'd you and Jayda become *a thing*?" she pressed.

"Well . . . honestly?"

Nala nodded.

"Okay." Graham swallowed. "I had been into her for a while. Everyone was. She was *that* girl. The same way you're that girl, now." He grinned teasingly. "Just what I hear," he shrugged.

Nala's smile beamed through the blackness. She didn't so much care about what the boys in the locker room were saying. All she cared about was what Graham was saying . . . or thinking.

She started once again to pick at the loose string on her shorts. Graham watched, but his mind was somewhere else. "I'll tell you about Jayda, but I just . . . I don't want you to judge the person I used to be."

"I would never judge you." Her fingers slipped away and clapped firmly in her lap. "Just so you know."

"I know. Thanks."

At some point, the blanket had crumpled across their ankles, and Nala and Graham were both thumped against the desk like a couple of curbside loiterers waiting for an ice-cream truck to roll around the corner. Someone had tampered with the thermostat, and the temperature was pressing 80 degrees. Graham swiped his sweat-glistening forehead with his sleeves, and popped up to mess with the air-conditioning until something croaked and another thing gurgled, and wafts of cool air began to tendril out of the ceiling vents.

"Looking back on it, I think it was a confidence thing. You know. She thought she was God's gift, and so everyone else sort of nodded their heads and agreed. In the first week of school, she turned down some senior on the lacrosse team. After that, everyone knew her name." Graham plopped down again with slicked back hair and gorgeous, tan skin sparkling with sweat. It looked like he had just gotten back from some jet-ski jungle excursion through the mangroves of Cancun. All that was missing was a thick, life vest tan-line.

"Sophomore year, after Turk moved out of the dorms—"

"Was that your roommate?"

"Yeah. Turk." He nodded. "So he moved out, and Jayda showed up at my door asking about a necklace she had left there. Silver. Expensive. Some kind of designer brand, I think. Went on and on . . . . Anyways, I'm pretty sure the whole thing was a trap. I mean, she was wearing a bikini, and I was an eighteen-year-old boy. She knew exactly what she was doing."

"So, you asked her out?" Nala asked.

"Yeah," he breathed slowly, trying to relax. Thinking about Jayda always made him jumpy. "We dated for three years. Can you believe that? Three years. I never dated anyone before her. Never dated anyone after her. Because—you know—I thought she was *it* for me. We had planned this ridiculous life together: I'd play football and she'd act, or model, or just lie around and play tennis with her friends, drink vodka tonics, tan . . . ."

Nala only heard three years before she tuned the rest out. Three years was like, a lifetime. "It sounds like you two really loved each other," she said, her face lit with jealousy.

"Well, yeah. I loved her. She was perfect."

Nala swallowed harshly. Hearing Graham describe another girl as perfect was more terrible than tacky, two-dollar stick-on nails grating against a chalkboard. Or fat, sweaty guys lecturing her on bone density and proper nutrition. Pure torture.

"So, what happened?" she finally asked, once the horrific vision of sumo-wrestlers shoving syrupy pancakes down her throat drifted away.

Graham took another drink of water and ping-ponged his eyes between the screen in the back of the room and the glistening, plastic bottle clung to his fist. "I caught her and Turk back together," he said. "Ironic, huh? Probably deserved it."

Nala grabbed her arms and frowned. Ironic? More like depressing. No wonder Graham never got married. Jayda had ripped his heart out and stomped all over it with her big, clunky stilettos. At least she seemed like the type of girl to strut around on stilettos.

"You must really hate her." Nala inched closer, hating the glumness in Graham's pale eyes.

"Actually . . ." Graham said, his hand slipping across the cool floor until their pinkies were almost touching . . . or slightly touching, she couldn't tell. He cleared his throat. "I never hated her.

Maybe I came close once," he shrugged. "Maybe twice. Up until August, I was thinking about her every day. And then, slowly, I just . . . stopped. I don't miss her anymore. I don't even think about her, really. There are days when something reminds me about a trip we took, or a dance we went to. Something happy. But even those days, I'm strangely unaffected. And I'm not sure when it happened, or how, but . . . glad it did."

Graham cleared his throat and gobbled down the rest of his water. All of the green in his round, hazel eyes faded as he yawned and threw himself back into the desk. His fingers grated the scruff of his tattered beard. "God, we're like little kids. Sitting on the floor, lights out, talking."

Nala collapsed next to him. If the night never ended, she'd be happy. "We're friends, Graham. Right? Can I say that? Friends."

"Yeah. You can say that." Graham nodded so that his full, beachy hair slid along the table. His mind was fumbling through the BU Instructor's Manual that he had somewhat memorized during training as he glared at Nala's manicured cuticle beds, which were—by then—barely intertwined with his. He was breaking some rule, somewhere, but he didn't really care. All along he had known what had changed since August . . . why he had stopped thinking about Jayda. Nala was it. The reason.

Graham kept his fingers perfectly still between Nala's, which was exactly where he wanted them. "I'm really glad you took the job," he said, clenching her fingers in his hands.

Nala stared down into their clasped hands, nerves rumbled beneath her pores. "So am I."

Pretty Eyes

"**D**o you mind? You're drooling all over on my bag!" Sosie Hinkhouse ripped her purse out from underneath Gino Blackthorn's humongous head and brushed it off with her sleeve. *There goes my chambray button-up*, she thought. She glanced down at the wicker basket that held her assignment. Crooked lips carved on a plump, spoiling watermelon glowered up at her. "So, we're supposed to kiss this thing, I guess. Want to go first?"

Gino squinted his dark, brown eyes. Making out with fruit wasn't exactly high up on his to-do list. Kissing class was a complete waste of time—time he could be spending on barbell deadlifts, floor wipers, single-arm clean-and-presses, or swiss-ball wall squats. But he was stuck here, instead, with a stupid watermelon that mocked him with its lumpy head. "Knock yourself out, Freckles. Wake me up when the bell rings." He yawned and cowered down limply on the cool wood table.

"Yeah, right!" Sosie shrieked, jamming her knuckles into his arm. "If I'm going to swap juice with the stupid freaking clown-fruit, you're going to, too!"

Gino rubbed his arm, blinking his eyes open. Sosie was a skinny little blonde girl, but she could punch like a skinny little blonde girl on steroids. "Fine. Have it your way." He snatched up the watermelon and began to jab it with his pencil and scrape away the rind. He wasn't going to make out with the watermelon, but he'd be happy to scribble all over it. "So . . . you talk to Rocko yet?"

"Rocko?" her voice cracked. She wondered if Rocko had ever noticed the huge clump of chewed bubblegum smudged in his ear-wax. "Other than when he showed up at brunch bunch? Nope," she shrugged, her eyes fumbling down the assignment. "Trying to get over my obvious daddy issues so I can stop liking assholes."

"Don't you have to meet your dad before you can have daddy issues?"

Sosie snarled, underlining a few words on her paper. "Fine! I'm mentally disturbed, regardless. Happy?"

Gino's neck stiffened beneath his collar. "No more assholes. Good," he said, nodding. "Decide on a new type yet?"

"Hmm . . . ." Sosie's hands fidgeted along the seams of her skirt. New type? "Still accepting résumés," she piped.

Gino winced, cocking a thick, black eyebrow at her. "I'll spread the word."

Sosie jumped as a tap fell on her shoulder. Behind her stood Kiki Weames in floral, flared-leg, pleated slacks and an aqua-hued felt hat that dipped over her un-plucked eyebrows. She had brown, ochre-colored lip stain smudged on her thin, cracked lips and ghost-white foundation caked in clumps . . . everywhere. "Want to sign my petition?" she wheezed. "Together, we can promote an all-natural organic hemp clothing line to replace these mass-produced, dictatorial zombie uniforms! I mean . . . if we have to abide by a uniform dress code, we should at least be able to rot in an eco-friendly fashion, right?" She breathed deep and exhaled hookah breath as she twisted the fringe of her tunic between her fingers. "It's easy. All you gotta do is sign your name on the dotted line. Free rice cakes for whoever signs!"

Sosie stared blankly up at her. Had Kiki honestly tried to bribe her with a rice cake? *Gross!*

"No thanks. I'm really digging *this* uniform, *man*." Sosie kicked out her belted wedge booties, flaunting her extra-stiff, twice-hemmed khaki skirt. "And I also dig steak. And leather. *And* mink coats. And I really, really, really hate rice cakes, so count me out of all future endeavors. Rainforest stuff too."

Kiki frowned as she scratched behind her ear. Sosie had been wound pretty tightly ever since they transferred to BU. She used to sign all of Kiki's petitions, but now, she rolled her eyes at every wildlife-reserve flier posted around campus. *Sosie could really use an all-natural anti-anxiety juice cleanse*, Kiki found herself thinking. "Screw you, Sosie!" Kiki grunted, moving on to Edward Pote. The stench of her mildewed scarf lingered in her path. Sosie watched as Edward signed the petition, just to get Kiki to leave him and his ballpoint-pen action figures in peace. Coward.

Gino was still scraping the skin off of the watermelon, trying to appear distracted. "Can you believe she just said that?" Sosie whined. "Screw me? Seriously? Screw her! I mean, who says that anymore? It stopped making since in 2003."

Gino rubbed his hands across the watermelon, and tilted his head to get a look at his masterpiece from a new angle. Damn, he was bored. "Well, you were a little rude . . . ."

Rude? "That granola-head was the one threatening me with rice cakes if I didn't sign her stupid petition."

"No. That 'granola-head' was offering to buy you lunch." Gino caught a glimpse of Kiki whittling the words "Organic or Panic" into her desk with a nail clipper. "Don't get me wrong—I think she's freaking weird, and not eating meat is just . . . insane, but she was just protecting what she believes in," he said. "Weren't you ever passionate about something, Freckles?"

Passionate? Coming from the guy who sleeps eighteen hours a day? Sosie stuffed her thin, yellow bangs behind her ears. "Spare me the sentimental pep-talk, Blackthorn. I have a diary; I've been collecting birthday cards since I was three; I freaking rescued a chipmunk that was run-over by a Moped, once. It died a few weeks later, but that's beside the point." She jabbed her finger into the desk. "Trust me—the word 'fanatical' is practically tatted across my forehead. Some have compared me to that fat guy who hot-dog gobbled himself to death. I *bleed* passion-fruit juice, okay? I'm freaking passionate!"

"Okay . . . okay . . . ." Gino chuckled, slamming his pencil onto the table. "You're passionate. Whatever."

"What are you so passionate about, anyways?" Sosie demanded. "Bacon doesn't count."

"No bacon?" He smirked. "Fine. No bacon." Gino's body just slightly budged. "I can't tell you what I'm passionate about, Freckles," he said, round and serious eyes burning holes in Sosie's skin. "But I can show you."

Sosie nodded, stabbing at her lips and trying to smudge her lip balm so that it didn't look so clumpy. How dare Gino accuse her of being dispassionate? That was just as rude as the time back in Bluffdale when Tess snipped Sosie's split-ends—and then some—when she had passed out on extra-strength allergy medicine in the dormitory chapter room. Or the time Juliet accused her of stealing strawberry truffles from Miss Iris Valentine's potluck. Or the time

Kiki told her to screw herself for not signing some stupid petition for new organic hemp uniforms. People could be so mean.

Gino flipped the watermelon around and handed it to Sosie. She held it, staring down at his passion.

"Think I'm the next Van Gogh?"

Sosie bobbed the watermelon left and right on her lap like she was burping a baby. She glared musingly at a stick figure girl with the name Freckles scribbled poorly into it, and a slinky, stick figure boy with big, bubbly muscles and the letter "G" scrawled over his shirt—all carved into the watermelon rind. "Bet you didn't know I'm an artist." He smirked, watching her assess his sad work of art. "Don't you think I got your hair just right?"

Three or four straws of hair poked on either side of the stick figure's head. She wore a paper-bag sundress and ballet flats, and had a lemon-shaped mouth.

"You didn't even give me eyes!" Sosie laughed so hard that her butt nearly shook right out of her chair.

"Yeah," he chuckled, trying to keep quiet. Kiki glowered back on them from her seat. *Screw you, and you! Screw you both!* Gino gently prodded his fingers around his carving. "Didn't think I'd do 'em justice."

"Oh yeah?" Sosie held her breath, feeling her heart drumming inside of her body. Gino had been so different, recently. Something had changed in him that night at Second Base. Something she hoped would stick around. Maybe forever.

He looked at her, smiling with ease. "Freckles . . . don't make it a big deal, or anything. You're still . . . you know . . . you," he added gruffly, smiling.

Then again, some things just never change.

Keeping Secrets

"Holy hotness!" Sosie Hinkhouse squealed, twisting her rose gold infinity bangle around her wrist as she checked out Professor Leatherwood behind his desk, licking salt off of his fingers. Had anyone ever made pretzels look so delicious? She looked at Nala Middleton, who was chewing on a vitamin C tablet. "I don't know how you keep your hands off of him when the two of you are all alone, in this big, dark room, doing . . . what is it that you do? File papers?"

The bell rang, and the girls jumped onto their Chelsea boots, their cute, cotton canvas backpacks draped from maroon cardigan sleeves like laundry bags. "We don't *file papers*, Sos. We just . . . you know . . . do normal stuff."

"Ummm . . . no I don't know, you snob!" Sosie's mind slipped away, wondering about Nala and Professor L's late-night TA sessions. Before long, she was picturing Nala in her primrose ruffle panties and a silk-blend, lace-trimmed bra, Professor Leatherwood's button down swathed over her eyes like a blindfold as she cried out "Marco" to Graham's rather muffled "Polo" and chased him around the room. *SMAAACK!* That's a desk.

"It's not like, a big deal or anything," Nala said, surveying the classroom for a wastebasket. Her sherbet-flavored gum was beginning to taste like an old-lady perfume sample swatch that had been passed around the mall.

Graham popped his head in the air suddenly and flagged Nala down as students poured out of the classroom door. He looked even more handsome now than he had the night they had unwound beneath that blanket, following the koi pond reflection as it pirouetted around the ceiling.

She walked up to Graham's desk and smiled down at him. "Mind staying after for a minute?" he asked.

"Of course not." She peeked back at Sosie, who was batting her big, green eyes mockingly as the rest of the students continued to race for the door. "See you in French?" she chimed, wishing Sosie would stop grinning so cheekily.

"Mmhmm," Sosie mumbled. "Bye, Mr. L!"

"Study chapter seventeen! I'm not saying there'll be a pop quiz . . . but I'm not saying there won't be."

Suddenly, Knox Ritchie appeared from behind, wrapping his arms around Nala and kissing her cheek. He was wearing a sports coat and slacks; his slicked hair and clean shaved jaw showing off his pretty-boy face. Nala cringed. He was kind of the last person she wanted to see. "I've been wanting to do that all day," he breathed into her ear.

Nala smiled painfully, feeling Knox squeeze her tight. "You staying after?"

"Yup," she said.

"All right. Save me a seat at lunch, okay?" he whispered, twisting her bangs in his fingers and pinning them behind her ears. "I have a surprise for you."

She nodded. "Sure."

All week long, Nala's fingers had been tangled up in answering Knox's seemingly endless texts, and she was starting to feel like he was days away from asking her to be his girlfriend, officially. Once or twice he had mentioned how he wanted her all to himself, and every day he'd bring her little surprises: fat-free yogurt, gift cards, flowers. It seemed they were heading toward being a "couple," which would be wonderful if her feelings for Graham weren't overwhelmingly present. Knox was great . . . she knew that. But he was little easy. Almost boring.

Knox's fingers slipped from her. "Later, beautiful," he called before swooping out the door.

She waved, whirling a loose, khaki-colored thread between her fingers. *Beautiful?* Now he totally felt like her boyfriend. *Ugh.*

The room cleared, and she was left alone with Graham. Finally. Though she was feeling a little anxious about it. Why had he asked her to stay back? Was she about to get canned from her TA position? Had she been talking in class too much? Had Kiki complained about the animal-tested, coconut-scented hand sanitizer she used? Or, perhaps, was this about the other night . . . .

Graham groomed his prickly chin with his fingernails and took a nervous drink of coffee. He choked on it a little.

"I want to talk to you about something," he said.

"Yeah?" Nala dropped her bag to the floor, wishing she had something to sip on, too.

Graham jumped onto his powder blue driving shoes and stuffed his knuckles through perfectly fringed strands. "Wanna sit down?"

"I'm fine." Nala blinked thick, mascara-black eyelashes at him.

"Well." He paused. The room was quiet for now, but any minute the classroom door would pop open and Milly Brown-Noser Hodge would poke through with her overstuffed book bag and solar-powered cooling water bottle. He cleared his throat, irritated by the familiar tick of the wall clock. "Remember the other night? When you called us friends?" he asked.

"Yeah."

Graham's face fell and this horrible feeling crept up Nala's throat. "Look . . . I'm sorry, Nala," his voice rattled. "I messed up. That was wrong of me . . . very unprofessional. I should have told you right then. As your teacher, I can't be your friend. There are rules . . . ."

Rules? There hadn't seemed to be any rules the other night, when they were watching movies together, fingers entwined. Nala felt her esophagus closing. Her bottom lip started to shake. Why couldn't they be friends? Was it her? She felt her cheeks turn an ugly shade of cerise, like the burned cherry pie Miss Iris had presented on Thanksgiving the year before; the one that tasted like tangerine and tree bark. Suddenly, she could taste tangerine and tree bark at the back of her throat, scraping at her taste buds.

"Okay. Fine." Nala curled her feet inside of her boots and tried to smile, but even her best efforts were grim. She felt like there was a puppeteer perched up in the ceiling vent, yanking on a string to tweak her lips until she was smirking like a possessed circus clown. "Shouldn't have said anything," she shrugged, stroking thick locks of cascading coffee highlights. "Can we just forget it ever happened? Because I really need this TA job."

Graham's lips frowned as his shoes stepped closer. "Mmm . . . I think you misunderstood." He snatched Nala's hands up in his, massaging their fingers together. *What?* Her eyes widened, goose-bumps crawling over her arms. "If it was up to me . . . we'd be more. More than this. More than friends." Graham's expression was stiff and serious. He flashed back to the first time he ever saw Nala, wearing her burgundy and khaki with hair tucked behind her ears and a "God is Love" pendant dangling from a vintage chain. She was the most beautiful thing he had ever seen. And he had wanted her every day since. "Sorry doesn't begin to cover how I feel. My feelings for you . . . they're wrong, Nala. Plain and simple. I screwed up. This never should have happened," he said. They blinked through painful gazes at each other. "So, I think it would be best if . . ." he gulped, "I have you transferred out of my class."

Nala stood, mouth wrenched open in shock. *Feelings?* Like, Graham-liking-her *feelings?* Feelings he maybe had all along? Her knees weakened as Graham reached out to catch her, and she shoved him away. "Not now," she said. "Give me a minute." Her head filled with his words . . . something about transferring her out? Like a little delinquent . . . so easily tossed aside. If his feelings were *so* authentic, then why was he pushing her away? Was it like cake throwing her out of his life, or was it like razorblades?

Nala stared into him. He looked so unsure of himself . . . regretful, almost. She could still see his hands reaching out for her, stretching, waiting for her to slip again so he could catch her this time; maybe to prove something. *No matter what, I'll always be here for you.* "Ummm . . . ." She stuffed her cardigan sleeves up her arms anxiously, clasping them in sturdy grips. "I don't think so, Graham," she said. "No. I don't think so."

"No?"

"No, Graham! No, I'm not transferring out of here! No, I'm not giving up my job!" she yelled. "Grow up, and keep your feelings to yourself like a mature adult. Be a freaking man, and leave me out of it!" Nala snatched up her backpack and threw it over her shoulder, stomping for the door. She needed something . . . a drink. Three drinks.

The door swung open, sunlight showering over her newly emerged adult silhouette, angrily and beautifully alive. She zoomed down the stairs to see Sosie and Knox giggling to each other on the lawn. Just what she needed. Her people. Their eyes soared toward Nala. Sosie's arm waved through the air. "There you are!" she screeched. "'Bout time! Guess what Knoxy Fox bought us?"

"What?" Nala grabbed the yellow strap of her canvas bag, and readjusted it on her shoulder, trying not to look so pissed off.

Sosie shoved a card of plastic in Nala's face. "Fake IDs!"

"We were thinking," Knox said, "if you want, we should skip class and go test them out at Cloud Nine. Drinks are on me."

Nala shaded her eyes from the thrashing sunlight, thinking about it. Baking class would be rather dismal since Miss Hart had contracted bronchitis and some old, perfumed-breath substitute was filling in for her. And Graham had just tried to kick her out of his class on account of his uncontrollable testosterone. Those three martini glasses danced around in her mind.

Knox's arm wrapped around Nala as she stared at her ID picture crookedly. Sosie must've given him that one. It was from their graduation party. She smiled intensely at the camera with crisp, bleached teeth. "So what do you say, beautiful? Come have a drink with us?"

She glanced through the classroom window where Graham was fumbling through a stack of papers behind his desk. Absentminded. Nerve-wracked. Served him right.

"Okay," she said, nodding and smiling a timid, plastic smile. "Why not?"

This School Would be Ours

Nala Middleton whirred her glass of merlot around and around in the air, smelling the familiar scent of fried jalapenos and vegetable oil that fogged the Cloud Nine patio. She glanced at Knox. He looked so sexy in his preppy, wool-blend blazer and tousled hair that she could barely stand to keep her hands appropriate to herself. Her feet flexed, grown stiff inside of her boots at the sight of him. Was he really so beautiful, or was her third glass of wine giving her rosé-colored lenses?

"Knoxy Fox! First beer on your twelfth birthday? That's like . . . equally as stupid as it is bad ass!" Sosie gulped her beer, running her grass green, chewed up fingernails through her hair. Blinking down into her bottle, she couldn't believe how *good* she felt—and at one in the afternoon. Beer was the new deep-tissue massage, although it totally took some getting used to.

"We were just bored kids," he shrugged. "It was pretty stupid, actually. We'd get hammered and jump off roofs. One of us should be dead."

Some fox-faced, redheaded waitress swooped by on her cheesy jelly sandals with a round of shots. "What are we celebrating this afternoon, folks?" she gushed so enthusiastically that Sosie thought she would throw her arms in the air and—what the hell—order another Vegas Bomb for herself.

Knox replied coolly as he snagged the shot glasses from the waitress's tray. "It's my girl's birthday. She turned twenty-one last night." His finger flexed toward Sosie. Nala set her then-empty merlot glass onto the table and sipped her Vegas Bomb delicately. Knox winked at Sosie, who then smiled back at him, and Nala suddenly felt—swallowed beneath burgundy and circle shades—like a hideously jealous third wheel. Her knees knocked beneath the table.

"Congratulations, girlfriend! Looks like you scored a pretty hot birthday present," Fox Face said. Her neck jerked toward Knox.

"Yeah, isn't he scrumptious?" Sosie licked her naturally red lips. Knox's hand grazed hers and they smiled two blinding grins up at the waitress, their fingers convincingly intertwined. Even though they were faking it, they did make a pretty adorable couple, both being somewhat blonde, and all.

The waitress grinned at their gathered hands, and then slipped away toward a table overflowing with pale skin and freckles. Nala sat silently, whiffing her shot and pouting at the familiar faces around her. She should have been happy in that moment. Graham had admitted two-and-a-half hours before that he couldn't stop thinking about her. Cheap merlot and butterscotch liquor were practically being shoveled down her throat. All classes were carrying on well without her, even though she was feeling a little crappy for skipping. Still, as she watched Sosie and Knox goofing around, she felt a weird urge to vomit in Sosie's crinkled, khaki lap. Perhaps it was her own fault for being so quiet. Forgive her for having so much on her mind that her head might explode if she so much as ordered something. Nala licked the brim of her shot glass, her nose scrunching at the taste of something bitter. Didn't anyone notice that she was about to take her shot alone? Didn't anyone care?

"Cheers to the hottest couple on the whole freaking planet!" Sosie gushed, clanking her shot glass against Knox's. They harmoniously tossed their sandy-blonde heads back as the liquor slipped down their throats.

Nala stared in disbelief, frowning back at their empty glasses. Did they honestly just forget about her? Were they seriously so hypnotized by each other?

"Ummm . . . ." Her voice stuck as Knox and Sosie cackled at something stupid . . . probably their fake relationship. "I'm gonna get going." Nala wobbled drunkenly to her feet, her brain whooshing inside of her skull. Three glasses of wine was apparently her limit.

"Aww, come on, La! Don't be such a party-pooper!" Sosie begged, her voice suddenly perky. "We haven't even ordered chili cheese fries, yet!"

Nala clung tight to her backpack, her gleaming brown hair tangling as the breeze blew over the terrace. "Yeah, I'm not hungry, anyway," she shrugged.

Knox's once bright eyes darkened. He knew something was wrong—he could tell by the way Nala was fumbling with her bag zipper. "You sure you don't want like . . . a salad or something? I'll get them to add some salmon on it."

"I'm fine," she resisted.

"We don't have to eat. We can just talk." Knox snatched up the lunch menus and casually tossed them over his head. Sosie giggled as they flip-flopped to the ground.

Nala glared at Sosie, maddened by the effortlessness of her laugh. Sosie's eyes squinted pale green as she hugged Knox's blazer and melted into him. They looked like a cute couple honeymooning in Tahiti, having brunch on the white sands of Bora Bora, preparing for their helicopter ride over Mount Otemanu, and their excursion of the blue lagoons. They were Swedish cyclists competing in the big race, checking out the local dives before hitchhiking their tiny, muscly asses toward Dirk Hill. They were a couple of models from New York City, showcasing Casio Castillo's newest clothing line in the October issue of *Jack & Jill: The Beauty Magazine for Him and Her*. Nala rolled her caramel eyes, petrified by the idea of Knox wanting anyone else.

"I'm fine," she repeated.

"At least let me walk you," Knox said, shifting away from Sosie who swayed drunkenly on her stool.

"You obviously have your hands full," Nala noted, and spun for the door. The wind whipped her in the eyes, making them tear up as she marched away. What the hell did Sosie think she was doing, drooling over Knox's crisp, white dress shirt, feeling up his biceps, gushing about his sharp, touchably smooth jaw? Knox wasn't hers to gush over in the first place. He was Nala's, wasn't he? Didn't he belong to her?

Nala's sunglasses bobbed on her nose as she approached the shimmering gold letters on the BU entrance gate, which bridged a short brick road ahead. Her temples were starting to throb from those three glasses of merlot, and all she wanted was to curl up beneath her addictively-snug, cotton voile quilt, pop in a romantic comedy, and binge-eat chocolate covered pretzels until the weekend. Like she'd *ever* binge-eat.

"Nala!" A deep, male voice yelled from behind. Knox Ritchie's hair flip-flopped in the breeze as he caught up to her, his darkly tanned shoulders roasting in the daylight. *Oh god. What now?* "Trying to break my heart, or what?" he asked.

Nala stared confusedly back at him.

"Look, I don't know what that was about," he said, pointing back at Cloud Nine, "but I'm sorry if I upset you. Did I buy you the wrong drink? Was it the Vegas Bomb?"

"No, it wasn't the Vegas Bomb." She rolled her eyes and stomped for the gate, her headache now wrought by Knox's vast stupidity.

"Then what?" He kept by her.

Nala's face fell to a perfectly incensed frown. The image of Sosie's body mushing against Knox's like sweltering yeast rolls made Nala's mind deluge with static. "I just didn't appreciate being, like, the third-wheel," she said. "And yes, all right, fine! I hated the Vegas Bomb, too. But I'm over it, Knox. Really. I don't care." She turned and cocked one perfect, black eyebrow.

Knox had never seen Nala so angry before. Her lips puckered fiercely as she turned and continued to march toward school, boots pummeling at the brick. "You don't care?" he asked, his voice muffled by his buzz as he realized that Nala was a little jealous. "Not even slightly?"

"Not even slightly," Nala pressed. She wished that Knox wasn't so dreamy; golden-sprinkled hair, gritting jawbone, cute, bending lips all up in her face. And he was sweet, too. Charming. He had followed her back to campus, after all. It had to count for something that he'd left Sosie alone with chili cheese fries and Fox-face. Nala was obviously the one that he wanted. And maybe . . . just for a second . . . she wanted him back. Slightly.

Knox's hands grasped her tiny waist, suddenly, driving her backwards toward a surfeit of weeping willows. Her ankles entangled in tall, gusty grass. She could feel his warm breath blowing in her ear. "You're so sexy when you're jealous," he said, steering her deeper into a cascade of green where no one could find them. Her back melted against a tree trunk, and there, where golden rays peeked through the dripping green willows, Nala's eyes flickered with impatience as if she wanted . . . no . . . needed him to kiss her. "You have to know how much you mean to me," he said, pinching the top button of her shirt teasingly. Nala's heart walloped crazily in her ears. "I seriously want you more than I've wanted anything else in my entire life." Knox's body crushed against hers.

"You're drunk, Knox," Nala said, turning her head away.

Knox kissed her long, thin neck. "So are you," he said. "But whatever. I mean it. Every day, I wish you were mine." Feeling her perfectly smooth, bronzed legs as her skirt lifted in a cool autumn wind, Knox's nerves deepened. He wished they were sober, so she'd believe him when he told her that every morning he showed up early for breakfast just in case she decided to stop by for a yogurt parfait or whole-grain pancake before class, or that he had spent eight hundred bucks on blue polos last week after she mentioned that they really made his eyes glisten. Maybe if they were sober, she'd believe him.

Nala's body tensed up as Knox's hand glided behind her head, his fingers knotting in brown baby hairs at the base of her neck. "I'm going to kiss you," Knox said grittily, his lips sinking toward hers.

Nala's eyes blinked shut; body humming. This was it. Her first kiss . . . .

"There you are, you asshole!" Rocko Borai stomped his double-laced, Prussian blue running shoes through the weeds. Thirty or so teammates trailed behind him in mock-neck jackets and perforated running shorts, exhaustedly wicking the sweat from their foreheads every other second. "Forget about practice, or what?"

Knox took an annoyed breath. Was this really happening? Now? "Just chose not to go," he declared, his hands tumbling from Nala's warm skin as she ducked behind him. "What is this? An intervention?"

"Don't be so conceited," Rocko snarled. "Today's the 5K. Or it was . . . . We just finished." His hands blundered over his short, black buzz-cut, which was lustrous with sprinklings of sweat. Then, behind Knox, Rocko barely spotted Nala's bony, suntanned shoulders peeping from beneath little cardigan sleeves. Nala? What was she doing back there . . . *with him?* Jealousy thundered through him as she tucked her face behind Knox's pretenticus, Ivy League hairdo. They looked like a just-caught Adam and Eve who'd been pitched behind the green of Eden, skulking in their own secretive sin.

"Damn," Knox managed (a little pathetically), searching the throng of teammates for Coach Mike. Missing the 5K would probably mean that, come Wednesday's practice, Coach would be kicking Knox's pampered, little ass all the way to Thursday. And by Friday, that pampered, little ass would be benched. Maybe skipping with Nala wasn't the smartest thing he had ever done, but feeling her nervous, trembling hand clasp around his reminded him that it was totally worth it. "I blanked, man. Sorry," Knox said, squeezing Nala's fingers like a toothpaste tube.

Rocko lumbered closer, shooing his minions of muscles and sports-bands back toward campus. All thirty-some trotted away, kicking mud up with their cleats as they sprinted collectively like a pack of gangly ostriches. Remotely, the quad was teeming with famished martial art students darting for the cafeteria doors, the poetry club reading from discolored diary pages beneath hickory branches, snapping their tobacco-stained fingernails and sipping espresso macchiatos, the debate team quarrelling over university politics, and the cheerleading squad flinging fliers into the cool, fall air. The three of them stood, scanning the clusters of intrinsically different students from beyond the BU gate, realizing that they too were an extraordinarily odd triad.

"Dude, you really put me in a bad position here," Rocko thumped his cleats, staring up into the thrashing hot sunlight. For a second, he almost sounded concerned for Knox—as if he gave two tenths of a shit whether he was punished for cutting practice. "Look, I'll tell Coach you ran the 5K, but you'd better get your ass back to campus and change before he comes looking for us. Otherwise, you know . . . ."

"Yeah. I know," Knox grunted. "Thanks." He grabbed the back of Nala's brown, shimmering curls and kissed her forehead delicately. She felt her muscles shudder at the feel of his warm, soft lips. The last thing she wanted was for Knox to disappear, just as their almost-kiss was burning a hole in her mind. "Call you when I get a minute," he promised, slinking toward the quad. His beautiful, sandy hair curled in the breeze as he went. The swarm of students swallowed him, and Nala realized that she missed him already.

"Sorry if I interrupted something," Rocko said, feeling the sweat trickling down the insides of his arms, pooling in his hands. "You skipping too, sweetheart? Never expected you as the type."

Nala blew at a strand of chestnut hair that had matted itself down with tangy lip gloss. She wondered how well Rocko thought he knew her. Her red shoes carried her just past him and toward campus. "I just had to get out." She shrugged her subtly freckled shoulders. Her once-there cardigan sleeves lolled over her elbows like a couple of grocery bags.

"Really?" Rocko rubbed his scruffy chin, purposefully bulging his dark biceps. He knew he was hot. He knew he belonged on the cover of *Sports Tomorrow*. The headline would read: "Rocko Borai, 'Like Father, Like Son': Willie the Wolverine's Little Wolf a Potential NFL Legend." Although there was no real proof that Willie "The Wolverine" Borai was his biological father, Rocko was sure he'd follow in Willie's very large paw prints, regardless.

He also knew that, because he was hot, and because he was such an incredible athlete, he deserved a girl like Nala. She would be his little trophy wife. She'd vaunt the finest designer totes around the shopping precincts, she'd sip the most expensive French wines, she'd catch a tan on the wood-planked sundeck of their newest luxury yacht in her hot-pink, vintage caftan and crochet swimsuit. They'd be the richest and sexiest couple on Cargill's Island. No, in America. No, in the whole freaking world.

Rocko's eyes lit up at the thought of Nala's cutaway swimsuit showing off her very-there hips. "Everything okay?" he asked. His eyes fixed on the top button of her blouse, wishing it would snap off.

"Yeah, just—you know—school and that TA position," she said, her mind a big, blurry splotch of Knox-kissing fanaticism. "I'm thinking about quitting."

"Really?"

"Yeah." She sighed noisily, a little surprised by her own words. She realized that she hadn't thought about Graham for a while. Well . . . for an hour, at least. Maybe quitting her TA position was the right thing to do after he'd blurted out his feelings to her. Maybe then Graham would realize how much he'd miss her if she was gone forever . . . flicked out of his classroom like old chalk. Or maybe she should stop thinking about Graham altogether, and start thinking about Knox Ritchie. Only Knox Ritchie. Sweet, pay-for-all-your-drinks, kiss-you-on-the-forehead, call-you-when-I-get-a-minute Knox Ritchie. *Gaaaaaw.* She hated comparing Graham to Knox, because they were two totally different, totally wonderful people.

"Next semester, I may try out for cheerleading so . . . I don't know . . . . I'd hate to take on too much at once."

"I could see why." Rocko nodded, suddenly envisioning Nala's perky ass peeping out of wine-red pleated skirts, her curls pinned back in a ponytail, her boobs compressed in a tight,

V-neck shell. She'd have his last name printed on both of her cheeks. Every high-kick, every back flip, every split she'd do for him. And, once the lights had powered down, once he had single-handedly destroyed the opposing team, they'd sneak below the bleachers, rip each other's uniforms off, and fool around until sunrise, their naked bodies splattered in mud, clinging together like sticky rice. "Well, I say you do it."

"Do what?"

"Try out for cheerleading," he said. "Quit that TA thing. Do what makes you happy." Rocko's feet trucked to a halt before they loped through the packed square of cloud-gazers and massage trains. Nala shared a marveled stare with him, admiring the aloof senior cheerleaders sprawled out across the Mediterranean fountain at the center of the court. Their long, golden hair flipped in the wind, dripped into the loch of water, cascaded over shimmering cast-stone. They took turns puffing cigarettes, painting their poorly clipped toenails, and blaring hip-hop from their cell phone speakers. Elle Moody, the captain, kissed her totally gorgeous junior beau on the lips and blew warm, grey smoke into his mouth. They were the most bizarre and fascinating group on the planet.

"I don't think I'd fit in," Nala said as Elle collapsed backwards into her boyfriend's lap, ripping a lighter from his straight-leg, twill pants pocket, and guardedly toking a second blunt. Her eyes rustled shut as she held the smoke in her chest. "I hear they do a bunch of drugs."

Rocko smiled satisfyingly down on Nala. She was so innocent . . . that silver cross pendant . . . those sweet, raspberry lips. There was so much he could teach her. There was so much she could learn. "Do whatever you want," he announced, holding her gaze with his big, honey-brown eyes, "But with that crowd and that sexy little uniform, this school and everyone in it would be yours."

Ours, he had wanted to say. *This school would be ours.*

276

Know that I Mean it

"**G**ross!" Sosie Hinkhouse squealed as she cracked another egg against Miss Hart's white-clay, hand thrown pottery bowl and yolk spattered into her mouth. She dunked her hands into a glob of flour and powdered the baking tray. That next day, Miss Hart would be breathing down Sosie's neck to assess every step of her marjclaire, multilayered chocolate cake, and she couldn't afford to fail after her lemon soufflé incident the week before. How was she to know that exuberantly popping open the oven would "quash the egg white protein and ultimately deflate the rise," as all of the gifted, yet pretentious wannabe chefs had chimed when her soufflé . . . flopped? Not everyone was like Nala and just *knew* that kind of thing.

The clock read nine just as the stadium lights powered down across the quad, and Sosie realized that she had been butchering marjolaine cake for the past two hours. Damn, she needed a break. Fast. As the oven was pre-heating for the next batch, Sosie sat and flipped through the glossy pages of the newest *Food & Fit to Fit,* kicking up her rad gold-link sneakers and mentally mocking all the anorexic models pouting at the camera. Sosie was skinny, sure, but at least she hated being skinny. She hated wearing a double-a bra like some kid in elementary school. And she especially hated trying to find jeans that didn't hang off her boney ass like flour sacking. It looked like someone had spanked the fat right off of her.

Pale, boney shoulders popped through a sheer, JM slip dress on the next page. Some model with sunken, reamed-out under eyes sucked on her cheeks. Sosie ripped out the page and crinkled it up. She couldn't begin to sympathize with those kinds of women . . . the type to sacrifice red meat and wild rice for rice cakes and juice cleanses just to look like pre-pubescent teens trying on their housemothers' clothes . . . 'cause it totally sucked!

On the next page she read a quote from supermodel Konstanze Eichelberger, who was depicted wearing a skimpy, triangle bikini top and linen beach pants as she straddled a jet ski and flexed her wimpy, tanned biceps. "Nothing is been more fantastic than look in the mirror and see—for first time—you as healthy and better you." Ugh. *The only thing Konstanze needs more than a burger is an English lesson,* Sosie thought as she cackled obnoxiously and ripped open a nearby bag of chocolate thumbprints.

Suddenly, a loud knock at the door . . . .

Sosie jumped, clenching her bag of cookies. It was late . . . nine or ten. The outside lights had faded. Curfew was rounding the corner. Maybe that noise was just the wind, or a falling tree branch. Maybe it was the air-conditioning. Then, fists slammed against the front doors again. Louder. Harder. Sosie popped up, throwing down her stash of cookies. Who would be showing up at the practice kitchen that late on a Thursday night? Someone with a vengeance for strawberry shortcake? She inched near the doorway, tip-toeing on her sneaker tops. "No one's heeerree! Come back tomooorroow!" she said, holding her elbows. Slipping closer, she pressed her ear into the door. Nothing. Crickets and Spittlebugs. *Phewww!*

Sosie started to tiptoe away when . . . again . . . a few knocks. Her bones froze. For a moment she couldn't breathe. Was the mysterious, angry fat chick actually a serial killer? Or a killer in need of some cereal? She clutched the door and pulled it open slowly, reservedly, peeking around it with wide eyes. Then . . . familiar, bushy hair. Behind it, Gino Blackthorn stood in a sweat-drenched muscle shirt and gunmetal-gray sweatpants, his sports duffle slung over his shoulder and his hands stuffed into his pockets. "Well? Aren't you going to invite me in, Freckles?" he asked. Sagging, tired eyes glared through the dark room at her, and Sosie guessed Gino had just been running suicides for the past thirty-nine hours. She felt kind of sorry for him. Being a boy would suck.

"Umm . . . whatever. Wanna come in?"

Gino stumbled inside, throwing off his bag and collapsing into a bluish-gray, velvet embossed side chair, just as uncomfortable as it was European. He licked his lips at a perspiring pitcher of once ice-cold water sitting on the counter.

"Mind if I . . . ."

"Nope. Help yourself."

The oven bell rang, and Sosie stumbled toward it. The smell of the burnt mozzarella cemented into the oven walls made her blench, queasy. She arranged the cake pan inside the oven and set the baking time. Now, all there was left to do was wait.

Gino poured himself a glass of water, ogling the *Food & Fit to Fit* peculiarly. His fingers flipped between the slick, waxy pages. "How to Bake Your Way into a Man's Heart," the cover read. Sosie peeped over his shoulder, reading along. So not only did she look like a loner who hung out around the kitchen in her spare time, she also looked like a loner whose idea of seducing a man was feeding him into a delirious food coma until he was too fat to be picky. Great . . . .

"So, why are you here?" Sosie asked as Gino skeptically read and re-read the lustrous blue words.

"Saw you in the window when I was leaving practice." He hunched his shoulders, realizing how crazy he must sound. Stalkerish. "Thought I'd keep you company. You looked bored." Gino took another drink of water and tried to get comfortable, although his chair was starting to give him blisters in his ass, and he was pretty sure he had just walked in on Sosie baking Rocko some sort of peace offering. Whiskey cake? Muffins? Something sweet.

Sosie staggered back toward the table, whirling a yellow strand of hair with a poorly painted polka dot fingernail. Even though her face was smudged with flour and her hair tousled into a messy bun — even though she was wearing a tiered ruffle, 1960s apron and batter-spattered chiffon shorts — Gino still thought she looked good. No makeup . . . like that day at the beach.

"Thought you were Jules knocking on the door," Sosie said. "She sneaks dessert out of here all the time. And every Monday, Miss Hart does the same song and dance. Takes inventory, and once she realizes that someone's raided the pantry, she blathers on and on about how it's 'so rude and un-lady-like to take things that don't belong to you.' As if that was her real hair." Sosie flung the magazine into her lap, and grabbed a cookie. "Want one?"

"Nah, I'm good."

The air whirled with cheese and chocolate fondue scents. Gino watched Sosie suck the chocolate glob out of the insides of her cookie. Weird. Strangely charming. "So, who's the cake for?" he asked, distracted. An image of Rocko spoon-feeding Sosie's whatever-it-was to a sophomore on the cheerleading squad in a plunging halter and denim cutoffs, pulled into his brain. She deserved better than Rocko. Rocko, who earlier in the locker room had shoved two baseballs down his briefs and started bragging about his "dangerously huge pitcher's mound."

Sosie glanced back at her cake, barely browning in the oven. She frowned. "No one. Just practicing for this *huge* exam I have tomorrow. And it doesn't really help that Nala is, like . . . the next culinary prodigy, and she bakes right next to my station. Using magic and fairy dust, of course."

Gino took a relieved breath of savory, mozzarella-infused air and gulped the last of his water. At least Sosie wasn't baking something for that asshole, Borai. Not that Gino would have cared. He had a plan . . . a playbook . . . and it didn't include a girl until junior or senior year. Even Freckles. Especially Freckles.

Sosie jumped up suddenly and refilled Gino's glass. "Between you and me, sometimes I hate having Nala as a best friend." She slammed Gino's water onto the cappuccino-stained hardwood tabletop and clunked back into her chair. "Don't get me wrong. Nala's like . . . the sister I never had. It's just . . . she's annoyingly good at everything. *Everything.* Cooking. Studying. And she's horrifyingly beautiful. Model beautiful, like Lily Collins. And then there's me. The weird, meandering dog tail latched to her butt that follows her around all day."

Gino laughed absurdly. Butt tail? Really? Then . . . beneath the table, Sosie's knee grazed his. They only touched for an instant, but it poked him awake. Whoa. Gino stared at her curiously through thick, black, smoggy classroom air. Sosie lounged, one leg hitched up on her chair, her bangs sweeping over her deeply blushing cheekbones. She was flicking crumbs off of the magazine and tracing her blonde eyebrow with a finger, like she was debating a tweeze or a wax. No way everyone thought of Sosie as the weird, meandering dog tail. She was beautiful. Really. Totally natural, easy on the eyes beautiful. Gino watched closely as her forehead crinkled with every absurd article title.

"Just so you know, I think Nala is . . . without," Gino blurted. Sosie's profoundly green eyes enlarged, wrestling back to his. Blackness sank in around their bodies. It was like they were quarantined in a beach home during hurricane season, the hauntingly dim windows blurring with heavy rainfall. Gino *wished* they were quarantined there, at least. They'd chug Cape Codders like they were on spring break. They'd make fun of the amateur surfers who wonkily dodged the remnants of burrito shacks, trying to catch the sick but deadly wave that would define their future and tragically mortal careers. They'd raid the not-so-impressive Pilates DVD collection, play Twister, sleep. Maybe then he'd get that kiss he had been wanting.

Sosie took a sip of Gino's water, remembering the time she stole some of his beer, too. "Nala's without what?" her voice rattled as she took another swig. No wonder she had always been so attracted to Gino, ever since he first stumbled into Bluffdale on his sun-tanned, sand-spattered feet. Somewhere deep down Sosie must have known that he was immune to Nala's entrancing beauty. The only guy on the planet.

Gino rubbed the knots in his hands. Ugly golf callouses. "I don't know. Just without."

"Okay . . ." Sosie cocked her head curiously, hair tumbling out of her bun in thin, golden splinters. That was all he had to say? Just without? "So, what *are* you into, then?" she badgered, wishing she had more crumbs to flick, and for that matter aim, between Gino's thick, black eyebrows.

Gino stole back his water. "Do we have to do this?"

"God! Seriously?" Sosie jumped up on her sneakers and darted moodily toward the oven. Gino was impossible to talk to. He was just like a slab of highly attractive plaster. "No, we don't *have* to do this," she grumbled, pressing her nose into the glass. She looked like a kid watching fresh calzones brown in an open kitchen bistro.

"Look . . . Freckles . . . ." Gino mumbled. "I'm not that kind of guy. I'm just not into like . . . talking about stuff."

Sosie observed as the minutes on the oven clock wound into seconds. "Why are you even here?"

"I didn't mean to upset you," he said.

Sosie swooped toward the classroom window, peering out into the shadowy lawn. Her arms folded as she blinked up into the hanging moon. The air was murky and whipped with fog. The last thing she wanted to do was walk through it . . . especially alone. She'd seen *Scream*.

"Why don't you just leave?" Sosie asked glumly. "Now." Her lungs plopped into her stomach. This always happened. Just when she thought Gino was finally changing. Just when she thought there was a chance. And then . . . warm hands molded to her shoulders. Soft, steady breath gusted behind her ears. She could just barely see the outline of Gino's reflection in the window; hands grasping her skin tight; everything still. His lips pressed into her scalp gently. "I'm sorry," he said. "I mean it."

Sosie could hear her heart thudding in her ears. Or was it the timer on the oven winding down? Or soft and sudden raindrops spattering over the window seal? Was it even raining? She couldn't think of anything other than Gino holding her, whispering. *I'm sorry. I mean it.*

Sosie's head wrapped around tentatively and caught Gino's sparkling, brown eyes. He pulled her bangs back, tucking them behind her ears. "You asked me why I'm here. I'm here because I couldn't help myself," he said, realizing how much he meant it. He took her face in his hands and smiled stupidly down on her. "Sosie, I . . . think about you, sometimes."

"Yeah?" She took in a deep breath, glossy-eyed and a little nervous. She couldn't remember when she last brushed her teeth. Lunch? Or had she skipped that to meet Juliet in Home Economics for that free meatball sampling? Or was that yesterday? *Shit!* Did her breath stink like onions and parsley?

Gino's fingers swept down her arms like cool spring water, grappling at her hips. He yanked her against him. She could smell the unfamiliar scents of deodorant, protein bars, freshly mowed grass, and sweat. The combination was so startlingly sexy that she wanted to ring his shirt into a perfume bottle and spritz it on her pillow every night.

Just as she was taking in another whiff, his lips blundered into hers. Sosie's eyes fluttered shut, his tongue slipping over her front teeth.

He tasted like pistachios and peppermint.

Sosie smiled as he pulled her in and kissed her harder. Deeper. Her toes tingled beneath tightly pulled shoestrings. All she had wanted since the first day she saw Gino trucking through the sand in cleats, staring out into the ocean as if he couldn't wait to hop a longboard and ride, was for him to want her seriously and greatly.

Oh yeah. He wanted her seriously and greatly. He wanted her big time.

If I Can't Go with You

"Tell me you're not getting stoned off book glue," Sosie Hinkhouse screeched as Nala Middleton buried her nose into the binding of her fusty, 1984 baking textbook. Sosie ripped off the thulite-pink infinity scarf tangled around her neck. Flakes of snow melted into her messy sock bun as the library's heating vents burbled scorching air.

Nala yanked out the nearest seat and patted the dust off of it. She was still a little pissed at Sosie for flirting with Knox the other day at Cloud Nine, but was trying to forget about it. Any effort thus far had been totally thwarted. "Can't believe finals snuck up on us so quickly. I'll practically be living here for the next two weeks," Nala groaned.

"Not me!" Sosie peeled open her new colorblock backpack and shuffled through the mess, ripping out one beautiful, sparkling, B-plus exam. "Marjolaine cake is my new specialty, I guess! With this grade, I'll pass Baking even if I totally bomb the final!"

Nala mused, blinking at the red ink. She never understood why Sosie refused to apply herself. "Congrats, babe! You totally deserve it. All those late nights in the practice kitchen . . . ."

"Well . . ." Sosie mumbled, studying the nearby students flipping through page after boring page of Stats and Home Econ and Finance; all with little iPod headphones plugging their ears. All distracted. She swallowed. "Actually, I didn't really practice much . . . at all."

Nala's eyes vacantly searched Sosie. If she wasn't practicing in the practice kitchen all night, then what the heck was she doing in there?

Sosie ripped a few books out of her bag, remembering Gino's lips smashing against hers like cool butter. *Mmm. Cool butter.* A book clamped shut nearby, and woke her up. Nala was staring heavily, waiting. Sosie's shoulders caved in. "Gino showed up that night."

"Gino?"

"Mmhmm," Sosie mumbled, wishing she had waited to consider her options in detail before she just . . . spilled. Would Nala tell Knox? And would Knox tell Gino? And would Gino care that Sosie told Nala, who told Knox, who told Gino? *Whatever.* Nala was her best friend. She deserved to know.

Nala's eyes shifted in curious stints as she slithered her highlighter through a few sentences.

"There's more," Sosie said.

"More?"

"A little." She tucked her knees gently below her chin, wobbling on top of her chair like an egg yoke. "Don't freak out, but . . . Gino sort of . . . kissed me." Her lips clamped shut.

Nala's gaze lifted, disbelievingly glassy.

"Wasn't like we planned it, or anything. One second we're fighting, and the next . . . ."

Heavily lit stoners poured out of the elevator, suddenly, and swooped across the second floor, hunting for seats in the black to roll their blunts and scrape together a few lines for their new reggae CD. Nala zipped back to Sosie, smiling cheesily. "You kidding?"

"Dead serious," Sosie nodded.

"Shut up!" Nala jumped, throwing her arms around Sosie and shaking her up and down like a hairspray bottle.

Everyone stared, pulling out earbuds. *Nothing to see here, folks.*

Nala brushed her crinkly lap and sat, still beaming insanely. "Oh my gosh, you've wanted this for, like, forever! How was it? Do you like him? Does he like you? Of course he likes you, what am I saying?"

"So . . . you're not mad?"

"Mad?" Nala gushed. "Why would I be mad?" Especially since I was totally convinced you were like, secretly in love with Knox, she wanted to say, but didn't. "You deserve this, Sos! And you deserve that B-plus! You deserve the *best*!"

"And so do you," a deep voice interrupted. Knox Ritchie leaned over and planted a big, wet kiss on Nala's forehead, hands clenching flowers. His intensely black sport clung to his biceps. "These are for you." He shoved blossoming white roses into Nala's lap. "Sorry I had to leave so . . . spur of the moment the other day." He smushed his combed part down into his scalp. "How you doing, Sos? Get home safely the other day?"

"I told ya I could take care of myself, Foxy!" She wiggled her small, bony butt in her chair.

"And I didn't doubt you for a second." He winked.

Nala stuffed her face deep into the roses and took a whiff. *Mmmm.* They were beautiful, just like him. Perfect, thornless stems. White, fluffy pedals. She buried her nose inside, enjoying the freshly blossomed scent until . . . suddenly . . . she felt something jab her in the cheek. Two sparkling, silver tickets buldged out of the bouquet.

"They're for the dance," Knox said, flashing snow-white teeth. "Go with me?"

"Is that a question or a demand, Foxy?" Sosie asked, a little turned-off by the haze of juniper cologne swarming Knox's slicked-back hair. At least he looked pretty! Like a European model, or a very masculine girl with chilling bone structure.

"It *is* a question," he replied. "Only accepting one answer, though." His bleached stacks of teeth nearly blinded the crowd, grinning nervously. "Look . . . I won't go if I can't go with you."

Nala stared down at his feet. New camel-brown boat shoes that swayed above swirling marble floors. It made her a little dizzy. Why wouldn't she go with Knox to the dance? He was the best-known freshman on campus. He was QB of the freshman team. He was sweet, handsome, adored her. Even Elle Moody, senior cheerleading captain, had been caught whispering teasingly to Knox outside a Friday assembly, slipping her fingers through his thick, sandy hair and moaning, "You're so hot, I could just eat you up!" And just the other day, Nala had wanted nothing more than to fall into a deep, mesmerizing, make-out coma with him; mouths melting together beneath the thrashing autumn sun. It only made sense for her to say yes. But in the back of her mind, she wondered what Graham would think, what he'd have to say. Even if he was her teacher, even if he was dating Miss Hart, even if his feelings for her had somehow . . . vanished.

Nala could feel Knox watching her, anxiously waiting. Sweet, considerate Knox. She cleared her throat, jumped onto her chartreuse loafers, and hugged his neck limply. "Sure," she said sort of lamely. "I'd love to."

Maybe she'd forget Graham after a while . . . after the dance. Or maybe she'd only miss him more.

Your Secret is Safe with Me

"Flowers, huh?" Graham snooped as he spread triple-cream terrine over a slab of pumpkin bread and took a bite. With Thanksgiving right around the corner, all of the female teachers around Blairstown were in a tizzy to create the most outrageous, most delicious dishes in all of BU holiday history, and Estelle Hart had promised her practice samples to Graham . . . even though he was mildly worried she had spiked them with a love potion, or something. But surely she'd wait until Valentines Day for that.

Nala flaunted her obnoxiously displayed white roses around the classroom as she found them some water and a ceramic planter in the back. She and Graham hadn't really talked since he had told her how he felt about her. She had even debated skipping her TA session once again, but after missing a few she realized it was affecting her work. Not knowing what Graham was thinking was severe psychological torture, so she showed up this time. Was he dying to know what she was thinking? What if he wasn't? Maybe confessing his feelings for her was just one of those in-the-heat-of-the-moment things. Maybe he didn't have feelings for her at all.

Nala fluffed the flowers in the vase, smiling back at them.

"Who are they from?" Graham's voice cracked jealously. He kicked his apron-toe derby shoes off his desk and clapped the crumbs from his hands against his pale orange, straight-leg twill pants. Nala's hair spilled down the back of her jungle-print swing shirt, where Graham could barely see her shimmering, tan shoulder blades. Beautiful. Even from the back.

"Knox." She shrugged, marching back toward her desk, the familiar scent of Estelle's homemade margarine drifting through stale classroom air. "Who made the bread?" She kicked a few chairs straight with the force of her lattice cutout boots, positive she already knew the answer.

"Would you quit doing that?"

"What am I doing?" she sputtered.

"Cleaning up," he said. "Avoiding me."

Nala blinked back agonizingly. *So what?* What did he expect?

Graham flung his hair back into a sleek Ivy League blow, dimples deepening into yawning black hollows as he watched her lean into her desk. She was supposed to be furious with him — for trying to transfer her out, for saying things he shouldn't have said, for confusing her, for ruining what they had — and all he did was make her feel all sorts of confusing, incredible things. Of course she was avoiding him.

Nala ripped her eyes away and collapsed into her chair. Angry. Confused. She could hear Graham clanking his pencil against his coffee mug, probably on purpose. *Look at me. Just for a second.* Nala flinched, thumping her hands over her ears to drown out the sound.

"So," Graham choked. "Guess that means you and Knox are officially together."

"Guess so," she said, scowling at crumbled pumpkin bits splattered across his desk. "Are you and Estelle?" Nala flipped through her backpack, ripping out an old magazine with a picture of spinach and brie-topped artichoke hearts sweltering on the cover. She had read it a bazillion times, using it for recipes and dieting tips. "I liked her pumpkin bread, too, until I found one of her weird surprises in it."

Surprises? Love potion surprises? Graham blenched, raking up his leftovers and tossing them into the trash. He wasn't hungry, anyways. He hadn't been hungry for days. Had other things on his mind. Other people. He plunged backward, the smooth, black leather sucking his body inside. "Whether you want to or not, we need to talk about this. What I said to you the other day . . . ."

"Do we?" She flipped through her magazine abstractedly, reading the same sentence on pineapple upside-down cake three or four times. "There's really no point."

Then . . . agonizing silence. Agonizing silence for minutes. Nala peered up, catching Graham with despairingly glazed eyes, scribbling on his notepad. Maybe that bit on Miss Hart's pumpkin bread surprise was too much. Maybe she was being too hard on him. After all, they were really just fighting about . . . what? Graham falling for her?

Graham's sad, glassy eyes flickered as outdoor wall sconces powered up and light crawled into the windows. Nala's bones ached intensely. Sad, glassy eyes like marbles. He looked so hurt . . . so broken. For an instant, she wanted to tell him how she felt about him . . . just so he'd know. If nothing else, they could share that secret. Her heart throbbed against her topaz-studded earrings. The truth was, she missed him. She missed what they used to have when their feelings were obscured by Twizzlers and indie flicks. She took a nervous breath of clammy, classroom air. "Graham, I . . . ."

"Konnichiwa!" a familiar voice chimed, fumbling through the door with Japanese takeout. Estelle Hart clomped on lilac platform pumps, sushi in one hand and a knock-off Michel St Pierre blush-pink tote in the other. "I brought Vegas rolls!" Her deep blue eyes surveyed the room. Graham. Nala. And . . . white roses? *For her?* Estelle wiggled her toes. "Nala! What a treat!" She wrapped her bony arms around Graham and pressed bright fuchsia lipstick into his beard, smudging it off — but only partly — with her thumb. "If I would have known you were coming, I would have ordered you a California roll. Bet you only eat the cooked stuff, huh? Am I right?"

Nala circled her rose-gold chain bracelet around her wrist, smiling insecurely at the word 'love' wired in it. So it was true. Graham and Miss Hart *were* back on. Was sushi some declaration of commitment? Estelle yanked a tower of rice from the bag, ripped it open, and began to smash it into a gooey glob with training chopsticks. It looked like tofu, soy, and some bizarre Japanese pepper. "Actually, I prefer it raw," Nala blurted, "But it's no big deal. Already promised Sosie I'd grab pizza with her on our way back to the library."

"Look at you girls! Such enthusiastic students," Estelle observed. "Graham here — errr, Mr. Leatherwood," she cackled vigorously like she was the only one who knew his first name. "Your teacher," she patted his shoulder, "told me you've been working hard as his TA. Snatched you up before any of us other eager staff had the chance to throw our names in the hat! He says you're a very hard worker, Nala. He even mentioned," Estelle leaned over a tub of soup, hovering her big, cheesy smile through egg drop steam, "that you were his *favorite*. And it was so ironic, really, because . . . I shouldn't even be telling you this . . . ." her lips curled into a maroon lemon wedge, "You're my very favorite student, too."

Nala gasped, catching Graham search through the takeout with embarrassed, blushing skin. Estelle's words—that he had talked about Nala, called her his favorite—they validated everything. Not being able to push her out of his mind, having to talk about her casually just to feel like an honest human being, just to put his mind at ease . . . that said a lot, didn't it? He *did* care about her, didn't he?

Graham's smile faded against the gray wash of the chalkboard, like he was remembering how good it felt to talk about Nala back when there was something between them. Was there still something between them? Estelle ripped out a tub filled with soy sauce, wasabi, and a few rolls. All she needed was a silk kimono, a Nagoya obi sash, a chopstick bun, and little, flat slippers, and she'd make the perfect geisha.

"Estelle," Graham said, flinging chopsticks onto his desk. "Think you could give us a few minutes, here? We were just finishing up."

Estelle's eyes jumped between Nala and Graham. Big, frowning lips pulled toward her chin. She had always been good at reading energy, and the energy between those two was electrifying. They were like two kindred spirits igniting the desert flames at Burning Man, and Estelle was just some awkward nomad being trampled by nudists and hippies on her venture through the Black Rock Desert. She felt her muscles spasm at the uncomfortable thought of being unwanted. "I suppose, Hon. But we shouldn't leave this out much longer. The drive back was already a little long, and I read something the other day about salmonella . . . salmonella and fish. Almost stopped eating meat all together because of it. You know . . . become a vegan . . . nothing with eyeballs and a head type-a-thing." Estelle grabbed her hands in her lap. "I'm just trying to say that we shouldn't leave the sushi out, all exposed. Just make it speedy. That's all."

Nala popped up from her chair and stuffed her magazine back into her backpack. "No . . . I'm in the way! I should get out of here. Sosie's probably wondering where I am anyways, so . . . ."

"But," Graham paused, upset as Nala zipped up her bag and slung it over her shoulder. "Didn't you have something you wanted to talk to me about?"

Nala slipped toward the exit. She didn't want to leave. She'd much prefer to kick Miss Hart out on the rear end of her moon-white, parachute-slouch jumpsuit, chucking a dragon roll at her poorly teased topknot, mocking her misconstrued perception of salmonella. But that wasn't an option, especially since Miss Hart had just called Nala her very favorite student.

The moonlight flickered just beyond the door. Nala twiddled the topaz-layered studs that pinched her ears as she hesitated to leave. She thought about Graham's future with that woman. Little, blonde-haired children and a welcome mat; exuberantly draped Christmas decorations; lots of soufflés. A normal life. She clutched the door-knob and tugged it open. "I just wanted to tell you that . . . since the semester is almost over and finals are two weeks away . . . today was the last day I could work as your TA." Nala glared vacantly at Graham, trying not to show how much it hurt her to hurt him.

"Umm . . . okay." He nodded. "I understand."

Nala smiled painfully, and then slipped into the cool winter breeze. Her white roses frowned at Graham from across the room.

"Great! No salmonella for us!" Estelle piped up, chewing on an edamame shell with her square, hamster teeth. "Hope you like eel. I went a little nuts!"

Graham shrugged, clunking into his chair. He didn't want eel. He didn't want Estelle. He didn't even want to escape that tortuous college town.

All he wanted was Nala.

The Hour After

"**W**hat do I look like . . . a philanthropist for a freaking geek dating service?" Juliet Bigsby carved into her chicken *ossobuco*, daubing it through a pool of olive oiled penne. Brains Fink was standing at the buffet, debating between gluten-free zucchini pizza casserole and the cheesy, cinnamony, sugary gluten-free Czechoslovakian Thoshky. Juliet gagged at the unattractive black hairs poking out of Brains's neck. She couldn't believe she was going to the dance with . . . *that*.

"He's not terrible looking," Sosie butted in, picking at her bacon cheese fries and attempting to memorize a butter-cake recipe for finals. 1.5 cups of sugar, 2 eggs, 2 tablespoons vanilla extract . . . or did that blue smudge of ink say teaspoons? *Ughhh.* Her mind collapsed into unalloyed disarray. Gino Blackthorn still hadn't mentioned the dance . . . not even once . . . . And even though he so "wasn't that guy," there was no way in hell she was going to that thing with anyone else. No way. No thank you, Brains Fink. Good thing that ship of stubborn, untweezed unibrow had already sailed into yellow, curly tufted abyss.

Maybe Sosie could threaten Gino into going. Tease about lighting his jersey on fire, or throwing his dumbbells in the lake. Or maybe she'd kiss him until he surrendered.

Miss Hart was in the distance, fumbling through the cafeteria with her little sidekick, Bill — the equipment manager — heckling instructions for The Winter Ball décor left and right. "I want white! Trees! Snowflakes! I see a gigantic ice sculpture here, with punch trickling down the slopes, gold Christmas ornaments dangling from the ceiling! Are you getting all of this?"

Bill's hand scribbled down a notepad. "Yes, ma'am," he chimed frightfully. He was like her little puppy, so starved for affection. Just wanting to be loved.

Suddenly, Knox Ritchie flew inside the cafeteria, scowling. His cheeks were flushed. His hair was still damp from the shower. He veered to the back of the buffet, where a pair of voluptuous juniors begged him to take their spot. "Look at you! You need to eat something," one girl with a tousled flapper bob and bright orange lips insisted. Juliet watched as Knox flashed a lazy smile at the girls and caught up with Brains. He was the hottest guy on campus, even to a couple of twenty-year-olds.

"So, I hear Knox asked Nala to the dance?" Juliet blinked thin, blonde, flimsy eyelashes at Sosie. "Is that true?"

Sosie took a large gulp of hot chocolate. It could use some more marshmallows and whipped cream. It could use some more cocoa, for that matter. "Mmhmm," she moaned to Juliet, flagging down a bus boy and ordering another mug with extra chocolate this time. "It was *soooo* embarrassing. He brought her these ridiculous flowers, which . . . you know Nala . . . she *loooov-vvvved* them."

Knox topped off his tray with some garlic bread, nudged Brains in the ribs, and started to walk toward the girls, all of them hovering their spoons over *dulce de leche* mousse. "Hey." Knox flung his hair out of his face, his kaleidoscope-blue eyes glistening naturally. Now he was just showing off. "Mind if we crash?"

"Why would we mind?" Juliet asked, trying to lick the mousse off of her spoon in the most sophisticated way possible. But Knox didn't look like he was in the mood to flirt. He looked sort of pissed off. Like someone had stolen his hair gel.

The boys yanked out two chairs and plunged into them. Knox loaded his meatballs with Parmesan cheese. "Anyone seen Nala? Think she'll be around any time soon?"

"Doubtful, Lover Boy," Tess piped up as she approached them, a fashion magazine clutched beneath her peacock-green manicure. Skater dresses floated across the cover like fog. "Something you should know about Nala. She's all straight A's and malnourished cuticles on the outside, but on the inside . . . just bones and bad taste in music. Beneath that big, goddess-like hair is a little brain, and that little brain has to study just like the rest of us mere mortals."

Malnourished cuticles? Yeah, right.

"She's in the library, Foxy," Sosie said.

"I should probably bring her a sandwich and a soda, then, huh? She's probably hungry," he said. They could study together, taking breaks at the coffee shop on the first floor every hour or so. She'd probably order something complicated. *A venti half-caf, no-foam, non-fat vanilla soy latte.* He'd wrap her up in the deep, black lambskin of his moto jacket when the air vents churned arctic-breeze. She'd take a twenty-minute powernap on his shoulder.

Dream big.

Gino Blackthorn ransacked through the buffet and slammed his tray of sea bass and brown rice onto the table. Swollen, bloodshot eyes surveyed the group. Grim, deeply frustrated eyes. Was he stoned, or just angry? Sosie dropped her spoon of *dulce de leche* and it hit her plate with a piercing clunk.

"Hey." Her voice rattled. Gino didn't respond. He looked furious, like a blood vessel in his forehead was about to burst. "You okay?"

"Fine." He fell into a chair, trying to find a comfortable seat amongst button tufts and embossed velvet. His mind was fused with a million different thoughts. What had just happened in the locker room . . . Rocko Borai . . . Sosie. He fidgeted. Left. Right. Uncomfortable position after uncomfortable position, until . . . finally . . . he sprung out of his chair and grabbed his neck in his hands. Sore, aching neck. "I think I need some air."

Tess rolled her eyes, watching Gino's hair flip-flopping in chilling breeze as he vanished through the patio doors. AXE Shock shower gel whirlpooled in his absence. *Mmm . . .* deep glacier mint.

"What the hell is his problem?" Tess snapped. Even though she hadn't talked to Gino in like, half a century, she still figured they'd go to the dance together. Why wouldn't he take her? Who else *was* there?

Sosie slowly stood to her feet. She could just barely make out Gino's shadowy figure pacing the veranda, all sorts of things on his mind . . . most of them about her. She couldn't stand to be left in the dark; vast, ghostly, bipolar dark. Why was he acting so weird? So different? Was this about the kiss?

"I think I need some air, too," Sosie announced, darting off as her mind stirred. She glanced back at the table to see Tess casually flipping through a magazine, Juliet clinging to Knox's swift movement, Knox and Brains mumbling back and forth about the locker room or football practice. Maybe both. No one cared that she and Gino had snuck away. Clearly their fling was still just a fling.

The patio door flung open. The temperature had dropped to a skin-biting forty, but Sosie roasted inside of her army-green bomber jacket. A cute, shag beanie drooped over her ears. There Gino was . . . off in the corner. He fumbled through his cell, clicking keys. Gravel cracked beneath Sosie's oxford flats. She appeared suddenly in crisp blue twilight.

"Hey," he mumbled, shoving his phone into his pocket, jostling his fingers through his thick, chocolate hair.

"Hey," Sosie said back. The waist on her loose hip-hugger jeans loosened as she breathed in deep, cold sky. Was she interrupting something? Wasn't he excited to see her? "Just wanted to make sure you weren't, like . . . dying or something. Cause how you were acting back there . . . that was kinda weird."

"Nah." He shrugged. "Not dying."

"Okay . . . ." They stood, staring at each other to the familiar sound of winter creatures scrabbling through the back woods. Sosie wondered if any minute some creepy, but totally cool bigfoot thing would come barreling out from behind the trees, picking bones from his teeth. She took a nervous breath, realizing they were totally alone. No Big Foot. "Is this about the other night? Because it's *so* not a big deal. It was just a kiss."

Gino fingered a smashed cigarette butt that was cemented within the jean of his pocket. "Nope," he said. A smoke would be just the thing to calm him down. Then, he wouldn't feel so pissed. Confused. Then, he'd just feel nothing. If he took a few puffs, he could tell Sosie what was really going on. He flicked the scorched, black butt through the air. It fell to the ground and he stomped at it angrily with his cleat. "We should talk, Freckles," he said finally.

"All right." Sosie glanced at him, nerves zapping through her veins. Something was wrong, she could feel it. "Then talk."

Gino looked her in the eyes — really looked at her — remembering how it felt to kiss her and how badly he wanted to do it again. His lungs burned. "So, about this dance thing . . . ." he said. "I was thinking about . . . I don't know . . . maybe taking Tess."

Tess? Tess Van der Pool? The same Tess he couldn't stand? Tess, the one he'd refused to walk home from their second, totally lame date? Tess, the person everyone hated? Was this a joke? Sosie nodded, her bottom lip pouting slightly. What was that kiss in the practice kitchen? Why did he even bother to show up that night? She yanked her beanie down over her frosted ear tips, gulping. What was she supposed to say? Congratulations?

Gino took a hesitant step forward. "What do you think about that?"

What did she think about that? He had to be smoking some junkie's crack pipe if he thought they were about to have *that* conversation . . . the one about Gino escorting The Bitch of Blairstown to the freaking dance. Sosie would have preferred him to ditch the dance all together for a post-apocalyptic video game and Hawaiian pizza, or a paint-ball tournament, or a colonoscopy, or a nap. Anything was better than him taking Tess to the dance.

Sosie smudged her thumb against her nose. She slipped further into her jacket, realizing exactly how cold it was outside. Or maybe Gino's cold heart was just paralyzing her. "Do what you want, I guess," she said bleakly, turning to head back inside. Her mind blurred with images of Gino and Tess slow dancing; lustrous, black hair dripping down Gino's suit.

Gino watched Sosie thump toward the cafeteria, her lazy hip-huggers just barely clinging to her narrow rear. She ripped the door open and stumbled inside, her blonde, knotted hair draggling out of her shag beanie. She was hurt, he could tell . . . and it killed him.

He should have told her the truth—maybe she'd understand, then. About what Rocko said. About what happened in the locker room. He blew out warm, smoky breath, surveying the back woods of Norfolk Island pines and peppermint trees. His lips tasted like sea salt, reminding him of his favorite baked potato chips. *Baked. Like he wanted to be.* His eyes pulled open, then refocused on a bushy, lemon bottlebrush plant. Suddenly, his cleats were yanking him toward the woods; dragging him like Siberian Huskies. He'd heard that one of the seniors on the golf team grew a few plants in there, under wraps. All he needed was to find one beautiful, green cannabis bud. He could smoke, get high, forget all about Sosie and Tess and that ridiculous dance, and when he started to remember, he'd smoke himself stupid all over again. He'd smoke the whole freaking forest if he had to, if it would help him forget what he had done to Sosie . . . the decision he had made . . . the mistake he was already regretting.

The Hour Before

An hour earlier, Gino Blackthorn had stood with a maroon, Blairstown embossed shower towel wrapped around his waist, his slick, chocolate hair speckled with shower water. Kiki Weames had made some donation that week to the boys' locker room—all-organic Turkish cotton towels for everyone—after getting the super-nerdy engineering professor, Timothy Tottle, to make a generous investment in her eco-friendly fashion line, Jute Jute Jooray!

Knox Ritchie was standing dead center on the massive BU logo, executing his touchdown dance with perfect agility with a few of his receivers. The locker room was like a festooned Mount Olympus. Everyone's voices echoed from behind wood-paneled doors with the utmost confidence of supremacy. There they were like the gods; like golden, Greek, may-statues-be-built-in-their-honor gods. But beyond it they were just a bunch of spoiled kids in a pigskin sanctuary flanked with gaudy marble pillars, flat screens, and surround sound.

Gino yanked out his sweats and stuck a leg through, listening to Chandler Vanderkrump yelp from inside the medical examination room. Silence rushed through the facility until everyone heard Dr. Clay's voice: "We're not certain about any of that . . . not yet. But we do know that you'll need physical therapy. Three, maybe four times a week. Probably Monday, Wednesday, Friday."

Yep. He was out for the season.

Coach Mike grumbled something.

"Okay. Shall we get going, then?" asked Dr. Clay.

Dr. Clay and Coach Mike jerked open the doors, wheeling Chandler on a gurney toward the exit. Chandler's shoulder was harnessed in a viscoelastic brace, his ankle wrapped up in fawn, and his head lying crooked on a slab of memory foam. May need surgery, but they'd take him to the hospital for a second opinion on that. All of the boys stared as Chandler's petrified green eyes paced the burnt umber ceiling tiles. He'd never gain back total strength in that arm. He'd never be able to make a near-impossible catch again. His athletic career was over before it had even begun.

But before being wheeled out, Chandler shoved the hand of his good arm in the air, making a trembling fist. They'd go on without him. They'd do just fine. The doors closed around the gurney, and the blathering began. Which second-string receiver would be the lucky bastard to replace him?

Rocko Borai ripped his midnight blue, long-sleeved tee over his head and layered it beneath a kangaroo-pocket hooded poncho. "What an asshole! Now, I'll have to change Chandler's underwear and shave his back and do all of that other, my-room-mate's-a-cripple shit."

Gino smirked, jerking his other leg through. Leave it up to Rocko to make Chandler's shoulder injury about himself. Oh, poor little Rocko. So deprived of a normal life. Stricken with the burden of an incapacitated roommate. Gino slipped his feet back through his cleats, starving for a medium-rare, blueberry-bourbon filet. But it wasn't Monday. It was Thursday. *Thoshky* Thursday.

"So Blackthorn," Rocko said as he stuffed his burnt-orange tarpaulin duffle bag with his practice jersey, cleats, some deodorant. He started to pull on a beanie, but noticed a big stain of protein shake on it. Chocolate. He'd have to give it to the redhead he had been hitting on in French so she could wash it with some of that lavender fabric softener. Made everything feel like whipped cream. Rocko pulled socks out of his locker. "I was thinking about asking Susie-Q to that dance," he announced.

Gino's jaw clenched as he watched Rocko toss a few more things into his bag. Cologne. A razor. Some aftershave. Susie-Q? As in . . . Sosie?

Rocko tucked his feet inside the warm, grey cotton. He wished that Knox Ritchie—who was still trampling his Bollywood touchdown dance all over the BU seal—hadn't paid Miss Hart's assistant, Bill, for two early tickets just to lock Nala down for the dance. If Rocko had as much money as Knox, he'd simply buy the freaking dance . . . or buy Nala, for that matter. But all of that was impossible now. At least by asking Sosie he could stare at Nala all night long. Tiny little bones prancing around. Glistening olive skin popping against silk that sucked to her like Crest Whitestrips. Maybe he could even snatch her up for a slow dance. That's all it would take, he was convinced, to make her fall in love with him. "Still haven't made up my mind about it,"

Rocko said. "Thought Nala Middleton might be interested, but . . . she's going with Slumdog Millionaire over there," he added, glancing at Knox. "Gotta take what I can get, I guess."

Gino glared back at Rocko harshly. "I don't know." He rolled his stick of Cool Rush Degree under his armpits and flung it into his bag. It struck his dual-density football girdle with a thud. "Don't you think that's kind of . . . messed up? Just takin' her 'cause the other one's busy?"

"Yeah . . . ." Rocko said. "What's your point?"

"Dude . . . ." Gino rolled his head on his neck until it cracked. "Sosie and Nala are friends. Find someone else to be your stand-in."

Rocko took out his protein shake—what was left of it—and took a swig. Why was Gino freaking out about which girl Rocko took to the dance? Why was he protecting Susie-Q? Since when were they even friends? Since Second Base? Rocko fumbled through the blurry memories of that night. Leapfrog, peeing in the woods, waking up with gum in his ear. He supposed something could have happened between Sosie and Gino when he wasn't around . . . or awake. *Damn it!* Why were all of his friends hooking up with his dibs?

"I know what this is," Rocko said. "You have a thing for her, don't you, Blackthorn?" He slammed his locker, stuffing his arms across his steroid pecs and staring Gino in the face. Why did Knox and Gino—his supposed friends—feel the need to poach all of the women he wanted? Or pretended to want? Why couldn't they go get wifed-up with some ugly, but equally sophisticated etiquette brats?

Gino fumbled through his pockets anxiously, twining a puff of lint between his fingers. Maybe he did have a thing for Sosie. After all, that kiss in the practice kitchen had been . . . well . . . incredible. But it was none of Rocko's business one way or the other.

Rocko put on his shoes. "Dude, chill. I don't give two shits. Have her," he said. "She's too needy, and not even that hot."

Not even that hot? Were they talking about the same girl? Gino zipped up his bag and slung it over his shoulder. His stomach was twisting in knots and his arms were aching. He didn't have time to argue with Rocko. All he wanted was to take an ice bath and go eat something: something other than *Thoshky.* "You have your opinion, I have mine," Gino said, stomping away, still wearing his cleats.

Rocko watched Gino catch up with Knox Ritchie. They both stopped by the Electrolyte Bar on their way out. Brains Fink, who was elevating his cast and flipping through a fitness magazine behind the bar, passed them two strawberry kiwi recovery drinks. They clanked them together, tossed their heads back, and chugged.

Gino won. Like always.

"4.5 seconds, Blackthorn. You kicked his ass!" Brains wailed.

They're such pricks, Rocko thought. *All of them.* Knox was some trust-fund baby who ordered Moscato with frozen grapes. He washed his hair with white truffle oil shampoo imported from the province of Cuneo in Piedmont, Northern Italy. He ordered lomi-lomi massage therapists to the dorms twice a week, and then passed them around like joints. And Gino was an even bigger prick. All he did was eat, sleep, and lift weights. Rocko was sick of Knox and Gino getting whatever they wanted. Nothing was work to them. Everything came naturally. Sports, school, girls.

Watching Gino and Knox smiling, bashing their drinks together, probably getting ready to meet up with their little girlfriends really started to piss Rocko off. He felt his muscles stiffening like left out cheese. Gino and Sosie. Knox and Nala. They were all freaking perfect. Big, perfect, wasted life.

"You know what?" Rocko blathered, chasing down Gino, Knox, and Brains. His fists flexed at his side like he was ready to swing. "I change my mind. Think I'll take Susie-Q to that dance, after all. And maybe . . . I don't know," he cleared his throat cockily, "maybe I'll take her home afterwards. Get her real familiar with my mattress."

Everyone in the locker room started to watch. A fight was about to break out, they could tell. The background filled with noise as guys gambled their receiver gloves and speed sleds and balance wristbands and protein powder on who would throw the first punch. Some peppercorn-haired boy sent out a mass text. *Borai — Blackthorn showdown. How many punches does it take to knock out a meathead? Place bets here.*

Gino took a breath against the array of eyes beating down on him like thrashing stadium lights. "What the hell's your problem?"

"Problem? No problem. Just letting you know that by the end of the night Susie-Q's going to be my little b . . . . "

Rocko's buzzed head smacked into a wall as Gino choked the air from his throat, fingers digging into his tight, dark skin. The crowd watched hungrily. Someone yelled, "Beat his ass, Blackthorn! Beat his ass!"

Rocko struggled for a breath. Wheezed. Choked. Punched at Gino's head. Gurgled. Nothing. Gino kept watching the color drain from Rocko's eyes, brown to yellowish to yellower. Finally, he let go. Rocko caught himself by his knees, breathing painful, sharp breaths. "Next time, you die," Gino said, ripping his bag off the floor and stomping toward the gym doors. He didn't have time to kill Rocko. Not today.

"Always the tough guy, huh Blackthorn?" Rocko barely managed to choke out. The entire locker room watched as he panted, grabbing his neck. Gino dropped his bag and slowly turned. He was starting to think that he could quench his appetite just by crushing Rocko's brains into his mostly-vacant skull. "How tough would you be if I told Sosie — if I told everyone here — the truth about you?" Rocko said. "About what a loser you are."

Gino stood, watching as sweat dripped from Rocko's short, black hair.

"About your loser brother and your loser parents . . . parents who couldn't even afford this place . . . who shipped you off to Elkins because they couldn't stand to look at you." Rocko's voice stalled. "People always said they didn't even drop you themselves. Did you know that? Your own parents didn't even care enough to say goodbye."

Gino's eyes sunk into deep, black bags.

"Blackthorn, even that *bitch* deserves better than you. Somewhere deep down you know that," Rocko said, chuckling. "Undeserving is in your blood."

And the room went silent.

Gino felt the fastening stares as he tossed his duffle bag over his shoulder, his pale, brown eyes veiled with unfortunate truth. Maybe he was a loser. Maybe Sosie did deserve better than he was capable of. Maybe he should just . . . let her go . . . for her own good. The door flew open under his fingers, and Gino vanished into the gym, his hair slicked with shower water and matted to the back of his head.

Rocko surveyed the room. All of his teammates were watching him, pissed. "What the *hell* are you all looking at?" he roared through the must of shower steam. No one spoke. "Well?"

Knox Ritchie grabbed his bag off the floor and shoved his cell into his pocket. He shook his head back at Rocko with deeply disappointed eyes. "Parents who couldn't stand to look at him, huh?" Knox asked. "Whatever makes you feel big, Borai."

Riddles and Pills

Estelle Hart clutched the tiny, silver microphone in her hand, glaring out across the feast of brine-soaked turkeys, fruitcakes, and eggnog. Her hair was bundled beneath a Santa Claus hat as she stood on stage, smothered in red and white fluff, one pair of hideous, green pilgrim-like shoes crowding her toes. "Welcome, starved elves," she chirped, "to the Winter Ball Feast; a tradition we cherish here at BU! Tomorrow, all of you freshman will attend your first Winter Ball, and I don't mean to toot my own horn, but . . . these may be the best decorations this school has ever seen!" *Toot, toot*. Estelle's yellow eggnog sloshed inside of her glass as she tried to clap a hand against her tights along with two or three staff members from the audience. The noise dissolved away, and Estelle was suddenly mute. "Well . . . ughhh . . . how 'bout a little Christmas riddle? What did Santa pay for his sleigh? Anyone?" She took a threatening gulp. "Nothing! It was on the house," she giggled. The audience yawned, rubbing their eyes and wiping the saliva from their lips as they imagined their first bites of sweet potato casserole.

Sosie Hinkhouse and Nala Middleton slipped between the cafeteria doors, tiptoeing on chunky, wooden-heeled stilettos and whiskey-brown ankle booties, their legs swallowed in tribal-printed skirts. Since Sosie practically had to pry Nala from the bathroom mirror and her tube of extra-bold mascara, they were late . . . once again.

Near the back, the two girls found flutes of champagne, glasses of merlot and eggnog near a giant sign reading, "Must Show I.D." A beady-eyed, black-haired bartender guarded the supply of bottles. As Estelle's voice rang through the corridor, Sosie ripped her I.D. out of her neon-blue patent leather clutch and passed it off, fumbling her fingers over two glasses of wine. "Merlot, champagne, or eggnog?" she asked Nala, giving her a nudge. "Show him your I.D."

"Merlot for me," Nala said nervously, passing her license off with tense shoulders. She was unimpressed by the distinct stench of cheap wine haunting the bar, but was far too worried about getting caught with a fake.

"Happy early birthday," the bartender nodded to Sosie.

"God," Sosie rolled her eyes, blinking down at the fake birthday embossed on her license. "Another year. I feel so old."

The girls snatched up their glasses and searched for open seating. Knox Ritchie was sitting nearby, his sandy-blonde hair slicked back like Bruce Wayne, wearing Michel St Pierre slacks and a pair of gorgeous, split-toe oxfords. A few chairs away,

Rocko Borai sipped his second glass of champagne, stealing peeks down Juliet's off-the-shoulder sweetheart dress. Tess was reapplying her lip liner, squinting at a silver spoon she used to see her fish-eyed reflection. Brains cleaned his glasses with a napkin. They were like little kids stuffed in a minivan. Fourteen hours until Disney World, and weeklong thunderstorms in Orlando.

Sosie set down her drink and collapsed between Knox and Brains, readjusting the straps on her stilettos before planting two frisky kisses on their cheeks. She couldn't help but wonder where Gino was. Even though he was taking Tess to the dance. Even though they had been ignoring each other in class. She was still bummed when she didn't find him at the table, drunk or stoned, Tess's boney fingers paddling through his scalp to the nauseating chime of Miss Hart's bangle set.

Sosie peered up at Estelle who was quacking like a duck. "How long has she been going for?" she asked the table, pointing to the stage. Estelle's hands patted her belly and reenacted a nineteenth century Dutch Sinterklaas. It seemed clear that she had been participating in their Jenever drinking traditions, too.

"Ten minutes, give or take," Brains piped.

"Ten minutes too long," Knox added gruffly, taking a long drink of wine. He was embarrassed *for* her.

Nala slipped into a seat on the other side of Knox, watching Estelle flop around like a jellybean. What did Graham see in her? An uncanny resemblance to Mrs. Claus? Nala quivered. She felt really weird about how she had left things with Graham. "Things" as in TA things.

Since that night Estelle showed up with Sushi, Nala just sort of . . . quit going . . . to make things less complicated, she told herself. But most nights—after Graham's last class let out—Nala would watch from the library as familiar, flickering lights poured out of his classroom windows. Lights bouncing off of a home cinema projector, she assumed. Maybe he was waiting there in case she changed her mind. Or maybe he had someone new to watch movies with.

Nala could feel Knox's eyes burning holes in her skin as she thought about things. TA things. Movies and Graham things. She tried to focus on Estelle. A tragically misplaced dreadlock of blonde hair tumbled out of the woman's hat and stuck to her neck. Had she forgotten to brush out her hair, or were dreadlocks somehow . . . festive?

"Hey," Knox said, noticing Nala's remarkably perfect skin. No blemishes, no blackheads like someone in a Proactiv commercial. She was as gorgeous as he had ever seen. Silky strands of straight, sleek, almond-brown hair dripped down her backless halter and shimmered in the torrent of dim lighting above. She smiled her wine-stained lips, and he became lightheaded. He was brainlessly and stupidly enthralled. He felt like a ten-year-old boy gawping at the malt-speckled shelves in a candy store. Or a fourteen-year-old sitting front row behind the pitcher's mound at the World Series, subdued beneath hot dogs and peanut shells. Or a young, rich Blairstown grad hypnotized by the words "I do" from his bride-to-be in Vera Wang. It literally hurt him to like her so much, to sense her next to him and to know that she wasn't fully his, to feel that his life was wasted on wanting and wishing, to imagine her wanting and wishing for something else . . . someone else.

"Hi," Nala finally whispered. Her smile widened at his dark blue, Milanese dress shirt. "See? Blue totally is your color," she said, leaning over, her lips grazing his ear. "Don't forget who said it first!"

Knox felt all sorts of boy juices revving up in his veins as Nala pulled away. She sipped her wine again, clueless. It was probably a good thing she didn't know how she made him feel. Would she still like him if she knew that his insides turned into testosterone mush around her? He cleared his throat and pictured Juliet sitting next to him instead, gurgling punch, as hopeless and harmless as ever. Things had always been easy with Juliet. She was simple and sweet. She was like . . . one of the guys.

Envisioning yellow, bouncy curls, Knox said, "I won't forget," and winked. His hand slipped over Nala's knee, pinching the stitching on her skirt. She felt warmness crawl through her belly button, a little tingly as Knox rolled his hand up and down her thigh. Further. Softer. Knox was just so adorable and charming; short, beach-waved hair and round lips; crushing smile. All Nala could think about was their "moment" in the woods, and how badly she had wanted that kiss.

Across the table, Rocko Borai glared at Nala and Knox as they flirted in ignorant bliss, guzzling down their merlot and giggling at the vigor in Miss Hart's voice as it whooshed through the surround sound. They were like those romantics in the black and white movies having coffee and biscotti on the veranda of some stuffy, old-world bistro, blathering about the weather and the war. There was always a war. He thought his eyes would start bleeding if he kept watching.

"Remember what we talked about?" Rocko nudged Juliet and ransacked through his pocket. Juliet's blonde lashes that were flaked with eye goop blinked open, and she noticed his hand appear with two white pills. "Chandler said they're harmless. It'll just give their drinks a little . . . boost," Rocko said.

Juliet nodded back unsurely. Just last night, Rocko had sat lazily in the cafeteria wearing a thistle mélange polo, bribing Brains with cauliflower pizza and Xbox for test answers to the stats exam when he noticed Juliet slavering over the dessert cart, her eyes fastened on buttermilk pound cake. She had been just the girl he wanted to see. He yanked her aside to explain that he could get some strong painkillers from Chandler, who'd been prescribed them for a shoulder thing, something that would help their "plan" to break up Nala and Knox. She had regretfully agreed.

"Just slip one in his drink when he's not looking," Rocko hissed, taking a gulp of champagne. The wearied crowd around him huffed into their sleeves, glaring at the headless, not yet carved turkeys stacked around the tables as if they were anomalous, mint-green Martians.

Starvation may cause hallucinations, some sign somewhere should have read.

Rocko nudged Juliet again. He had spent all of last night coercing her into being his little, frizzy-headed sidekick, and there was no way in hell he would let her back out. Not now that he was holding the freaking mind-erasers in his calloused hand.

"I don't know," Juliet mumbled, peeking up at Knox and Nala whose minds were so brainlessly and frustratingly bonding over the color blue. She slipped back to that moment with Knox on the dock when the sunset had trickled down Rocky Pines ski lift, and they were staring clear across calm, blue lake. Even as the pain of remembering stirred through her body, Juliet realized she didn't want to go through with it. Any of it. Knox was already adorning his flagpole with a pennant of victory, it seemed, and NALA was written on it in glistening gold sunset. What was the point of fighting for what she wanted if Nala was the freaking destination and Juliet was merely a red dot on the peripheries of Knox's radar?

She glanced back at Knox only for a second, noting that his rows of perfect, bleached teeth were in sync with Nala's. His happiness was enough. Wasn't it?

"Here." Rocko whacked Juliet's leg, annoyed. He assessed the crowd for snitches who might be noticing the drugs clamped tightly in his fist. Pain pills were practically illicit, and the Blairstown administration was amassed with silver-haired snobs from the '60s. Not the Zeppelin's '60s, either. If caught, he'd probably be sat down by Principal Dotie, told some weird, back-in-the-day story about how—believe it or not—Dotie was quite the party animal himself, but after months of waking up in a puddle of his own vomit, vodka bottle fused to his hand, blunt burning through his Italian-leather money clip, he'd realized he was wasting his life away. And then he'd casually mention how he had always wanted to be a principal since he was just a wee, little lad, and after the partying, the fooling around, and the 3 a.m. pizza runs, he got his shit together and made it happen. He'd brag: look at me now. And Rocko would see a fat, smelly, lonely old man standing before him with nothing to show for his life but a Jon Matinee wallet and an ego the size of Jupiter . . . one pant-size less than the bread baskets latched to his hips. Maybe Rocko would be put on probation, kicked off the football team, drug-tested every two weeks for the rest of his college career. Or maybe Principal Dotie would let him off in exchange for some high-grade marijuana. Either way, it all sounded really, really dramatic, especially considering he wouldn't even be getting high off of those pills himself. "Come on, Blondie!" he snapped. "Take one before someone sees!"

Juliet shoved Rocko's hand out of her lap, patting down her sheath of floral print. His eyes were big and scary. "Sorry. It just sounds dangerous," she whispered. "I'm out."

Dangerous? What the hell do you think harmless means, you stupid, fickle girl? Rocko turned away angrily. He chugged the rest of his champagne, glass flute clenched beneath his fist, which was seemingly too fragile for his rage. Jumping out of his chair, Rocko stormed for the bar, one glass of merlot on his mind for Nala and the anticipation of one tiny, white pill dissolving in its bask. Maybe two now that he had an extra.

Rocko would be sure to take great care of Nala once her body reacted to the meds. He'd skip dinner to carry her somewhere safe. Her dorm. His dorm. He'd hold her hair back as she puked in the toilet. He'd change her when she complained about the vomit on her halter. And in the morning when she peeled those sparkly, golden eyes open, she'd see him . . . her knight in shining armor . . . her hero.

Although heroes weren't typically the sketchy guy at the bar slipping pills in your drink . . . .

You're the Only Girl for Me

The turkeys had been carved, the empty wine bottles had been stacked into a pyramid, and drunken bodies failed around beneath beautifully chipped crown molding. Knox Ritchie took his last sip of merlot hesitantly and stared back into the same pair of round, sparkling eyes he had been gazing into all night long. Eyes like butter-pecan ice cream. "Christmas is my favorite holiday," he said to Nala. Groans reverberated off of dinner plates as the waiters swooped in and began to clear the tables. "Everyone is always weirdly happy."

"Yeah," Nala nodded, blinking at the crowd of people floundering in food comas. "People always transform into like, saints around the holidays. Like every other day people are just walking around town, taking things for granted. Shoes and feet. Or even simple things, like public transportation and . . . burritos!"

Knox laughed. *Burritos. As if she ever ate those.* He grabbed her knee beneath the table and squeezed it. "God, I love it when you say stuff like that. I'll never take it for granted."

Nala gasped, feeling his hand linger in place, stroking the tier of shea butter lotion on her bare skin. Honest Knox, always saying what was on his mind. Genuine. Real. He was great . . . really. Why didn't she appreciate that until now? Maybe because of Graham . . . because he was this giant fog that had clouded her sensibility, keeping her as naïve and unaware as Estelle Hart's wardrobe. Maybe all along, Knox was meant to emerge from Graham's long casted shadow as the safe but obvious contender. Maybe those strands of gorgeous, dirty-blonde hair had been made just for her. Maybe he was her *one and only.*

As Nala meditated in a tipsy stupor, she noticed Rocko Borai across the table, wrinkling an eyebrow at her and grabbing at a glass of red wine. It seemed as if he had been watching her all night long, just waiting for his moment. Just like Ted Bundy. Rocko's voice caught in his throat as Nala locked eyes with him. "I, ugh . . ." he stammered. "I saw you were out." His fingers slowly pressed the glass of merlot across the table, staring into the mere of smushed grape whirling inside of it like a vortex. He wondered if the pill had dissolved totally. Had he chopped it up acceptably? Had he spiked it with too much? Had he spiked it with enough? *Shit.* What if Nala was allergic? Would she die? And what would happen to him if she did? Would he spend the next 60 years in prison, clenching his bar soap like the last pair of size thirteen Air Jordans? Those thirty freaking minutes in a restroom stall hacking at a pill with a butter knife better not have been a complete waste.

By the time Rocko made it back to the table, glass of wine in hand, the turkeys had been carved and the people were grumbling with fullness. He was still starving. But taking Nala home — making her fall in love with him — was more important than the Winter Ball Feast, anyway.

It would work, because it had to work.

Nala reached for the glass confusedly. Something about Rocko just seemed a little off. His body was propelled by her every move, his eyes were narrowed with black haze, his confidence was exhausted with a stutter. He just wasn't his usual bigheaded self. He seemed . . . almost . . . scared.

"Thanks," Nala mumbled, collapsing back into her chair. She swirled the glass in circles, staring into it. "But to be honest, the last time I had three glasses . . . I was kind of a mess."

"Nah, come on. You weren't a *mess*," Knox interrupted, stealing the glass from Nala's red manicure, remembering the day they had skipped class for Cloud Nine. He thought she had been completely charming after three glasses. Damn, he wished he'd had that chance to kiss her. "And even if you were, I think the day turned out all right. Don't you?" Suddenly, Knox's lips met the glass, and the wine slipped between his teeth. Spiked wine.

Rocko felt his heart pummel against his green, gingham-checked dress shirt as Knox took his second, third, and fourth sips. There was nothing Rocko could do but sit and wait. Wait for something peculiar to happen . . . something that hopefully didn't end with flowers and an open casket.

Ten minutes later, as waiters lurched through the dining hall in pursuit of cold beet-casserole and turkey scraps, the crowd began to vanish into the moonlit square. Knox Ritchie stumbled for the steps outside, and instead face-planted onto the lawn. His only thoughts before he dozed off were of the familiar scent of recently trimmed grass and the hovering glow of moonlight.

"Did anyone see how many drinks he had?" Sosie asked, jerking on Knox's sports coat sleeve and nudging him with a chunky wooden heel. Rocko marched forward and grabbed Knox, slinging him over his back coolly. Effortlessly.

"He had three or four, I think," Nala said, "unless he had a few at the bar before dinner."

"Don't worry about it, ladies," Rocko interrupted. "Knox has always been a lightweight."

Sosie, Nala, and Juliet frowned at Knox's totally flaccid, but deeply tanned arms which stretched for the ground like pancake batter from a bowl. He was somehow still beautiful, even though his hair was no longer trapped in a stiff, shiny wave of gel, and his face was now matted with filaments of grass. "All right, girls. Say goodnight to the big baby," Rocko finally said. His shoulder was starting to ache. "I should get him back before he starts puking up red and green."

Nala and Sosie walked up to Knox and planted two wet kisses on his cheek. Nala couldn't help but think how Graham would never get so stupidly drunk. It was kind of embarrassing to see Knox like that.

"Thanks for taking care of him," Nala whispered to Rocko, stroking the strands of Knox's hair which glinted with shards of green lawn. "It's really sweet of you."

Rocko shrugged, grinning smugly. Maybe all along, all that was needed was for him to make Knox look like drunk, lethargic idiot. Maybe Nala would see Rocko as her knight in shining armor, after all. "This is just something you'll learn about Ritchie," Rocko said, feeling the 180-pound pile weighing heavily on him. "He's a little . . . immature."

Juliet's eyes welded with Rocko's. She knew exactly what was going on.

As Nala and Sosie waved goodbye and began to waltz toward Alistair Dwelling with a throng of their wide-eyed peers, Juliet stayed with Rocko, who walked at crawling speed toward the male dormitory. Her mind was hazy with a million different thoughts. Nothing was said . . . not immediately, at least. And before she knew it, Juliet's back was buried against a wood planked elevator wall, and she was pretending to admire the lame jazz that trickled out of the speakers as Rocko pushed the fourth floor button.

"So, did you mean to . . . ."

"No," Rocko interrupted. "Not exactly."

Juliet nodded, patting down the wrinkles on her floral print. She didn't need to know any more details. She didn't even want to. All she needed to do was figure out what the hell she was still doing there.

The elevator doors slipped open, and Rocko carried Knox down a black-walled hallway lined with giant, grey, contemporary art and white-marble tiling. Heavy European rock and house music blared from behind bedroom doors. Electric guitars hung from above where Alistair Dwelling similarly glistened with jewel-strewn chandeliers. Dusky lighting flickered from wall sconces. Juliet gaped. Everything was so freaking cool in the male dorm. It was like being backstage at a concert in Sweden, where rock stars chugged beers, painted on their eyeliner, strummed their guitars, and thrashed their drumsticks against vintage, tobacco-stained wallpaper.

"This is his place," Rocko said, stopping in front of a smoky, grey-oak door. "Check his pockets for his key, would ya?"

Juliet stared blankly at Knox's black slacks. They seemed so ominous and scary . . . full of unmentionables. Even though she had been desperately in love with him since the first time he had said *"bonjour"* in his awful French accent, she had never hugged him, let alone searched his junk for junk. Maybe his arms had grazed hers once or twice. Maybe she had fantasized a million times about his lips on her neck, his fingers tumbling through her hair, his hands massaging her perfectly rosy shoulders with sunblock. But their bodies had never purposefully collided.

"Don't dally now, Blondie! My shoulder is about to implode," Rocko snapped. "Hate for my blood to ruin that pretty dress."

Juliet trembled. She slipped her fingers into Knox's pocket. What if he woke up to find her ransacking through his pants, groping his thigh through pocket lint? Would he ever forgive her for being so forward?

Would he be into it?

Inside, she could feel his cell phone, a packet of mints, and something else. Something sharp. Ripping her hand out, she peered down into it. The silver key glowed in her fist, and Rocko snatched it up and shoved it into the door. The three of them barreled inside.

The door closed behind them and Juliet skimmed the room, instantly hypnotized by Knox's uber-urbane boudoir. Everything about it was insanely perfect. White leather club chairs were littered around a gorgeous, rustic trunk coffee table. Copies of horseracing magazines and vintage rock-and-roll record shells wreathed the lounge. Big, bronze, velvety drapes poured down the tall, glass windows. It was as if some snobby New York interior decorator flew in from Manhattan just to drown his room in Egyptian cotton and plasmas. No clothes were slung across the palettes of black shag rug. All of the trashcans had been emptied, the countertops wiped down. Juliet felt dirty just being there, as if she might contaminate his purified air.

Near the mirage of flat screens, Knox's head flopped into the black and gold bedcovers of his gigantic California King with a thud. Strands of hair flopped into his eyes as grass scattered across his covers. "We should get going," Rocko said to Juliet, rubbing his shoulder where Knox's lifeless, potato-sack-of-a-body had once dangled. "Before we have to hold Princess's hair back."

Juliet wrinkled her nose, glaring down at Knox's sunbaked skin. He was squandered in total obliteration. He was beginning to drool. They couldn't just leave him like that. What if he woke up? Would he do something that could get him expelled? Or worse . . . something that could get him *killed*?

"When does his roommate get back?" Juliet asked, plopping down on the bed next to Knox, staring at his pale, squinting blue eyes.

"Roommate?" Rocko almost choked. "Knox is way too pretentious to have a roommate, Blondie."

Well, that explained the one bed . . . .

What would Rocko have her do? Leave him there to choke on his own puke? Juliet skimmed her fingers through Knox's scalp, imagining that they were the only two people in the room. She could pretend that they'd just flown back from a rowing tournament in Connecticut, where his team had secured a fifty-pound plaque for the Blairstown Trophy Room. Knox was just relaxing, jet-lagged, his face glowing with a perfect winter tan as he received a scalp massage from his fiancé, Juliet. Or she could pretend that they'd just returned from a date and after eating burgers and getting drunk off of mudslides, Knox had drifted to sleep, the last words from his lips a muffled, "I love you."

Juliet sighed noisily. "I'm gonna stay with him for a while," she said. "Just until he wakes up, and I know he's okay."

Rocko stuffed his hands in his pockets and shrugged. It seemed kind of unfair that Juliet was reaping the benefits of his mistake. "Fine. Just don't tell him anything you shouldn't."

"I won't." She stroked Knox's head carefully. "Promise."

Rocko vanished in seconds, headed for the upstairs kitchen to make a microwavable pizza and watch MMA in the lounge, leaving Juliet and Knox totally alone. The last time they had been so alone, Knox was pathetically awaiting a text message from Nala, and Juliet had realized that it was time she let him go so that he could be happy, with or without her. She wondered if she still meant that "with or without her" part.

Juliet laid her head next to Knox's, peering over at the wide-set windows. The drapes had been secured back so that the glass exposed the gorgeous, glowing, moonlit skyline, where stars kindled in clusters and hickory-strewn mountaintops blackly stretched for the smear of clouds above. She imagined how Nala and Knox would be around Christmas time . . . bundled up in robes, sipping creamy hot chocolate near the fire, collapsing into each other's enthralling scents as they gazed upon the sward of snow below. Her heart thumped jealously inside of her and tears collected in her eyes. Knox was incredible, and Nala didn't even notice. She probably never would.

Juliet twirled a strand of his hair around her finger. Now that she had felt a piece of him, she never wanted to let go. It was the closest she had ever been—and maybe ever would be—to something more.

"Knox?" she whispered. His body remained limp and lethargic. "I just wanted to tell you that . . . even though we're just friends, I think you're really . . . great. I like you more than that."

Knox continued to breathe in drunken bubbles, and Juliet hoped that on some unconscious level he had heard. Maybe it was like hypnosis. Maybe she was channeling his inner psyche. Maybe Rocko's plan wasn't so lame after all. Maybe Knox would wake up, and it would be like he had been struck in the ass by Cupid's arrow. The first thing he'd see would be Juliet's glistening, crooked teeth hovering over him, smiling into his soul.

He snored mildly, and she took that to mean that he was trying to speak through the drugs. "I keep hoping that one day you'll see me in class, or at dinner, or on campus, and it will hit you suddenly: *she's beautiful. Why couldn't I see it until now?* And you'll know that every time I do my makeup, or every time I fix my hair, or every time I buy a new shirt, it's for you." Juliet's eyes flooded with tears again, mostly from feeling sorry for herself.

"It's always for you," she added, wiping her cheeks against the covers, leaving a streak of pale concealer behind. "Even if I'm never yours and you're never mine, I'll always have tonight."

Juliet's fingers slipped from Knox and she scrunched her toes inside of her big, chunky platforms. She knew Knox would be okay by the morning. Tomorrow he'd wake up and aside from the headache, the muscle cramps, and the smog of poor memory, Nala would still be the first thing on his mind. He'd still want her so badly he couldn't see straight. He'd still wait for her text messages on that dock, scrubbing the grime from his oar with impatience, peering out into the lake with a morose flicker in his eyes. Come morning, Nala would still infect him in the most beautiful and frustrating way. And in the meantime, Juliet would waste her love on this boy who couldn't love her back.

Juliet stood and began to brush the creases from her dress when she felt a hand grab her wrist and jerk her back toward the bed. Her heels flew out from under her as her body sank into the duvet and she was swallowed in juniper cologne. Knox lay, his eyes wrenched shut, his hand bonded to hers. She couldn't believe he was holding her there. If he let go, she'd sail through the windows and fade into the night sky.

Then, Knox mumbled.

Juliet's eyes opened wide. "What?" she screeched, assembling on her elbow, shaking him. "What are you saying? Speak up!"

She threw herself closer, her ear practically smushed against his lips. Knox's breath warmed her. "Yougarine," he said.

"What's that!?"

"Youmarfine," he said.

Youmarfine? Juliet listened intently, her body buzzing with nerves. Perhaps Knox was trying to say something, anything, to let it be known that he was still in there. Or maybe he was sleep talking. Maybe Youmarfine was some one-eyed alien leading the Youmarfees into victory, pummeling Knox beneath his big, three-toed foot.

Juliet pulled away, watching Knox's lips tremble with effort. Her head drifted closer, admiring his long, curled eyelashes. He was even more beautiful up close. Dreamy. Perfect. Then, she suddenly pressed her mouth against his. He tasted like wine and grass. It was as wonderful as she had imagined. Soft, like whipped cream. It almost felt like he was kissing her back.

And then she heard him clearly.

"You are mine," he said, eyes still clamped shut, body still torpid. Juliet's eyes filled with tears as she peered down on him, feeling his fingers entwine with hers. Had her kiss woken him up, just like in a fairytale? Had it cleared his mind? Could he finally see what had been standing in front of him the whole time? Her lips grinned down on him as she reveled in the possibilities. Maybe now they could be together, now that he knew she'd always take care of him.

Then Knox spoke again, this time as clear as day. "You'll always be mine, Nala. You're the only girl for me."

Winter Wonderland

Juliet plodded along on her nude, nubuck pumps, her arm intertwined with the sleeve of Brain's oyster-gray, two-button poplin suit. Miss Hart had really outdone herself with the décor for the ball. Everything was frosted with fake icicles and snowflakes. Even the hammer-beam trusses dangling from the stenciled ceiling were spattered with sparkling snow-powder. The cherry brick walls were hidden by beautiful green quaking aspens whose branches were bleached snow-white. One thing was for certain: they had just stepped foot into Winter Wonderland.

Juliet ran her eyes over the Christmas lights dangling above and yanked Brains toward Sosie and Rocko who were sipping apple cider through crystal champagne flutes at a table nearby. Juliet's white, sequine-bodiced sweetheart dress entwined with glitter and scraps of plastic snow as she stomped across the room. Flinging her arms above her frizzy, knotted up-do she squealed, "Sos! Is that champagne? You're so naughty!" and hugged her neck.

Sosie looked really pretty in her classic but simple corset gown, her lips smothered in MAC's Lady Danger lipstick and her golden highlights arched out of her face. Juliet was a little intimidated just breathing next to her. Sosie took a sip of apple cider and yawned. "No, but can you find me some? These shoes are killing me!" She kicked out her new patent leather, studded bow platforms and glared down at the shockingly tall heel. They were like, five inches! Of course they were killing her!

Juliet compared her measly, two-inches. She had felt so beautiful until she saw Sosie and Tess strutting around on their long, skinny legs, puckering their bright, red lips in the air, flaunting their skinny, concave torsos beneath sheaths of glistening fabric. Where was Tess, anyway? She hadn't seen her since they shared body butter in the dorms. Hopefully she was de-beautifying somewhere. Juliet took a long breath. Tonight, she refused to be background noise. Tonight, she was going to be the center of attention even if it killed her!

"Brains, can you get us something to drink? You know," Juliet nudged, "something with alcohol. And make it quick, puh-lease! Our shoes are killing us."

Because Juliet's two-inch pumps were so very *risqué*.

She fell into a seat, her blonde, wisped bangs stabbing into her makeup, which had taken about a century to apply. She noticed Rocko nearby, humming drunkenly into his glass as he examined some activity on the dance floor. He had pre-gamed with

Chandler Vanderkrump and eight Manhattan Dries, and totally reeked of whiskey. But at least he looked good.

Juliet's eyes shot across the room. Black sports coats and floral applique fogged the flat of dancers. A few sophomores and juniors huddled around the punch bowl, emptying their flasks of vodka inside. Elle Moody swayed her flimsy hips to the acoustic chime, smothered her lips against her boyfriend's, and stroked her fingers over his stubbly neck. Ed Pote unsuccessfully attempted the robot. Then, someone familiar flickered into view. Knox Ritchie was slow dancing in a silvery-gray, Neapolitan tailored suit, his hair slicked into a flowing side-part. He looked gorgeous. Happy. Too happy. Her eyes followed his body, swaying along with someone else's. Someone tiny and beautiful. Nala. A long, sleek, champagne gold-sequined gown streamed over her in trundling waves. Her eyes fluttered shut, showing off her thick, black lashes as she twined her arms around Knox's neck. Her lips were pouty and pale, and her face glowed in the clutter of hang lighting above. Juliet felt sick to her stomach just watching them dance. She wondered what it would feel like to wake up every morning, to look in the mirror and to see *that* staring back at her; how good it would feel to not pick herself apart before her chipped toenails slithered inside soft, pink butterfly slippers. She wondered what it would feel like to have a boy like Knox pursue a girl like her.

Juliet snatched Sosie's flute of cider and took a long gulp. "Didn't she get the memo? Girls wear white to the Winter Ball. Not gold! It's like, symbolic or something."

"No, it's tradition." Sosie rolled her green eyes and pried the flute out of Juliet's hands. She hated when girls just assumed they could share drinks, and lipsticks, and bathing suits with her. She never cared with Nala, but with everyone else . . . .

Sosie looked back at Nala and Knox, who swayed to the beat of some cheesy vintage record. They looked so happy. Maybe tonight would be the night that they finally kissed. It was about time she had *someone* to compare notes with. "Besides, we both know that Nala's way too beautiful for white. Isn't she, Rocko? Too beautiful for white?"

"Mmhmm. Beeeaaaauuuutiful," he whirred drunkenly, licking his whiskey-flavored lips. He stared along with Juliet and Sosie. It should've been *him* wearing that Neapolitan suit. Those should have been *his* hands on Nala's waist. That should've been *his* chest her hair spilled down and *his* collar smudged in lipstick. That should've been him.

But fortunately, Rocko was almost too drunk to care.

Brains arrived back at the table with two glasses of white wine. He passed one to Sosie and the other to Juliet. Water for him. "Just be smart, okay? There are teachers lurking around every corner."

Duh. This is the dining hall, after all.

Sosie took an annoyed drink of chardonnay. Since when did she belong with the drunk, the wannabe, and the narc? Since Gino didn't ask her to the dance? Is this what her life had come to be? Rolling with *this* crowd? Thinking about Gino, suddenly, she still couldn't believe he had picked Tess over her. She had thought after their kiss that night in the practice kitchen . . . .

Whatever.

She flicked a blonde curl out of her lipstick. It didn't matter anymore. She had a date. A fumbling wasted, embarrassing date. She turned just in time to catch Rocko burp and blow the warm gas through the air. When he had called Sosie up and asked her to the dance, she had almost considered saying no, but then she wouldn't have been able to wear her new dress. Now, with every burp and every blow, she couldn't help but think that no dress on the planet was pretty enough to compensate for putting up with Rocko's miserable ass.

"So, has Knox fully recovered from last night?" Juliet asked, admiring him from afar. Rocko suddenly popped awake, and tried to listen in. After all, it was sort of his fault that his friend had made a complete ass out of himself at that dinner thing last night.

"Nala told me he was throwing up all morning," Sosie shrugged. "And you *know Knox*. He still claims he only had three drinks last night. Even says he may have been drugged . . . which, call me batshit but it actually makes a little sense."

Juliet's insides plunged into her milk-white ass. "It does?"

"Yeah," Sosie said. "I mean . . . what girl wouldn't want to drug straight Ricky Martin?"

Juliet and Rocko swallowed, and gave each other a look; the, this-secret-dies-with-us look. Rocko's look kind of screamed: this secret will die with you tonight if you keep asking questions.

"Jules, thank God! Tell me you have mascara!" cried someone familiar just in time. Tess kicked a bare, tanned leg through her dress slit as she shoveled through her rainbow-glitter clutch, hovering over them like a skyscraper in heels. Her hair was a big, teased, curly mess.

"You changed your hair," Jules noticed as she snapped open her purse. "Love it!"

"It took, like, an entire bottle of hairspray," Tess bragged.

Sosie's heart was thumping, suddenly. If Tess was strutting around on her obnoxious, cap-toe pumps hunting for mascara, then Gino had to be nearby . . . probably stalking the liquor bar. Would make sense. Tess was quite a headache.

"Where's your hot date?" Juliet asked Tess as she passed over a tube of extra-bold mascara.

"Grabbing a beer, I think," she said.

Sosie's eyes carried toward the back, searching.

"Yep! What'd I tell you?" Tess whined when she found him. "At the bar already and it's not even nine. If gasoline could get him drunk, he'd sacrifice grilling out and cigarettes so he wouldn't catch fire as he chugged. Swear! Right hand to Gucci!"

Tess's voice faded to static as Sosie searched, and searched, and searched, until finally . . . there. Gino. He was sitting across the room at an Amarello bamboo granite bar scattered with liquor bottles and white-chocolate covered pretzels, both of which had been scrounged from the Blunderbuss cocktail lounge in mid-town. He was sipping from a lowball glass, fiddling with his cell. Sosie had been secretly hoping all week that he'd show up in slacks and a muscle tee looking like a hobo, maybe even missing a few teeth or experimenting with some weird facial hair, but that wasn't the case. His sharp, black Italian suit and slicked-back hair were far from hobo. His jaw clinched as he sipped his sour drink, and his slight, five-o'clock shadow drew light attention to the hollows of his cheeks. He looked like some foreign model for an aftershave commercial. Not pretty boy American, but Spanish or Greek. The gold in his eyes glimmered as he debated another swig. Maybe four. Sosie had never seen him look so clean-cut and cool before. She had never seen him look so frustratingly perfect.

At least he was bleating in boredom to his something on the rocks.

Sosie peeked over her shoulder, where Rocko was still drooling over the back of Nala's head . . . or maybe just drooling after one too many Manhattan Dries. Perhaps they had all lucked out and he had drunk himself into a permanently vegetative state. Tess was applying her umpteenth layer of mascara nearby, and Juliet was begging Brains not to do that "eye thing," whatever that meant. Sosie clenched her wine stem so tight that the chardonnay splashed around and almost escaped the rim, still marked with Juliet's icky, pastel lipstick. *Appetizing.* Sosie wiped at the smudge with her thumb as she stared at Gino. Maybe she could sneak by the bar, grab a new glass of wine, and escape before he even noticed her. Or maybe it wouldn't be so bad if he did notice her. After all, she was wearing concealer and a push-up, which like . . . never happened.

Sosie's twiggy legs stumbled as she noticed a big carnival of antlers hung across the room, attached to a giant, mounted deer's head. *Cool.* She was impressed that Miss Hart had really captured the masculine interpretation of Winter Wonderland instead of just spraying glitter everywhere. Hunting. Cabins. Whiskey. All that was missing was pot and a hot tub.

Her feet continued forward as her mind fogged with memories from that night on the patio . . . when Gino told her he was taking someone else to the dance. Even though she'd never admit it, it had practically destroyed her. That was twice that he had stomped all over her mojo. Twice.

Then, Sosie's body froze. Her eyes raised and she saw those same giant antlers. She was right there. Right next to Gino. She could barely make him out in the corner of her eyes. When did this happen? How'd she get there? Her heart began to race.

She brushed her fingers through her blonde curls distractedly, trying to remain calm, trying to avoid contact with him at all costs. She thought she should order a drink to appear busy — or to help calm her nerves — so she stretched over the bar top and tried to flag down the bartender. No success. Her hand flipped through the air again. No success.

"Hey," Sosie heard. She jumped inside her shoes at the deep, all-too-familiar voice. Two seats away, Gino was staring at her blankly, eyebrows slanted, glass raised, considering another sip. "You look," he paused, "great."

"Thanks." Sosie rolled her eyes and pretended to debate between a vodka soda and a glass of champagne. She wasn't ready to forgive Gino . . . not yet, and maybe not ever. Even if he did say she looked "Great."

Gino waved over a bartender with the name Vic stamped across his nametag. Vic had a black, batty beard and thick eyebrows. Sosie recognized him, but she wasn't sure where from.

"Ready for another?" Vic swooped up to Gino's glass and poured a second shot of amber liquid.

"Not for me. For her," he said. "Whatever she wants."

Vic latched his eyes onto Sosie, particularly her sad, under-developed rack. "Umm . . . is *whatever* your friend wants apple juice? Or an apple martini? Because I'm walking a tightrope as it is, man."

"Look, I'll take the fall if she gets caught," Gino said. "Just get her something."

Vic's dark brown eyes hunkered down on Sosie again as she watched him back. It wasn't like she had gotten her period yesterday. She was eighteen-years-old. The same age as Gino, the same age as plenty of other wasted minors in the building. Why should she be chastised when there were hundreds, if not thousands, of equally qualified lawbreakers cutting up the dance floor in ugly oxfords, spiking the punch, poking at the finger foods with their unwashed hands, and toking on blunts in the restroom stalls?

A minute passed, and Sosie was debating whether or not to whip out her fake when Vic finally nodded. "All right. What do you want?"

"Just get me another chardonnay, I guess." She clanked her old wine glass across the granite, and then nicked a cluster of pretzels from a bowl of snowflake shaped party mix, chewing them anxiously while she waited.

"So, where's Rocko?" Gino yanked out a barstool for her. All week he had been thinking about Sosie. He had been wondering what she thought of him for kissing her and then asking Tess to the dance. He wanted to explain why he did it, but it almost seemed too late for that.

Sosie lunged for the barstool, her eyes bouncing between the stash of chocolate-covered pretzels and the massive deer head that hung above them. Its antlers were entwined in bright Christmas lights. "Oh, Rocko's off somewhere, probably grinding on some cheerleader or passed out in a urinal. He made it pretty clear to-night that he wants nothing to do with me. But I guess I knew that already."

Gino's eyes fell. He hated that Sosie's date was a piece of shit. And he hated that it was kind of his fault. Vic handed Sosie her wine and offered Gino a beer "for the road." He looked from side to side. "Dude, I'm sorry, but you guys really need to get lost. I can't afford to lose another job."

"It's cool. Thanks."

Sosie hopped out of her barstool, nearly rolling an ankle as she lost balance in her impossibly tall platforms. Tess was sitting back at the table with Juliet, running her half-moon polished fir-gernails through Brain's quiff cut and making a half-interested comment about his hair. Tess was probably wondering where Gino had run off to. He had probably promised her a strawberry vodka sparkler or a cosmopolitan or a frozen blueberry cocktail. She was probably counting down the seconds until he arrived back, giving Brains a minute-long makeover as she waited.

Gino followed Sosie's gaze toward Tess and stuffed his beer bottle between his lips. Tess probably still reeked of carnations and spray tan. He blinked down at Sosie, drinking her wine and admiring the dancers bumping to some electro-trance European single out on the dance floor. She giggled as a senior did the worm. She certainly didn't smell like carnations and spray tan.

He took a serious breath as a cascade of artificial snow trick-led down from the ceiling vents. A flake landed perfectly on the tip of Sosie's nose. Gino carefully dabbed it with his thumb, catching Sosie's eyes with his. She looked so startlingly beautiful, and he lost himself for a moment. "So . . ." he mumbled a little nervously. "Want to take a walk?"

Not Easy to Forget

"**Y**ou cold?" Gino ripped off his black suit jacket and threw it over Sosie's shoulders. The smell of the freshly trimmed lawn and garden ravine grew sweeter as they walked across the courtyard. The sky was pale blue and the air thick and cold. Naked hickory branches cowered over their heads. Still, both were happy to escape the blustering dance-off inside, where some break-dancer was at this moment spinning on his cricket-green slouch beanie to the beat.

"Thanks." Sosie slipped her arms through the bulky jacket sleeves. The lining smelled like pine wood and mint; like Gino or

Christmas, or maybe both. She wasn't sure. Her mind was a big, blundering mess. She couldn't stop thinking about what was on Gino's mind, so she fiddled a loose thread between her frostbitten fingers, trying to relax. "So . . . you think Tess is wondering where you are?"

"Who knows," Gino shrugged coolly. "Her mirror's probably keeping her company."

"Probably." Sosie laughed. Her blonde, stringy bangs flip-flopped in the breeze as she wondered how much more walking she could take in her dangerously high platforms. Her big toes were starting to look like ripened cherry tomatoes, while the others had evolved into purple veggie sticks. Annoyed, she kicked off her heels and scooped them up in her hands. "Sorry, but these are such a pain in the . . . *butt*," she said. "I quit cussing."

"I noticed." Gino collapsed onto a white pine garden bench, slipping his hands through his waved hair. Sosie looked so pitiful and adorable, squeezing her studded-bows against her white corset gown as her lips exhaled tendrils of smoky air. She crumpled onto the bench beside him and curled her legs beneath her dress for warmth. The long train flowed to the ground and gathered in a silky, silvery puddle at his feet.

"Can I ask you something?" Sosie asked.

Gino's eyes dithered on her licorice-red lips. "Yeah, whatever you want."

"Okay." She breathed noisily, absently squeezing her silk-donned, pedicured feet in her hands. She was freezing. "Who was that guy working the bar back inside? He looked so familiar."

"Oh, Vic?" Gino stuffed his hands in his pockets, toying with his cellphone and his room key. "He bartends up at Cloud Nine, remember? He waited on us that one time."

Oh yeah, how could she forget? That had been the afternoon when Gino insisted, "You don't want to know me" like some tragic martyr in a mid-century play, and Sosie had tried to get wasted off of three sips of draught beer. It hadn't been their finest hour.

"Oh, maybe that's it." Hugging her legs, she blinked back at the cafeteria doors. No one was cartwheeling through the square or streaking near the lakefront bluffs. There were no drunken buffoons watering the clumps of woodland phlox with urine and no lovebirds snuggling up on the gothic stoops. Gino and Sosie were completely alone . . . just their thoughts and the birds above.

"Or maybe you recognize him because . . . " Gino's voice paused, "Vic's also my older brother."

"*Brother*? Really!?"

"Yeah," he said. "Graduated a few years ago, and since he never got married . . . ."

"He never left," Sosie filled in.

"Pretty much." Gino's black, button down smacked into the white pine bench as he leaned back and rolled his head on his neck. It was supposed to be a secret, but he didn't care. It was nice to tell someone who wouldn't use it against him.

"Do you have any other brothers or sisters?" Sosie asked. She had never met someone who knew what it was like to have a sibling. None of the students at BU were supposed to know about their families until spring semester. There was a lavish sibling ceremony held every four years, where freshmen, sophomores, juniors, and seniors would all come together to meet their on-campus relations and learn all about their off-campus relations. It was all *very* dramatic, like a cult gathering or a comic book convention. Although some people figured it out on their own, like the Bleaker twins and Saturn and Jupiter Flonk. Last names were sort of a dead giveaway, though the school went to extraordinary lengths to keep siblings from meeting each other accidentally.

"I only know about Vic," Gino said. "He doesn't want to ruin all the fun, I guess, so he won't say if we have any others." He glanced at Sosie, who was elated with curiosity. "No one knows this except you and the guys, so if you could just . . . ."

"Keep it a secret?"

"Yeah."

"Okay," she nodded. "No problem."

They sat silently, taking in the evening air gulp by cold gulp. Sosie looked at Gino, whose head relaxed against the bench and eyes were wrenched shut. He looked like he was sleeping, or listening to Imagine Dragons on his iPod, or meditating with Mother Nature to channel his inner chi or something. But he was *way* too manly to meditate, of course.

Sosie yanked her eyes shut, too. Maybe she could even have relaxed if her stomach wasn't whimpering for fried food. She had caught a glimpse of crab hushpuppies drenched in tartar sauce on her way out, and had felt like she was slowly, and frozenly, starving to death ever since. Maybe if she could gain a few freaking pounds she wouldn't be so pathetically cold all of the time!

"Sosie," Gino's voice cracked. His eyes were opened. He suddenly looked so worried. "I need to tell you something. Something I should have told you a long time . . . ."

Just then, the cafeteria doors swung wide open behind them. Rocko Borai appeared, joined by a pair of campus patrolmen decked out in navy-blue uniforms, gray badges, and bulky combat boots. Rocko seemed to be the ringleader of their very somber circus.

"That's the guy," Rocko pointed to Gino as the patrolmen clunked doggedly down the stairs.

Gino stood. "Is there a problem?"

The taller of the two men had thin, black hair and beady, blue eyes throttled behind a pair of square, tortoise-shell bifocals. He smelled like Swiss cheese and applesauce, and Sosie was pretty sure he had week-old mustard stains dribbling down his cotton crewneck undershirt. The other was greasy and round — definitely the all-you-can-eat Chinese buffet type. Moo goo gai pan was practically tattooed across his blackhead-infested forehead.

"Gino Blackthorn?" the tall one asked as they clomped through the grass.

"Yeah?"

"Yeah, we're gonna have to take you in." The shorter patrolman wiped his sweat-spritzed, blonde bowl cut and whipped a canteen from his knock-off S.W.A.T. accessory belt. He took a swig, and a liquid with a distinctly blue tinge slipped from the corner of his mouth and dripped down his chin.

"Take me in *where*?"

Sosie slid her feet out from under her dress, staring at the patrolmen blankly as they fiddled with their handheld transceivers. Couldn't they go back inside for a minute so Gino could say what he "needed to say?" Why were they there, anyway?

"To the main office, so you can have a chit-chat with the principal." The short one flashed a yellow snaggletooth at Gino. "And he'll decide what to do with ya."

Sosie lunged onto her feet, her patent leather platforms rolling out of her lap and plummeting to the ground with a clatter. Rocko leaned cockily against a pillar of Tuscan marble, perched up the steps near the cafeteria doors. His crooked lips were smiling into her eyes.

"No way!" Sosie blurted out. "He's not going anywhere until you two assholes tell us what the hell is going on."

So much for not cussing.

"Watch it, kid!" the short one ripped out a flashlight and blazed the light right in her face. "We'll take you in, too. Assaulting a police officer is a felony in some places."

"Well, everywhere . . . ." the taller guy helped.

"Oh, puh-lease." She rolled her eyes. "You're not *real* cops. That law doesn't apply to you two. I'm not an idiot."

That taller patrolman, who appeared to be the nice guy in their poorly rehearsed good-cop bad-cop duo, interrupted quickly. "All we know is, that guy up there," he pointed out Rocko, "claims Gino Blackthorn threatened him. And we take threats *very* seriously here. So, we have to take Gino to the principal, and he'll deal with the situation as he sees fit."

Gino stared up at Rocko who was drunkenly shoving a spinach and mushroom flatbread between his teeth and sizing up the lawn like snotty alumni would do before whipping out his checkbook to make a generous donation to project Campus Facelift. Was this about the argument in the locker room? Because Gino had approximately one million buddies who would testify on his behalf. Even if he did sort of tell Rocko he'd kill him next time, whatever "next time" meant. But that was an empty threat. It was the testosterone speaking. Boys will be boys, right?

"Are you kidding me?" Sosie growled. "That guy up there is wasted out of his mind! Last time I saw him, he was falling asleep in a plate of macaroons! You can't possibly believe a word he says!"

The tall guy shrugged. "It's protocol, ma'am."

"Isn't it also protocol to apprehend minors who are drunk off their asses?" Sosie accused.

The two patrolmen ignored her and advanced toward Gino. "For a punk like you, I bet you get expelled," the short one said. "So say goodbye to your little bundle of blonde drama, 'cause you probably won't be seeing her again. Except—you know—from behind bars."

Like that wasn't dramatic.

They led the way to a rusty old car with a "Campus Patrol" decal crookedly slabbed to the side, flanked by black racing stripes. They had parked on the curb, of course, because they could.

Sosie kept pace with Gino, hardly noticing the cold earth that squished up between her toes. She had left her eight hundred dollar heels back at the bench, but what did she care? She didn't want to leave Gino. And, as the bad cop had so rudely pointed out, there was a chance that Gino would soon be expelled.

And expelled meant gone for like . . . ever.

"You aren't gonna do anything funny, are ya? 'Cause I have handcuffs, and I *will* handcuff you." The short one cocked his yellow, caterpillar-thick unibrow at Gino.

"No."

"Then," the other added, "We'll go have a cigarette, and give you two a chance to say goodnight." He ripped the short guy away, soothing him with the bribe of smokes. They walked toward a maple tree, fumbling for their cigarettes and a lighter.

Gino grabbed his face and grumbled noisily into his hands. He couldn't believe that he was about to be tossed into the back of a weird campus cruiser by two pimply, beer-bellied losers. If he ever saw Rocko again, he'd . . . he'd . . . well, he couldn't exactly kill him as he had threatened to before. But he would do something. That was sure.

Because now he had let Sosie down three times: by lying about the Bluffdale beach, by asking Tess to the dance, and by getting hauled away like a criminal. He watched her toiling with her blonde curls as the thrum of wind wallowed in their ears. Behind them, the smell of willows and moss oozed from the lakefront bluffs. Gino imagined it was a beautiful, warm day, and he and Sosie had taken a paddleboat and a six-pack onto the lake. He would hold Sosie until they both dozed off, not waking until small waves reflecting the beating sunrise splashed against their boat.

"Sorry about this," Gino said, posting up against a thicket of rust growing on the car's bumper.

Sosie clasped her ruined corn silk gown in her hands and shrugged. "We'll figure this out. There's no way you'll get expelled over this."

"Yeah." Gino grabbed Sosie's hips from inside the jacket and pulled her close. She looked *seriously* beautiful that night, he didn't mind admitting. "But just in case, maybe you should know something."

Gino glanced back at the two patrolmen who were arguing about pit bulls and water polo as they sucked poison from their shriveled, little sticks. He and Sosie were alone again. Finally. His chest congealed beneath his shirt. He cleared his throat. "I always remembered you, Freckles, from that day at the beach."

Sosie's eyes plunged open.

"I never told you because I had these plans . . . plans I made a long time ago . . . plans that didn't involve you," he said. "But then I wanted them to — you know — involve you."

Sosie paused, trying to collect her thoughts. Was Gino saying that she was his new plan? She smiled, and hugged her arms around his waist, feeling his hands blunder through her thin, golden hair. She knew it! She knew it! She knew it! She wasn't crazy after all! Gino *remembered!*

The short guy was toying with the butt of his cigarette — flicking it, smoking it, pattering it against the bark of the tree. Any minute, he'd return with his blinding flashlight and nasty yellow bowl cut, waving his handcuffs through the air and barking, "Now, we can do this the easy way, or the hard way." But Gino didn't want to leave Sosie. He wanted that paddleboat, and that six-pack. He wanted *her.*

Gino held Sosie's chin and pulled her face toward him. Her green, glowing eyes reflected the evening sky. "Truth is, you just aren't that easy to forget, Freckles," he said, planting a soft, wet kiss on her forehead. He had wished the evening had turned out differently, with her falling asleep in his arms somewhere. That was as simple and as perfect to him as life could be.

The sound of four muddy boots clomping against the pavement interrupted them. "Ready to go, Gino?" the tall patrolman asked gently. His breath reeked of cigarettes and oranges.

"Can I have one more minute with her?"

The shorter guy wrenched the driver's door open and plunged into a seat filled with shreds of sandwich lettuce and potato chip crumbs. "You got thirty seconds," his distinctively shrill voice squawked.

The tall guy walked off quickly, probably planning to take a quick leak in the woods . . . because he could. Gino held tightly to Sosie's hands. They were so cold it felt like he was squeezing icicles. He closed his eyes, remembering the first time he saw her: freckled skin, gleaming white teeth, beachy, crimped hair. She had been twirling in the sand like she didn't have a single care in the whole freaking world, and it captivated him. She was so spontaneous. So alive.

"You know I'll be thinking about you, right?" she said, smothering her face against his chest.

The sound of lake water sloshing the dirt banks behind them was like the ticking of a clock. Their lips met and they kissed until Gino was pried away. He thumped across the backseat of the car, blinking at Sosie from behind the glass. "I know," he said. *Me too.*

"Sorry to ruin your night," the tall patrolman said genuinely to Sosie, who looked bewildered as her hands twined around the jacket sleeves. It was kind of sweet for him to apologize, even though his banana-yellow briefs peeked through his jammed front zipper. Or was that, perhaps, just a pee stain? *Gross.* "If it helps, I never even had a date to the dance freshman year. Or any year, for that matter."

Sosie shrugged. "He's not my date," she said. The guy gave her a strange look before marching for the passenger seat door. "By the way, I'm sorry for calling you an asshole," she yelled just before he lunged into the campus cruiser. "But, I'm not sorry for calling *him* an asshole," she added, glaring at the driver's window.

The car veered out of the parking lot, leaving behind a powerful stench of scorched rubber and gasoline. Sosie watched until the taillights vanished amid the Coral Bark Maples, her lips still tingling from that kiss.

Gino's jacket clung to her shoulders as she returned to the garden bench to retrieve her platforms, her eyes grown murky with tears. Rocko was still perched up on the stoop outside the cafeteria, toking a blunt and trying to blow smoke rings.

Sosie snatched up her heels and stomped toward the cafeteria, where the Winter Ball was currently alive with techno and strobe lights. Rocko mused there on the highest step while twining his joint, watching the clouds forge above him. He was like some deep, contemptuous critic evaluating the sky, with the earth as his guiding spirit. His eyes were pulled closed and he hadn't budged in minutes when he felt something sharp smack him in the face, whacking the joint right out of his pinched fingers. He found Sosie gripping her heels and hovering over him. Whoa. Hadn't she just been in the parking lot? He blinked his red, swollen eyes. "What the hell, Susie-Q?"

"You're seriously getting *stoned* right now?"

"I was until you knocked my—ummm—my . . . ."

"Joint?"

"Yeah!" he squealed. "My joint. Until you knocked my joint out of my hand!"

Sosie's wicked eyes stared down on him. "You are such a loser!" She flew toward the cafeteria doors. "And by the way, if you don't fix this *right* now, I'm gonna go tell Coach Mike you've been smoking pot for the past three weeks beneath the bleachers, and taking snapshots up girl's skirts. He'll drug test you, and when it comes back positive you'll be kicked off the team. And probably expelled."

Rocko jumped onto his polished, baroque oxfords, his blood-shot eyes glowering up on Sosie as she marched barefoot into the building. "But that's a lie! This is the first time I've smoked in months! You can't just ruin peoples' lives like that! Karma's a bitch, you know."

She peeked back, her lips curling maliciously toward him. "Well," she paused, flashing him one tantalizing wink. "Better start calling me Karma, then!"

The Last Two People on the Planet

Tessa Van der Pool watched Brains Fink skim the finger food buffet and stab a prosciutto pinwheel with a toothpick. Juliet Bigsby sat next to her at the table, sipping her fourth glass of Chardonnay and jealously studying Nala's perfect, tan arms resting on Knox's shoulders as they slow-danced. She could remember Knox—drunk and drugged—confessing his feelings to a blurry version of her, somehow misconstrued as Nala. His lips had tasted like cinnamon that night, and she missed them. Or was that just the alcohol? By then, the wine was seriously whirring through her body, and she was starting to feel a little parched. Parched and sad.

"Do you think I'm pretty?" Juliet mumbled drunkenly, pushing her wet, floppy curls out of her face. She wished she had Nala's long, sleek hair. She wished she had Nala's *everything*.

Tess looked Juliet up and down, stabbing a crouton with her fork. "I've told you this a million times. You're *cute*. You'd be hotter if you lost some weight," she shrugged, "but you already know that."

Juliet's face crumpled.

"I'm only telling you that because you're my friend. You know that, right?" Tess asked.

"Yeah, I know."

Brains Fink returned with two plates of hazelnut-crusted duck breast and sun dried tomato cobbler. He sat next to Juliet and handed her a plate. "Don't eat too much. You'll start to *QUACK!*" he joked.

Juliet yawned, finishing off her glass. She was starving, and duck was her second favorite thing in the whole world behind pizza, but Tess had pretty much just told her to either lose weight or else die a cute but worthless human being.

"Thanks Brainiac, but I'm really not hungry." Juliet clinked her glass against her plate. "But I could use another drink. I'm *very* thirsty."

Brains blinked down at the plate. He had spent fifteen minutes begging the chefs to prepare it just right, insisting on prickly pear sauce over cherry, cobbler over Gorgonzola biscuits, and garlic mashed potatoes over almond rice. But none of that mattered, because Juliet was thirsty, not hungry.

"So, ice water?" he asked, rolling his fingers around the loose change in his pant pockets.

"No, not *ice water*. Vodka water, or vodka tonic, or vodka soda. Something low in calories."

Brains nodded, stumbling toward the glob of antlers mount-ed to the wall. Tess eyed him as he went. Even Jules had some poor dweeb running circles around the ballroom for her, and Tess couldn't even get her date to come out of hiding. Where was Gino, anyway?

Just then, Knox and Nala stumbled back toward the table, their hands clasped together and their fingers intertwined. They were like a couple of honeymooners in the Cook Islands, grin-ning stupid, spritely grins and waltzing until their legs fell off. Knox flashed a glowing smile down on Tess and Juliet. "Wow! You two look great!" he said sweetly as his hand trickled down Nala's spine. He looked the happiest he had ever looked, espe-cially for being seriously drugged the night before.

Nala's nude, sparkling lips mouthed, "Hi!" at her friends as she gasped for air. She and Knox had been dancing for half-an-hour, and she was way too exhausted to speak.

Juliet caved, taking a nervous bite of duck and waving up at them with her fork.

"Have you girls danced yet? The DJ's pretty good. I think he's Norwegian, or something," Knox said.

"We don't dance," Tess sneered.

Of course she didn't dance. She was a living, breathing Barbie doll with plastic for joints.

Brains returned to the table with a sparkling vodka tonic and a root beer. His bulgy, bug eyes bombarded Knox's silvery-gray Neapolitan tailored suit. "Dude! You're like, the Duke of Wellington. Only better dressed!"

"Thanks," Knox said, squeezing Nala's hand under his. "I knew I was going to have to look sharp. Look what I have to stand next to."

"Yeah, I know the feeling." Brains blinked down at Juliet wishfully.

Nala's attention began to drift from Brains and Knox's conversation about pleated trousers and gingham raw silk ties as she observed the thicket of bodies frolicking across the room. Another round of fake snow sprinkled over the copse of quaking aspens where a couple of sophomores were having a very unsuccessful fake-snow snowball fight in their gold-trimmed vests and cocktail flapper dresses. Everything was beautiful: the decorations, the food, the people. She glanced back at Knox, who had borrowed Juliet's vodka tonic for-probably-ever and was laughing with his beautiful, white teeth at something Brains had said; something about the food. Knox was the sweetest guy in the whole world, and he was brilliant, and gorgeous, and crazy about her . . . and yet, something was missing. And it wasn't *just* his alcohol tolerance, though she had been a little turned off after he face-planted on the lawn last night.

She accepted a flute of ice-cold water from a nearby waiter and stared over the crowd again. This time, she fluttered to a gorgeous head of short, chestnut-brown hair peeking from the behind the mosh pit of thumping indie-rockers, skull-spiked studs, and white leather mini-skirts who were having their turn on the dance floor. He was sipping on a beer and talking sports with a couple of the other professors. Graham.

Suddenly, her body felt limp and lifeless. She took an anxious sip of water as Graham spoke, laughed, drank, clanked his beer bottle against Coach Mike's beer bottle, and drank again. There was no sign of Estelle's firm, blonde beehive or snowflake getup. Graham appeared to be flying solo.

Suddenly, Nala felt an iron hand clasp around her shoulder. Knox was holding a half-empty vodka tonic, his eyes drifting up and down her face. "You okay?" he asked worriedly, noticing her glazed eyes.

"I'm fine."

Nala felt suddenly dizzy. Her mind was a total and terrible mess. Why couldn't she just *love* Knox? Why wasn't it that easy? She toyed with her patchwork wristlet, feeling a sudden wave of nausea climb over her. "Kind of have to . . . pee. Mind?"

Ugh. It was so unlike her to use the word "pee," but it just sort of . . . fell out.

"Of course not." He shook out his hair and a small crease formed above his eyebrows. "Want me to walk you?"

"No, thanks." She took a quick drink and then passed Knox her lipstick-kissed water glass. "Save this for me?"

"Sure."

Knox could tell that something had been upsetting Nala all evening long. She seemed distant. On the dance floor, she barely looked at him. Her body was like an empty vessel, swaying to the meaningless melodic beat. For a while, he had convinced himself she was just nervous, but now he knew differently. Something was seriously off. He hoped it wasn't because of last night. He couldn't even remember last night. Did he say something terrible? *Oh god.* Did he tell her he loved her? As he watched her slip away through the crowd, he imagined her slipping like melted butter between his fingers . . . unattainable once again.

"Oh, Kno-ox!" Juliet called nearby. She batted her clumps of black mascara. Nala had vanished, Knox was gorgeous, and she was drunk. This was her chance . . . her "everyone's coherent" chance. She patted an empty chair next to her. "I believe you're enjoying my vodka tonic without me," she said. "But I don't mind sharing."

Nala quickly moved on tapered heel pumps, vanishing into the mob. She needed to be alone for a minute, to think or to not think, to breathe in white orchid fragrance wicks instead of roasted duck and goth sweat.

She wobbled toward the restroom door, her thick, brown locks flapping angrily between her tanned shoulder blades. She was almost there when, out of the corner of her eye, she felt Graham catch sight of her. His mouth plummeted open. His bottle shuddered beneath his grip.

They trapped each other's gazes for one breathtaking instant. The room slowed down, and everyone faded to black and white static. It seemed that they were the only two people left on the planet. She and Graham.

And then — before anything could happen — Nala slipped behind the bathroom door of cool, driftwood gray. And the world rushed in on her once more.

Love Me Forever

Graham's beer sloshed inside of his bottle as Coach Mike rubbed his tobacco-stained fingernails against his bald, polished scalp and whacked the back of Professor Tuttle's silver, sharkskin blazer. "Tuttle! You dirty, old bastard! You've been working out behind my back."

Tuttle flexed his lean, wiry arm. His square, tortoise-shell rims slid down his hawk nose as he grinned back at Mike. "I have, in fact."

Graham smiled weakly, his body still ringing. He couldn't focus on Professor Tuttle's absent biceps. He couldn't even focus on Estelle Hart's atrocious, rhinestoned snowflake wear, which she flounced about in a never ending search for intoxicated minors. All he could think about was Nala's bright, golden eyes blinking back at him just before she slipped into the ladies' room.

Coach Mike flagged down a waitress carrying a tray of sour-cream potato cakes and grabbed a handful. "I really should be watching what I eat, but this is a special occasion, right?" he asked Tuttle and Graham, hoping for reassurance as he popped one between his teeth and patted down his flabby stomach. "I'll start my diet Monday."

Graham emptied his beer. The crowd began bumping to house music, arms whipping to the beat, bodies moving mindlessly, hair flipping through waves of sound. Everyone was so full of life. Everyone but Graham and his boring staff friends. Was this what twenty-three was like for everyone? Was this his future? Potato cakes and people watching?

"There's a very popular nutrition fad arising in Europe. The studies are off the charts," Tuttle butted-in, grabbing a few potato cakes himself.

Had it really come to this? Talking European weight loss regimens as a crowd of young-adults explored fist pumping? It was just yesterday that he was at this dance himself . . . as a student. In his senior year, he and his three buddies wore white tuxedos with satin lapels, drank greyhounds, and smoked cigars on the patio. Jayda, his ex, had dragged him out on the dance floor and stomped her chunky heels all over his feet for two straight hours. He had woken up in a lounge chair at the pool with frozen eyelashes, a few broken toes, and a serious winter tan. It had been the time of his life. And no matter what boring sport coat he was wearing, or what boring beer he was drinking, or what boring conversation he was having, he still wanted to be that guy . . . tuxedo, or no tuxedo.

"Hey." Coach Mike nudged Graham's arm. "You holding your liquor all right, Leatherwood? What is that . . . two beers now?"

Graham nodded. He did feel dazed, although not from the beer. All he could see was a replay of Nala in that beautiful, champagne sequined gown, her eyes sparkling in the baby-blue lights overhead.

Mike ordered another beer for Graham and wacked him on the back. "So, you still with *Estelle?* I hear she purrs like a cat when, you know . . . ." He laughed with a disgusting mixture of shame and anticipation. "That true?"

Graham took a deep, drawn-out breath. "How 'bout I tell you when I get back? Too many beers." He patted his stomach.

"Two too many, huh Graham?" Mike called after him. "And another one on the way, you lightweight!"

Graham thumped away, trying to knock Mike's annoying voice from his skull. *Estelle and cats and Europe?* It was all too much. Way too much. The buzzing slowly dwindled away as he realized where he was. The ladies' restroom. His espresso brown perforated ox-fords were right at the threshold, and suddenly all he could think about was the girl behind the door. It wasn't like he was going to go in, or anything; he just wanted to know what the hell was going on. He inched closer, scuffing the handle with his badly chewed finger-nails. Should he go in? Just for a minute? All he had to do was sneak inside without anyone noticing. Luckily, the restrooms were buried behind a tacky shrine to the Himalayas, so it couldn't be *that* hard to sneak in. He swallowed loudly and gripped the handle. Was he seriously about to do this? Then, suddenly the door flew open and three little Japanese girls with pink hair extensions spilled out of it, giggling into their porcelain-white hands.

"Hey Mr. L," one said determinedly. "If you're looking for Miss Hart, she's not in there. Just some freshman," she said, roll-ing her eyes although she was also a freshman and kind of wor-shipped Nala, just like all of the other freshmen girls.

"Thanks Cindy," he said as the girls toppled off, their hot pink extensions floating after them. Just some freshman. One freshman. *Nala.*

As the door was creeping shut, Graham took a deep breath and, without thinking, slipped inside. His heart started to hammer in his throat. What the hell was he even doing? What was he going to say? He glanced around nervously. The bathroom walls were painted in deep rose, and the crown molding was trimmed with crystals. The entire room was drenched in aromas of orchids and vanilla, and the black slate floors were decked with peacock-blue shag rugs. No wonder girls were always going to the restroom together. They had a freaking lounge next to the chrome sinks!

Graham slowly inched around the corner. Nala was standing in front of a vanity, staring blankly at her reflection as if she was unpleased. She'd raise her thick, arched eyebrows and watch them sink, just like a bored child on a rainy day. Bored and beautiful. He felt his heart race just looking at her.

Nala zipped her wristlet closed, poking her lipsticked lips with her thumb. She didn't want to leave. She was happy in her little hiding spot surrounded by fluted glass soap dishes and retro, jungle-red settees. Although, she began to feel that she was missing something . . . or rather someone. Where the heck was Sosie, anyway?

"Ahem," someone grunted from behind.

Spinning around, Nala's hair whipped through the vanilla-infused air and she grabbed her pounding chest. "Graham! You scared me!" she gulped, slipping her hands over the swirling marble countertop. Was her heart racing because she was surprised, or because she was surprised by Graham . . . there . . . in the girls' restroom?

"Sorry," he said, stuffing his hands in his pleated khakis and rocking inside of his shoes. "I just saw you walk in here a minute ago, and I just . . . needed to see you."

The walls were thumping along with the stage speakers outside. Nala twiddled her wristlet in her hands. She had practically dreamed Graham up after fifteen worthless minutes of begging the sink deities to help her forget him, and then on top of it, her brain was suddenly whooshing inside of her skull to the jolting instrumentals. Had someone spiked her drink or something? Were spiked drinks an arising fad at BU now? Or was she just going crazy?

"You having fun?" she finally asked.

"Not really," Graham admitted. "Honestly, I just feel out of place here."

"You too?" She twined a loose sequin from her dress and flicked it into the sink. She still thought she might have been drugged, but one thing was for certain: Graham looked so happy to see her, and she was definitely happy to see him back. He was one beautiful, unexpected, totally off limits dream she must have conjured up, because there was no way it was actually happening: Graham standing in the ladies' room for her.

"So, I've been thinking about you a little," he said.

"A little?" Nala replied. All of sudden, she was dying for a drink. All she needed was one drink, just to kill the nerves. Something classy, like a glass of merlot or shiraz. "I mean, it's not like I expected you to be thinking about me a lot, or anything, but it's kind of offensive to say a little." She giggled, blushing.

The music slowed outside, and they could hear the very faint strains of slow dance melody trickling out the bathroom speakers. They could finally hear themselves think. "Okay, I've been thinking about you a lot," Graham admitted, his eyes locked on her. "The last time we spoke, I should have told you . . . there are things I really . . . ."

"Don't worry about it," Nala interrupted. Her hair spilled down her shoulders like she was modeling for a vintage perfume ad. *Aime-moi pour toujours* by Michel St Pierre. *Love me forever*. She relaxed against the counter, her toes scrunching up. "I forgive you," she added.

"Oh. Good," Graham said. He fiddled with an old gum wrapper stashed in his pocket as he debated what to say next. It was great that Nala forgave him, but he wasn't sure he wanted her forgiveness. He knew that he had totally screwed up, but more than anything he just wanted to pour out his guts so that she could know his heart. He wanted her to know that before he met her, he was as monumentally broken as a poorly packaged vinyl record, and . . . what? She was the glue that bonded the sharp remains together again?

Graham gulped nervously. What if Nala didn't want to be his glue? What if she just wanted to be his student? What if that was why she didn't say anything in the classroom that day after he told her how he felt? Because she just wanted to be a normal, 18-year-old girl who wasn't *involved* with a teacher. There was always the slight possibility that he was making everything up in his head. Maybe this whole flirtation was as ridiculous and illusory as the weird, scratched record metaphor.

Graham and Nala watched each other through the silence when suddenly . . . *creeeeeaaak!* The bathroom door flew open. Through it, Cindy and her two pink-streaked girlfriends clomped inside on snakeskin platform wedges, one of them squealing about her ruined, banana-yellow, sculptured couture shoulder. Graham snatched Nala by the hand, yanking her into a stall before anyone could see them.

"Brad is totally dead!" Cindy blabbed as she stomped around the corner. She blotted her friend Veronica's fitted, French 75-soaked sleeves with a hot towel as Veronica bawled until her mascara streamed down her cheeks. "First he cheats on you, then he pours a drink on you, then he laughs with his stupid, jock friends. Don't worry, honey! We'll get him back."

"But I—I—I don't want to get him baaaaack!! I mean, I *want* him back. I just—I—I looooove him!" Veronica moaned.

Graham and Nala stood still in their tiny stall, trying not to breathe too loudly or fidget too much, especially trying not to laugh too hard. Veronica's crying sounded like a whale going through labor. Graham smirked, realizing they were both feeling tortured by the noise. He mechanically pulled a strand of almond hair out of Nala's pale lip gloss and tucked it behind her ear. *There. Better.* They stared at each other, blinking and breathing, bobbling inside of their shoes.

Suddenly, Veronica's crying faded. Nala gulped. The feel of Graham's fingers on her skin made her squirm beneath her layer of glistening gown. His hand lingered on her neck, his hazel eyes beating down on her like the heat of the sun. "You okay?" he mouthed.

She nodded, looking around the stall for a distraction. A three-tiered chandelier shimmered above their heads, spangled with crystal droplets. The walls were Tuscan red and stippled with black and white portraits of gorgeous runway models. The toilet seat was literally embossed with rhinestones. Everything was so luxurious, but she couldn't focus on anything else. Graham's glowing, hazel eyes watched her as his hand just barely brushed her neck.

"Hold still, V! You're like, a little caterpillar!" Cindy squealed from beyond.

Nala blinked back at Graham. His lips twitched into a smile as if he had always wanted this . . . exactly as it was. Wonderfully and strangely captivating. Then, his head slipped closer to hers. Their noses almost touched. She yanked her eyes shut, holding her breath. It had always been Graham, hadn't it? He was the one that she had wanted all along. Her muscles tightened as his skin grazed hers.

And then . . . it happened.

Graham's lips turned to milk against Nala's mouth. She felt tingly and light. Her body molded to him as he pulled her closer. Tighter. His hands buried into her curls. She could feel him smiling against her lips as he kissed her again. And again. And again. She felt like her soul might fly out through her mouth if he stopped.

And he kissed her again.

Cindy, Veronica, and their tagalong clunked out of the bathroom, their snakeskin platform wedges drawing dim silhouettes of shadows across the slate as Nala and Graham attempted to remain upright. They stumbled against hard metal walls, their mouths fused together like vacuums. The door squeaked shut and Graham pulled away, Nala's body clasped in his arms. He kissed the top of her head. "God, I've been wanting to do that for a long time," he mumbled, his glowing red lips buried deep in her coconut-shampooed tresses. He could have stayed there all night, he realized, in that tiny confinement. Holding her and kissing her, feeling her lips on his.

"Me too," Nala whispered, grinning stupidly.

They stood, holding each other, listening as classical violin rang through the speakers. They kissed senselessly again, stumbling against the walls. Their fingers fumbling all over each other.

Finally, they were together like they were meant to be. Only in the girls' restroom where someone could walk in at any minute . . . Cindy and Veronica . . . Estelle Hart.

"Nala," Graham blew into her hair as he spoke. "This was . . . amazing. You're amazing, but . . . ."

"You should get going," she filled in.

"Yeah . . . ."

He wished they could spend all hours of the night talking about vintage films and the art districts of Paris, planning their vacation for the summer, but he was a chaperone at a college dance and she was a student, and he didn't think getting caught like that go over too well with the administration. He swallowed loudly. "Before I go, you should know . . . ." His hands held hers as he twirled her pink chalcedony ring around and around on her finger. "When I stepped through those doors earlier, I had every intention of kissing you." His lips fell near hers again. "So everything that happens from here on out . . . it's all on me."

They kissed as Graham unlocked the stall door, and both fell out into the haze of white-orchid air-freshener. Nala was leaving for Bluffdale soon for winter break, and she wouldn't see Graham for an entire month . . . and she missed him already. They stared into the crisp reflection of a beautiful, happy couple through the collage of vanity mirrors stacked before them. Graham's arms wrapped around Nala as he noticed her swollen, cherry-red lips shimmering in the glass. "Now that we have this, I never want to let it go." His mouth brushed her neck carefully. "Stay here with me."

Graham imagined whisking her away, taking her back to his apartment, falling asleep next to her, waking up next to her, beating chocolate chip pancake batter for breakfast with hand-squeezed O.J. They'd stay in bed all day watching documentaries and ordering Chinese. They'd be one of those totally boring couples everyone secretly envied, who could be so happy with just each other. Maybe he could convince her to stay with him over winter break . . . to skip Bluffdale Prep's rather traditional holiday extravaganzas. He'd roast a turkey on Christmas. They'd attend church, too.

Maybe, somehow, they could make it work.

And then, as Nala stretched onto her toes to kiss Graham one last time, two pale, razor-burned legs wobbled inside the rest-room, a pair of familiar nude, nubuck pumps hugging around her ankles. Graham ripped himself from Nala just in time to see Juliet, a champagne flute wedged in her hand, blinking back at their blur of shock. "Shit! Sorry!" Juliet squealed, twisting for the exit, a clump of blonde frizz pouring out of her poorly pinned up-do. The flute slipped from her hands and shattered against the black floors. At first, she thought she had stumbled into the boys' restroom by accident, but then she realized that Nala's big, worried eyes had been in the picture, too . . . filled with guilt. Nala? With . . .wait . . . Mr. L? Were they . . . kissing? What the hell was going on?

"Juliet!" She heard Nala's voice cry out and an assemblage of loud heel stomps chasing her down. Juliet zoomed past the weird mirage of the Himalayas, trying to wrap her mind around what she had just seen. "Juliet, wait! Can we talk for a second?"

The dance floor roared with sweat-infused suits, white flapper dresses, and one non-existent ass smothered beneath olive tuxe-do capris, all dancing drunkenly to British electro-pop. Through the chaos, Nala caught Juliet's hand and spun her around. "Hey, didn't you hear me?"

"I heard you!" Juliet screamed over the music. "Everyone always hears you! You never have to worry about whether people notice you, Nala, because you're all anyone is ever looking at all the time! And it's so infuriating for people like me! Sometimes — you know — sometimes I have something to say, too. Sometimes I want to be heard, or seen, or noticed."

Nala watched as tears pricked Juliet's cheeks, her mind jumbled with a million different thoughts. Would Juliet say something? Would Graham get fired? Would Nala ever see him again? And where were those tears coming from? Was this about Graham — err, Mr. L? Because it felt like something else . . . .

"Look." Juliet pushed her yellow hair out of her eyes, assessing the crowd of drunken body parts flapping around her. "The only reason you're talking to me right now is because you need something from me."

"No, Juliet, that's not true . . . ."

"Stop!" Juliet snapped. "Just stop! It is true! You know it. I know it. Regardless of how you see me, I'm not just some frizzy-headed idiot!" She pushed her yellow hair out of her eyes, feeling totally spastic. Was she really yelling at Nala? The most beautiful girl in the world? She gulped loudly. "Whatever. This isn't about you and me. This is about you and Mr. L. And . . . Knox."

Knox?

Nala blinked back at her group of friends who still crowded around their acclaimed dinner table, picking the arugula from their salads and chugging flutes of champagne. Then her focus narrowed and she saw Knox, his elbows propped on his knees as he stared out onto the dance floor, patiently waiting Nala's return. He was like a dog . . . hopeless and inanimate without her.

"He's been like that since you left," Juliet said. "We literally just sat there and talked about you for fifteen minutes. Fifteen minutes of him telling me that his heart literally pounds inside of him when he sees you. Fifteen minutes of him asking me if you maybe feel the same. Fifteen minutes of him admitting that it wouldn't matter if you didn't, because there wasn't a runway model or a lapse of amnesia that would make him feel any differently about you. And he thinks he screwed it all up. After last night, he thinks it's over between you two. And it's killing him." Juliet trembled, remembering how it wasn't even Knox's fault that he had been such a drunk, drugged-up mess in the first place. "And the sad part is . . . I think I love him. I seriously do. I think I love him," she said again. Nala stood, shocked. "Isn't that the most pathetic thing you've ever heard? I love him. He loves you. You clearly love Mr. L . . . ." she cackled a little obnoxiously, glaring back at Knox's slouching shoulders. "But Knox is yours or he's no ones. So don't be stupid. Be his, back." Her eyes remained there. For a second, she wished they were back in Knox's room, his hand clasped tightly to hers, his mind so obliterated by pain pills that he had actually thought she was Nala. It had felt good to be someone else—someone beautiful—even if it was just for a minute. Even if it was all a lie.

"Look, you and Mr. L . . . whatever that was, it doesn't matter to me. Frankly, I'm not even that surprised. But Knox? I'm not going to let you toy around with his feelings anymore." She took a threatening glance back at the table. "Either forget Mr. L and be with Knox—really be with him—or tell him the truth," she snapped, disappointed, "or I will."

Nala watched as Juliet plodded back to the table, grappling at a freshly poured champagne flute and tossing her head back angrily. Nala suddenly realized what Juliet must think of her. Hooking up with a teacher in the girls' bathroom. Sneaking behind Knox's back. When had she turned into this beautiful, little bitch?

Her eyes clamped shut as she listened to the thunder of cork shoes and loafers pummeling the floor. When had she become so selfish? When had she stopped caring about anyone but herself? And where the hell was Sosie when she needed her?

There. Heading toward the punch bowl with . . . Rocko Borai?

"Susie-Q! You get your skinny little ass back here, now!" Rocko screeched, his face furiously red. "Don't do anything stupid! You rat on me, and I'll make sure that Blackthorn never sets foot in this place again!"

"Watcha gonna do? Tattle-tale on him from your timeout chair?" Sosie's body fluttered past a table of sophomores and juniors eating spinach and brie artichoke hearts. They all looked up, cheese dripping from their fingertips as the pair passed by. "You'll be gone too, you idiot! Somewhere where you can smoke all the stupid ganja you want amongst plenty of dreadlock-headed dropouts! Peeing in sand dunes and eating whale crap."

Rocko rubbed a hand through his stubbly buzz-cut, eyeing Principal Dotie across the dance floor. Dotie was shuffling on his ugly, dirt-brown derby shoes and sucking on the green olive he had stolen from Estelle Hart's martini. If Sosie alerted the administration that Rocko had been smoking pot, and his drug-test returned positive—which it totally would—his football career would be over. And even though he was sure he was sexy enough to pull off dreads, he wasn't sure he could handle living in some stoner's shack on the beach. No air-conditioning. No Sunday Night Football. Eating whale poop. He had to do something . . . fast. "Susie-Q!" he yelled, snatching her by the arm and yanking her against him. Her body struck into his with a thud as he grabbed her face and . . . unable to think of anything else . . . smushed his lips into hers.

His mouth tasted like cigarettes and skunk as he stuffed his tongue between her lips. His rough and equally slimy tongue Sosie felt the sudden urge to vomit. What the *hell* was he thinking kissing her like that? Peeling back, she managed to whack him in the face once or twice, her silver-adorned wrist jingling with every blow.

Rocko's cheek swelled with a painful, pink handprint. The nearby table of spinach and brie-eaters sat watching Rocko Borai simmer, his palms holding his face, his eyes jet-black. He looked like he was trying to count back from one zillion, or imagine his happy place, or channel Zen in order to calm down before he did something else stupid.

"What the hell was that?" Sosie screeched, wiping Rocko's spit from her mouth.

"What? Too much of a good thing?"

Sosie rolled her eyes. "Do you like . . . love me or something? Is that what this is about? Did you send Gino away so you could, like, have me all to yourself?"

"Don't kid yourself, Susie-Q," Rocko said, hawking a wad of saliva onto the ground and stomping at it with his shoe. His eyes shifted to Nala as she swooped up behind Sosie, her long, silky dress wrapping over her toes, her face totally confused. Damn was she sexy. He deepened his voice. "Whatever you thought there was between us was just a myth . . . like flying squirrels."

"Yeah, those are real," Sosie said.

"The truth is, blondes have never really been my cup of whiskey. Never wanted you, Susie-Q. Made you think I did. Even convinced myself that your kiss was like Hawaiian pizza . . . just the right combination of spicy and sweet. But nope . . . never had my eyes on you. Only on her." He nudged his head at Nala. "That's right, Bambi. You. Only asked Sosie out on a date because Knox had scooped you up before I got the chance. My first football game, I was waving at you in the stands, not her. And that night she kissed me?" He took in a deep breath and zipped his eyes down Nala's body. "I was watching you get undressed through your bedroom window." Rocko struck Sosie with a sharp glare. "So, Susie-Q, the answer is no. I don't, like, *love you, or something*," he mocked. "Bambi on the other hand . . . . The offer still stands, sweetheart, and I pay in hundreds."

Sosie and Nala blinked at each other, totally shocked. It was turning out to be the strangest night of their lives. All they wanted was to remember what life had felt like before boys . . . back when everything was simple and boring. Back when their lives didn't revolve around testosterone and making out.

Rocko's shoe stomped against the floor, waiting, bringing the girls back to the Norwegian house music as a puff of snow drifted upward. Sosie and Nala gave each other a look and their heads turned in uncanny unison toward Rocko. To everyone else, he was just some handsome and harmless jock with great bone structure and an MMA obsession, but they knew him far too well to buy into any of that crap. He was a jerk, and he needed to go.

Suddenly, Nala and Sosie stretched out their arms, narrowed their recently waxed brows, and shoved their hands into his chest. Rocko's polished, calf-leather oxfords shot out from under him, his body crumpling backward into the bowl of deep carmine-colored punch stationed near the finger foods. His expensive Italian suit absorbed the red beverage like a sponge, and the vodka-laced fluid smelled almost flammable as the stench rose from him. Fried filaments of coconut shrimp sprinkled softly over his dark skin. He pouted, licking the punch off his lips.

Nala and Sosie linked arms and strutted for the cafeteria doors, smiling dazzlingly. First semester at Blairstown University was nearly over. After Christmas, they'd be back again to face the music of this hellish and frenetic night. But until then . . . as always . . . at least they had each other.